W9-BGE-287

Acclaim for Caitlin Macy's
THE FUNDAMENTALS OF PLAY

"Well-written and thoroughly conceived. . . . Macy has crafted a well-honed story that builds with tension and surprise. It's a promising beginning." —*The Washington Post*

"A noteworthy debut." —*Los Angeles Times*

"Reading Caitlin Macy's fine first novel, *The Fundamentals of Play*, is a bit like being invited, unawares, to the party. . . . Macy's portrait of prematurely conservative rich kids . . . is richly evocative. Her narrative swings gracefully from present to past and back, slowly revealing the secrets in the shadows." —*Salon*

"An insightful first novel. . . . What resonates is the style and sharp eye for detail. . . . Macy finds the poetry of regret without stumbling into sentimentality." —*People*

"A slick drug-free *Less than Zero* for the relatively buttoned down '90s set." —*Entertainment Weekly*

"*The Fundamentals of Play* is a graceful, poignant tale of thwarted love. . . . The book works because of an all-too-rare quality in first novels—its grace." —*The Hartford Courant*

Caitlin Macy

THE FUNDAMENTALS OF PLAY

Caitlin Macy graduated from Yale and received her MFA in creative writing from Columbia. She has been published in *The New York Times Magazine* and *Slate*. She lives in New York City.

THE
FUNDAMENTALS
OF PLAY

CAITLIN MACY

THE
FUNDAMENTALS
OF PLAY

A NOVEL

Anchor Books • A Division of Random House, Inc. • New York

First Anchor Books Edition, July 2001

Copyright © 2000 by Caitlin Macy

All rights reserved under International and Pan-American Copyright Conventions. Published in the United States by Anchor Books, a division of Random House, Inc., New York, and simultaneously in Canada by Random House of Canada Limited, Toronto. Originally published in the United States by Random House, Inc., New York, in 2000.

Anchor Books and colophon are registered trademarks of Random House, Inc.

This is a work of fiction. The characters and events in it are inventions of the author and do not depict any real persons or events.

The Library of Congress has cataloged the Random House edition as follows:
Macy, Caitlin.
The fundamentals of play : a novel / Caitlin Macy
p. cm.
ISBN 0-375-50413-3
1. Young adults—New York (State)—New York—Fiction.
2. New York (N.Y.)—Fiction. I. Title.
PS3563.A3387 F86 2000
813'.54—dc21
99-086625

Anchor ISBN 0-385-72112-9

Author photograph © Sara Barrett
Book design by Helene Berinsky

www.anchorbooks.com

Printed in the United States of America
10 9 8 7 6 5 4 3 2 1

For my father,
Peter Tarr Macy,
and my mother,
Claire Canapary Macy

I would like to thank the George Gorham family; the Carballals—for letting me keep my hand in; Tim Scott, Ron Irwin, Jenny Offill, Jeremy Barnum, and my sister, Jem.

I would also like to thank Daniel Menaker, whose editorial presence had a wonderfully steadying effect; and Dan Mandel, this book's first friend.

"He calls the knaves, Jacks, this boy!"

—*Great Expectations*

THE
FUNDAMENTALS
OF PLAY

I went to Paris after graduation but it was too late to do me any good. Under the stipulations of the fellowship, I was to stay for a year; I barely lasted the winter. I cited, in my letter to the committee, the weakness of the dollar, which had eaten up the stipend. Touching down in New York in gray, frigid March, I had a great sense of relief. The truth was I couldn't wait to put on a coat and tie and go to work and have the next ten years go by. It was only later that I associated the feeling with the realization that Kate was right. She had always maintained that she and I shared this quality—call it a fundamental conservatism, associate it with whatever you like: the Latin motto of your youth; Budweiser in cans; the moral imperative of fresh air. Or as Kate would have put it, I am one of those Americans who would rather go to Connecticut than France.

It was the year they changed the name on the building that ruins the view down Park Avenue. My firm was midtown—Fordyce, Farley—and I was that lowest form of post-undergraduate life: the first-year analyst. We worked hundred-hour weeks in fabric-upholstered cubicles of four feet by six. The guy in the one next to mine didn't so much as acknowledge me till one morning when he came in late and was compelled to share the latest outrage. "They changed the name!" I was indignantly informed. "They went and changed the name!"

I remember I told Robbins not to worry, that everyone would go on calling it the Pan Am Building. I was wrong. Everyone started calling it the MetLife Building. This isn't really important—I certainly never heard anyone try to make a metaphor of it (the change in the city's most visible corporation from airplanes to insurance)— but it stuck in my mind, and it is from that point that I always date my arrival in the city.

I was like any other foolishly young face in pinstripes. I lived on the barren top of the Upper East Side in one of those high-rise dormitories called the Something Arms. My roommate was Geoff Toff— Will Toff's brother, whom I'd known at Dartmouth. Geoff was paralegaling as a means of getting into law school. We didn't live together so much as run into each other in the apartment every couple of weeks. When we did, Geoff was amiable, aggressively amiable, agreeing with my opinions before I had fully uttered them.

"I really think this whole mess about the Long Island—"

"Yeah, yeah, I know—me, too."

The television was Toff's. So was the sofa bed, and a large fake-leather reclining chair from which he affected an ironic distance that I didn't quite believe. I had the stereo and a glass coffee table and hung three prints of the Seine on the wall.

In my bedroom (the smaller of the two; I lost the coin toss), as in the living room, the floor was carpeted blue. I slept on a mattress on the floor which I planned to upgrade to a bed. The night I moved in we made spaghetti and jar sauce, and that was the last time either of us opened a kitchen cabinet.

Recently I was depressed to read in the *Times* that the idea of catching up on sleep is a myth. Nevertheless, I'm planning my Rip Van Winkle revenge. I took a poll of some friends of mine, and we all agreed the last time we were well rested was in 1982. I remember one particular morning that first spring at Fordyce when I discovered myself lying on a stretch of the blue carpet, the L-shaped inlet which joined my bedroom to the hall. I did not know how long I had been lying there. I believe that I was having a breakdown, from pulling two or three all-nighters in a row, but I don't know—maybe I was upset about something. Eventually I stood up and went to work. It seemed funny to me, in the cab downtown.

But then everything seemed funny. The money—or the idea of money, for I had none yet—and the never-ending work weeks gave the year a wired, comic tinge. It was all such a ruse. One pretended to be an adult and did adult-like things: one had the *Journal* delivered; one had a morning coffee order. The coffee order—*order*—was everything. If you imposed enough order on your life you would wake up your boss, you would wake up old, the imposition would no longer be necessary because the habits would be fully acquired. And in our generation we wanted to be old. Not all of us, of course, but among those of us who went to Wall Street, it was a prevalent posture. I looked forward to the day when I could creak around in threadbare seersucker and indulge in my baffling idiosyncrasies; when I would be chastised by my wife for sneaking out to the local diner for an old-school, high-cholesterol breakfast. My parents were a little older than most parents with kids my age—closer to World War II than Vietnam—and I and a number of my peers were of the opinion that their generation had gotten it right. And perhaps the habits had stuck all the more in my family because they were all we had been able to hold on to. I hadn't come to Wall Street for nothing.

I thought of calling Kate—of course I thought of calling her—but the time was never right. Monday was too early in the week and Wednesday too late. The daytime seemed too casual for the initial call, the evenings much too formal. The weekends were impossible. Chat Wethers would know where to find her, but I didn't want to go through him. And in the back of my mind, I cherished the idea of running into her. I had envisioned various settings, each triter than the next—crossing Grand Central, hailing a cab up Park on a rainy night. Then one evening she materialized, right where you would expect her to, at the Town Club, on Sixty-second Street.

The partner in a deal I worked on took us there the night the company went public. It was the partner and I, a director and two associates, shooting endless after-dinner pool in an inner sanctum three or four flights up. My direct boss was the associate Daniels. He was the kind of man who buys the Harvard Business School sweatshirt, the Harvard Business School key chain, and any number of Harvard

Business School bumper stickers. He got drunk and said more and more loudly, "You're having a good time *now*, eh, Lenhart? First time at the Town Club, eh, Lenhart?" Eventually he picked a fight with me over a shot I didn't call, and looking for an excuse to escape the scene, I volunteered to put him into a cab.

I had intended to head home myself, but after hesitating a moment outside, I let myself back into the foyer of the Club. It was well lit; standing just inside the door you could see up a wide marble staircase that rose for several steps, split in two, curved around a gold bust, and rejoined in time to deposit the climber onto a brief mezzanine. Like all stairways, it gave the best view coming down, but the ascending prospect was more enticing because it was in looking up that one anticipated the rewards that lay beyond the mezzanine: ballrooms, there were, and bars.

Contrary to what Daniels had said, it was not my first time at the club. My grandfather had been a member, and I had childhood memories of drinking Tom Collinses "without the Tom" in the men's bar upstairs. Looking back, I'm sure I returned to seek some evidence of this—our residual belonging: Grandfather's name on a roster; a face staring out from the photograph of a men's dinner half a century ago; or perhaps his old chesterfield hanging still in the coat check, the claim forgotten after a particularly raucous night.

But of course there was no coat. My mother wore it now. And as I stood there, looking up the stairs toward a muted, urbane din whose source the mezzanine concealed, my disconcerting childhood seemed to creep up and surround me. We didn't, for instance, own our own house. My father ran a tiny pre-adolescent boarding school in western Massachusetts called the Rectory, for sixth- through eighth-grade boys, of the kind that the last thirty years had nearly wiped out. And so the school provided a house. My grandfather's apartment had been sold years ago to settle some of his debts. There was more—a whole host of recuperative fantasies which someone like me swears by, growing up: I was going to buy back 1100 Madison . . . ! Buy back Nantucket . . . ! And I suppose the Town Club figured in there somewhere as well. In the meantime the running joke between my sister and me was that we had the only kind of money that was respectable these days—the kind that was all gone.

I am not sure how long I had lingered there, just inside the door, when somewhere above me I heard a loud party come down from dinner and take over the main bar. Then, over the sound of men's voices, I heard a girl laugh. "I'll see if I know anyone," I decided, and I went for the stairs. At the top I turned to see who was laughing. There were a couple of others passing with me, and they turned, too. It was impossible not to follow that laugh to its source.

A group of men her father's age with big old-fashioneds in their hands were standing in a circle around my old friend Kate Goodenow. I remember, in the moment before she saw me, I had a dread Kate wouldn't recognize me, and it seemed to me her face took an instant too long to change. Then she cried my name.

"George!"

Anointed, I stepped forward to embrace her.

"Why, it's the most fun possible," Kate declared.

With us both there, the men seemed to remember themselves, or their collective age, and rather than be introduced they turned in a single motion toward the bar.

She was all grown-up in a navy blue suit with a sprout of scarf blossoming from the neck. The cut of her suit was too severe to be becoming, but then Kate had never been stylish, really. Like a lot of thin girls, the clothes tended to wear her.

"I've been looking all over town for you," I said.

"And where all over town did you expect to find me?" She was as tranquil as she ever was, and I suppose I had known she would be. That was why it wouldn't have done any good to seek her out. One wasn't allowed to want things of Kate. I had meant to "catch up," for instance, and in a hurry, but against my intent was Kate's demeanor—denying that there was any catching up to be done.

"I've been in Paris, you know," I said anyway—to establish myself somehow.

"Really? I've been right here every minute."

"Then it suits you to be home," I said.

For though Kate was not beautiful, hers was a fresh face, to which you found yourself applying old adjectives—she had been called "game," for instance. "Attractive" wouldn't work, either. Attractive tells a slightly different story. The preternaturally pale boy who emerged, presently, from the bar would not have gone around with "attractive" women. In the first place, he wouldn't have found them attractive. He had to squint at me through his wire-rims—

"Lenhart! Christ almighty!"

—and then I was wringing hands with my college roommate Chat Wethers.

"It's about time you turned up! I thought we'd lost you to the demimonde. Didn't I say, Kate, George'll shack up with some Frenchie, start wearing berets, heh-heh?"

Chat's bank had sent him to China for three months, but he seemed more concerned with matters on the home front now that he was back. "Business school applications—they're hell, George! What am I supposed to write about a major setback I've encountered? You tell me. The time the Diesel died on the way to Vermont? But maybe I won't go next year. I don't know. See if my recommendations pan out. Otherwise do a third year—"

"I'll bet George wouldn't do a thing like that for a living," said Kate, who could interrupt a conversation without raising her voice. "Would you, George?"

"I'm afraid so," I confessed.

Chat drained his glass. "They got you, too, Lenhart?"

I nodded. "Corporate finance. Fordyce, Farley."

"What about the expat plan?"

"I just couldn't—I don't know," I started, struggling toward an articulation I myself had not quite formed.

But Chat nodded as if he understood. "I know exactly what you mean," he asserted. "You think *Paris* was tough."

"No, not exactly—"

"Try China, George—*Chow-jang, China.* Two Western bars in the whole town."

"Yeah?" I couldn't picture it till Chat added, "One newsstand." Then an image came to mind of a tall, oblique scowl on legs trying to get hold of a *Journal* in a remote Eastern city, then settling grudgingly when by some miracle somebody produced a day-old *Trib*. He had always been bent on travel, yet travel without any wish for, or—my mistake—pretense of, assimilation. I guess he was the old sort of American abroad.

I had stories of my own to tell and was about to expand on Paris when Kate announced, looking pleased with herself: "If someone gave me the chance to go anywhere in the world, do you know where I'd choose?"

"Where?" said Chat and I.

"I'd choose Maine. I'd choose Cold Harbor, Maine. I'd choose it over France, Italy, Spain—" She ticked continental Europe off on her fingers. "Is that horrible of me? Is that the most horrible thing you've ever heard?" Her gray eyes looked happily from one to the other of us for confirmation.

"I'll drink to that," Chat said curtly.

"You?" Kate said, affecting scorn. "You were hardly up at all last summer. George, he was hardly up at all—do you believe that?"

"I *work*, Katie, remember?" Chat said, and gave me a burdened look that seemed to say: "Women!"

And yet from the inflection he put on the word I got the sense that the job remained a novelty. "Guess what, George?" he'd announced our senior spring, with the air of someone who has done something rather devilishly clever: "I got a . . . *job.*"

"Now who's having what? George? What are you drinking now, straight absinthe, heh-heh?"

I hardly needed a drink. Kate's patriotic provincialism—and Chat's cinematic picture of Paris, with men in berets sipping liqueurs—went down like a tonic after my sojourn across the pond.

We had settled on something when Kate got a silly look on her face, like she was going to tell a joke. "No, Chattie," she said. "I have a better idea."

"Yes?"

"George will have a vodka and lemonade."

"Sorry?"

"A Popov and lemonade," Kate went on, making her voice silly and dreamy. "*Dining* hall lemonade. Dining hall lemonade mixed in an athletic department water bottle."

"Oh, yes," I said warmly, catching on. She was referring to a habit of ten years earlier. Kate and I had gone to boarding school together; I had met Chat in college based on our mutual acquaintance. Or to put it more precisely, our friendship there had been predicated on my knowing her.

"Will you have one, too?" I asked quickly, flattered by her turning this into a landmark, and in front of Chat.

"Of course." She laughed.

"One quart, you mean," I supplied.

"Yes! And if I drink too much—!"

"If we should get sick, you mean—"

"Why, we'll go and vomit our guts out behind the science building!"

"I don't want to hear about you and George behind the science building!" Chat bawled. "Wouldn't surprise me if you did want vodka and lemonade!

"I'm telling you, George," he went on, petulant, gesturing with his empty glass, "I don't know what anyone drinks anymore. In China, it's one thing, get a little tropicallee, but I swear, the next corporate *tool* I hear ordering a Kamikaze, I'll—"

"I want a Sex on the Beach!" cried Kate. "I want an Orgasm!"

"Don't say that word, Katie. I hate that word. You know I hate that word."

"Get me an Orgasm!"

"They should never have let women into the Town Club," said Chat gloomily.

"Oh, have they?" I said. I meant this to be ironic somehow—as if I would know the inner workings of the admissions policy—but the irony was lost on Kate.

"Well, not really," she said seriously. "Only till we're thirty."

"Then what?"

"Then we have to marry in or we're out."

"Put out or shut out," they both said, and they both gave half a laugh.

Chat took himself off to the bar.

Alone with Kate, I was self-conscious, suddenly, as if I had forgotten my lines. Their particular brand of droll urbanity was not entirely new to me, but it was the first time I'd seen them in situ, as it were, and their casual indifference to the setting made me feel like a very young boy, with shiny shoes and his hair slicked down, who has been allowed to make an appearance at the grown-ups' party before bed.

I thought that Kate and I might now talk for real, but she said, rather annoyed, "Did you hear Jess Brindle was engaged, George?"

"No, I hadn't," I said.

"Yes, but she broke it off."

"Oh, good," I said, glad of this, for some reason, though I wasn't sure I'd ever met the girl.

"Yes, bit of a . . . random choice . . ."

Kate proceeded to give several more names I had never heard and to account for their whereabouts. Marnie Pall was in town, and her cousin Dick had married Loribelle Betz up in Maine, and Granny had gotten drunk at the wedding—which was a rather *elaborate* affair—and Granny had said, "That girl is climbing as fast as she can, isn't she?" and it was very embarrassing . . .

I heard it said once, by whom I can't recall, that true beauty always has one flaw. As Kate went on, blithely chattering, I fell into the habit I had of looking for that flaw—the thin lip or feature out of place—which might have meant her entry into that elite society. And yet those frank good looks of hers had always seemed to suggest that there was something distasteful about beauty, something a little tacky about a quality that by its very nature draws attention to itself, like coming overdressed to a party, or throwing a black-tie wedding in the country. But Kate—Kate was what you wanted, somehow, in this infinitely ironic age. She was the kind of girl about whom other girls used to say, "All right, so she's *thin* but," trying vainly to suss out the appeal. And even now, when her name comes up, and with it the sulky protest it invariably evokes—"She's not *that* great"—I do not feel compelled to argue in her defense. That was the whole point: she didn't have to be.

"You're not still with that one girl, are you?" she wanted to know.

"Hmm. What else do you want to know?"

Kate thought, frowning. "What you ate for breakfast."

"Poached eggs on toast," I lied, finally getting up to speed.

She liked it. "Where did you eat a poached egg? Where did you *get* a poached egg?"

"In my kitchen."

"You poached the egg yourself, George? How did you learn to poach eggs?"

"My mother taught me."

"She did? I wish my mother—"

"Come over sometime; I'll make you one."

"Breakfast date?" she said curiously. "Do you think Chat would approve? You know he and *I* are supposed to be engaged," she added, as if it was an afterthought, and she grinned.

"I lied," I admitted suddenly. "I didn't eat breakfast."

"You didn't?"

"No, I just had coffee. That's all I ever have."

"That truly disappoints me."

"I meant to say—best wishes."

"Oh, it's not . . . *official*," she said. For some reason this made both of us laugh. There was no promise in Kate's laughter; in fact it was just the opposite note that seemed to resound, an expression of utmost faith in today, of total absorption in the moment as it passed. "You know, George, the main thing is to have fun," she asserted.

"I don't know," I said after a moment. I put my hands in my pockets and took them out again. "It's just New York, I guess. I'm still getting used to it."

"I understand completely," Kate said. "Isn't it dirty and awful?"

"Yes," I said.

"But it's fun," Kate continued. There was something in her voice that made platitudes like that sound fresh. "It's so, so, so, so fun. You just go out and everyone's around and—and you don't have any homework. It's so *nice* not having any homework."

"Oh, Kate."

"And you know, George, what else would we be doing? We have nothing better to do, do we? Or . . . ? I should speak for myself, shouldn't I? *I* have nothing better to do." She said this cheerfully. "Do you?"

"Well, sometimes I work about a hundred hours a week," I said.

"Right," Kate replied. "Work—play—that's what I mean."

Presently Chat returned with the drinks.

"Cheers, then," I said, making an effort to rally. This was cardinal with Kate; one always rallied. I think she had invented the word, at least in this context. She and Chat lived by certain imperatives, such as "You have to rally," and "You never bail out on a scene," and the principle, when throwing parties, of never running out of tonic.

"To what?" said Chat, drinking off the top of his glass.

"Well—to our generation," I said. "Because we have nothing better to do."

Chat, good sport—best sport—laughed a little too hard.

We stayed for two more. Waiting at the coat check, I cursed the middle of the week. There were not five minutes to turn into an hour to turn into a night out. "Get used to it, buddy," Chat advised. "I'm telling you. I did. All anybody did in China was drink and work."

"I'll bet," I said.

"Guys getting plastered—American guys—same goddamn two bars every night. Pure liver torture." He eyed me then, seemingly on the brink of a confidence. Perhaps these many months apart were what made him hesitate, or the fact that our friendship in college had been born not of late-night intimations, but of certain fundamental agreements about how things ought to be done. We had never seen the need to bog each other down with exposing the more sordid corners of our souls. "Tell you, Lenhart, it's different over there," Chat said finally.

"What's different?"

"The drinking."

"Really."

"Same thing as here, same as school, but it's different."

"Come on," I said, "a hangover's a hangover."

But he replied coldly, "No—I'm not talking about that."

"What, then?" I really couldn't guess what he was getting at.

"It's like—it's—well, you work so hard, you know, and you're all alone over there." Chat took off his glasses and rubbed them absently on his shirtfront. "You end up hanging around with people you wouldn't hang around with here."

"Oh."

"Kind of . . . *random* sometimes."

"Sure."

"I'll tell you who I ran into."

"Over there? Who?"

He hooked his glasses back on and ran a hand through the colorless strands of his hair. I remembered his saying in college, "See, some men thin and some men recede, but my dad did both and so will I—I'm doubly fucked," and laughing then, too, because of his many vanities, physical beauty was not one, or if it was, he saw it as so far beneath himself he would no sooner indulge it than sleep off a hangover.

"Hell with it, I didn't just run into him," Chat said, looking me in the eye as if making a decision to come clean about a crime. "I'm not going to lie, why should I? Truth is, I spent time with him. I drank with him nearly every night." There was another fraction of a pause before he pronounced the name, a fraction of a pause during which Chat and I were alone in the foyer, waiting for Kate in a kind of disgruntled sympathy that was the usual state of things between us. Then he said: "Lombardi."

"Harry Lombardi? My God."

It was the last person on earth I would have expected Chat to name, and I didn't know quite how to react. But Chat seemed to take my remark for general derision, and he gave a harsh, approving laugh. "He *surfaced*, George! Reinvented himself as a go-getter, a fucking entrepreneur! High-tech venture capital: who would have thought? Ambitious, evidently."

"But—of course," I said. "We always knew that."

"We did? *I* didn't. I had no idea."

I had to think he was joking, but the long blank face was void of humor. The unbelievable, and sometimes delightful, thing about Chat's myopia was how astoundingly vast it was in scope. Rumors of Lombardi's success had reached me even in Paris.

"Guy had quit his job—was knocking around China for *kicks*, Lenhart—finds this electronics factory . . . *takes it over.* By the time Broder sends me over he was king of the goddamn hill! All these factory manager guys were like, No, Mis' Lombardi, Yes, Mis' Lombardi—"

"You mean you worked together?"

Chat nodded. "You know he'd been at Broder, too?"

"God," I said, trying to get my head around it, "that's some crazy coincidence." I was only voicing the obvious, and yet this element of the encounter hardly seemed to have occurred to Chat.

"You think?" he said with a shrug. Then, seized by a fit of impatience, he drummed the coat check on the counter. "Gilberto! You dozing in there? We need our jackettos, guy!"

We shrugged into our overcoats. I'm sure I would have grilled him about Lombardi right then if there hadn't been another, much more pressing question I wanted answered. "How long have you and Kate been going out?" I asked, as if the answer would shed light on their relationship, as on any old couple's.

Chat guffawed. "Three months? Fifteen years? Hell if I know! You think she deserves the ring?"

I was saved from answering when Kate herself emerged from the ladies' room, her long blond bob curving to her shoulders. Chat got her into her camel's hair with a neat toss and watched her button it up. The expression on his face—it wasn't affection, it wasn't remotely affection. It was the way I'd seen him, a thousand times, look at himself in the mirror after shaving—with approval for a job done, if not perfectly, then well enough. He approved of her, that was all.

I followed them through the revolving door. I felt as if my thoughts were spinning, too, trying to catch up with the evening's revelations. Lombardi . . . and Kate and Chat . . . I wasn't so much crushed by Kate's announcement as I was conscious, again, of my own backwardness. Until then I hadn't been aware that people could—well, *bore* themselves into marriage engagements, was the way it struck me. Why now? When she had known Chat her whole life?

Outside it occurred to me that I had not asked Kate what she was doing.

She pretended to be offended. "I *work*, George."

"Oh, right—you and Meems and Annie Roth," Chat interrupted, chuckling, with a wink in my direction. "They're in the art business, George. They're all—"

"You're *extremely* funny tonight, Chat—"

"—objets d'art."

"I'm in American paintings, George, at Sotheby's."

"You work, Kate Goodenow," Chatland Wethers sententiously pronounced, "because you live in an age when it is considered appropriate for rich American girls to work."

He would get drunk and come out with things like that. But somehow I felt that this made sense of the whole evening, much more so than their putative engagement.

We walked to the corner, and Chat hailed a cab going uptown. Most men would hold a taxi door for a girl, but Chat knew better: he did the slide himself.

"We'll drop you off, George," offered Kate. "Chat? We'll drop George off."

"Sure, hop in."

"Oh, no," I said quickly, "I want to. Walk."

"Shoot yourself, Lenhart."

Kate cranked the window down. "Sure we can't take you somewhere?" she called. They were very polite, the two of them. They were always very polite. When I declined a second time, Kate warned, "You know, you won't be able to hide your mysterious double life from us forever!" and I forced a laugh, too late to hide the solemnity that had stolen across my face. I remember resolving, as their cab sped off and I started on my solitary way uptown, to do better the next time. With Kate I was forever trying to live up to an ideal, but when you considered what that ideal was, it made no sense at all, my striving: it was an ideal of carelessness.

The next week at work I reached into my suit pocket and drew out a balled-up cocktail napkin with the Town Club logo crumpled across the front. I tossed it into the wastebasket, only to retrieve it a moment later. I smoothed it out and stuck it in the top drawer of my desk. I think I kept it because it made me think of luck. They were the most conservative people I knew, and yet I had walked home that evening thinking the two of them seemed to represent everything that was worthwhile in the city, everything that was respectable, solid, even hopeful. Their lack of ambition struck me as wonderfully smart against the vulgar striving I witnessed by day. My own ambition for Kate suddenly seemed vulgar as well, like a bold, alcohol-induced comment that one would never make sober. How much better, it seemed, to have her taken, and to get the two of them in one package, so we could all have a lot of fun together. I wasn't exactly sure what she meant by fun, but I felt as if I had been running in a boring, drawn-out race called New York until that evening, when my old friends stopped me and pointed out the rest of the fair. And if Chat and Kate said it would be more fun over where they were, then I believed them. They had grown up here, after all, whereas I had just arrived.

CHAPTER 2

It was hard, with a roommate like Toff, to confront him about anything. The fear was that he would agree about his failings but do nothing; that further confrontation would mean a scene; that a scene would make his wiring go berserk. But after I had to wait for the shower several days running, I made up my mind to say something about coordinating our schedules, and one morning I waited outside the bathroom door. When the water stopped, however, a girl came out in a towel.

"Sorry."

"Oh, that's all right," I said. I went into the bathroom and closed the door.

The girl's name was Cara. I used to see her late at night from time to time, because she liked to come over and watch television and get away from her roommates. If it was I and not Toff who found her there on the couch, she would apologize and make herself smaller on her cushion, curling in around her frozen yogurt; I got the feeling Toff had told her she should. Some nights the two of them slept together, and other nights Toff wouldn't come home at all and she would crash on the couch, though his bed stood empty and unmade. She was tall but fighting slim with the haircut of the moment—a layered helmet—highlighted blond. I gathered she hoped to marry Toff.

You know how it is when you learn a new word and then all at once everyone seems to be using it. That spring it happened not with a word but with a man: Harry Lombardi. A week or so after my reunion with Chat and Kate, when Lombardi's name had so improbably come up, I was riding up in the morning elevator; it stopped on four, the trading floor. Two men shouldered out and one of them distinctly said, "You'd have to go to Harry Lombardi for that now." It gave me an odd feeling all day, that name—part curiosity, part dread— though I hadn't laid eyes on the guy in four years. Nor, I hasten to add, in the months that I had known him, had Lombardi been either close friend or enemy. I ought to have forgotten him entirely, the way Chat had, until the two of them ended up whiling away the Pacific nights together, ten thousand miles from home.

And while there was some justification for my curiosity— Lombardi's wild success on Wall Street as tracked by the Dartmouth grapevine—there was less for my dread. The only way I can think to put it is that he got to me, Lombardi did; he always had. He was one of those people who, even in absence, take on an annoying, insistent presence in one's mind, like the bang of a shutter or the whine of an airplane ruining a summer's day. And though Chat's introduction of the name had seemed the one discordant note in an evening with old friends, it only made sense that with Chat and Kate, I would get Lombardi as well. For if they were the evening's unexpected pleasure, Lombardi was the unavoidable reckoning of the morning after. And get him I did.

That same week I was pushing through a subway turnstile at Grand Central when my eyes happened to meet those of someone pushing through the opposite way. I couldn't place the face, though it stared up hard for an instant at my own, with blue, bloodshot eyes.

With a jolt it came to me, sitting at my desk that afternoon: it was Lombardi I'd seen. He was losing his hair, that was all. Later that day I was tracing the name on a piece of paper when the phone rang. I picked up the receiver and—by this point I was rather expecting the call—it was Harry Lombardi.

"I thought I saw you!" he gushed, in a way no man ought to. "Had a buddy amine look you up in the Fordyce directory. How do you like that? It must be fate, huh, Lenhart?"

I felt the old defensiveness come over me, and wouldn't admit to having seen him as well. "You work around here now?" I said instead.

"Naw, I was in to see you guys for a meeting. I'm not really 'office-based' these days. Couldn't stand the heat, you know?"

Despite the disclaimer, there was something in the way he answered that made me think he was doing very, very well, perhaps even better than I'd heard, and on an instinct I congratulated him.

"Yeah, thanks, it was time I got out on my own," he said briefly.

"So, what are you, starting your own fund now?" I pressed him. "Advising the Feds?"

"I hope to be getting something off the ground soon," Harry said, automatically, like a witness taking the Fifth.

I tried it one last time, but beyond mumbling an acknowledgment of his "stake in China," he wouldn't be tricked into elaborating.

He hadn't changed. In an inverse of the rest of the world, when talking about himself Harry Lombardi was permanently distracted. Chat had been his roommate at Dartmouth for a year, and yet we'd been the last to know he was some kind of computer genius; it wasn't until Eastern European graduate students started leaving messages on the answering machine and lurking around the room discussing theoretical cryptography that we got him to admit to it. He had never so much as alluded to any such ability. It seemed that nothing the man had been born with, no natural faculty of his own, could hold his interest.

"So speaking of China, I guess your buddy Chat probably told you I saw him over there this winter?"

"I guess I did hear that," I said slowly.

"Hell of a time, George. Hell of a time. Chat's a riot." That voice, coming at me after so many years, inevitably pumped enthusiasm. Lombardi could spin anything—even Chat's disgusted commentary—into a "riot."

"I heard you saw a lot of each other."

"A lot?" Harry's tone was reproachful. "We met up every night! We were drinking buddies, George!"

I had to stifle an urge to congratulate him again; no doubt in his mind this achievement was by far more laudatory than anything professional—like, say, starting his own venture at the age of twenty-three. As we spoke I found myself turning the fact over again and again, like a coin, in my thoughts: he was twenty-three years old—he was a twenty-three-year-old college dropout, rather, and he was hoping to "get something off the ground." There was no way around it. It was unique as hell.

"So what about you, George? You heading into your second year now?"

"First year," I said stiffly. "I was in Paris till last month."

"Paris?" He was clearly—needlessly—impressed. "That's original."

"It's anything but," I protested.

"Do you speak the language? That is, do you speak French?"

"I get by."

"Yeah? You're lucky. I got a tin ear. *Juh nuh parlay pah fron-say*. Although even I was better than Chat. You should have seen him trying to pick up girls in Xiaojiang."

"Well, for Chat it's a matter of principle to speak all foreign languages abysmally," I explained, half-jokingly, before I remembered that the grossest of ironies were lost on Lombardi.

Sure enough, he said earnestly, "He's a very principled guy, isn't he—Chat?"

It was absurd: Lombardi *didn't* speak the language. Either that or he wasn't listening, which I suspected as well. Harry's mind raced rudely ahead in conversation, seizing on points that could be of further use to him, discarding the rest. It could be trying, or downright offensive. In college I had given up introducing him to people, even open-minded people, who might have seen what I saw in him—for even then I'd had some perverse investment in the guy, against my better judgment. But even then it wasn't worth the effort. He couldn't stick around long enough to get their names.

"So you see him a lot, George?" he wanted to know. "You see Chat a lot? Funny, his starting out at Broder, isn't it? I mean, just the way I did."

"Look, I really just got back," I said.

"Oh, right, right. . . . You probably haven't had time to . . . connect. He's probably with Kate all the time—his girlfriend, Kate? They hang out, like—like most couples but probably even—"

"Something like that," I interrupted.

"And I bet it's hard for him to get out—or for *you* to get out, for that matter! Do you get out much, George? Do you get out at all?"

"As a matter of fact," I replied, provoked, absurdly, into a retort, "I'm seeing Chat tonight."

You could almost hear the mind turning, processing the information in ones and zeroes, before the deathly casual: "Oh, yeah? Where are you guys going? You having dinner—you going out for real? Or you just—"

I named the bar.

"Killian's on Lex? Sure! I used to go there all the time."

"Did you." It was the obvious midtown pub, and had been for thirty or forty years.

"Oh, sure, sure—"

"Join us if you want."

"Join you? Tonight?" Harry stumbled audibly. "I think I'm— well, what time? What time were you thinking? I wonder if I could make it. I don't know if I can make it. I've got a dinner with these guys—Europeans—Eurotrash, ha ha—gotta take them out."

"Oh."

"You know what? I'll try to make it anyway. What time you think you'll be there till? Eight? Nine?"

"We're meeting at eight."

"Oh, *meeting* at eight. I didn't realize that you were meeting at eight. Then I'll definitely see you. I should be there nine, nine-thirty latest. Does that work for you? If you're not there, where will you be? Think you'll move on somewhere—go downtown maybe?"

"Nnn . . . I doubt it."

"I tell you what, let me give you my mobile phone number just in case, okay?"

"Your *what*?"

"My phone—I've got a mobile phone—you know, one of those things you walk around with. That way you can reach me, you know, if your plans change."

He was the first person I knew to have one. Everyone else thought they were a joke. He read off the number, and feeling a bit ridiculous, I copied it down.

"You got it?"

"I've got it."

"If we don't connect, if I miss you for some reason, tell Chat I said hi," Harry urged. "Tell him, you know, I'm back, and I say hi."

The fawning repulsed me, and that evening I made a joke of it to Chat. It was a Thursday, the best night of the weekend, and Chat turned up a little drunk already.

The long narrow bar was jammed with guys like us, no more than two or three years out, and the occasional corporate girl holding court. You couldn't get near the bar, but Chat's high-pitched whine easily asserted itself over the crowd, to whose chagrin we were served right away.

I thought I had better get the worst over with. "You know Lombardi's back in town," I announced, when we had found a corner to protect.

Surprisingly, this elicited a dismissive shake of the head. "I don't think so."

"No—I saw him."

Chat, surveying the crowd with a lax expression, did not seem to have heard. "Those guys look alike—short, you know?"

"No, but I *saw* him—"

"Really short," Chat insisted. "A couple of times I thought I saw him, too. He's got that kind of face. But it was some other short guy."

"Christ, he's not *that* short."

"He's five *seven*, George! He's down *here* on me." Chat held a hand to his hip. "He's like one of those little guys in the cartoons— you know those guys, their legs go around in circles to keep up."

"In any case—"

"Six two's not even tall anymore," Chat added disconsolately. "In the old days, that was tall. Now it's only average."

"Look: Lombardi's back," I affirmed. "He called me, and he's showing up here later."

Oddly, it was not the prospect of seeing the man that seemed to concern Chat. "He called *you*? What'd he want with you?"

"You, I think," I said honestly. "He told me to tell you he says hi."

Chat snickered. "What a little suck-up. How'd he find you?"

"Saw me going into Fordyce. He was there for a meeting." I looked sidelong at Chat. "I do believe he's doing pretty goddamn well."

"I'm sure he is," Chat admitted. "Conniving little bastid." We both chuckled.

"I always wondered if the rumors were true."

"You would, Lenhart."

He had me there. "Didn't you?"

"What rumors? I never heard any."

"But you must have—of his hitting it big? Come on—didn't you ever wonder what happened to him?"

Chat shrugged, draining his beer. "I figured he found his own scene."

"He did." I laughed. "The mail room of Broder, Weill, and Company."

Harry had dropped out after freshman year. He had dropped out without any notice, any hint to Chat or me, or expression of dissatisfaction—just simply had not returned to Dartmouth with the sophomore class. It was a fact I had privately come to admire. It was the one cool thing about Lombardi—infinitely cooler now, in the light of his success. That whole first year in New York, I used to think that if only he had learned how to capitalize on it, the way he did on the fluctuations of the market, he might have seen phenomenal personal returns.

"He didn't really come up from the *mail* room?" Chat pressed me.

"No," I admitted, though I knew Harry would prefer the old-school sound of it. "Systems, I think. With that computer brain?"

" 'S true. Even I remember that—he was taking comp sci ten thousand freshman year."

"What the hell—none of this came out in China?"

"I guess not," Chat said, as if he hadn't been there himself.

"Didn't you wonder how he happened to be running things over there?"

"I'm telling you, Lenhart," Chat protested, "he used to drink me under the table! You have no idea what that guy can put away."

"You must have made conversation," I insisted.

Chat considered the question blankly for a moment before answering: "Kate. We talked about Kate . . . and Nick. We talked about school . . ." All at once he seemed overcome by the perplexity of it, and put on the set, obtuse expression I associated with his having an economics test in the morning. "God, that place was strange!"

"Dartmouth?" I said, surprised.

Chat gave me a pitying look. "Dartmouth? No. Dartmouth was not weird, George. Chow-jang was weird. It was all just . . . the landscape wasn't normal."

"Huh."

"Do you know how normally you have—well, pine trees or buildings? Buildings if you're in New York, say, or maybe palm trees if you're in the Caribbean? Well, this wasn't like that."

"You were in China."

"I know, I know! I'm just telling you, George! It was strange!"

As I waited for him to say more, it crossed my mind that the Eastern sojourn might have warped Chat's outlook a little bit. But he seemed to shake off whatever was bothering him and gave a peremptory laugh.

"What a freak. He'd always be grilling me in the strangest way. Asking me all these questions about things—school, you know, after he left." Chat focused suspicious eyes on me. "*Your* name came up more than once. It's funny—I think he respects you."

I had always rather suspected this as well, and tried not to dwell on the suspicion, for it failed to produce a corresponding desire on my part to live up to Harry's respect. "Well, *naturally*—"

"No, listen, when I told him you made magna or summa or whatever the hell it was you got, he was all . . . excited. He acted like you'd named your goddamn first kid after him. He kept saying, 'I knew George Lenhart had it in him.' "

I was silent under Chat's scrutiny; I hadn't asked for the guy's faith in me, and I didn't want it now.

"Anyway, we used to drink a toast to you at the end of the night, Lenhart. You could at least be grateful."

I drained the foam from my glass. I, a financial aid student, had gotten good grades; Harry had dropped out of college and made bonuses I could only imagine. But I wouldn't have traded places with him for anything. One doesn't, after all, wish to trade places with the man one pities. And despite the trajectory his career seemed to be taking, I pitied Harry. I pitied him for a hundred things—his physical clumsiness, his utter lack of social grace—but most of all I pitied him for the nakedness of his ambition, for his inability to cop an attitude or bluff through a hand in sync, for once, with his blasé generation.

What can I say now, other than that things are, naturally, quite different. Now I can see that like all pity, mine was misguided. It's not that I don't pity him anymore, for even with his success and everything else that happened, I do. But now I understand that my pity is my problem.

I took out my wallet to get the next round. I assumed that having been interrupted, Chat would drop the subject, but he had that confessional air about him again, and, as it had previously, it seemed to be driving him to speak. It didn't suit him any better tonight. Chat never talked about people; it was understood that the habit was a weakness of smaller men—the Lombardis of the world—and his usual conversation had two topics: things he did and places he went. But three months in the Far East having his life story wheedled out of him would have been hard for anyone to shake.

"He's got this bizarro memory, George," Chat continued, as if the fact were an indictment. "It was really . . . weird. Like, once I got confused and said I was hanging out with Kate up in Maine and he said, 'But you can't have been hanging out with her—she didn't come up at all that summer.' Bizarro, no? I mean, tell me that's not the limit of a warped mentality."

As one who had kept a chronicle of Kate's life myself, what was stranger to me was that Harry was evidently still broadcasting the habit. I couldn't understand why he never learned, but went on exposing himself again and again and again. He seemed to have no pride.

"It happened a couple of times: 'No, no, you've got it wrong. That was the year it rained all summer—come on, don't you remember— and you and Nick just hung out at the yacht club playing chess and she never showed up.' That kind of thing. Or, 'I thought you said *you* were the first to kiss her.' Annoying as hell. So one night I took matters into my own hands, kind of . . . turned the tables on him.'"

Chat glanced at me to see how this would settle in. When I failed to reply, he broke out angrily, "Damned if I was going to be corrected on—on *Kate*—on my own *childhood*, for Chrissake—by some fucking . . . Lombardi! I can't remember every goddamn little thing that happened when I was twelve!"

But Harry could. And if you met him now, when men twice his age fly across the country to drink a cup of coffee with him, he could tell you what sport your brother played and how cool you were in eighth grade and whether you summered in town or up-island. He wouldn't be embarrassed to tell you, either—any more than you would be to show him your vinyl LPs or your model train collection. Harry has a collection, too—he collects backgrounds. And like many collections, his had started with one prized, chanced-upon item, given him for free: in the year he spent as Chat's roommate, with me next door, he had first heard talk of Kate.

"So what exactly did you tell him?" I asked.

Chat snickered. "Most of what I said was true. Some of it I made up, gilded the lily a bit. I told him she's never been the same since Nick, you know, showed his true colors."

I caught my reflection in the mirror above the bar and looked hurriedly away. "So you told him about Nick?" I said.

"Oh, yeah—Kate, Nick, boarding school, golden couple—you would have loved it, Lenhart. I was quite the narrator. I kind of got used to it—looked forward to the session every night. Oh, get this: at the end of it all, when Broder was packing me home, I told him if he ever got back to town he should look her up."

I looked at him sharply. "Why'd you do that?"

"I thought it would be funny! Can't you just see him calling Katie now? 'Excuse me. You don't know me but I can recite every detail about your life and I thought we could, like, get together for drinks.' " Chat broke off, laughing hysterically. " 'Don't worry, honey, I'll keep it tied around my leg so it doesn't get out and bite you!' Is that the funniest damn thing you've ever heard?"

"Do you think he'll call her?" I asked.

The question disappointed him. "Hell if I know, George," Chat said bitterly. "Or care."

"Right," I said.

"Oh," he added, "I told him she might 'never fall in love again. . . .'"

"Oh yes?" I tipped my glass up, but there was nothing left.

"Yup."

"Gee."

"Hell!" Chat exclaimed vehemently, setting the empty stein down with a crash. "Maybe it's true!"

By nine the bar had emptied out except for some old guys in corners, partners in law firms you'd never heard of, plying secretaries with drinks. It was refreshing to know that sort of thing still went on, but whether it appealed to my generational cynicism or my own relative innocence I couldn't have said.

When Harry had not shown up at half past nine, Chat begged out of the second act.

"You're just going to go?" I hadn't counted on this possibility.

"Part of me wants to see the freak, but, alas, I am wanted at home."

This was a favorite joke. Home was Bobby Renfroe's girlfriend's couch in the Seventies. Chat had been crashing there for the three months he'd been back, smoking Pam's cigarettes, hanging piles of dry cleaning from the lamps. Pam didn't mind; she liked having people around. Kate would never have put up with something like that. I was beginning to surmise that they kept each other on very, very long leashes; that they could, and that this was a source of not a little pride to them.

"You ought to come with me. Say you waited and missed him."

I shook my head. "He gave me the number for his mobile phone."

Chat's eyebrows went up in an expression of ultimate amusement, as if he'd been given a key to Harry's character, and to all that was absurd in the world. "Why is it," he said, "that all of the jerks who nobody wants to get in touch with are buying phones? If I ever get one of those phones, take me out behind the barn and shoot me, George—all right?" He twisted a blue school scarf rather foppishly around his neck, perched a ridiculous fleece hat on his head, and strode toward the door, defying, with his imperious stare, the world to laugh.

C H A P T E R **3**

Then there was nothing to do but wait. I had learned from experience that it was better to get this kind of meeting over with than to keep postponing it; to skip out with Chat would have been like eating dessert first.

I got a seat at the bar and took out a *Post* from my briefcase. Turning the pages of the latest scandal, I tried to remember the last time I had seen Harry Lombardi up at Dartmouth. Finally I placed it: it had been exam week at the end of our freshman year. I'd been walking back to the dorm after my last final, in that overly calm, hallucinatory state induced by sleep deprivation and hope. Nothing then made me so hopeful as doing well on a test; now that the tests were over, I was beginning to wonder if anything ever would. Someone had shouted to me from a taxi. It was Harry, packed and taking off for the summer, or so I thought. He hadn't brought much stuff with him to school, compared to me, compared to Chat; two big suitcases would have done the job.

"How'ja do?" he called.

"God, I don't know," I said, as rigorous self-deprecation, particularly when it came to academics, was the expected mode of discourse. "That last question really—"

"Aw, come on!" Harry broke in. "You know you aced it!"

And I was startled into grinning out the truth. "Yeah, I guess I did!" I admitted, and I ran up to the cab to say a proper good-bye.

Harry waved this off, however, and leaning out the window, he said, "I've got no worries about you, George."

His remark annoyed me, because I felt I should have been the one offering reassurances. But I had thanked him with what humility I could muster, and sitting in the bar waiting for him, I was glad that I had at least done that.

After Harry's cab drove away I had continued toward the dorm full of promises to myself. I resolved to boldly eat with him in dining hall, for instance. But when term started the following fall, it was three weeks before I thought to formally inquire of the guy. I was relieved, at first, to be informed that he had withdrawn from school, but on second thought felt duped: quite conceivably his dropping out was not an admission of failure but a daring leapfrog. I honestly didn't know which one it was. I could see that it irked Chat, too, so we didn't talk about him—not that we ever had, much.

One thing Chat did always say was that Lombardi's head was too big for his body. It was true, his head was massive, and he had a large toothy grin to go with it—a tortured disembodied grin, I thought— which he turned on and off to great effect; I imagined he had gotten a lot of mileage out of that grin, over the years, from people who didn't see the torturedness in it.

At finding me alone in the bar, it was abruptly quenched. He shook my hand, gravely pronouncing: "George."

He had learned to dress at the firm and the look suited him. It wasn't the French cuffs, though, that made me want to call a timeout for reassessment. His hair had receded halfway to the crown. But I noticed that the blue eyes blazed, brighter now, against the bare forehead.

"Chat go home?" he said right away: get the worst over with.

"A little while ago."

"He probably had to meet Kate."

"Hmm."

"You told him I said hi?"

"Would you like a beer, Harry?"

Watching him try to refocus was painful. It seemed to take a huge mental effort for him to recalibrate the evening in his head, salvage a few points after heavy losses. "Jeez, it's been a while, huh?" The grin was turned on again. "A beer? That's a great idea. Let's have a beer. Lemme get it, though. I want to get it. You don't mind if I get it, do you? Although . . ." He surveyed Killian's divey interior. It seemed to embarrass him, and he passed a fidgety hand over his skull. "You know what? Let's go somewhere else. What do you say we go somewhere else? Somewhere a little . . ." He mouthed the last word: "nicer."

"Nicer than Killian's?" I deadpanned.

"Somewhere, you know," Harry persisted uncomfortably, glancing over his shoulder, "downtown."

"Oh, *down*town! But you just got uptown."

"Doesn't matter," he mumbled. "Come on, let's get outta here. This place is—it's just, I don't know. It's okay after work, but you don't want to hang around here—you know what I mean?"

I went, just to see what he would pick; or, more likely, because I had nothing better to do.

Down we went to Soho, Harry making calls to answering machines on his mobile phone. "Promised some people I would call."

"Sure."

"Here, you wanna try it?"

"No, thanks."

"No, seriously, call anyone you want. Long distance—anything."

"I can't think of anyone."

"Call Chat, why don't you? See if he wants to meet us. He might change his mind if he knows we're going downtown."

"That's all right," I said. "I thought of someone."

"You did? Here. Dial away."

I punched in Kate's number. She answered after a couple of rings.

"Hello, it's George."

"Oh, George!" She always sounded faintly appalled when she picked up the phone, and the tone of her voice made me shiver a little, imagining what the rejoinder would be to the man whose name she didn't recognize. "Where are you calling from?"

"I'm calling from a mobile phone in the back of a car."

"You are? You must be very important, to have one of those!"

"It's not mine."

"It's not? Well, whoever you got it from must be very important."

"He is. Very."

"Well, have fun. Where are you going? Do you want to come over?"

"We can't—we're going downtown."

"Are you? Gosh, that's a big effort. We were thinking of going out, too. But I don't know if we'll leave the apartment. Dick and Loribelle and some people just came over with a bottle of Mount Gay."

"That was nice of them."

"But I don't think we have any limes. I wonder if the deli would send over just limes."

In the background a man's voice said, "The deli'll send over anything!"

"I think he's right," I said.

"Good, I hope so. Well, have fun, George! Come over if you change your mind. There are some people here who'd really like to meet you."

"Who was that?" Harry asked.

"A girl."

"Does she want to join us?"

"No."

CHAPTER **4**

For half an hour we trawled the warehouse streets south of Houston looking for the place Harry wanted to go. "I'd go somewhere else, but I really think you're going to like this place, George, I really do." And five minutes later: "It's not that we have to go there, but I think we should go there if we can." Eventually the driver dropped us off, cursing, in front of a line of people standing, literally, behind a red velvet rope. "I knew we'd find it!" Harry exulted. He walked directly to the front of line, spoke to the bouncer, and turned around and beckoned to me. I was lagging back, like the bad friend that I was, certain he would be rebuffed. "Come on!" Harry called. "Come on, George! We're in!"

As we walked through the chrome doors I felt a curious rush of excitement. I could only conclude that this latent side of myself—the side that got a real thrill out of being plucked from the crowd to enter a nightclub—had been aroused by New York.

"Pretty cool how I got us in, huh?"

It was two floors inside, with dining upstairs and dancing down, and a steel staircase spiraling between. We sat down and ordered a pair of extra-large cocktails—the drinks came in sizes—and sipped them and, from the vantage point of a corner table, looked around. The crowd had not quite gone bridge-and-tunnel; amid guys like us and an optimistic group of South Americans, a handful of hipsters were enjoying their last supper. Harry and I must have looked ridiculous—two guys in suits sitting across a chrome table the size of a record album. Almost in spite of myself, however, as I sipped my drink, the scene and the Latin beat put me in an immoderately good mood.

"You like it, huh?" Harry said diffidently, understanding that if pressed, I would shut down into disapproval. "See? You see what Chat's missing? He doesn't even know what he's missing! I mean, this is great!"

He drank in the funniest way, pushing his head down and out through his shoulders, picking up the glass in one trembling hand with the other spread on the table for balance, and funneling liquid off the top. His eyes would get wide as he slurped, like a child's.

"Where you living?" Harry asked.

"Uptown."

"You live alone?"

"No, I've got a roommate."

He paused to consult the menu of hors d'oeuvres. They were all sucker appetizers, Tex-Mex plates you'd never see west of the Connecticut River, various skewered items with incongruous sauces. Harry ordered half a dozen of them.

"Do you have a lot of parties, George?"

"We haven't had one. We ought to."

When the food came he gobbled up a shrimp quesadilla, wiped his hands on his napkin, and tossed the napkin back in front of him. "If you had one—if you had a party—when do you think you'd have it?"

"I don't know, Harry."

"If you have it—"

"I'll invite you, I promise."

His lips turned up wanly. "No, hey, I wasn't going to ask that. I know you'd invite me, George. I know you're my friend. I was going to say—I was going to ask, actually, what does your, uh, roommate do for a living?"

"He's a paralegal," I said shortly. You had to keep it brief with Harry; the more information you gave him, the more his mind would want to do something with it, project something on to it. Give him an inch and he'd *pave* a mile.

"Paralegal?" he repeated. "Okay, okay . . . I don't know what they're paying you to start at Fordyce these days, but I know it's not a hell of a lot, and I wanted to say, if you want me to pay for some of the booze—you know, I could bring some really top-shelf stuff"—he caught my expression and kept going—"top-shelf stuff really gets a party going, I find."

"Why don't you just give me a hundred dollars cash right now and I'll put it toward the Mount Gay?" I suggested.

"Yeah. That's what I mean, like Mount Gay rum, Stolichnaya vodka . . ."

"Thanks, Harry," I said. That was all you could say.

I finally got him to talk about work. There was a gracefulness in his self-deprecation that you never saw elsewhere. He answered my rudimentary questions about the market in a tone that was almost gentle. When we spoke, presently, shouting above the flutes and drums, of his own career, Harry reminded me of an aging athlete recounting the big game, having to go through the whole spiel again not because he particularly wants to but because he knows it's expected of him. His modesty was both false and true, and the conflict of it made him shy.

I myself was probably at the height of my susceptibility to the romance of Wall Street that evening. Impoverished beginner that I was, I loved to hear the stories of the players, the winners and losers, and the allowances made for the eccentricities of the former. So I would have been happy to shine the spotlight of a disciple's attention on Harry for a good couple of hours. But I could hardly hide my disappointment when he cut short his personal history and started in telling me about the company he wanted to start.

I have to laugh now when I remember the exchange.

"Computers?" I said with distaste. "But I thought you were through with the techie stuff." To me, computers smacked of mediocrity—guys who wore short-sleeved shirts to work, the engineers of the nineties.

"Now it's not computers per se, George, you've gotta understand. It's a computer *network*—"

But he could see the way my eyes glazed over at even the briefest of details, and he smiled benevolently and said, "Well, nothing's happening quite yet."

I will say that despite my own lack of enthusiasm, I had no doubt Harry would do as he said when the time was right, when he got the capital, or just got bored. He had done it before, two years earlier: when he was at the top of his game he had quit the desk at Broder— just like that—to go off backpacking in the Far East. That was how he'd ended up in China.

I didn't have to ask Harry why he left Broder, or why then. Naturally, the first thing he did when he had some money—the first thing anyone who never had much does—was go and try to give himself a few of the privileges he'd missed out on, growing up. It wasn't that he had been poor—"But in my hometown kids didn't, like, spend their summers abroad, you know what I mean?" But I did ask him why Asia, why not Europe.

"Keeping my eyes open for deals," Harry explained. "Indonesia, Malaysia—very hot right then, George."

He sounded disingenuous, and atypically so, but I let the comment pass, for of course that's exactly what had happened. Harry couldn't help doing deals; he walked out the door and a deal accosted him. He had stumbled up Nepal and through to China, found an undercapitalized electronics factory, and set them to making the new telephones. When the project was under way, he had called up his old Broder mentor for capital to finance the expansion. And then fate had intervened—at least that's how Harry told it—in the form of Chat Wethers, who had been sent over on due diligence for the firm. The deal had brought Harry back to the table; the coincidence had legitimized him to himself. There is nothing like running into someone to replace ambition, or chance, with fate as the apparent governing influence in one's life.

"See, what I really wanted to do was to see some concerts," Harry admitted, on our second XL margaritas. "That's why I quit. That's why I went to California: to see a show." He named the peripatetic rock band he had hoped to follow around—by VW bus, no less.

"What show was it?" I asked, inanely. The conversation seemed to have taken a precarious turn.

"New Year's Eve. San Francisco."

"And how—how was the show?"

But Harry shook his head, staring down at his lap. It was horrifying: he suddenly appeared to be holding back tears. Or perhaps it was the alcohol that made his eyes bloodshot; he was a sweaty, unhealthy drunk. I could see him in twenty, thirty years, nodding off in the bar car of the Long Island Rail Road, mouth open, shot bottle of Wild Turkey on the grimy little table, breath spray in his coat pocket—except he was going to be too rich for that destiny.

"Canceled. They canceled it because one of the guys got sick."

"God, I'm really sorry," I said, as if someone had died.

He went on miserably, "I didn't belong there anyway. Those groupie kids. . . . You know where I was staying? Just take a wild guess where I was staying."

"I don't know. I give up."

"The Four Seasons. The *Four Seasons*, George. It was the only hotel I knew in San Francisco! We used to stay there on the firm."

"But, Harry," I said impatiently, "you know all those kids are from Greenwich."

"But they *were* kids," Harry said. He blew his nose into his napkin. "Maybe twenty-five-year-old kids, George, but kids. I was no kid."

He looked at me dumbly for a moment, as if hoping for a refutation of the statement. When none came he sighed and said, "Once I was out there, I couldn't go back. I stayed in San Francisco a week, took some tours, watched videos in my hotel room. Then I booked a flight to Hong Kong."

"Hong Kong?" I felt the seesaw of my respect for him teetering up a notch.

"Yeah. You ever been to Hong Kong?"

"No."

He sniffed; sighed; seemed to find security in that. "Did you ever see them?" He named the band again.

"Yeah—twice," I admitted. "Just twice, and one time the show wasn't even that great."

But it was no use apologizing: he looked wounded anyway.

The waitress came, and I excused myself and went to the men's room. There I leaned against the sink and gave myself up to a kind of mirthless laughter. I kept picturing Harry in tie-dyes with crunchy hair. It was the saddest thing I had ever heard, or the stupidest or the funniest—Harry's stealth mission to the West Coast, his elaborate acting out of the desire to acquire a teenager's pop culture references. No doubt he'd been planning to buy some overpriced weed and figure out how to smoke it, too. I laughed, not quite drunk but pitying him. The man at the urinal must have thought I was on drugs. He kept turning around to stare.

We went to two more bars, or three or four, working our inevitable way back up to the Upper East Side. At the last bar, a place in the Sixties with sand on the floor and plastic beach toys on the wall, Harry fell in love with the bartender.

She was older than we were, with long bare arms sticking out from her overalls. She ignored him at first, and who wouldn't: big-spender short guy and his I-banker-bozo pal, all dressed up in Daddy's clothes. But I learned something that night. Harry went on, unruffled, persistent. *This your regular night? I don't think I've seen you before. What time do you get off?* I envied him for being able to say the things he said with a straight face. And the crazy thing was that soon enough he was getting somewhere. The girl would make a drink, take her time about it, but edge back to our corner eventually, until she had taken a proprietary stance there. Time and again Harry got that from women—a second look—and there were a handful of reasons one could have proffered as to why: a sense of the money, or the power, or something more profound—the intelligence that lay beneath them. He had the kind of face, too, that demands a second look, not because it was good-looking but because it so nearly was. He had large blue eyes, penetrating when they looked directly at you, more often restless; but the mouth was more sloppily drawn. It was too big, with a slight excess of lip whose slack ought to have been taken up. With a certain type of girl he had been very popular in his year of college; a fact that had mystified and then enraged Chat. But it was easy for me to see why. Even though to us his name became a synonym for the hopelessly uncouth, Harry was one of those men whose modest growth tends to encourage the development of "personality" early on. There was a vitality about him, an alacrity to his movements even in their clumsiness, which bespoke an urgency in every moment.

There was one more thing going on with the woman behind the bar, something I had never quite understood before. At some early point in their flirtation, she must have sensed that she herself was not the focus of Harry's ambition; the distracted quality surfaced even in the midst of his pursuit. And because he didn't like her any more than she liked him—though, for a million reasons, he should have—she liked him much, much more. It was like his telling me, freshman year, when I thought I was condescending to be civil to him: "I've got no worries about you, George." Lombardi threw the playing levels out of order.

"I've gotta work tomorrow," I said to Harry, and then to the young woman standing to my right.

"So go home," the woman replied.

This struck me as an excellent idea. I still had a drink to drink, though. It was fresh and seemed a shame to waste so I took it with me. It was one of those nights in early, early spring when people go prematurely coatless and late at night are overcome, tumbling out of bars, by a desire to walk a few blocks. I started up Third Avenue, and thirty-three blocks later tagged home. I looked forward to having a word or two with Toff—he was more relaxed late at night after a few drinks—but I found his bedroom door closed. There is something so dismal about a roommate having sex.

Then I thought I would watch some television, but that thought depressed me, too. I wasn't exactly lonely, the way I had been in Paris, where loneliness had taken on the form of an enjoyable pastime. This was somewhat worse. I had the horrible conviction that somewhere in the city at that very moment a great party was going on without me. All of my friends were there and I had been invited, too—I knew the date and time—but I had either forgotten to write the address down or had lost it, carelessly, or thrown it away. And as I emptied out my suit pockets, I had a dreadful premonition that this was to be the case, a permanent post-collegiate syndrome of missing out, of driving around in pointless circles the way Harry and I had earlier, just to have something to do. When the reason for my rotten mood came to me, it was more humiliating than any homesickness. I was school-sick. I missed school, the lovely order and the sense of limitless yet defined forward movement. Kate had said it was so nice, but there were men at work who ran marathons and jumped out of planes just because they didn't have any more homework.

In college Chat and I had had an endlessly evolving roster of character tests and dire predictions for people who failed them: like the man who won't take a dare, or the man who fixes himself a drink and doesn't drink it. I remember making a promise to myself that night not to admit a relaxing of standards now that I was in New York, not to become one of those people who yell at one another on the subway—not to end up a Lombardi. I still had the vodka tonic; it was watery now, but I sat on the edge of my mattress and downed it. But the truth was the fridge was empty, and I drank it out of thirst more than anything else.

CHAPTER 5

I had a single my freshman year, which meant it was up to me to make friends. There were two rooms of guys on the hall—at least two that anyone noticed. The first, and by all accounts the dominant room, was Mike Murray and Craig-O's; they cornered the hall the way a department store anchors a mall. Mike was a scrappy kid from southern New Hampshire who looked like he ought to play football but didn't; Craig-O was a half-back from Detroit. Privately I was rather fond of Mike and Craig-O because they did all of the things I and my putative friends never would have—shooting hoops in the courtyard, collecting money for kegs; they even had a moose head hanging above their fireplace. At parties it would have a long straw in its mouth so it could reach its drink. Most people you met, if you told them you lived on Mike and Craig-O's floor, that was location enough. At the beginning of school they had a keg every night, and except for the half hour of silence from seven to seven-thirty when Craig-O watched *Jeopardy!*, blared WDCR out the window from their massive, shitty speakers. The whole freshman class must have passed through that room, with the exception of the other two guys on the hall.

Next door to me lived Chat Wethers, with a roommate he detested. Before I knew Wethers's name I had a nickname for him. I called him "Portrait of an Ancestor," and hung him in somebody's living room beside "Martha, his wife." Shining above the boy's pallid, peaked nose was a forehead so high you could have dived off it. His chin was a touch weak, which added to the eighteenth-century look, and he moved like an arthritic old man, creaking down the hall to the bathroom in a dressing gown and a preposterous pair of velvet slippers, black, with red devils on the vamp. That he couldn't stand his roommate the entire hall knew. Before I'd identified either of them I heard Chat whining through the wall, "Lombardi, what—what kind of a weird freak are you?" and giving Lombardi hell. It was easy enough to figure out who was who.

Several times I was taken to task for the pair's bad behavior, sheerly on account of the proximity of my room to theirs: "You *live* next to them: what the hell, Lenhart?" Those first few weeks of school, around Mike and Craig-O's kegs of ever descending qualities of beer—and after, I'm sure, when I was no longer privy to such conversations—friendships were formed over what a total fucking asshole Chat Wethers was. He incurred hatred just walking out the door: a girl claimed she had met him at the freshman tea and that now he pretended not to recognize her. (She also claimed he had let the door slam in her face, but I didn't believe that part.) Then there were the disinterested, impersonal forms of arrogance, which, oddly enough, people seemed to take even more personally: the stupid tape Wethers always played, for instance, whenever he was in his room, the same stupid cliché of a reggae tape, on and on and on inexorably. As I later learned, it was one of two tapes Chat had brought to school. It was the tape that got to Mike; Mike who prided himself on a collection of CDs two hundred strong. "Wouldja knock it the *fuck* off!" he used to shout, and then he would bang on the walls, and, rather than confront Chat, turn up his own stereo even louder, to the approbation of the entire hall, who would toast the asshole's impending demise at the pigskin-callused hands of Mike and Craig-O.

But though I dropped by the parties for a beer or two, I couldn't summon the requisite animosity, in the form of a grievance of my own, to really belong. Nor could I join in corroborating the initial judgments as they were handed down. I am as happy as anyone to make friends over a common enemy; the trouble was that I'd sensed Chat and I should probably be friends. It wasn't that I particularly liked him—not from what I saw, anyway. It was more a suspicion I had that he would not annoy me, as ridiculous as he was, nor I him, and that this vague mutual approval would prove more sustaining than any instant, dazzling alliance formed of open admiration and emulation.

There was one quality Wethers possessed, however, which I did admire. I couldn't have put a name to it at the time, but it had crept under my skin at Chatham—where I'd gone after finishing at the Rectory—and, as it turned out, was there to stay. It was a weakness, I suppose—a peculiar weakness for unexpected, contrarian surfacings of originality. Even the muted idiosyncratic strain in Chat was enough to get my attention: that same embarrassing tape played over and over, when the depth if not the breadth of one's musical taste said— Well, everything in college. What the hell did it mean?

I knew that Chat had gone to Hotchkiss. Boarding school was as good a jumping-off point as any, but neither of us, I think, wanted to be too crude about it, like some desperate types who had put on their Exeter sweatshirts and gone running around the Green.

So I held out for a few days when everyone was madly meeting and greeting, and by the end of the week my neighbor needed a fourth to play cards. Actually, they needed a third *and* a fourth, but as the rest of the dormitory had gone to hear an orientation address, Chat was willing to settle for dealing out the two and playing a limp game of three-person hearts.

I had not skipped the address for any reason other than I knew I ought to. If I had learned anything at Chatham, it was the simple dictate that to get anywhere in life one had to skip required events. To not skip would have been contrary to my personal code, so when three o'clock arrived I was lying fugitive on my bed, toying with a book and congratulating myself for being such an independent, rebellious soul. There was a knock at the door and Henry Lombardi came in. He was Henry then; Harry, with its echoes of princely sobriquets, came later.

"Hey—George, right?"

"Yeah, hey."

I sat up to be polite. It was funny, but he was the last person I would have expected to ditch the schedule.

He did not introduce himself then; in fact, we were never introduced. He came to me as Chat Wethers's emissary. "Chat wants to know if you want to play hearts."

"He sent you?" I said skeptically.

"Yeah, he's . . ." Harry said, and put a fat stubby index finger and thumb to his mouth and sucked in air in the least convincing pantomime of smoking a joint I had ever witnessed.

"Are you saying he's in your room smoking marijuana?" I said coldly—cleverly, I thought. For I was not so grown-up, after all, as to deny myself the easy target. Besides, the guy had irritated me on sight, and besides that, it was the first week of freshman year: one had to draw the line somewhere.

I still remember the look of reproach I was given. When I went on in a more conciliatory tone, startled into graciousness, Harry made an odd gesture, batting the air as if in pain, to stop me from being nice. It was to become a pattern with us. He would embarrass me with his clumsy attempts to drop into the vernacular; I would pointedly dissociate myself from these attempts; he would register my scorn; I would try, too late, to soften the blow; he would wave my efforts off. From Chat, Harry took it all, every baiting, insulting word; but even from the beginning he seemed to expect something more in the way of tolerance from me.

We went next door. How incongruous it was to see the Portrait of an Ancestor firing up a two-foot bong. It was duly held out to me, but I shook my head. I didn't like to get stoned with people like Chat, people who were meant to be drinkers and who got stoned simply because they thought they ought to. I like to think Chat respected my abstaining. He gave me a look that was both measured and measuring as we shook hands, and I saw that he had registered the point I was making, and it seemed to me that in that moment we understood each other. For the other great theme that had been borne in on me in my adolescence was that while it was always cool to partake, it was sometimes even cooler to abstain. It meant you were above all that. I had learned it at Chatham from Nick Beale, Kate Goodenow's boyfriend, who some would say forgot his own lesson. I didn't know it yet, but Chat had learned it from Nick, too. There was a whole generation of us who had learned everything we knew from Nicholas Beale. He was constantly being quoted by people who didn't even know they were quoting him. But Chat and I had learned firsthand.

We sat on the floor, Harry and I on one side and Chat on the other, with a wicker settee between us. On the opposite wall was a huge black-and-white photograph of one of the old J-boats that raced for the America's Cup in the thirties. It reminded me of my father; I remember thinking that Pop would have known the boat's name, her history, perhaps, as well. My father had grown up on Long Island Sound, sailing every kind of boat, and he had made a habit of taking me down to Newport when I was little, to watch the trials. Looking at the picture, I could hear the stories he would tell—of escapades at Indian Harbor, Larchmont, Manhasset—the great American yacht clubs which are strung along the Sound like pearls—

"Enterprise," Chat said, not unkindly, catching my glance.

"Right," I said. I had learned to sail, as well—on the pond behind my father's school.

Chat dealt, explaining the rules to his roommate as he snapped the cards down.

"You've never played before?" I asked Harry.

"No, no—I think I did," Harry said. "I'm pretty sure I played, but we called it something different."

"Spades?" I inquired. "That's a different game, you know."

"No, no—I know. I think—"

"He's never played before," Chat said. "Have you? And yesterday," he went on, brightly, "we tried to get 'high' for the first time, didn't we, Henry? It's a whole new world up here in 'college,' isn't it? You've got a checking account now, and you're responsible for laundering your own clothes." Beside me Harry was methodically arranging the cards in his hand, suit by suit, panting a little as he worked. Chat lit a cigarette from a pack in the breast pocket of his bathrobe. "Tomorrow I'm going to teach him how to use a fork."

Harry giggled. No sound brings back freshman year to me—not the songs they played in the basement of Psi U, not the maniacal musical interlude in *Jeopardy!*—more sharply than that low uneasy giggle which was Harry's response to each of Chat's taunts.

"Do you want to play one hand open?" I asked. "We'll lay our cards down?"

"Oh, no, I'll be fine."

"He'll be fine," Chat said.

"I'll pick it up," said Harry.

And he did. He was a natural card counter. I don't think he even knew that card counting was a thing people did, playing cards—it was just the only way he could think of to stay alive: to remember every card that was played. He ate the hearts on the first hand, but it was strange the way he cursed himself. Not for misunderstanding; no, he was angry at himself for making mistakes. It was like watching a natural athlete pick up tennis. I played the same game I always did—conservative. I stayed at zero for several hands, and I was beginning to think I would pull out the win when Harry blew my defensive game away. "You little bastard—you got aggressive on us!" cried Chat, when he realized what was up. "How fucking dare you?" Harry giggled the even, low-pitched giggle; evidently it could mean anything he liked.

When people at school would ask me if Lombardi was as smart as everyone said, I never thought to cite the crazy computer invention he was supposedly working on or the astronomical-level math classes I heard he was acing. To me the more plebeian achievement was infinitely more impressive: he shot the moon, I used to tell them, on the third hand of hearts he ever played.

"You realize you have to mix the drinks now," Chat announced.

"Oh, sure, Chat," said Harry. Amazed, I watched him hoist himself to his feet, kneel down again in front of the mini-fridge.

It made me nervous just to see the vodka bottle in a dorm room in daylight. I almost wanted to get up and check the hall for teachers—a reflex from Chatham. "I feel like we're going to get busted," I confessed.

I felt foolish the minute I said it, but Chat cleared his throat and said, "Yeah, I know." Then some mutual fear or indecision seemed to silence us for a moment. We both looked down at the pile of cards, then away, listening to Harry crack the ice trays and rattle cubes into the glasses. I think it was the first time either of us had tried it out on anyone else—saying "I got through it, too"; the four previous years of cold comfort—and we had to wait a moment to see if the other would let it stand. The falseness of the notion struck me at once. I thought of the appalling first nights away from home third-form year, as Chatham, fancying itself an English public school, had eschewed "grades." But in the next moment Harry came rattling back with the drinks, and Chat and I had tacitly agreed to hold up the one thing we had in common as the greatest of connections. Chat asked me: "You went to Chatham?"

"You went to Hotchkiss?"

"*I* should have gone to Chatham." He laughed a laugh so affected one suspected it might have been natural. "I could have been Chattie the Chattie! Ha, ha, ha, ha, ha! Instead I was Chattie the Kissie!"

Harry sat absolutely still, his hands folded in his lap. It must have been then that my host realized his roommate might have a purpose beyond the occasional bartending: he was that rare thing, the perfect audience, trapped and interested. His presence somehow lessened the subsequent embarrassment of our stooping so readily to play do-you-know.

"So you know Kate Goodenow," Chat said.

"Of course—Kate and Nick," I answered, for I thought of them only as a pair. And who didn't? At Chatham they had been the couple, *the* couple that transcended other high school romances as surely as God and country, in its happily myopic motto, transcended Yale. Kate was there now; I'd had a postcard from her with the phrase on it, and had stuck on my bulletin board.

"You talk to Nicko recently?" Chat inquired, eyes downcast, taking a last drag on the cigarette.

"No."

The cards lay thrashed on the table from the last hand. Harry began to pick them up and turn them over quietly.

Chat scowled: his roommate was a mouth-breather, as oblivious to the sound he made as a sleeping child. "Think I've heard your name."

"How do you know Kate?"

"We go to Maine."

At this oddly chosen moment Harry interjected: "You went to Chatham?" Pronouncing it wrong, as if he hadn't been listening at all, he rhymed the first syllable with "bath" instead of "bat." Neither Chat nor I corrected him. "That's on the Cape, right?"

"Near it," I said. It was a common mistake; the school was across Buzzards Bay and thirty miles west of the town of the same name, which marks the tip of the Cape Cod elbow.

"Did you know John Lash?"

I nodded. "Of course."

"John's a great guy!" Harry gushed. "John's from my hometown!"

As he clearly wanted me to feed him the next line, I asked him where he was from.

"Glen Cove," he said.

"Oh." Except that he wasn't. The sophomores had put signs on the doors with our names and hometowns. Chat was from New York. Henry was from Millport. I didn't know Long Island—the discrepancy would ordinarily have meant nothing to me, other than its *being* a discrepancy—but I wanted to sit the guy down and tell him to play life like cards. Surely he could make the discards less obvious.

He went back to reassembling the cards.

"We ought to go down to New Haven some time," Chat said. He laughed deprecatingly. "Road trip!"

"I'd love to see Kate," I said.

Chat nodded. "So you haven't talked to Nicko recently?" he asked again.

"No. Why? Have you?"

"Well, I mean—I saw them in Maine this summer."

"Well, anytime you want to go . . . I haven't seen Kate since she graduated. Or Nick." They were two years older than I. And Nick, keeping himself legitimate, had gotten himself kicked out their fifth-form year.

Harry had the cards in a neat stack ready to deal, waiting for his cue.

"You know," Chat volunteered, with a touch of sheepishness, "I should have graduated with them."

"Really."

He twisted the end of his cigarette in the ashtray. "I kind of did the five-year plan at Hotchkiss."

I opened my mouth to reply but found, to my embarrassment, that Chat's admission had left me tongue-tied.

"And then, you see, I traveled for a year," he went on, in a rather mechanical tone of voice. "I went to Africa—went on a safari. You see, I've always had an interest in traveling, and my parents support that. It was a great year."

Still I was silent. I didn't care, I didn't give a damn if it had taken Wethers two extra years to get into college, and yet I couldn't think of a single thing to say that wouldn't sound patronizing.

"Hey!" Harry piped up, to my relief. "At least you got in here! I mean—eventually!"

The response seemed to both delight and astonish Chat. He looked amazed that Harry had spoken—impressed, almost, that he would dare to. "What the hell, Lombardi! 'I mean—eventually!' What are you, my little consoler?" He clobbered him, but good-naturedly. "Can't you breathe through your goddamn nostrils? Come on, try. You can do it! In-out! In-out!"

After endless hands and long after our hall had come shouting back from orientation and left again for dinner, Chat's roommate stood up and rather formally excused himself. He was leading by such a large margin that Chat and I were taking bets on who could lose worse. "I have to go to a meeting," he added.

It is always awkward in a room after someone tells an obvious lie for an unknown reason. None of us spoke until he had left, lugging a small duffel.

"Guy has a job delivering pizzas," my host informed me. "I saw him trying on the fucking outfit. It kills me about him—kills me!"

Chat stood up from the floor, stretched languidly, and lay down on their long shabby couch. "That's why I'm not letting up. I figure if I'm a big enough asshole to him, see, he'll get fed up and tell me to fuck off and the net result will be positive. Right now, for Chrissakes, I'm like a goddamn Pygmalion. Why won't he just admit he has a goddamn job?"

That reminded me. "Christ, I skipped the job fair."

"You're getting a job?"

"Have to," I said.

Chat stretched again and yawned. After a second or two, he sat up and said, "That's a drag."

"Yeah."

I felt him look at me and away. "How many hours are we talking?"

"I don't know yet."

"Might cramp our style," Chat added thoughtfully. He reached underneath the table for a pair of cards.

"Yes, well," I said, as he held them up, frowning, to examine them.

We wandered to the dining hall and back; I went to my room and he to his. I had only been back a few minutes, and was wondering what I would do, when Chat paid me his first visit. I invited him in but he remained standing, just inside the threshold. It was barely eight o'clock, but he had already gotten back into his robe and slippers.

"This—this is appalling of me but—but how much do you need?"

I thought about it, understanding now the formality of the posture, dreading what was to come. But it was a fair question. "A couple thousand this year for books and, I don't know . . ."

"Books and beer," Chat supplied.

"Right."

"Look, why don't I lend you the money."

"Oh, no."

"You can pay me back later."

"No, I just couldn't."

"I mean much later, when we graduate."

"No—but thank you, Chat."

"You're making a mistake."

When I continued, naturally, to protest, Chat grew more and more uncomfortable. He shifted his weight from foot to foot, and a stutter appeared, which quickly worsened.

"This is a hell of an awkward conversation, and I wish you'd put—put—put an end to it right now, George. In two days you'll have forgotten you—you borrowed it and I'll have forgotten I lent it. And that's—that's—that's all there is to it. Other option is for you to work fifteen—twenty hours a week. And—and I don't see that kind of effort fitting in with the—the grand scheme."

"Absolutely not."

"No, no, listen here—don't be stupid about it. Simple business transaction. In—in—interest-free, of course," he added gently. "I'll talk to my . . . guy tomorrow." He was too delicate to say "accountant." It was only later, after I'd heard him snap into the stutter half a dozen times, that I realized the whole thing was an act. He put it on—his discomfort—to make it possible for me to take the money. For it was strange how it happened: I suddenly began to feel that I was protesting too much. It started to feel like a tacky scene in a restaurant, when the people next to you argue over the check so vehemently—and neither couple will back down but each of the men is deathly set on paying, driven by some perverse egocentric need of his own—that you want to lean over and yell, "Just let Bob pay the goddamn check!"

The subject of money embarrassed both of us; I felt myself going hoarse from arguing and heard my fatuous arguments with distaste. I couldn't back them up with any kind of support, nor, most of all, did I want to go into the details of exactly how poor I was. Part of the problem was that I was not—had never been—quite sure myself. There had never been enough money, but I knew that more from feelings accumulated over the years than from empirical evidence. In our odd kind of poverty, puzzling inconsistencies had existed side by side for years. My sister had had a pony growing up, for instance. But we couldn't afford a color TV, and every towel in the house was stamped with the Rectory's athletic-association blue. And as I pondered how to explain all this, Chat would not come in and sit down but stood in the threshold, where I knew he was uncomfortable.

"My parents—my father would not approve of this," I said finally. I had the feeling Chat's father wouldn't, either.

"Your father go here?"

I nodded. "Yours?"

"Forty-eight."

Before I knew it, he had thrown me the change of topic, another consideration, and dropped down into the club chair I had salvaged from home. We got to talking and I told him the easy things to tell, how Pop had gone to Chatham in the school's best days, the days of *ora et labora*, and cold showers, and baggy knees from so much kneeling in chapel, and then to Dartmouth; and that I, lacking inspiration, had always figured I'd do the same. We discovered that we both had fathers who were a little older than most of our classmates' fathers—the Ice Box Age, Chat called their generation—and mothers who had dropped out of college to marry young. We both had much older siblings, but while Chat was the last in a long line of Wetherses, my sister and I were the two lonely Lenharts. The longer we talked, the more little similarities we turned up—we had both taken Latin, we had both taught sailing a couple of summers; we even figured we had been at one of the same rock concerts, in Massachusetts two summers earlier. I think that night with Chat, comparing our relative experiences, was the first time the pointlessness of it truly struck me—that my family simply hadn't been able to figure it out—something so basic: the simple having of money.

I didn't tell Chat everything. There were a few points I might have added but left out because they seemed redundant, revolving, as they all did, around that central fact. I didn't add, for instance, that my mother had gone back to college eventually, to the local branch of the state university, so that she could finish her degree and earn money tutoring. I neglected to mention certain benefits of growing up at the Rectory, such as the milk we could get gratis from the old school dairy. I had made a friend that evening, and I didn't want to bore him with the details.

A week later, in the mail alongside a letter from my mother, there was an envelope from a Manhattan accounting firm with a check inside for ten thousand dollars. I went straight to the bank and deposited it. A couple of times in the next few years I woke panicked from my sleep, overcome by a black dread of the size of the debt. But undergraduates are largely indifferent to money, so long as it's there, and the rest of the time I hardly thought of the loan at all, except to make sure a decent amount remained. It seemed a perfect piece of good fortune had befallen me, like manna from heaven; frequently I forgot to attach the good luck to its source.

Chat's reputation on the hall never lost its initial taint, but we found our group of friends in time, and in the spring we rushed and were accepted at our fraternity of choice. Say what you will about Wethers, and people said plenty—and I myself might reluctantly cede a point or two today—he is the only man I know from whom I could have accepted a loan like that and not felt ashamed, beholden, and a dozen other debilitating emotions. Chat himself almost never had cash on him, and it became his habit to borrow from me—tens, twenties, once $250 to buy an amplifier. There was never anything odd about the way he asked, however, as there would have been with most people, and he always paid me back right away.

As for Chat's roommate, we saw less and less of him. Classes started, and Harry spent his time holed up in the basement of Kiewit, where the computer lab was. He quit the pizza delivery job before Chat got him to admit to having it, and instead troubleshot for humanities majors like me, casting spells on our printers to make them spew out papers that had been eaten, making himself the object of daily prostrations of love and gratitude: "Oh. My. God. You saved my *life*!" About the middle of the fall, one of the girls whose deleted document he salvaged took a fancy to him. Around the same time I kissed Ann Callow from my Shakespeare class, with the result that the two of us found ourselves with girlfriends. Each of us made an independent decision to downplay, in my case, or to hide, in Harry's, the existence of said girlfriends from Chat. Harry's girlfriend was called Marie. She was a Mike-and-Craig-O regular—a smart, determined girl from Rochester, half a head taller than Harry, who eventually did big things for student government. Chat found out about her soon enough. He had to be polite to me about Ann, no matter that he thought my married state was putting a damper on the fun, and I'm sure this constraint, doubled with the fact that he himself remained girlfriend-less, increased his venom toward Harry.

The tone changed in their room. Before Chat had been outrageous, certainly—there was no escaping it—but there had been a kind of creativity in his attacks, and a certain underlying hope. Now Chat lit into Lombardi in a way that was just boring. He made fun of the way the guy dressed, right to his face. He used to take periodic inventories of Harry's wardrobe, of his black concert T-shirts and his two ugly ties and his quasi-oxford shirts in odd patterns.

Harry got so much flak from Chat about Marie that finally he dumped her rather than deal with it, and went around looking hunted. She really liked Harry, though, and one night that fall she came over, blind drunk and blubbering, to see why they couldn't give it another shot. Marie didn't usually drink. That was one of the many things Chat had found to ridicule about her. She didn't drink, she didn't put out. As it happened, Harry wasn't home; Chat and I and Will Toff were sitting around trying to get a plan together. Toff finally gave up on us, and I went to my room without much hope to call Ann, who would have gone out to get drunk long ago, disgusted with our lethargy. I couldn't get hold of her, so I went back next door. Chat had fixed another drink for Marie and she was drinking it and talking about Lombardi. "It's really over now!" she cried. "And I don't even care!"

"Yes, dear," Chat was saying, and stroking her hair. "Now drink your drink."

To me he murmured, marching me smartly back out the door, "Very sorry, George—party of two, you understand?"

In the morning I started at Chat's light rap on my door. We prided ourselves on getting up and going to breakfast, and belittled the others who slept the day away and tried to make up for it at night. This morning, however, I stalled. I folded up the newspaper on my desk and took my time about finding my keys. We were supposed to take the road trip to New Haven that weekend or the next. I imagined Kate's approval when she found out that the two of us had become friends. It struck me how melodramatic it would be to start a fight, to make an accusation. I think it's safe to say that was the very last thing I wanted to do.

"While we're young, Lenhart," remarked Chat. I opened the door. He was wearing a gray overcoat over the dressing gown, a wry look on his face.

"I wasn't sure you'd make it this morning," I said stiffly.

Chat feigned insult. "Christ!" he said. "Give me some credit, will you?"

CHAPTER 6

It was fitting he should say "While we're young" in that sarcastic tone—Chat, who had never felt the exigencies of youth. He had felt no obligation to "make the most of it"; he did not go around saying, as so many did, that those years—or these in New York, for that matter—were the best of our lives; or berating himself, as I did, for failing to live up to their promise. I guess that was the other thing I liked about him right from the beginning: Wethers took the edge off my moods. As we walked to breakfast through that fine, cold morning, the foliage—the color—was gone, and the trees were bare. The sense that I had backed down from a moral crisis quickly dissipated. Chat and I were up early, as we always were, while the rest of the college slumbered on, and I saw at once the wrongheadedness, the self-indulgence, of painting the world in gaudy colors of morality and crisis. Chat's dour expression and the gray overcoat seemed more to the point, and much more reliable, than any overwrought conscience-wringing of my own. "Grow up," his presence seemed to be saying. "Grow up and enjoy life."

It is tempting, looking ba̶ ̶ ̶ ̶ ̶ ̶
favored outings—to say "We̶ ̶ ̶ ̶
curred perhaps twice. And ̶ ̶ ̶ ̶
that in Manhattan I was im̶ ̶ ̶ ̶
engagements with Kate a̶ ̶ ̶ ̶
happily for me, as Kate's̶ ̶ ̶ ̶
have otherwise. I got th̶ ̶ ̶ ̶
fits together and that C̶ ̶ ̶ ̶
as he frequently called me ̶ ̶ ̶ ̶
vinced that the excuse of my job was ̶ ̶
cret double life of mine.

But I had no such gratification.

It was a dismal spring of five-dollar umbrellas, the rain seep̶i̶n̶g̶
down the collar of my coat and Daniels on my case with a dreary
kind of vengeance. One week, the week before we left for a road show
out west, I saw the sun rise from the thirty-fifth floor of Fordyce three
mornings in a row. Or I would have seen it, if I'd had a window, and
it hadn't been raining. In the antiseptic hours before the dawn of
those all-nighters, I fell back into a sad habit I'd had in college, of
picturing the world asleep in their beds. I wasn't choosey; anyone
would do. I would think of Toff and Cara, passed out after their perfunctory amours, the bottom sheet shrunk from its corners revealing
naked Dial-a-Mattress underneath; or of a girl I'd known briefly in
Paris, who had a brass bed; of Daniels, the bastard, dreaming of
Y-curves with Mary Ellen Flynn, the secretary on 19 who commuted
from Croton. Sometimes I would think of Nick Beale, strung up in a
pipe berth in some stripped-down maxi off Bermuda, off Barbados,
or anywhere the wind blew; or even—and here I would chuckle,
laugh in the face of my dull fate—of Harry Lombardi here in New
York, slack-jawed on his back, clutching some fantasy girl. I envied
them all their slumbers, but it was Kate's image that haunted those
sterile vigils most, and hers that I ground away toward through the
nights, as if I were striving to meet it and not the FedEx deadline. I

would one day possess eight dreamless hours
n-sheeted, and that my darkness, as hers no
be still as a reflecting pool.

to see her apartment, and so one night when I was
waiting for the graphics guys to come through, I
and met her and Chat for a game of cards.

ved on Sixty-sixth Street, off of Lexington; her father had
her the place, "simply because it's a good investment,
ge. You should think about buying, you really should. It's point-
ss to keep paying rent; you're just throwing money away, you
know." Indeed, Goodenow's investment probably doubled in value
during the years she kept it. I wondered, later, what Kate did with
the place when she got married, as it was a perfect Old New York
apartment, with molded ceilings and tiled bath, hissing steam heat,
and the impression I always have in this type of Upper East Side
place, of Antique White emanating from the walls, the fixtures, and
the air itself.

They had just come from dinner with the circle of cousins and
childhood acquaintances from New York who predated me as their
friends, and it made me glad when Kate made a point of saying I
ought to come out more. "Work is not an end in itself, George," she
reprimanded me, as Chat shuffled and dealt the first hand with Kate
sitting on his lap. "It's a means to an end."

"Tell that to my boss, Daniels," I said, picking out two lousy cards
to pass.

"I'd be happy to," Kate said. "What's his number?" and her eye
got that prankster's glint in it. "Chattie, let me go!" She was on her
feet. "Come now, George, give me his phone number."

"Crank call?" Chat inquired merrily.

"It's all right, Kate," I said, knowing she would ignore me. "He's
not *that* bad." She got the number from information and made a
pouting face when Daniels failed to pick up. I saw my livelihood
snatched away as Kate began to leave her message: "Hi, this is Annie
Roth and I met you about a week ago? At that Fordyce party? It was
great talking to you and I'd love to, you know, finish what we started.

I don't know what your schedule's like—I hear you're a total slave driver—but please give me a call as soon as you can."

"Annie's going to *kill* you!" cried Chat. I made a weak effort to keep up, laughing hollowly. And yet I wasn't sorry she had made the call. I thought of Daniels coming home to the blinking light, playing his messages, racking his addled brain, but though I projected the most personal kind of sympathy onto the man, I began to glow with a strange kind of gladness, with the leaping us-against-them superiority of being in on a joke.

"See, George?" Kate joined us at the table. "I put my money where my mouth is, didn't I?"

"I hope you washed it first!" Chat said, and cracked himself up. "Money's dirty, you know."

Hearts was still our game, and Kate played the quick, sure game I remembered from Chatham—she sat right up at the living room table, back straight, feet on the floor, and threw the cards down with a snap. She played each hand hard, to win, but she wouldn't stop to think, and when she lost, it was from careless mistakes. Beside her, Chat was cold and methodical, inexorably sipping his drink; and across the table from them, I did all right. My problem was that I hedged my bets too much (I don't mean literally; there is, of course, no betting in hearts), but I felt rusty after Paris and wouldn't shoot the moon for fear I would fail and embarrass myself.

So the three of us were evenly matched—too evenly matched, perhaps: I found myself thinking we could have used someone or something to shake up the game. As it turned out, though, I was the one to do it. After a couple of hands, I ducked a trick full of hearts and made the mistake of attributing the move to a classic Nick Beale strategy I had learned to imitate long ago.

"Nicko all the way, baby!" I shouted, tallying up the scores.

"That *is* Nicko's move," Kate said slowly as if to herself. "He always holds the queen and the ace, but I get rid of them as fast as I can."

The present tense threw me, and I took it to mean she had seen

Nick recently. "Where is Nick now?" I asked, shuffling the deck. "Does he ever come through town?"

Chat took a slow sip of his gin. "This could use another lime, Kate," he said.

Kate looked up brightly. "Could it? I'll get you one. Don't get up—let me get you one."

She rose from the table and I shuffled the cards feeling I had made a blunder of some kind, and disliking that feeling with friends. "Does he ever come through town?" I repeated.

"George, have you ever heard of making polite conversation?" inquired Chat.

"I'm sorry," I said, surprised by his tone, as he had never taken it with me before.

"There are certain things you don't want to go dredging up." He had pushed his chair back from the table as if to give me a little talking-to, and crossed his legs at the knee, the way some men won't.

"Of course not," I agreed. "But—"

"When she talks about him that way," Chat instructed, checking my protest, "it's not a good sign, all right? It's not something you want to dwell on. Her doctor thinks—"

"Her *doctor*?" I interrupted.

"Look, she's over it now," Chat said dismissively, lowering his voice with a glance toward the kitchen, "and we all want her to be well."

"What the hell are you talking about?" My voice trembled slightly with some sudden emotion I struggled to suppress.

"It's not something I can go into now," replied Chat. But then he seemed to relent and, leaning forward, confided, "In my opinion the whole thing was overhyped. It's just a little trouble she had last winter. She wasn't getting out enough, she wasn't having fun—"

He broke off as his girlfriend returned to the table, bearing a tray.

"Look what I did, you two—I made everyone another so we won't have to be interrupted again," announced Kate.

"That's lovely, sweetheart," said Chat, lighting a cigarette.

I thanked Kate and took up my glass, baffled and annoyed. With almost any other girl, Chat's intimations would have been grave but understandable. But Kate—Kate was supposed to be above the psychological fluctuations the rest of us had to endure.

Chat stood up to look for an ashtray.

"I'm going to beat you both now," boasted Kate. She gathered up her cards. "I'm unbeatable now, aren't I, Chat—I mean, when I try."

"Yes, dear—unbeatable."

"You see, George? And oh, what you've dealt me. You are not going to believe the brilliance—"

"Christ, is there a goddamn ashtray in this apartment?"

"I don't *smoke*, Chattie—"

"Well, I do."

There were two floor-to-ceiling bookshelves built into the walls of Kate's living room. In the open spaces, where the books left off, Kate had put framed photographs, vases, candlesticks, and the like—and, resting at eye level, a little silver cup.

"Here, I'll use this." Chat plucked the cup from the shelf, set it on the card table, and retook his seat. "Is it my go?" He took a long drag on the cigarette and tapped the ash into the cup.

The John Scarum Memorial Trophy, 1979, I read. *First place: Nicholas Beale, "Lucky Duck."* The trophy had been offered by the Cold Harbor Yacht Club. "Kate," I started, "are you sure—?"

"Is there something you're trying to say, Lenhart?" Chat inquired.

Kate caught my glance and, when our eyes met, looked scornfully away. I stared dumbly at Nick's little trophy. At the end of the hand I excused myself and went back to work. The next time we got together it was with other people.

As for the rest of what passed for my "social" life that spring in New York, the particularities I can remember are pathetically few. The parties were all the same, and the same people threw them. When the girls threw them there would be refrigerator Brie and the beer would run out and the mixers would run out, but you would have a slightly better time, drinking straight Popov on ice. Some of the girls who threw parties worked in publishing and were temporarily impoverished but had character, or their apartments did—crummy, crammed sixth-floor walk-ups, with alphabet magnets on the fridge and an antique or two slowly getting trashed. This was when that trend of childhood regression was flourishing. Like talking about what television shows you used to watch—endlessly. Or the girls would play *Grease* on the stereo. The stereo would be a cheap one. All girls have cheap stereos.

When the guys threw them, there would be top-shelf liquor and a subwoofer and too many of us standing around. Harry had been right about the liquor. Often, while searching through the rubble to fix myself a drink, on York Avenue or Eighth Street or up at Columbia, I would think of him and of our odd, isolated gesture toward resuming a friendship—if that's what the evening had been—that had never really existed. It crossed my mind to wonder whether he'd gotten the bartender into bed with him; either way, he wouldn't have dwelled on it. I figured I would throw a party myself one of these days. I wanted to see if I could pull one off. But there was no time, and there was Toff to deal with. I would run into my roommate occasionally, with Cara doggedly, unhappily, staked at his side, fending off other girls like herself, with equally aerobicized arms. I always got a kick out of seeing him, though the neutral settings didn't change the fact that we never had much to say to each other. Still, Toff, I felt, in some obscure, fundamental way, was toeing the line.

As for me, I worked, doing spreadsheet homage to Daniels, nursing paper cuts that wouldn't heal and other emasculating office injuries, like backaches and desk bruises, until a week or so before Memorial Day, when the weather stayed absurdly pleasant for days on end, and I got sick. It was a spring flu that was going around, but I liked to think I had made myself sick from working so hard. And what with the flu and the perfect days that I read about on the 6 train, one day I lounged into work late and interrupted Daniels's morning castigation of me and told him he had a stain on his tie.

Or perhaps it was the time of year. Nick Beale had gotten kicked out of Chatham on Memorial Day weekend eight years earlier, and as it was the defining event of my adolescence, ever since then I'd been wont to cop a devil-may-care attitude around the end of May in memory, and imitation, of Kate's old boyfriend.

When she herself called up saying it had been ages, I told her I would meet her for lunch, and left the office pumped up with about a minute's worth of attitude, mumbling the weak man's mantra: "What are they going to do? Fire me?"

We went to one of those big-menu coffee shops on Lex and got hamburgers. That's all you ever ate with Kate. You could reel off half a dozen suggestions of places to go, and she would half listen and get a look in her eye and say, as if it were a rather subversive suggestion, "Or we could go to X—— and get a *burger.*"

When the food came, however, Kate surveyed it impassively. I was starving and couldn't seem to eat fast enough.

"And? In the mad, mad world of finance?" She salted a fry and ate that.

"Oh, you don't want to hear—"

"Yes, I do!" she insisted. "Tell me about it, George. Who your friends are and—and everything."

"Well," I said dubiously, "I suppose there's Robbins . . ."

"Oh, Rob Robbins?"

"No."

"It must be his brother, then."

"No, this Robbins has sisters."

"Cousin, then."

"I doubt it."

"Should we put a little money on it? Lady's bet?"

"My Robbins, Kate, is so far from being the cousin of anyone you know—"

"How do you know? Have you asked him? I know a lot of people."

"You do not. You know about . . . ten people."

Kate considered. "Yes, that's right—ten or maybe twelve. Don't you love getting hamburgers?"

"Yes."

"And Cokes?"

"Yes."

"Me, too."

"But you're not eating yours," I pointed out.

She took a large, fake bite. "Yes, I am. See? Anyway, I don't want to talk about what I'm eating, George."

"All right. How's your job, then?" I asked.

"It's great. I love it." And there was that topic gone for good.

I was so delighted to be out of the office and out with her that it took me a little while to notice that Kate wasn't quite herself that afternoon. I suppose I didn't particularly want to notice, as I hadn't particularly wanted to dwell on the revelations of the evening at her apartment. I had not broached the subject with Chat since; it just didn't stand to reason, knowing Kate the way I did, that she should suddenly fall prey to that kind of internal uncertainty. When I did notice what was different about her at lunch that day, it, too, was a quality so atypical that I had trouble associating it with Kate. To put it simply, there was a restlessness about her.

"You like it here, don't you, George?" she asked me at one point, and before I could answer, she had called the waiter over to ask for a new Coke, as hers tasted funny. That was the way it went: she spoke briefly, intimately toward me and then past me, unable to concentrate on whoever it was sitting across from her, making plaintive, pointed pronouncements, such as: "I grew up here, but I would never raise children in New York."

"Nor would I," I said, for I could conceive of no childhood that wasn't lived mainly out-of-doors.

"It's so dirty!" Kate went on, her gray eyes resting, disturbed, on a point outside the window. "Look at that woman out there. How could anyone let herself get so fat? If I weighed that much, I'd go on a diet! I wouldn't sit there stuffing a hot dog into my face." She gave a vacant, perturbed glance around the diner. "You know, I can't ride the subway anymore. It's like the Third World down there. It's worse than the Third World, it's . . . the Fourth World! These men leer at you! These people come on with strollers . . . and everyone's so unbelievably rude!"

Again I took notice slowly, for while this trait was not new in her, it was something New York had brought out, or something about a particular kind of money that I associated with New York: girls like Kate really detested the middle class. I can remember the first time I saw it, in a girl at Dartmouth. Then, as now, I found the attitude a rather repellent fascination, with its disregard for the most basic lesson of the nursery, to pity those who had less than you.

Also, she was amusing. "People *are* getting ruder. I've noticed it, and Chat's noticed it. Why is that, do you think?"

"Hmm."

"And here's something else, George: Why is it that secretaries don't have to wear pants to work? Do you know what I mean? Do you know the kind of *ensemble* to which I refer? Annie and I have noticed this, and we think it's very unfair. *We* have to wear dresses or suits to work, but the registrar's office is allowed to wear those— those maternity tunics and stretch pants, or whatever they are. Now, why should that be?"

"I can't imagine," I said gravely. For while many responses were possible, the only one that came to mind, as ever, was an infinite indulgence of Kate. She was made to be indulged; she made you believe in predestination—or something.

"My mother thinks I ought to get married, but why should I be in a hurry? I like Sixty-sixth Street. I'm going to live there until I do get married, I always said I would. And besides: I'm young!"

This fact was asserted not to me but to the general audience in the café. It was as if she suffered from the affliction schoolchildren claimed of late: attention deficit disorder. I had an urge to say, as if she were one of them, "Kate, you need to sit quietly and drink your soda."

Halfway through the meal she got up to go to the bathroom but returned almost at once.

"George, dearheart."

"Kate?"

She pursed her lips for a moment, studying my face, and it was odd: I suddenly got the feeling that there was something she had to say to me, something she had to sell me on, but she couldn't quite work her way around to mentioning it lest the pitch be too obvious. I sensed, too, that everything up to now had been a warm-up—vocal scales of nonsense syllables—and that I had been an idiot to try and discern meaning in any of it. She tapped her fork against her plate distractedly. It was quite loud, and I said, "Aren't you going to eat any more?"

"No, it's too rare. You know, I haven't seen Nick in almost two years, and frankly it's a relief."

"I . . ." But the juxtaposition left me speechless.

And yet here, where anyone else would have leaned forward, Kate sat up straighter.

"Two falls ago he came to town—it was in October. He used to make one of his 'appearances' every six months or so. He would show up in the city and call me, leave me a message—'It's Nicko, Kath, I'm in town,' as if I was supposed to invite him over on the spot and tell him nothing had changed. I really think that's what he expected to hear. It's so . . . grim, George, it really is."

"Where is Nick now?" I asked finally, regaining my voice. "What does he do?" I clarified this: "For money?" It was a stupid question. It wasn't as if Nick himself, wherever he was, would have been worried about money. But for years I worried for him, not seeing the patronization in this.

"Oh, I can't keep it straight," said Kate, and proceeded to give a detailed account of his endeavors the last two years. "He was going to do an Olympic campaign but he couldn't get the funding. Then for a while he was working at a sail loft in Newport. Last winter he delivered a boat down to the Caribbean with Donny. They got jobs working on a charter . . ." Unexpectedly, a lone spasm of emotion twisted across her face. "Why doesn't he learn, George? It's not *cool* to be the way he is, to smoke pot every day! He doesn't have resources, George! He does. Not. Have. Resources! Chat's tried to reason with him, but what can he do?

"I almost do want to see him, next time, and tell him, 'Nick, we're not in boarding school anymore. You can't sail for the rest of your life! We're too old for that, for God's sake. We're old!' "

It was a phase, I decided later. She was going through one of the few phases of her life that didn't suit her. She had been out of school nearly three years now; perhaps she no longer saw any point in being a young unmarried woman in New York. Possibly, there wasn't so very much to think about; the distractions were not quite so absorbing as they once were. It was only natural that she would set her mind on what next.

As for why she didn't give Chat the nod and have done with it—well, one didn't ask that the week before Memorial Day. No doubt I was vain enough, too, to see an opening in her distraction, however temporary, for myself.

As the scattered, frenetic meal ended, Kate regained her composure so quickly and thoroughly it made me think she had never truly abandoned it, that perhaps even the "trouble last winter" Chat had referred to had been a symptom of boredom alone.

"Dad's tried to speak with him, too, but Nick doesn't listen—not anymore. . . . You know, I really can't get over how second-rate this place has become." With a violent motion Kate pushed the untouched plate to the edge of the table and squared her shoulders as if to wrap up an unpleasant bit of small talk. "Do you have five minutes? Because I took the afternoon off and I'm going to Bergdorf's. I'd love it if you came. You can be my second opinion, George."

We hurried up toward the park in the afternoon sun, speaking hardly at all. There was always that distance you could count on with Kate, to balance out the afternoon. Even in the warmth her smooth coloring did not change. I seized her hand and pressed it to my fore-head. "My gosh," she said, laughing, "what will you do in August?"

In the high hushed room of the old store, Kate tried on twenty or thirty dresses. She wanted my opinion on each one, but they all looked the same—becoming, appropriate, pretty on her.

Afterward we stood on Park, and I found I couldn't even live up to Nicko's example for an afternoon. All my AWOL attitude had seeped away in Women's Designers. As I was composing my umpteenth excuse for Daniels, Kate rested her hand on my arm. "I have to cross here."

"Can't we trade?" I said. "My boss would like you better."

"I would have been good on Wall Street," said Kate, without irony.

She was right, too. I was exhausted just thinking about the after-noon to come, but Kate exuded well-restedness. As long as I had known her, she had been a healthy girl. I had never seen her run-down or exhausted; I had never seen her with a cold. I would have put money on the supposition that she had never stayed up all night finishing a book. I gave voice to this theory.

"What on earth do you mean?" Kate said. She wasn't really sur-prised by the comment, though. Many men had been moved to make pronouncements about her, of one sort or another, and to her face.

"You know—just read all night and then find you've read too long because it's getting light out."

"But that's not fair! I don't think I've ever come across a book worth staying up all night *for.*"

"I never thought of that," I said.

Then there was a curious moment. I bent to kiss her good-bye, and she turned her face so I caught her lips. They were quite dry. The downtown traffic had stopped for the light. "It's funny," Kate murmured—murmured against my lips. Her face was huge in my vi-sion, magnified; a flower under a glass.

"Is it."

"No, I don't mean that. Come back." For I had straightened up.

I did and then stopped. I glanced across Park, to where the cross street started in darkness. The May recklessness beat against my skull.

"Let's fly to Paris," I said. "I could show you around."

Kate cocked her head back to look at me, and the light covered her face.

"We'll go for the long weekend."

"You'll book a midnight flight out."

"Why not?"

"Chat will be gone," she added, "and I haven't a thing to do."

Kate could get out a neat response, no matter what the situation. She was the kind of date who knew her lines. And she was only answering in kind, banter for banter, mindless chatter for mindless chatter. For instance, she might have said: "Wonderful. What shall I wear?" or half a dozen other things. What I mean is, it was probably only by chance that she happened to mention Chat.

But I thought suddenly, blindingly—for the first time in nearly a year—of the money I owed him. Chat had never mentioned it; he would not mention it. But I saw all at once that it was going to prey on me. We weren't in college anymore; I was a debtor now, a man in debt—suddenly the fact seemed to define me. I even felt a touch of paranoia that it was the money that had been behind the supercilious tone Chat had taken with me at Kate's, and I wondered if New York hadn't changed him, too. In college, even a conservative place like Dartmouth, he'd had to endure a fair amount of resentment about his background, and ridicule for the attitudes he assumed; perhaps now, in his hometown, he was basking defensively in his entitlement.

I watched Kate's unchanging face as she explained that he was going up to Maine on Thursday to open up and would stay the weekend. Chat was famous for being fanatical about that, about never missing certain weekends—Memorial, Commissioning of the Yacht Club, Fourth of July—even going to infamous extremes like driving up on a Saturday, eight hours, spending twelve hours in Maine, and turning around to drive home on Sunday.

"And I just don't know what I'll do . . ." Kate was saying.

I was sure she had half a dozen offers, from Blue Hill to Watch Hill, but with a last flash of bravado, I took her up on it—on this last point at least.

"Well, that's too bad," I decided. "Because he'll miss my party."

"You're having a party?" she said curiously. "What kind of a party?"

"Nothing special," I said. "Kick off the summer."

"Oh," said Kate. "Goodie."

The light changed. I hurried away.

I was a literature major in college, but I never went in for the criticism that was popular with most of my peers. "I'd rather just *read* the books," I would smugly declare. So when I say now that I have subjected the afternoon I spent with Kate and the events it germinated to a truly rigorous deconstruction, I have to confess I never knew what the word meant. Still, I couldn't help myself from trying to understand certain things that happened afterward in and of themselves—I mean, to imagine what would have happened without me as their inadvertent author. I don't know why I decided to throw that party, except that I couldn't let the day slip away like that, not without salvaging something for myself.

CHAPTER 7

When I got back to my desk, the phone's red message light was on. Before I checked it, I mentally updated my résumé and composed the gloss-over: *Yeah, I wanted to land in a smaller shop, anyway—less red tape to deal with* . . . The message was from duplicating. They had called to say my Xeroxing was ready. Robbins looked up from next door. "Long lunch?"

I tried to read meaning into this but failed. "Yeah."

"Get a load of this," he said.

He forwarded me a phone message that had been forwarded to him. I wasn't in the mood for Robbins's kind of humor, but this one was a keeper. By the time I got it, pretty much all of Wall Street had heard it. Anyone who was our age in New York at the time will remember it. It was the story of a blind date, a blind date in the age of voice mail.

"You're never going to believe this," said the unsuspecting woman, who talked straight Queens oh-my-gawdese. Oh my gawd, indeed. She'd had sex with her blind date in a movie theater, and then again back at his place. His place had mirrors on the ceiling, and the woman said, "Oh my gawd, I was climbin' the walls! I was buggin'—you could fuckin' see everything," and then she told what she saw, in the most extraordinary detail. It was gorgeous, that message. It was rich. It was the kind of thing that made you love New York like a little kid.

I spent the afternoon forwarding it to everyone I knew, with a witty preface inviting them to my party. The last person I invited was Lombardi. I hated to do it, in a way. I could almost hear him panting over the message, replaying it, acting, for his colleagues' benefit, as if he and I went "way back, way back—Lenhart and I—great guy, great guy—oughta be a good time, if I can manage to turn up, a'course . . . don't know, schedule's pretty tight"—but I had promised, and when I thought of going back on my promise, the sneaking guilt that I associated with Lombardi drove me to the phone.

As for Toff, he got a note on the bathroom mirror.

Thursday night when I got home from work, I found Cara McLean waiting on the couch. "You still having it?"

I told her I was.

"I'm here to help you carry."

The two of us went around the corner to the liquor store and bought gin and rum and as much tonic as we could carry. "I really think we ought to get tequila, too," Cara said. "People like tequila."

I was out of cash, so she paid for it herself. "You're not going to regret this, George. I promise you. Wait'll you see—people'll be getting wild. Tequila really makes a party wild."

We called the deli for beer, and then we got the place ready as fast as we could. I took out the trash and cleaned the bathroom sink, and Cara set everything up on the kitchen table, a bit too tidily for my taste. At the last minute Toff—God bless him—Toff came through brilliantly. We had forgotten the ice, and he said he would buy it on the way home.

I didn't particularly want to sit on the couch with his girlfriend, who had staked it out, so I fiddled with the stereo and went into my bedroom to change my shirt. When I came out she handed me a shot glass and said, "Come on, George, you and I are going to do a tequila shot to get this party going, 'cause we did everything else, didn't we?"

"I guess we did," I said.

We did the shot and the buzzer rang.

Cara ran over to it, pressed the intercom, and yelled, "Send 'em up!" With some displeasure I recognized it: her wild-'n'-crazy party mode. I had seen it once or twice before, when she and Toff came home late, and I just hoped Toff would have plenty to drink himself.

There are many ways to show up at a party. One can show up late hoping to create an impression of being insouciant, wildly busy, and sought after. One can show up on time, because one is beyond needing to create that particular impression. Chat Wethers always showed up on time. "Come *on*, George," he would urge seriously, in college. "They said the party's starting at *nine* and it's quarter to!" One can, of course, show up incredibly late, at one or two in the morning, because one *is* insouciant, wildly busy, and sought after. Or one can show up the way Harry Lombardi did, exactly half an hour after the party is slated to begin, expecting to be quite late but instead finding oneself the very first to arrive. He stood for a moment in the hallway, peering fearfully into the empty rooms.

"Would you like to come in, Harry?" I asked.

He took a cautious step through the doorway. Then he seemed to make a decision to face the facts squarely. "Don't worry, George," Harry said in a low voice. "More people will show up soon."

"I was hoping they might," I said.

Dispensing with further pleasantries, he walked past me into the kitchen. He was lugging a paper bag from which he removed three large bottles—of gin, vodka, and Scotch. My bottles were hidden under the table. Having this task to do seemed to put him at ease.

"You can use these for backup, George—nothing wrong with that." I was on the point of arguing with him about a thing called trying too hard when I remembered a particular habit my mother had at dinner parties. Her silver set was missing so many pieces that there weren't eight complete settings to go around. It was my job to set the table, and she would tell me, "Give me the flatware, George. No one will notice." I would do it, but it used to bother me enormously, the one dull setting that didn't belong; her, not at all. I don't know why the memory came to me just then, but it stayed the protest on my lips. My parents were never very far from my mind, and I would think of them at the oddest moments, especially since coming to New York—when I spent more on cabs, for instance, than they spent on a week's groceries.

I took an ice tray from the freezer to make us drinks. "That all the ice you got?" He was frightened again; scandalized.

"Yes, don't you think it'll be enough? I mean—three trays—"

But Harry never got jokes, even stupid ones, so I had to give up and explain that my roommate was on his way.

"Thank God!" he burst out, taking a rumpled handkerchief from his pocket and wiping it across his brow. "I didn't want to say anything, but Jesus Christ! You can't throw a party with three trays'a ice!" He surveyed the living room with a disapproving frown. "Coulda had somebody in, but oh well."

I had proposed a toast when Cara came out of the bathroom, into which she had disappeared for a final reckoning—or in order to make an appearance. She had abandoned her usual attire of black leggings, athletic shoes, and an oversized T-shirt for black leggings, high heels, and an undersized T-shirt. At the strip of linoleum that marked the beginning of the kitchen, she paused, looked sharply at Harry, and made a purposefully audible intake of air. This drew no immediate reaction, as Harry was busy readjusting the liquor display—at any moment I thought he was going to take out the handkerchief again and go to work dusting—so Cara shrieked his name.

"Henry! Oh, my god, Henry!"

Harry's hands clenched themselves into fists; he turned as if someone had shouted an insult at him on the street. But before he could give back worse than he'd gotten, Cara had her arms around him and was pressed against him in an ecstatic, vocal embrace.

When they parted he shuffled back a step and picked up the bottle of gin he had brought and examined it as if it puzzled him in some way.

"Jeez, Henry!"

"How you been, Cara," he said to the bottle. "Long time no see."

"You don't have to be embarrassed, Henry!" she exclaimed, touching his arm. "We were kids, for Chrissake! It's me, for Chrissake!"

What significance this last remark entailed I couldn't venture to guess. She herself was over the moon. Between tugging on my sleeve and, with the evening's newly coined flirtatiousness, demanding that I make her a Tanqueray and tonic—"I always switch to gin in the spring!"—she reeled off tidbits from Harry's and her wild and crazy days at Millport Junior High. She seemed to exult in the connection; there was no end to her reminiscences. "When I was a freshman and you were in seventh grade! Oh, my god! We were so bad! I taught him how to smoke! Remember that? Sure you do! You didn't know how to inhale! You weren't doing it right!"

Harry's head sank farther into his shoulders where his neck ought to have been. He still hadn't looked her in the eye. His focus, when it encompassed her at all, remained firmly fixed on her taut midsection.

"The parking lot at Brady Beach!"

With something like fondness, I recalled a favorite in Harry's freshman-year wardrobe—a shrunken black concert T-shirt, "Brady Beach," with something or other obscene on the back. Chat liked to try it on from time to time and come out in the middle of the room and play a vigorous air guitar with his amplifier turned up too high.

"Hey, you want one? You want a cigarette now? Look: I still smoke Marlboros. I never changed my brand!"

"You smoke?" I said.

Cara put an arm around my shoulder. "Only when I party, Georgie!"

Releasing me, she stuck a cigarette in her mouth and looked around the cramped excuse for a kitchen as if at a great view, as if there were twenty men who might have come running from the esplanade with matches.

The matchbook Harry removed bore the logo of the bar downstairs. He must have been waiting down there, I realized, watching the clock, for the previous half hour to be up.

When the buzzer rang again, I excused myself and went to get it. It was Toff, haggard from lugging the ice, and a few guests of mine he'd ridden up with, to whom he had, in Toff-like fashion, not introduced himself. "We thought he was going to another party," said one of the girls, "or we would have helped."

The early turnout was a bit *too* promising. A number of people slinked in whom I didn't recognize, and as I couldn't believe Toff had that many friends, it seemed to mean that word had overly gotten around, as sometimes happens. But then I noticed that a lot of them seemed to know Harry. In fact he was hosting a sort of sub-party in one corner of the room, taking drink orders and pointing out the bar. A little while later, I caught him pointing me out, so I went over and thanked him for inviting all of his friends to my party. "Hey, anytime, George. I know how it can be—first party in the city. . . . No worries, no worries . . . all is good among friends." Cara, standing beside him the way she normally protected Geoff, looked at me contemptuously and remarked, "Looks like half the people here are friends of yours, Henry."

"It certainly does, doesn't it?" I said.

"Hey," Harry said, "don't feel bad or anything, George—"

"I'll try not to."

As I turned away, Cara smirked and put a hand to her mouth to whisper in his ear.

When I next remarked the two of them, she had him monopolized on the couch. By then, however, I could see that it was no one-sided communion.

"You're kidding me! You gotta be kidding me—that's crazy!"

"I know it's crazy, but it's the goddamned truth! You wanna hear how it happened? Lemme tell you how it happened."

Harry had warmed to her considerably; he looked relaxed, expansive, as he pontificated to his circle of guests for her benefit. It dawned on me that perhaps it had been my presence that had cowed him earlier, not Cara's. I looked around for Toff, to see what he made of this, and found him in the kitchen pounding beers, the flirtation was so obvious. "Great party, George!" called the poor guy, straining for a lighthearted note with a grimace of a smile. What was even stranger, at least to me, was that the new Cara McLean, flushed and animated under Harry's steady, rather menacing gaze, had all but obliterated our forlorn weeknight couch denizen. She looked robust; she looked as if she'd had a steak for dinner. I remember thinking that Harry *ought* to take her out for a steak—it would do her good, from time to time: woman cannot live on fro-yo alone—and thinking also that a maniacal commitment to aerobic exercise was not such a bad thing after all.

Or perhaps I had simply had too much to drink. There were shots to be done with my roommate, shots to be done with Robbins, shots to be done with Daniels, whom I had rashly invited and who had, predictably, come. A guy I didn't know in a cap was working the door, and another guy in another cap was roundly and vocally dismissing me as "the freak who never got out of vinyl," when an hour or so into the full swing there was a flurry at the door, and as the song on the stereo ended a clean, dry voice across the room said, "Oh, so this *is* George Lenhart's place, then. I'd better introduce Delia, what was it, Ferrier? Delia Ferrier, we've just met in the elevator."

Not just the song, it seemed, but the entire album's side had ended, so that as Kate came in with this other girl, the entire party stared across the room at them. Cara McLean, I'd venture to guess, stared hardest of all.

I went to greet them. The girl with Kate was taller and brunette, with glasses that were rather severe and obscured her eyes; she was dressed all in black. It was a look, and not one I disliked. It impressed me that Toff had procured her when, even more improbably, Harry Lombardi stood up yet again and claimed her as his guest. This he did by shouting her name across the room. "Delia!" But the name was an aural fake; he barely looked at the girl. She seemed to take this with a certain amount of irony, and on this shared note the two of us shook hands.

"You look familiar," I said, already too drunk to be embarrassed at starting so poorly. And I would finish worse.

"We all do," came her unexpected response.

"Really."

"Yes, except we've all dropped a size and started waxing our eyebrows." She looked straight at me and you could see why she wore the glasses. "New York does that to girls." I absorbed this as, with his usual finesse, Harry walked heavily—I might now say inexorably—through the crowd to Kate Goodenow. I remember thinking that he walked like a man defeated—a man who, lacking alternatives, keeps going, his shoulders hunched into the wind, his cross on his back. Yet there was something reassuring about his resignation in the midst of all our glib expectations. I hoped he wouldn't take it too hard when Kate shot him down.

He stared at her for about three seconds—she was charming the Cap at the door with some nonsense about a cab shortage—before interrupting her with an important bulletin: "I'm Harry."

Cara he had utterly forgotten about the instant the door opened. She was left openmouthed and furious on the couch, her knees tucked up underneath her in a provocative pose, now provoking no one.

"I'm sorry?"

"I'm Harry."

Something about the stolidity with which he repeated this seemed to amuse Kate. She shot me a droll look. "Just 'Harry'?" she said. "Harry, Harry, quite contrary?"

Harry failed to get the implication; what was more, he didn't pretend to get it. I think the latter might have impressed Kate ever so slightly. He said—nothing; he stared at her, unembarrassed, his large head poking out through his shoulders. In the background, music started again, after a moment of static, as the needle touched a new record.

Kate didn't have the kind of complexion that blushes, but she lowered her eyes for half a second to indicate where the blush might have come. "Do you have a last name, Harry?" she said softly.

Harry grunted. "Lombardi." He took her hand and shook it, methodically, serious, not smiling. Kate fluttered her eyes in my general direction, as if for help, but not particularly wanting help.

"Kate Goodenow."

"I know who you are."

"You *do*?"

"Sure."

"And how—"

"I wenta Dartmouth."

"You—you went to Dartmouth with—"

"Chat Wethers. And George here. They told me about you."

"You did? George?"

"I never said a word."

"Well," Kate said happily, "I've never heard of you."

"Yeah, I dropped out."

Kate seemed to miss a beat as, against all expectations, her curiosity was piqued. I had missed nothing, but I was giving Delia Ferrier short shrift as I observed this encounter. Of course, I thought: Kate would cotton to that fact—his dropping out—as much as I had. It was something new in her world, at least new in her New York world. He was talking so closely to her that she was pressed up against the wall. I stepped forward to assert myself. Instead I heard myself asking what I could get them to drink.

"You choose," Kate demurred.

"I'll choose," said Harry. "I know what you want. I'll get you something good." He ordered by brand name; fortunately, we had his brand on hand.

"Shall I help you, George?"

"I'll manage," I said, and realized that my girl had slipped away—as, of course, she ought to have done.

"All right," Kate agreed. "I'll stay and hear more about myself from your charming friend."

I tried to press forward, but the way to the kitchen was blocked.

"You'd be surprised what I know," Harry asserted.

"Would I," she said, unimpressed, not really believing him.

"Sure—like, Wednesdays were square dancing," Harry offered. And he began to recite the facts of her childhood like multiplication tables. "Thursdays were Coggywog nights, and Fridays were—wait, hold on! I know this. Fridays were—Fridays were—shit, what were Fridays? Don't tell me!"

Kate's face was immobile but her eyes were paying attention to him, something they almost never did.

"Don't tell me! I know this."

"Don't tell him, Kate," I mumbled. "Don't tell him what Fridays were."

"Fridays were Top of the World," Kate said. I pushed my way into the throng.

I laughed at a dirty joke of Robbins's and was aware of Cara's unmerited attack on Geoff coming from their bedroom. I agreed with Daniels that all was forgiven—of course, of course—in the interest of friendship, and somewhere between the door and Harry's top-shelf liquor I understood what had passed between Kate and me on the street before. I labored the ten feet toward the kitchen, and all the time it was dawning on me until I knew it as surely as I knew her name. She would have gone to Paris with me. A large bag of ice was melting in the sink. She would have gone, only I hadn't seen it quickly enough, or clearly enough. You couldn't throw a party with three trays of ice. Toff was a good roommate to remember the ice. She would have gone, only I had thought of the money. It was still the same question it had always been. I had missed my chance because of the money. At the moment I'd realized she was playing to my hand, I was down an enormous sum.

Or so it seemed to me at the time. It is only recently that another idea has come creeping into my consciousness—that it was not the ten thousand dollars I owed Chat but the sum, rather, of my years. Twenty-three was a stupid age, a know-nothing age. It was the age when it seemed quite likely that that kind of debt could have consequences. It was a guilty age. And I was guilty enough already, guilty of the same old thing since grade school, guilty of having come from a family that had had the lack of foresight—the poor taste, really—to come down in the world. It was almost anti-American, losing money the way we had.

And yet there was Kate, nodding at me across the room, perhaps saying something about me to Harry. Her face hadn't changed. But to act now? Under false pretenses?

"Lenhart, how many feminists does it take to change a light-bulb?"

"I don't know, Robbins. Is your mother one of them?"

I gave Kate a pointless little wave through the crowd. It was like the feeling you get in bridge when the bidding ends and you see you are to lay down your hand as dummy. You see you are going to sit this one out. And in my place Harry Lombardi, of all people, had stepped in. I felt my jaw clench with anger. What right had he? I wanted to go over and invoke Wethers's name, even if he was eight hours north. But there was, of course, no point in mentioning Chat. Unlike me, Lombardi didn't owe Chat Wethers a thing. Unlike me, Lombardi had found it more practical to trade debt than acquire it. I took my hands away from the block of ice as the chill penetrated my fingers.

When I had the two drinks made, I elbowed my way back through the jammed kitchen. At the refrigerator I met Delia Ferrier all in black wedged between the open door and a wall.

"For me?"

"No," I said thoughtlessly, "they're for Lombardi." I ought to have taken that as a sign—that with her, I would never get a decent line off.

"Harry can take care of himself," she suggested.

"I meant yes, by the way," I said, and handed her a drink.

"I know you did."

"Harry brought you?"

"Invited me. I brought myself."

"How'd he happen to—"

"He thought we might get along."

"He's smarter than he looks."

"If you haven't learned that yet, I can't help you."

"You probably can't help me, anyway," I said.

She had great teeth when she smiled.

CHAPTER 8

The party peaked and went inevitably downhill. Toff had invited an unsavory bunch of people from the law firm who kept turning the television on. Daniels got trashed and made further apologies to me while hitting on Robbins's date. A handful of girls, including Cara, wanted to dance in the helplessly determined way that drunk girls want to dance, and they were dragging people off the couch to dance with them. And in the early hours of the morning Harry had, as it turned out, a final request: "Borrow a pen." He held up a gnawed ballpoint. "You got a pen? Mine's out." I had finally gotten Delia Ferrier onto the couch with me, and I shook him off two or three times. But he was as persistent as a mosquito in a silent room. Excusing myself finally, I went into Toff's bedroom and rummaged around on his desk, a great pen repository, and found one of the cheap Parkers he liked to use. When I came out I saw that the party had thinned to practically no one. The few that were left had the stupefied air that overtakes a party at which there is nothing left to drink.

Delia was reclining on the couch, watching one of the remaining pockets of people with her eyebrows raised in a detached air. Her face in repose wore a curious, ready expression; she looked as if she were going to be delighted or appalled by whatever happened next.

It was painful to watch the other two women interact, or rather fail to. Cara was trying to get her arms around Harry's neck while he, awkwardly, with both hands on her forearms, attempted to keep her from doing so. "I wanna dance, Henry!" she was yelling. "Come on, le's dance! Wha's a party if you don't dance?" Beside them Kate was standing quite erect, quite sober, with a pleased expression on her face which indicated: "This has been such a nice party, George. I'm so *glad* I came—it's really been fun!" She said as much to me, as I joined them and, leaning close to my ear, murmured, "Where did you find him? He's *unbelievable*."

"Gotta get your number," Harry asserted. I handed him the pen. Cara took the opportunity of his lowered guard to get her arms around him. "Let's dance, Henry! I wanna dance!"

"I don't give out my number," Kate said.

"Address, then."

"It's no party if people don't dance!"

"One-ninety East Sixty-sixth Street," said Kate.

Harry sat down to write out the address on the back of a business card, squeezing himself onto the couch with Delia and me; Cara moved with him, sitting as he sat, settling for the arm, glowering up at Kate.

"Apartment fourteen."

He didn't know how to use the pen. He held it too tightly, the way a child holds a crayon, and pressed down hard, so that the point scratched and the ink came out unevenly. It was a small thing but it embarrassed me, and I looked away, the way I'd pretend not to notice when Daniels scraped up his food with his knife at our "team" dinners.

"Now I'm afraid I must fly."

"Coach turning into a pumpkin?" Delia Ferrier remarked.

"Never," I asserted. "That will never happen."

"Walk out with you," offered Harry.

"Oh, no—no, no—I'm gone."

He stood up with Cara like a poncho around his neck. "I wanna dance, Henry!"

"Kate." It was the first time he said her name to her, and I seemed to hear it anew, all dentals and stops—it was a clean, hard name. "Kate, are you doing a share or anything this summer?" he got out.

"Am I—? What did you say? Am I 'doing a share'?" She turned around with a studious frown. "Is that something financial?" I walked her to the door. "I think my investments are sound! At least," her haughty voice came back to us from the hallway, "they ought to be!"

When she was gone, we seemed to have lost all impetus for conversation.

"Good riddance!" said Cara, and no one bothered to reprimand her.

I was the host and I ought to have broken the silence, but no appropriate comment came to mind.

Cara seemed to take our silence as an insult. "Fine!" she snapped. "Go home alone!" She stalked off to Toff's bedroom, whence another quarrel presently arose, followed by Toff's emerging, saying nothing, walking directly to the front door, and closing it behind him. In the bedroom Cara began to sob.

Harry, breathing heavily through his mouth, and alternately tucking the business card into his breast pocket and then removing it to gaze on it further, didn't even seem to hear her.

"Kate Goodenow strikes again," remarked Delia Ferrier coolly, from her corner of the couch.

I very much wished she had not said that; it was a deal breaker for me, that kind of comment about Kate.

"It's just—I've met her before," she added.

"Oh, well, you can't blame Kate," I said.

"Hmm . . ." She pushed her glasses up the bridge of her nose.

"No, but you can't," I said, wishing I could explain myself without making the situation worse. So many girls, so many people who knew her, thought Kate was a bitch, and would have released a litany of complaints if I had ever indicated the slightest sympathy to their position. She was thought to be shallow, a snob, overprivileged, rude, cold. But Kate herself had hardly any criticisms to make. Occasionally I had slipped, with an offhand remark, disparaging someone we both knew. "You think so?" Kate would say doubtfully, if she even acknowledged the comment. Her mind simply didn't work that way. She had one litmus test, which she herself was subject to: she hated it when people got in the way of having a good time. The worst indictment Kate could hand down was that someone was "un-fun." Over the years this had come to seem rather profound.

Of course, as I have already observed, I was twenty-three. And even at the time, it could be hard to explain to other people, to other girls.

"I took four classes with her, and she thinks we met in the elevator."

"No, but you know what I mean," I persisted miserably. "You can't *blame* her for something like that."

"Oh," said Miss Ferrier. "*I* see." She sat forward and gave Harry's arm a tap. He started in his seat. "Huh."

"Shall we share a cab?"

"Oh. Yeah. Yeah, yeah, yeah. You bet. Drop you off on the way home."

I showed them to the door, and she and I looked at one another across the threshold for an unhappy moment. Lenhart! Lenhart! What kind of an idiot defends one girl to another? Defends a girl like Kate to a girl like Delia Ferrier? My kind, the evidence overwhelmingly indicated.

The elevator came. Delia got in and Harry made to follow her when suddenly he remarked, a little too loudly, "You know what? I forgot my jacket."

I almost laughed in his face. He was still telling bald-faced lies without any embarrassment at all.

"We'll hold the elevator," Delia said, with the forcibly patient intonation of one who has endured much for a friendship.

Harry appeared momentarily stumped, as if he hadn't thought of this possibility. "Uh . . . you know what? Don't bother. It might take me a while to find it. George—could you, uh . . . ?"

"Come on, I'll put you in a cab," I volunteered equally impatiently. I always did feel that his rudenesses were reflected onto me.

It wasn't until Delia and I were riding down in the elevator that I realized I owed him for this second chance—this moment alone with her. I took her down and a bit too solicitously got her tucked into a taxi: that was easy to do.

"Listen, can't I call you?" I said.

"I'm in the book."

"Really?"

"Really—Ferrier on Ninth Street."

"So this wasn't a total fiasco."

She was kind. "Hardly," she said.

"Then we have Harry to thank."

"Inadvertently."

"No, I mean for right now."

"So do I."

"But he must have gone back to . . . give us a moment alone," I suggested.

"You think so? I'm sure he's gone to seduce your friend."

"Kate?" I nearly cried, at once losing all the ground I had regained.

I still remember her expression, full of comprehension and foresight, and a touch of a kind of pity I had no interest in but would have to take. I had betrayed myself again.

"No, George," Delia said. "Kate's gone home. I was talking about your homecoming queen."

Indeed I met the two of them coming out of the elevator, Harry and Cara, she triumphant, cozy, Harry licking his chops until he saw me and dropped her hand guiltily. That he could on the same night meet Kate Goodenow, after five years of anticipation, and leave with Cara McLean—but perhaps that was the key to his triumphs on the Street. He set his sights high but took what he could get.

"Heya, Georgie—*great* party," Cara said.

"Yeah," Harry corroborated, eyeing his watch nervously, wanting to be on his way, "good effort. Good call on the tequila shots. Oh, and hey," he added, not meeting my eyes, "sorry it didn't work out with Delia."

"Didn't work out?" I repeated. "But I just met her tonight."

Harry shuffled nervously. "Some girls take a while . . ."

"Hey!" Cara gave his arm a friendly whack with her handbag.

"They like to be taken out to dinner," Harry went on, grinning now. "You'll learn, you see. Just takes time. It's different from college."

"Thanks, Harry," I said, as Cara snuggled into his arm, "for the advice."

Up in the apartment, I walked through the beer bottles and ashtrays to the kitchen, trying to remember the misguided inspiration that had given rise to the party. The place seemed strangely deserted, and I realized that what was missing was, of course, Chat—not so much at the party, but at the end of it. At the fraternity parties I'd arranged he would always stay till the bitter, bitter end; you could count on that; you could count on him. He wouldn't help clean up, but he would sit and talk and smoke cigarette after cigarette and fix himself drink after drink, if there was anything left, and when he finally got down to the desperate measures he would say, "Gin and orange soda—is that a drink? I think that's a drink," and he'd mix one up for each of us. I'd sit down and have a cigarette—I smoked about one a month—and we'd get into an argument about what the temperature of the water was when the *Titanic* sank and where the Donner party went off course and how long you could survive if you had all the beer and water you could drink but you had to drop acid every day. When the sun rose he'd rise and lean on the windowsill like an old man and say, "It's going to be a great, great day. Think of all the goddamn lazy Lombardis who are going to sleep the day away"—because Harry would sleep all day if you let him—and then, "Dining hall opens in two hours. Quick hand of gin?"

The thought of college gave me a mellow feeling, and I must have fallen asleep, because when I awoke, it was three or four in the morning and Toff was coming in the door.

"George."

"Geoff."

He went to bed. I decided to turn in, too, but about a half an hour later, the buzzer rang. Cara was, unbelievably, back. I couldn't ignore the ringing, but I didn't want to deal with her, so I left the door ajar and went back to bed. Presently, half-consciously, I became aware of someone crying, and I realized it was coming not from my dreams but from our bathroom.

Cara was half sitting, half sprawled on the floor for maximum effect, in her T-shirt and underwear. She raised a red face to me, distorted by alcohol. "Geoff threw me out and then he locked me out! Geoff locked me out of his room!"

When I didn't respond at once, she cried, "He hates me! He's evil! He hates me! He's evil! He hates me!"

I knocked on his door, rattled the doorknob, said his name half-heartedly, but it was no use. It never was any good arguing with people like Toff. There was nothing to do but give her my bed and take the couch. I got a pillow and my trench coat and a couple of bath towels and cleared off the cushions and lay down. I desperately wanted to go to sleep, more than I ever had in my whole life. Cara called me back to thank me, tearfully. "You won't hold this against me, will you, George? You promise you won't!"

"I promise," I said.

" 'Cause you and I have always gotten along so well. I love you so, so, so, so, so much, George! I know this sounds awful—but sometimes I think I love you more than Geoff. We have something, you and I—a rapport, you could say—and he can't take it away." She called me back a second time; this time I stayed where I was. Nevertheless she made her point. "Your friend Henry Lombardi still likes me!" she proclaimed into the trashed room, into the cigarette air. "I know he still likes me! I know it! I would have stayed over tonight if it hadn't been for my having a boyfriend! *And* for my being too loyal to wake up in another man's bed! It was never just about sex with Henry and me! Never! And that"—she struggled briefly for the insult—"that *girl* is all wrong for him. I know! You know how I know? George? Are you listening?"

I suppose I could have at least made it clear that on this point, she didn't have to convince me.

"He lost it to me!" Cara cried. "That's how!" As I was trying, half asleep, to remember what "it" signified in this context, she clarified the reference: "On my parents' water bed!"

CHAPTER 9

Just last summer I was finally able to complete an empirical proof that I began to lay out my first summer in New York. I call it the Law of Summer Displacement. This is how it works: my parents' friends the Beverlys live on Sixty-eighth and Third and spend their summers in Litchfield, Connecticut. But Mr. and Mrs. Beverly's neighbors in Litchfield, the Clarks, make Connecticut their home all winter, so they like to spend July and August on Martha's Vineyard; they have rented the same house in Tisbury for fifteen years running. Now, a guy I know from Chatham called Billy P. made the bold move after college to become a year-rounder on the Vineyard. The idea worked out well for a while; he sailed and washed dishes and played guitar, but eventually he couldn't stand the summer crowds, so a couple of Junes ago he took off for Nova Scotia, where his grandparents have a farm. He met a girl there named Val Breton; they went out for two summers, then last summer I heard that Val, who was still in college, had gotten herself an internship in New York and was subletting the Beverlys' daughter's apartment in the East Village. *Quod erat demonstrandum.*

That was the way it worked. I remember how amusing I found it when I first became aware of the phenomenon—that people in Manhattan went to, say, City Island; people from City Island went to Stamford; people from the suburbs went to the country; people from the country went to the islands; and people from the islands came here. And I used to look forward to the day when I would hear that people from Soho were summering on Fourteenth Street, so that I could prove the absurdity of it all—that one man's meat is, in fact, another man's grilled steak. But after a few summers of my own, I came to understand, as even the most benighted New Yorkers eventually do, that the important thing wasn't where you went but *that* you went, that you committed yourself to the drives there and back, to the endless coming and going. The getting there wasn't the point, because summer, at least the American summer, is one long moment in the present. The other seasons have their years and their private histories, but every summer is a part of every other summer. Different rules apply, which one must learn in youth.

"In the summer," Chat put it to me once—the summer we spent up at Dartmouth—"nothing counts."

I had, nevertheless, paid Robbins fifteen hundred dollars for the privilege of showing up every other weekend in Southampton, well north of the highway, to share a room with one of his fraternity brothers from Pennsylvania. On the two or three weekends I made it out there, however, hastily formed couples took the rooms and the beds and I and two other luckless guys flipped for the good and bad couches.

I couldn't have made a move for any of the girls Robbins drew. They were friendly, cooperative girls, and good sports; when we barbecued, the lot of them would go to work rustling up platters for their signature hors d'oeuvres. But I couldn't get a handle on their muscular arms and plain faces. And I couldn't remember where any of them were from. Like an idiot, I kept repeating the question until one girl complained, "I've told you three times!" and named a town upstate. I had a horrible sense of vertigo those weekends. The entire time was like one afternoon when I had to go to the drugstore for aspirin and a buddy of Robbins's offered me a ride to the mall. It was a strip mall, and the pharmacy was one of a discount chain. I went inside the store and walked up and down each aisle, but I couldn't find the right one. I kept wandering around looking for the aspirin under the fluorescent lights until, standing by the greeting cards, I suddenly felt as if the air inside the store were thinning. It was difficult to breathe. My headache was so bad by this point, it occurred to me that I must have a brain tumor. So this was it: death at the strip mall. At last a middle-aged clerk showed me to the painkiller section. I walked back out to the parking lot and swallowed two dry and waited for Robbins's pal. Something was wrong. I was standing in a parking lot of a strip mall on the nicest day of the year. Something had simply gone wrong. My ride came trundling across the parking lot clutching a bag of fast food. "Hey, you wanna go ride the go-carts?" he asked, stuffing in a bite. I declined as politely as someone in my condition could.

The Long Island Rail Road on Sunday, with the passengers sunburned, bitchy, defeated by the size of the *Times*, standing all the way from Bridgehampton with rackets sticking defensively out of their bags—that at least was a lovely embraceable misery. And every Monday morning was like a baptism. There was work to be done, money to be made. Without the money I reckoned we would surely have all gone away for good.

Once in a while there would be an empty Saturday, devoid of plans and meaning, and on one of those Saturdays I got a call from Harry. It was a few weeks after my party, a day in late June; sticky, with a high, halfhearted overcast, as if the weather were hedging its bets. I had worked most of the night before and was contemplating how to endure the next day and a half—it wasn't one of my allotted weekends in the share—when Harry offered salvation in the form of brunching with him. It was his verb, not mine; I myself have never been able to eat pancakes after ten o'clock without a kind of moral malaise setting in. He named one of the popular brunch spots in my—both of our neighborhoods, actually, there being a branch on either side of the park. It was one of those pseudo-fifties diners that advertise a free mimosa or Bloody Mary with your $12.99 eggs, as if life weren't tragic enough. The choice of restaurant was so repellent to me that I hesitated, as much as I wished to leave the apartment, when a woman's voice spoke up in the background and a moment or two later Kate got on the phone and told me I had better come, because if I didn't, she wasn't going to go, either. "It's true," Harry said, reclaiming the receiver. "She says she won't go unless you go, George. She's been saying it all morning." And that was how I learned that she had taken up with him, just like that.

I was the first to arrive; it was a depressing two o'clock when I got there. It was late enough so that a few minutes' wait yielded a table, a booth no less (the hostess indicated that this was a great stroke of good fortune for me) and late enough also that the booth wore the effects of the ten previous parties it had seated that morning. Bits of egg and mayonnaise clung to the surface of the table, and you could see the hasty path the busboy's sponge had taken, drying now in a gray-brown figure eight. In the next booth I watched a heavy, sunburned young man with a crew cut pour ketchup on his eggs and eat them in a continuous shoveling motion, hunched over his plate as he highlighted for a buddy the sexual conquest of the night before. When their plates were nearly clean, the two of them came up briefly for air, pounded their Bloody Marys, and set the empty glasses down. The buddy took up his fork to spear a last bite when his face suddenly resembled that of a man who has been punched in the stomach. He gripped the table, eyes goggling wildly, saliva forming at the corners of his half-open mouth. The ketchup-and-eggs man suspended his shoveling to watch. After a moment the stricken man lurched to his feet and made for the men's room. He returned a few minutes later, wiping his mouth on his shirttail with a gratified air. "You lose it?" grunted the companion.

"Lost it all," the man confirmed, making a loud vomiting noise.

I ordered tea and a negligible cup of water appeared, too cold to bleed the tea bag. I sat dunking it anyway, waiting.

They were half an hour late. Neither of them seemed to notice the place, which irked me, since they had chosen it. Floating in like a tractable kite on Harry's arm, Kate alit on my side of the booth.

"Oh, you wanna sit with George, huh? You wanna sit with George?"

I felt my hand seized by both of her cool ones. "Of *course* I want to sit with George!"

"Oh, you do, huh?"

I began to dread the rest of the afternoon.

There is a phase in every new relationship when it cannot be seen to exist by its constituents unless reflected by a third party. During this phase one makes plans ardently, exacts double dates from any existing twosome, and preys upon mutual friends for dinner. For Harry and Kate this phase would be dramatically foreshortened, or at least narrowly focused: I was the only person both of them knew.

"So you wanna sit with George, huh?"

"Read your menu, Harry."

As Harry dutifully scrutinized it, Kate flipped her sunglasses up on her head and whispered in my ear, "I'm *so* glad you could come! *You're* the reason I came out at all." She was tan, but not ostentatiously so; Kate was one of the few people left who got tan from sport.

The waitress came. Harry did the ordering for the two of them, or, rather, the two of them and the six imaginary friends who were to show up later: waffles, French toast, eggs over easy and scrambled, a Spanish omelette. "That oughta do it."

"But I want french fries," Kate said pleasantly. "Did you order french fries? That's all I want."

"Awright, add a fries to that. And Bloodys all around. You'll have a drink, won't you, George?"

As the day was lost already, I could think of no reason to refuse.

"The Bloodys are free with the meal," Harry announced. He pulled a fistful of paper napkins from the dispenser and shredded them methodically. "Not that I care, but you gotta live it up when you get the chance, right?"

"Absolutely," I said.

"See, George knows what I'm talking about. You gotta live every day like it matters—like it's your last."

I glanced at Kate. It was her practice to live no day like it mattered. She sat demurely, pressing into me slightly, utterly retracted into herself. From the blank, pleasant expression on her face, you would have thought she could see no farther than the inner surface of her own eye. At last the drinks came.

"They call this spicy?" Harry protested. He seized the pepper from the next booth, deserted now, and shook it methodically into his glass, ten or twelve shakes. Then he repeated the procedure with the Tabasco sauce. "But you'll burn your mouth off!" cried Kate, aghast.

"No, I won't—I *like* it hot!" declared Harry. "The hotter the better!" He drank it down and his eyes watered terribly.

"How *could* you?"

Choking, he summoned the waitress and ordered another round.

"I'll skip it," I said, with a view of what was to come. Harry was evidently bent on getting trashed in the middle of the day.

"Don't be a teetotaler, George," Kate chided me, though she had not touched her drink.

This was her way of telling me I had better be a good sport. "All right," I said giving up. "I don't care either way." And I really didn't.

"There's nothing Dad detests more than the teetotaler," Kate went on contentedly, as if a string in her back had been pulled and she had been mechanized into conversation. "Dad's always saying that Alcoholics Anonymous is ruining this country, and Mom and I just say . . ."

There is a certain kind of person who refers to his mother and father as "Mom" and "Dad" instead of "my mom" and "my dad," as if his parents were the only parents in the world, and the listeners are presumed to be acquainted with Mom and Dad and their endearing idiosyncrasies. Previously I had taken this as a minor flattery from Kate; now, watching Harry make the same assumption, it occurred to me that it was in fact a minor rudeness. He breathed a little more heavily at the mention of Mr. Goodenow.

"When do I get to meet your dad, Kate? He sounds like my kind of guy. I'll bet he and I would get along great! Didja ever think of that—that your dad and I would probably hit it off? We got lots in common, you know. I mean, when you think about it."

"Dad?" Kate said coolly. "You'll get to meet him one of these days."

"You promise, Kate?"

I shot her another look; I couldn't help myself.

"Why shouldn't you meet Dad?" she said mildly. "Maybe you'll come up to Maine—"

"Maine?" Harry shouted. "Kate, you mean it?" If the table hadn't been in the way, I believe he would have jumped into her lap. As it was, he made a helpless, truncated gesture in her direction, as if to embrace her across the expanse of Formica. "You and me at Chilly-ick? Jesus, Kate! That'd be the best!"

"Well, we'll see," said Kate, retreating into herself once more.

"I mean, Chillyick—!"

My hamburger came and I ate it, studying the blue plate specials above the grill as if to memorize them. Chillyick was their nickname for the yacht club, Kate's and Chat's and Nicko's, the Cold Harbor Yacht Club—C.H.Y.C.—they called it Chillyick.

Harry had ordered so much food that the plates wouldn't fit on the table, so he scraped the three egg dishes onto one. "That oughta do it!"

He got down to eating. Kate didn't want to eat, not even the fries, but he cut off a square of waffle and ran it through the syrup on his plate and poked it toward her. "Just try it." She took it, gingerly.

He inquired politely after my job.

"Harry's starting his own company, did you know that, George?" Kate asked.

"I did hear that," I said. Both of us spoke to Harry as if he had suddenly become the satellite through which we beamed our communications.

"Give this software thing a shot," mumbled Harry. Midbite he seemed to be weighing a conversational risk. He swallowed, put his knife and fork down European-style, sat back in the booth, and spread his palms on the table. The nails were bitten down to the quick, but at the thought of the company he was going to start, his face went absolutely clear and focused. "I'm looking for backers, George. This could really be a good thing for you . . . I wouldn't even mention it if I didn't think it was one hundred percent rock-solid. I mean, I don't know where you've got your money, but—"

"What's the idea?"

"The idea? Awright, awright." Harry cleared his throat, contemplated me for a moment with some consternation, and then gave a barely perceptible nod, as if he had answered some internal question for himself. "Okay, okay, George—I'm going to lay it on you. You know how up at Dartmouth all the computers were, like, connected? Yeah? You with me?"

"I'm with you."

"You're with me?"

"Yes." It has crossed my mind more than once to wonder what another man would have given that year to have heard a speech like the one that followed.

"Okay, okay. So there's all this information, right, flowing between the computers. You see what I'm saying?" I nodded. "Great, great. So now forget about school, because I'm not talking about school. I'm talking about networks everywhere, George. Picture this: there are all these *different* networks, and they're connected up, too. This information is everywhere and anyone can access it through their own computer—George, you with me? Now this is a great thing, right? I mean, this is what it's all about: *access to information*." Harry's tongue lingered lovingly on the words. "Access," he breathed. "To information. You have that, you have—I mean, damn it, you have everything! And technologically, it's all there. All I have to do, with your support, a'course . . ." He glanced at Kate. "But you know—why don't we, uh, talk about it later," he muttered, clearing his throat again. "You and me."

As I have said, Kate had expected me to be a good sport about this brunch. I very nearly let her down. I nearly let her down, but I have always been susceptible to the oddest, most sudden sympathies. And the joy with which Harry made this last suggestion, with which he reined himself in at last, to assign men's affairs to the realm of men and spare the little woman the boredom, aroused a wild charity in me. I turned shyly away and ordered another round. Harry insisted on going with the waitress to show the bartender how to make the Bloody Marys. After he got up Kate and I sat in silence, looking out into the afternoon. You could see people through the glass door, scowling on their ways, made angry by the heat. But inside it was cool. . . .

"Think I straightened this guy out!"

"Oh, good!" we both cried.

Later on, I became the topic of conversation. They were going to find a great girl for me. That is the other thing a newly minted couple is compelled do for their only mutual friend: set him up. "I know a girl for you, George," Kate said. "She's a great girl. Virginia Prince, Hotchkiss, Trinity. We'll all go out next week."

"What about Delia?" Harry said. He wiped his mouth and threw the napkin down on the table. "What's wrong with her? If you'da given her another try, I'da bet—"

"Delia? Who's Delia?" interrupted Kate.

"Girl from the party."

"What party?"

"George's party."

It was my cue to tell them I had called Delia Ferrier after the party and that I was taking her out on Sunday. We had a dinner date, just as Harry had recommended. But I didn't mention Delia; somehow I felt it would be rude—rude to Kate—to bring her up. I sat there and let them discuss me.

"Oh. Oh, you mean—yes. The girl from the party. She seemed fine. But I don't know, I think George wants someone really . . . *fun,* don't you, George?"

"You come out to the Hamptons, you'll find the funnest girls around," Harry asserted.

"That's an idea . . ." said Kate.

"You mean you'll go?"

"Go? Well, we haven't been invited—"

"Invited! Kate, you *know*—I've asked you ten times. I mean, if you'd go . . . Jesus!"

Turning to me: "I got a house out there," Harry said apologetically.

It spoke to my particular capacity for mythologizing that I believed Harry meant he had bought a house. I didn't find out till the weekend was over that he was renting, just like everyone else. After the introduction of the possibility, Harry was bent on going that very afternoon.

"Why shouldn't we? Gimme one good reason why we shouldn't go!"

"Oh, I don't know," Kate said carelessly.

"What do you usually do on the weekends?" I inquired.

I didn't mean to imply anything with the question, but Kate said, a touch indignantly, "I've been busy, George. I've had sailing. I've gone out on Uncle Goodie's boat almost every weekend."

"Oh." I hadn't realized until then that she was interested in stooping quite that low—in having a boyfriend she didn't go out with in public—and it made me feel a little sick.

"George, you'd be up for it, wouldn't you?" Harry demanded. "Why not, right? What else are we gonna do?"

"What else . . ."

"Come on!" he urged. "Say you'll go—we leave now—what is it—three-thirty? Four? We can have swordfish on the grill at eight.

Seven, the way I drive! Come on, whaddaya say? Let's do it! We'll have swordfish, tomatoes, corn on the cob—*corn on the cob*, you guys! George, come on, you talk her into it."

"I think we ought to go," I said. I didn't even bother trying to plead third-wheel; they never would have gone without me.

"See? George is up for it! You *gotta* be up for it! I mean, wait'll you see it! I got everything! I got a grill in the backyard, a hot tub!"

"Oh," Kate murmured, elbowing me under the table, "you didn't tell me you had a hot tub."

"No, but—I'm serious!"

O love affair that cannot wait a week but must go forward now. To show—this I did, all of it, for you! Harry, the newly minted lover, must have felt that there was no time for them, that there would never be enough time—in spite of the information he had acquired, in spite of the access he had gained—and even taking into consideration the way he drove.

The restaurant was nearly empty by then, except for a disheveled couple with two whining children and an Hispanic busboy who, having given up on getting us to leave, had begun to mop the floor. He was younger than we were, though it was hard to tell by how much. Over the course of the meal Harry had developed a rapport with him, or believed that he had. Harry was the type of person who considers a meal a failure unless he relates successfully to the wait staff.

"Yo, Carlos!"

"You need something, sir? More coffee? I get the waitress."

"Naw"—he batted the suggestion away—"I had enough caffeine; drank like five cups. Listen: I wanna ask your opinion. You know the *Hamptons?*" His voice rose a little to help the foreigner understand. "Like *South*ampton, *Bridge*hampton, *East* Hampton?"

The boy nodded, smiling faintly. "Yes, sir. Long Island, sir."

"Okay. Now if you got a chance to go out to a house in the Hamptons, you know, go out to a really nice house with a big pool—huge pool—and a hot tub and everything, would you go?"

The young man grinned. He had a quick, knowing smile, insolent and deprecating at the same time. "Oh yes, sir."

"That's what I'm tryin'-a convince these two, and it's like pulling teeth!"

The young man looked from Kate to me, nodding as if he understood a joke. "More coffee?"

"Oh, no—no, thank you. But thank you."

"You want something else, sir?"

"Naw, thanks—you been great. Now, guys . . ."

Harry drummed his index fingers on the table as if waiting for inspiration. Kate and I began a silly conversation about nothing at all, teasing him, which Harry half listened to until, in a perturbed fit of energy, he burst from the booth, threw a handful of bills on the table, and announced we were leaving. "We gotta go now if we're gonna go!" he said miserably.

"All right, Harry," said Kate with the greatest indifference. "So we'll go now." She stood up and walked out.

In his rush to follow her, Harry tripped over the busboy's mop bucket and sent the dirty water spilling across the floor. "Jesus Christ!" He took several thudding steps to regain his balance, cursed again, brushed off his pant leg, and hurried toward the door.

I counted the money on the table. The tip was a little shy, especially with the spill, so I took a five out of my wallet and added it to the pile. When I stood up I realized I was drunk. On the way out, I apologized and shook the busboy's hand. It seemed wrong not to, seeing as how for that day, anyway, he and I were in the same line of work.

I am no teetotaler—that fault, at least, Mr. Goodenow couldn't pin on me—but I can count on two hands the number of times I have been drunk in daylight. It is the guiltiest feeling in the whole world. The sky that day might have cloaked the knowledge with a considerate meteorological opacity, but the ceiling had lifted while we ate, and by the time we stumbled out of the diner, the sun had come out to vilify the lot of us—except that Kate had barely touched her drink.

When I got back to the apartment, I wanted to crawl into bed, stand them up, and call it a day. But I knew how I'd feel later if I passed out now, so I threw a few things into a duffel and met them at the garage where Harry kept his car.

After several minutes of anticipation in which the humidity pulsated through my brain, they brought the car down.

I had traveled a bit in Europe, and, as everyone knows, in the global jokeplace the Bavarians are the easiest targets of all; one can make fun of those beer-swilling, wurst-eating, lederhosen-wearing folk for all of the obvious reasons. But one thing the southern Germans are is sincere. You would have to be, to build a car like that. It popped into sight like a blown-up balloon, plump through its curves and glistening faintly like an erotic toy.

"Blue," breathed Kate. "My favorite color."

And settling into the passenger seat and finding her hipbones with my two hands—she had to sit on my lap, it being a two-seater—I understood that she had every right to be loved in the old, high way of love; that she had every right to be driven out to Southampton in a fifty-thousand-dollar convertible, and that every girl did. It was my problem if I lived life ironically, if indeed it was the only way I knew. It wasn't as if I even believed in it. I saw how thin it was, I saw the poverty of it—that I couldn't make love to her because it wasn't an ironic act.

CHAPTER 10

We made the kind of picture you make once or twice in a lifetime. Harry drove a thousand miles an hour and I kept my arms around Kate so she wouldn't blow away, and the wind we created in that airless day whipped her blue, polka-dot scarf in a crazy, intractable rhythm. Near Millport, Harry shot out onto the shoulder to pass another convertible. It was the same model as Harry's, but they had left their top up, perhaps to keep the air-conditioning on—more presumably to make our day. Harry double-clutched to get by, the car seemed to gather itself for a split second, and I caught the helpless glance of the other car's cuckolded driver before we went screaming down the expressway.

The house was sincerity itself. It was a big, comfy nothing—you couldn't have even called it a contemporary—overgrown by at least a few bedrooms. We left the car on a gravel half-circle drive, landscaped straight out of the suburbs fifty miles west, and went in through a pair of mini-Doric columns. We could have been anywhere, in that house, anywhere in America. I guess that was the point: to make one feel at home.

"Look around, make yourselves at home," Harry advised, and left for the store, refusing help. When he had gone, Kate and I tripped up and down like thieves. I myself felt gloriously far from home. There were six bedrooms upstairs. In the self-consciously superior master bedroom, the bed took up the entire room, and a few hundred geese had been kind enough to make an offering for its pillows. Kate threw herself onto the bed the way you belly flop on a hotel bed.

"Do you think Harry'll come around tonight and leave mints on the pillows?"

"I don't know. Do you think the service is any good in this place?" I kicked off my loafers and flopped facedown on the bed, too. It *was* just like being in a hotel, where the one-size-fits-all luxury is such a nice, nice joke. The house had no obligations in it.

"Get under the covers, dear," said Kate, "where it's warm."

I did as she said and then we were sitting up in the bed together. "I'm a little worried about Mary, dear," I said. "Her last report was rather disheartening."

"Yes, dear, I'll speak to her about it. Now, did you take Rex to the vet this afternoon?"

"Yes, I did. The vet said you mustn't spoil him the way you do. No more steaks and chops. From here on in, strictly dog chow."

"Dog chow? What a bore for poor Rex."

"Well, we can still have steaks and chops."

"That goes without saying, dear."

Kate settled down into the bed and turned over on her side so her back was to me. Her shoulders were wonderfully rigid against the piles of pillows. "Will you get the light, dear?"

"Yes, dear." I yawned and scrunched down as well, pushing my legs under the tight, cool sheets. "Now about Mary, dear."

She rolled over on her pillows so she was facing me. We were lying about six inches apart.

"You're not really worried, are you, darling?" whispered Kate.

"Shouldn't I be?"

"She'll reform soon enough, dear."

"You think so?"

"Oh, yes. We all do eventually."

"Well, I hope so. Good night, dear."

"Good night." But she didn't close her eyes. Laughing, impenetrable, they stared into mine.

"Truth or dare," I whispered, when I couldn't stand the silence.

"You know what I always choose."

"Truth or dare," I repeated.

"Dare."

"I dare you to take off all your clothes."

Without dropping her gaze, Kate's hands went down to her skirt. There she paused, as if daring me to dare her for real.

Children came banging out of the house next door. A voice cried, "Mo-*om*!" My eyes flickered away from Kate's face.

"I win," she mouthed.

"What is this—"

"We ought to—"

"—satin?" I said, pushing back the coverlet.

"—see the rest."

She stood up from the bed and arranged her hair in the mirror above the dresser. I watched her reflection.

"Kate," I began, "about the other day—on the street, I mean . . ." But she stopped me with a look, a stubborn hardening of her eyes that yielded to disappointment. I closed my eyes and turned away from her. It was the disappointment I couldn't stand.

The only thing I had that was different from the others was that I knew it was a game—all of it—and I played it with her. It wasn't a game for Chat or Nick, certainly not for Harry. But I had played it with her from the moment I learned the rules. I wasn't supposed to forget them now.

"Come on, then," I said, "let's go see the rest."

"George?" Kate had moved from the dresser and she wasn't looking at me, but at the square of the sea visible through the window.

"Yes?"

"You know. . . . You're a very good sport, you know."

I nodded. It was cold comfort, but I preferred my comfort cold. She knew that about me, perhaps better than anyone. In that way, we understood each other.

"Yes, dear," I said after a moment. I ran my hands down the coverlet to smooth it out for Harry later.

Downstairs, traditional living and dining rooms had been abandoned in favor of one vast carpeted space minimally furnished with a long table and chairs at one end and a long, beige, L-shaped sofa "unit" at the other. Along the far outside wall, a pair of floor-length blinds, also in beige, sheathed a length of sliding glass doors. These opened onto the backyard. You could just see the pool, curving like an amoeba, and the tall Southampton hedge that flanked it, the one natural touch, the one touch of authenticity.

"Oh, my gosh—come, come and look at this!" came Kate's voice from below me. "I've found it!"

I went through a large, new kitchen, glittering with appliances, and down into a basement room.

Kate was standing in the middle of the room pointing, with a strange expression on her face. "It" was a large sunken Jacuzzi, landscaped by a mass of green plants and topiaries. "Look—watch." She flipped a switch on the wall and the overhead light changed from white to bright red. "What do you think it's for, George?" She flipped it to white again. "Pornography?"

"No." I laughed. "It's to keep warm after you get out."

"To keep . . . warm?" She'd hardly had a sip at brunch, but she was very nearly giddy. I was suddenly giddy too, in a way that had nothing to do with the alcohol. She turned on the spigots of the Jacuzzi to show me the overwhelming force of the water pressure. I laughed, nervously, and then she did, and we both stood there giggling. It was as if in that house we had been granted an unexpected reprieve, which we weren't sure we deserved.

Upstairs, Harry started to call for us from the driveway.

"Guys? Guys? Hey, guys?" He sounded like a kid who wants to call off the hide-and-seek game. "Guys? Guys? I got mixers! Kate? George? Gonna make drinks in the blender! Guys?"

I caught her eye.

"Be quiet," she mouthed, pointing toward a closet in the corner of the room. We crept over and I opened the door. It was a linen closet, stuffed with clean towels. Kate snatched them from the shelves two at a time, dumping them behind the Jacuzzi, mashing the top ones down so they wouldn't show. I gave her a leg up and she wedged herself, doubled over, into the middle shelf. "Ow! Dammit!" She had scraped herself on the way in. I crouched myself down onto the closet floor below her and grabbed the door shut.

We could hear Harry searching the upstairs with increasing desperation. "Guys? Hey, guys? You out at the pool, guys?"

"Christ!" Kate hissed. "My neck is in *pain*!"

"Do you want out?"

"Of course not! Do you want to ruin it?"

It was the Kate I had met ten years before—the old wicked Kate, skipping chapel in the boys' dorm. And just like then, my heart was pounding with the fear of being caught and the joy of the secret.

We gave up after half an hour, when we heard Harry dialing the Southampton police. I had never seen Kate so disdainful.

"But how was I supposed to know you were hiding down there? I mean, why would you go and do a thing like that?"

"Why *wouldn't* you?" Kate said coldly.

The ocean air drove the humidity away. Upstairs, Kate turned on the shower. I meant to get that swim and changed into my trunks but dithered instead, eyeing the blue water, circling the pool. I gave up, finally, and took up chaise-longue position and a beer. It was touching to see how solicitous Harry was of a guest's comfort. He toiled between the kitchen and pool, panting a little, getting out the grill, setting it up, lugging a bucket of ice poolside, poking beers into it. On the last trip he produced an opener and a pair of cushions. "Sit up a minute. There you go. Isn't that better? Huh? Isn't that way better? Make yourself at home, George—really, I mean it. Comfort is everything. You want another beer? I got lotsa beer in the fridge after this, and if we run out there's another fridge downstairs."

"Why don't you have one with me?" I suggested.

He passed a hand over his head distractedly. "Oh—yeah. Yeah, I'm going to. Thanks." I opened a bottle and passed it to him. He took a long drink, and the Lombardi grin flashed on as he surveyed his surroundings. "This is it, isn't it, George? I mean, this is *really* it: barbecue by the pool, beers in the great outdoors. It doesn't get much better than this, does it?"

"I can't imagine it does," I said.

"I come out here, I think to myself, Christ—this is really it!" And yet almost before he had gotten the words out, the grin had ebbed from his face. He took a cigarette out of his breast pocket and smoked it miserably.

The shirt, a muted mauve, was cut Hawaiian-style, with a long open collar, and went halfway down his shorts. Like many men who had learned to dress at the firm, he hadn't quite mastered the leisure-wear. The old trader's habits were catching up with him, and he had put on another five or ten pounds.

"You comfortable, George? You need anything?"

Embarrassed, as if he could read my thoughts, I took a swig of beer. There were details about his life that I had always wanted to know. I found myself asking him, point-blank, to fill me in.

"You serious?" I kept prodding him when he would have changed the subject, and so that evening, on the lawn of Harry's rental, I finally got the full story of his astronomical rise in finance. Harry didn't brag, but the false modesty was gone, perhaps because he was moving on now and could think of the Wall Street chapter as closed. He was the kind of person who is forever passing the present into the past at a desperate, sweaty-palmed rate, like nothing so much as a kid playing hot potato; nothing was real to him unless it was over, lost, cast in color-by-number sunset yellow and orange, and he was as comfortable in the nostalgia of the past as he was ill at ease in the present.

"Gonna tell it to you straight, George, 'cause I know you won't do anything with it. I know you just wanna know."

"Go," I said. "I'm listening."

I had been right about systems.

After quitting Dartmouth, he'd gone home to Long Island, lied about his age, and talked himself into a summer job at Broder. "Don't ask me how I did it, 'cause I'm not sure myself. I kept my head down, that's for sure—did my work, made sure I didn't make enemies. So after a couple of months I kinda got a reputation, you know? I was, like, the psycho computer guy. Everybody on the floor knew you went to Lombardi when things fucked up. Lombardi would deliver. Lombardi would put in the extra time."

When he fixed a systemwide bug that had stumped his bosses, he caught the eye of one of the partners, Donald McCance, and McCance took him under his wing. He was trading by Christmas. He hadn't exactly lied about college, just fudged the details—he certainly didn't look too young to have graduated—and by the time the truth about his degree surfaced, first in murmurs around the trading floor, then in self-congratulatory tones upstairs, he had already made the firm so much money that his lack of a college education became the stuff of insider legend. McCance had known from the beginning; he had guessed the truth and called Harry on it, and with a trader's instinct for a position he should get out of, Harry had been straight with the guy. Most of the old guys took it as a good joke, but it just about floored the Ivy Leaguers. Lombardi had done it the old-school way, back office to front, no B.A. That took *balls*.

As for the new company, I still couldn't make heads or tails of it. I wasn't sure I wanted to. I had always been a bit of a technophobe, and proud of it. At least I made the most of that attitude, for it was the last year one could wholly get away with it.

"You don't hafta understand it, but understand this: it's gonna be huge."

"What is?"

"The computer network—the interconnected networks. The 'World Wide Web.' And I'm going to be providing a, a, like an entrance to it. Or like, like a navigation tool. A, ah, whatchama call it—on a boat. You know. . . . A six ton—"

"You mean a sextant?"

"Yeah! Just like that, right? You'll use it to get around. Navigate your way through choppy seas to a new world." He took a swig of beer. "I got guys throwing money at me. 'Nother frienda mine came in for fifty yesterday."

"Is that the minimum?" I inquired.

"Naw, I'd take half that, a quarter that. Hell, I'd take anything from you, George. You wanna give me ten, twenty thousand, I'll put it in water and grow it like a Chia Pet."

"By when?"

"Mmm . . . better be by Christmas. You know," he added, juggling the barbecue fork, the cigarette, and the beer, and still managing to get his hand to his mouth to bite off a hangnail, "I'm pretty sure Chat Wethers is going to come in for fifty thousand."

"You spoke to Chat?" I said, surprised. "Recently?"

"Yeah, we took Chat out to dinner the other week. He's a great guy, that Chat—a real original."

"So the three of you . . . ? Wasn't it—a bit—"

"Naw," Harry said casually. "Chat's not gonna get upset over some girl."

"Some—girl?" I repeated blankly.

"Yeah, you know"—he flashed a guilty grin—"pals before gals."

Even the expression was Chat's. Harry eyed me over the top of his beer. "I helped him outta something once, you know."

"You," I said, trying to get it straight. "Helped Chat." I seemed to be out of my league. I couldn't seem to keep up.

"Yeah . . . in China."

"Oh."

"He's a funny guy, that Chat. He just about attacks this girl—"

"What? You mean a Chinese girl?" I said.

"Naw, it was nothing like that. She was like us, over there with the firm. You know, I take it back. What do I know, right?" He snapped the grin on; it had never looked more grotesque. "It was just, this girl . . . she was so, so, so drunk. You ever have that, George, when they're just so drunk it'd be, it'd be . . . well, you just can't figure out how it would be . . . enjoyable?"

He looked so guilty by this point I could barely look him in the eye. But with Harry you never knew what that look meant. Some men achieve guilt; many more have it thrust upon them by their fathers. But Harry had been born guilty.

"How exactly," I asked with distaste, "did you 'help him out'?"

"Aw, it was no big deal. I just took the girl out to dinner and cooled her off a little . . ." He left a rather pointed ellipsis. "It was a really nice dinner, I'm telling you. I musta spent three hundred bucks, with the wine."

"Did you."

"Oh, yeah. . . . Shit, what'm'I'unna do! This thing finally gets going and Kate's still upstairs!"

"Why don't you drink another beer."

Harry contemplated this. "Okay. Okay, good idea. That's what I'll do. I'll drink a beer."

We were on our third or fourth when the screen door banged and Kate flip-flopped out into the evening, combing her wet hair into straight lines. She was wearing a man's shirt, a long white oxford shirt, and she had her bathing suit on underneath.

Despite the setting, I got to my feet. "Will you go swimming with me?"

"No," Kate said. "I just took a shower." Harry glanced furtively at her and away, as if she were someone else's girlfriend.

"You can take another one."

"No, I don't think I'll swim at all this weekend. I'll tell you what I'd like to do—I'd like to go get in the hot tub."

Harry beamed. "You mean it? Great! Lemme go down and get it all going and everything and you guys can come down."

"What about the grill?"

"Aw, hell, it doesn't matter, George. We can eat anytime. Anytime we want. We got no hurry, do we? We got all night! There's no need to rush things, is there?" But he himself was in a rush and panted off to the screen door.

I retook my chair feebly. I felt the old sense of vertigo returning. I couldn't get my head around any of it: Harry's having come to Chat's rescue, Chat and Harry and Kate's having had a pleasant outing together in New York. It was as if the world had suddenly turned professional, and all engagements were to be of a business nature, and those who struggled along as I did, with a remedial—or perhaps a romantic—conceptualization of how things worked, would soon be obsolete.

Kate sat down at the foot of my chair facing the pool and dangled her feet in the water. I kept focused on her hair. It reassured me, somehow, that the top of her head was ash-blond to the scalp.

"Sip of your beer?"

I passed it over her head. Kate took a sip and held it up, and we shared the rest of it as the last of the sun set through Harry's hedge. You could smell the next-door neighbors' barbecue through the hedge, and hear them jumping in and out of their pool and crying out. A child screamed, "Cannonball!" and there was an emphatic splash.

"Did you have a pool growing up, George?"

"No," I said.

"No? I thought—in the country—you might have had a pool."

"No."

"Oh, well, it doesn't matter."

"We lived at the school," I reminded her.

"You lived—"

"At the Rectory."

"Oh, that's right," Kate said. But her boredom with the subject made it seem as if she hadn't heard.

She set her legs on the surface of the water and let them break the surface and float down to the side of the pool.

"Don't you want to go in?" I said.

"No. Not this weekend."

The way the ground floor was laid out, you could sit in the hot tub and watch television on the big-screen TV at the same time. We made a cozy après-ski party—in the middle of June. Kate seemed to have become a cold-blooded animal that turns the temperature of the environment. "Aren't you hot?" I asked, perching on the side for one of my breaks.

"No, I could sit here all night." Her face wasn't flushed, but her eyes were so bright I worried she would faint.

Like me, Harry could stay in only so long. He trundled up and down the stairs, working the blender and bringing down daiquiris and plates of food from the grill which nobody ate. Every time he came down, he made a big deal of settling in, only to jump up five seconds later with something he had to "take care of." The room began to smell of barbecued meat. After a few of Harry's trips the tile floor was covered in water and used towels, and here and there were pink splotches of spilled daiquiri.

When Harry came down a final time, I announced I was going to bed.

"Oh, do you have to get up early for chapel?" Kate inquired. I had risen from the tub to dry off.

"That's right," I said. "Acolyte duty tomorrow."

"Torch or cross?"

"Torch."

"Harry is a Catholic," Kate remarked. "Did you know that, George?"

I didn't say anything.

Our host took a breath and slid his head down the edge of the tub till it was fully submerged. He came up, loudly, for air. "Yup," Harry said for me.

"I'll bet you're a very poor Catholic," Kate teased him. "Can you say a Hail Mary?"

"Hail Mary, full of Grace," he recited. "The Lord is with thee. Blessed art thou amongst women—"

"All right, all right." Kate thought for a minute. "Can you do the seven deadly sins?"

"Pride, envy, anger, lust, avarice, gluttony, and sloth."

"Say them again!"

Halfway through the list, Kate began to laugh, a rather derisive laugh. "That's the funniest thing I've ever heard!" she cried. "The seven deadly sins in a hot tub!"

I'm not quite sure how he did it, but Harry managed to clamp a hand over her mouth and pick her up and get the two of them out of the tub. "Past your bedtime, too," he grunted.

"No!" Kate protested, and wrenched his hand away. "I don't want to go to bed! Don't make me!"

"Come on, Kate—don't you wanna go to bed?"

"No!"

"Aren't you tired?"

"No!"

"Well, whadda you wanna do?"

"I don't know . . ." Her eyes sought mine.

"Let's dance," I said. "Fox-trot."

I took her, dripping, in my arms. She was just the way she had been on my lap in the car—her balance was light but firm—and she let me lead.

"Slow, quick-quick, slow," chanted Kate. "Slow, quick-quick, slow—but you're good! Did I know this about you?"

"You did, but you forgot," I said.

Harry couldn't stand it and cut in. "Here, let me! I'll show you some stuff." He had flipped the stereo on and he began to dance her around clumsily, because he wasn't tall, and roughly, and to sing the lyrics of a popular song. There was one like him at every high school gym or college party, in every club, on every dance floor: the guy who thinks he can dance. Not that Harry's rhythm was bad—it was probably better than mine—he just didn't know any steps. It took him all of two minutes to get Kate doing the Pretzel.

"Don't spin me!" cried Kate. "Don't—you'll drop me!" Clutching for her as she fell, Harry knocked one of the daiquiri glasses off the side of the tub and it shattered.

"Oh my God, Kate—I didn't meana—"

From the floor Kate began to laugh the high bright laugh again, and when Harry offered her a hand, she tried to yank him down with her.

"Watcha glass!" Harry yelled, struggling to keep his footing. A line of blood streaked the tile. Kate reached out her hands to him, and he scooped her up in his arms like a bride or a doll.

"God, you're something, Kate," he said huskily.

In my elevated consciousness I remember I saw her, kicking in Harry's arms, as the embodiment of some primal girlhood. I tried to imagine the two of them in bed, and my imagination failed me.

At the door Harry stopped. He stretched his face down to hers. It was too quiet, I thought; I realized he was kissing her. Then Kate spoke up—

"Now, George! You go to bed, too!"

—and I was alone in the room.

In the middle of the night I found myself standing at the deep end of the pool, steeling myself against the cold. I dived in. But the shock never came, and I realized, as I paddled to the shallow end and floated languidly to the top, that the pool was heated, too.

CHAPTER 11

The next morning I woke in the fine, condescending mood that comes of believing one is the first awake in a house. I threw on a shirt and a pair of shorts and stole downstairs, not wanting, in my condescension, to wake anyone. I did a few stretches and was contemplating a grand pancake-making gesture when I heard a car in the driveway—*the* car, rather—and who should come through the front door but my host, in a rumpled suit and tie, carrying a box of doughnuts, with the newspapers tucked under his arm like mounted guns.

"You're up early."

"No, you are," I replied.

"Hadda go to Mass. Now I'm going back to bed." Harry surveyed my attire. "What're you up to?"

"I don't know. I don't have a plan," I admitted.

"Here." He pressed the keys into my hand. "You wanna drive somewhere, take the car." He left the *Times*, tucked the Long Island paper under his arm, and trudged upstairs.

I went out to the driveway. I'd been itching to get my hands on the wheel. But the more I thought of it, the more the idea was too stupid, driving around in a car like that with no place to go. And the possibility of running into Robbins or someone else I knew was intolerable. It seemed to me there were two kinds of men in the world: men like Harry, who were ridiculous enough to buy a car like that and drive it; and men like me, who would become ridiculous driving it. I went for a run instead—just like that, in my flat old tennis shoes. I was so out of shape I turned back after a quarter of an hour. When I staggered in, Kate was sitting in the passenger seat of the car with the door open and her feet up through the open window.

"Where've you been?" she said crossly. Stretched out like that, her legs looked much longer than they were.

"Down the road and back. Barely."

"I've spoken to Harry. We're going as soon as you're ready."

"Fine," I said. It was all the same to me whether the weekend had turned on us now or would turn on us later, for it would turn on us. That much I had understood from the outset.

We packed the car in ominous silence. Harry couldn't do anything right. He beat on his suitcase with a frenzied determination to make it fit. "It'll go! It'll go! It went in before!"

The car itself seemed to have changed sides: it was no longer a favorite toy but an eyesore of ostentation. It was annoying to have Kate sit on my lap, whether she liked it or not. There is nothing more depressing than having to hold a carefree pose when one is full of cares.

Breakfast in Sag Harbor cheered us a little, and we might still have gotten away in the hopeful hours before noon except that in dropping us off, Harry had parked in a lot behind the main street, and to get the car we had to walk by the harbor front. The marina was crowded, it being June; the masts stretched on like a forest of emaciated trees.

"Oh!" cried Kate. "Let's go and look at the boats!"

"Sure, sure," Harry agreed. "Whatever you want, Kate. We got plenty-a time." But he looked at his watch as if to convince himself of the fact.

We walked down the pier along the water, stopping here and there to admire the boats. It was a perfect day for looking at boats. The stalled front had passed, there was an eight- or ten-knot breeze out of the southwest, and in Shelter Island Sound a fleet of one-designs were racing; you could see the uniform set of white triangles tacking and dipping in the distance. "There must be a regatta on," remarked Kate. Her voice had a bright, hard tone, as if it alone could persuade the day to behave itself, as if she were saying, "Now isn't this pleasant?" the way you speak to a child, to force him into good behavior after a temper tantrum. "What do you think they're sailing, George?"

I guessed the name of a racing sloop. "Do they sail them out here?"

Kate shook her head. "You're wrong, George," she said lightly. "It's a dinghy regatta."

"Dinghies?" I protested. "They wouldn't look that big from here!"

"Still," insisted Kate, "I say it's a dinghy regatta. The hotshot skipper's a fourteen-year-old from the high school out here."

"The hotshot skipper's a fat old man from Greenwich," I countered happily.

We ambled on. We passed a pretty sloop with teak decks and a black mast. A gray-haired group having a picnic on their old wooden yawl raised their glasses to us. "That'll be us someday," remarked Kate. A little farther along there was a tender the size of a small house.

"Talk about big—get aloada that!"

Harry had been trailing a little ways behind us, and it seemed to startle Kate when he spoke up then. She turned around with a vague look of annoyance, as if she'd been jostled in a crowd.

He pointed toward an enormous cruising boat—the companion, evidently, which the power yacht tended. I made this assumption when I saw a boy come down from the top deck of the tender and hop across to the other boat. There was no denying the sailboat was huge—120, 130 feet, and fat through the middle like a giant's bath-tub. Her hull was painted bright aqua, in contrast with which a lurid hot pink script proclaimed her name: *Oral Fixation.* At one time peo-ple had named their boats *Reliant* or *Courageous* or *Intrepid.* But nowadays people would name a boat any stupid name. They would name it after a rock band or a bad movie; they would name it after a psychological disorder. People would build ignoble boats and give them stupid names.

"Whaddaya think?"

"It's not my kind of thing," I said. She was tricked out with every kind of gimmick: Jet Skis, mountain bikes, a sea kayak, a rubber raft.

"I don't know," Kate said. "It might be fun."

I didn't answer, as she was only enjoying being contradictory.

"How much you think the owner's worth?" Harry asked.

"A hell of a lot," said Kate. The little tour had improved her spir-its immeasurably, and like most people with money, Kate loved to talk about how much money people had.

"Why don't you ask him?" I said.

"Who?"

"The boy."

"You think he works on the boat?" she said.

"Works?" I said. "I bet it's the guy's son."

"I bet you a dollar he works on the boat."

"Dollar it is." We shook hands on the bet.

"He's gone below." Indeed the boy had vanished from view.

As we waited, I chided Kate for not taking a more democratic view of the world. "But my view *is* the more democratic," she protested.

"You think the boy's a little lackey," I said.

"I think he's a kid with a great job," she said. "You always ro-manticize things, George—unnecessarily."

The stereo came on playing Caribbean music, and a few minutes later the boy reappeared through a hatch in front of the mast. He was barefoot now, and began to spray off the top deck.

We stood watching him; it is always pleasant to watch someone take care of a boat.

When he came around to our side of the bow, the sun was to our right and the boy's profile was toward us, outlined by a long lock of hair. "So, ask him," I prodded Kate.

"Why—"

"Go on." She didn't answer. I was about to call out myself when the spray of water stopped, because the boy had let it stop, and as the last few drops evaporated into the air, Kate clutched my arm and my own heart began to pound wildly. The boy bore a dead-on resemblance to Nick Beale.

"It's not him," Kate murmured faintly, steadying herself on my arm. "My God, I thought it was Nick."

It was Nicko ten years earlier. The kid couldn't have been more than fifteen, but he had Nick's brown coloring; he had Nick's thin, lithe body. He had Nick's hair in his eyes, and as he looked at us with no more than mild curiosity, he had the same habit: he put his hand under his shirt and absently stroked his stomach, squinting into the sun. It was not only Nick's gesture but the universal gesture of thin pothead boys with hair in their eyes who worked on boats.

"Do you work on this boat?" Kate demanded, going up to him.

The boy looked her over in a squinting manner. "I do, indeed." You could hear the derision even in the one phrase; you could see he thought we were tourists—non-sailors—going to waste his time with foolish questions.

"You do? Where's it out of?" She walked around to the stern, very businesslike. "Says Anguilla. Is that true?"

The kid shrugged. "Guy's from L.A."

I was watching him to see if he would do something else like Nick. I was sure he would if we waited long enough; I think Kate was half waiting for him to recognize her. When we didn't go away, the kid turned the hose back on, and when we still didn't go away, he stopped the water again and said dubiously, "You wanna . . . check her out or something?"

"Oh, no," said Kate. She had an odd, abstracted look in her

eyes that was not like Kate at all. "No, no. We just . . . we stopped because . . ." She swallowed and tossed off the last remark: "Well, you reminded us of someone we know."

"Yeah?" the kid said, bored. "I get that a lot."

"No, but you really look like someone we know," insisted Kate. She held up a hand to block the sun. "In fact you could be him— couldn't he, George?"

"Ten years ago," I said.

"Oh, no," Kate objected. "Not that long."

"What happened," the boy asked skeptically, "the guy die or something?"

Kate gave an artificial laugh, walking down the dock as the kid walked aft on the boat. "Hardly. The guy leads a very nice life not doing much of anything, running around the Caribbean all winter. He doesn't do much more than sail."

"Oh, yeah?"

"Oh, yes."

This drew a long understanding nod. He wasn't, after all, as good-looking as Nick. The nod made him look dull-witted, whereas Nick had an omniscient expression. "I just came from there," he volunteered after a moment.

"From where?"

"B.V.I.'s. Brought her up from Lauderdale to Hatteras and from Hatteras last week."

"You and who else?" Kate said, calling his bluff.

"Just a couple other guys!" the kid said hotly. He had gone from writing her off to trying to win favor in about two minutes.

There was a silence then, not unpleasant, and I thought we would take our leave. Harry had wandered on ahead, as if to assert his independence. But Kate wasn't quite ready to leave. She coaxed another invitation from the boy—it was easily won—and this time she said, "Yes, I wouldn't mind having a look, after all." A certain change in her voice made me wonder what she had in mind.

The gunwales were quite high, and the boy took Kate under her arms, leaning over the lifelines to hoist her up. It was wonderful to see someone take that liberty with her.

I went over to the side of the boat and reached up and belatedly shook the kid's hand. Immediately I felt the pointlessness of the gesture: the boy had a weak, noncommittal handshake, as if he didn't quite believe in the custom.

"You coming on, too?"

"All right."

To help me aboard, he gave me his hand for real. He was very strong, despite being so lean and slouchy, stronger than you would have thought. He had no idea what to make of us, that was clear. Kate was looking at him with an almost parental expression, pleased and patient. "Are you here for the regatta?" the kid inquired finally, directing the question to me.

"No, no," Kate explained, "we're here . . ." But her voice drifted off absently; she couldn't seem to remember why we were there.

"Wow—late night, huh?" said the kid. "I'm all messed up, too, 'cause of the delivery."

"I'll bet."

"Starving, too—it's Cook's day off."

With a diffident eye on Kate, Harry came shuffling over.

"Guys?"

The whole exchange was beginning to feel rather surreal to me: the boy looked so much like Nick, and he was living Nick's life. And yet it is never as rewarding as it should be, in life, to meet a representative of one of the types you know. You want to sit them down and have them confirm your suspicions—"And don't you do this? And don't you do that?"—but unless you are a sleuth in a detective novel with a murder to solve, the implications remain inconclusive. There is nothing at all to be done with the information. All you know is yes, they are just like someone you know.

From the dock Harry set about coughing and clearing his throat. That way he had around Kate, of hanging back—presuming not even so much as an introduction to a stranger—seemed pathetic to me. I wanted to tell him to speak up for himself for God's sake—have it out with her.

"This is a friend of ours," I said.

Turning toward the pier, Kate seemed to consider the premise of my statement. "Why, yes," she corroborated, "he is."

There was an awkward moment when Harry boarded and got tripped up on the lifelines and fell to his knees. His eyes watered, as when he'd drunk the Bloody Mary in the diner. "Oh, gee, I'm sorry—" The kid was beside himself, but Harry wouldn't take the apology. "I'm fine! I'm fine!" He was clearly in pain. The kid suggested a shot of rum and darted below to get the bottle.

"You know I'm fine," Harry claimed, limping forward and aft with a proprietary frown, as if to establish himself as a Man Who Knew Boats.

"Take the shot of rum," ordered Kate, ever so pleasantly.

We went and sat in the cockpit and passed the bottle around. "Isn't this funny?" Kate said. It seemed to please her enormously that we had been able to make inroads with the boy. She was strangely, overly friendly. They began to talk about the delivery, and Kate plied him with questions. Was it cold? Was it lonely on the watches? Did it blow hard? A gale? A real gale? I didn't like to see her like that. I didn't like to see any woman with an agenda, but particularly not Kate. I didn't like to see her stooping to draw a man out.

The kid's jaded manner fell away (but we, knowing Nicko, had known that it would) and he carped happily about the owner of the boat, who didn't know the first thing about sailing. "Not the first thing. We're taking her out of the harbor for the first time, going out the channel, and he says, 'What do I do with that red thing?' and I say, 'You leave the nun to port,' and I go below and come up two minutes later and he's leaving it about two inches to starboard!" Kate gave the pleased, patient smile, but Harry guffawed loudly. Meanwhile his eyes looked up the rails desperately to see—would there be some indication? Did they label port and starboard? Wasn't port the one, on the cruise that time—or was that starboard? I wanted to reassure him that there would be no test.

"You see the name?" the boy asked.

We nodded.

"You hear about these dentists? These celebrity dentists?"

"Um—" I said.

"*What* did you say—celebrity *dentists?*" exclaimed Kate. "George, did you hear that?"

"My gosh," I said.

"Must be pretty successful, though," said Harry, asserting himself into the conversation at last. "I mean a boat like this must cost, well, at least—"

"Five," said the kid coldly, picking up immediately, as teenagers do, on whom he could be rude to without repercussion. "Five and six zereos." He stretched the tail of his T-shirt out to wipe off a winch. "I have to get her in shape, 'cause the kids are coming," he allowed.

"You mean the dentist's kids?" asked Kate.

"Yup," he said, "and they don't even like sailing. They don't even like sailing! Dentist has to force them to come out at all, and then they just take the Jet Ski out, and go out for dinner."

"How do you put up with them?" cried Kate. "It must be awful!"

"Oh . . . they're not *that* bad." The kid relented, with sudden largesse. "Actually, they're not really kids. They're about . . . our age."

"Our age!"

"Well . . ."

"How old do you think we are?" I asked.

"I duh-know," said the boy with a scowl.

"No, how old?" Kate insisted.

"Maybe twenty," said the boy, after a long hesitation. He had to keep Kate within his range, or the whole conversation—and the day and his job on the boat and probably his life—were pointless. I understood this need; I had played the same game at Chatham, when she was sixteen and I was fourteen. But Harry cried, "Twenty?" and smacked his thigh. He seemed to be made up of a series of broad theatrical gestures—a thigh-smacking, throat-clearing, fist-clenching player. "Ha, ha, ha, ha, ha."

"Not you!" cried the kid, indignant. "You're older! But you other two?" He turned to Kate on a note of appeal.

"You're right!" Kate spoke up in his defense. "We *are* about twenty. And you're also right about him." She pointed at Harry as if he were her wicked stepfather. "*He's* older. Much older!"

Even Harry didn't know what to say to that, but he seemed determined not to take offense, to prove that anything—anything— was all right by him, that he was just a roll-off-your-shoulders kind of guy. "Say, you got a bathroom on this thing?"

The kid took him below to the head and returned, coiling a length of line into a long, lazy circle.

"So who'd I remind you of?"

"You remind us of a kid who was the best sailor—" Kate began, her voice softening to paint the picture.

"Yeah?" the kid broke in impertinently. "Was he all-American?"

"No."

"No? Well, then he can't have been that great," concluded the kid. "Anybody who's good in college—"

"He didn't go to college."

"Oh. Okay." He took this in. "Why not?"

"He couldn't afford it," I said.

"Now, George, you know that's not true. He didn't apply himself."

"I don't 'apply' myself either," said the kid.

"I know," Kate said simply.

"What's the guy's name?"

"Nick," she threw out, after a fraction of a pause.

Then it was funny, because the kid said, nonchalant as hell, "Oh, I know Nick."

"Of course you don't know Nick." Kate laughed. "You have no idea who I'm talking about."

"Still—I know him."

"No, you don't," Kate said. "That's stupid."

The kid shrugged. "Works on a boat called *Troubador*. Hangs out down the Caribbean."

It was as if he had now called her bluff of flirtation—and was demanding that she reckon with him. Kate turned cozily, patronizingly, to me. "George, wouldn't it be too funny if—"

"Look, I know who you're talking about. Tall kid . . ."

"Not that tall!"

"No, not that tall," the boy said quickly. "I mean, pretty tall. He's built . . . like me. Brown hair."

It was impossible to read the emotion on Kate's face. "I don't believe you," she said evenly. "You don't know Nick."

"Yes, I do. I *do.*"

"How could you?"

"I just do!" The kid was utterly frustrated, practically to the point of hysterics. "I'm telling you, I *know* the guy."

"What's his last name?" Kate inquired.

An indifferent shrug. "Got me."

"Then how do you know him?"

We waited, acutely tuned to the boy's answer.

"Just 'cause . . . everybody knows Nick," he said helplessly.

"That's a stupid thing to say," Kate said. And yet oddly enough it was the kind of thing someone would say about Nick, and I know that's when I, at least, made up my mind that the kid probably did know Nick Beale. His description sounded like Nick, for one thing. For another, every experience seems to prove it: the world isn't just small, it's smaller than you would ever think.

"You haven't told me one thing to make me believe you've ever laid eyes on him," Kate said.

She had him stumped for a moment, and he repeated, "Thin guy, really good sailor. . . . Wait, I know! Ha, ha! I got you!"

"What?" Kate said carelessly. She had lost interest in the game.

"I know his wife! Stacy! See, I do know him! I know Nick's wife!" The kid threw his head back and reveled, laughing, in his victory.

"His wife," I said.

"It's not the same Nick."

There was a creak down the line of boats as they adjusted themselves, unhurriedly, to a three- or four-degree shift in the wind.

"Stacy! She's an Aussie. I met her in a bar last Race Week. She got

bumped off her charter, so I was gonna get her a job on *Fixation*—
she's a cook. Blond hair. Dyed blond hair." The boy appealed to me:
"I'm right, aren't I? I know I'm right!"

"When did they get married?" I asked.

"Last winter," he answered triumphantly. "She didn't take me up
on *Fixation*, 'cause they'd just gotten married."

"Where did they meet?" I said.

"Same as everyone—in a bar down there, right? And wait, I
know." The kid finished coiling the line and looped the end that was
in his hand through the coil. Then he slung the coil over his shoulder
and patted it against his side, companionably, to neaten it out. "This
Nick's from Maine," the kid said.

Across the Sound a new race was starting. The mass of white quiv-
ered together, fluttering along the line in an agony of anticipation for
the gun. Then they were off. It was a clean start. We heard the echo
of the shot.

"Where are you from?" I inquired.

"Marion," the kid said proudly. "Massachusetts. It blows all summer."

"A nice southwesterly."

He met my eyes quickly. I think he was surprised I knew anything.
"You got it. I mean, out here it's cool—you can see they're getting
races off—"

"Not like Sippican Harbor, though."

This got a laugh, again, of surprised recognition. "We used to sail
on Buzzards Bay," I volunteered.

"Whereabouts?"

I told him. "We went to Chatham."

"Yeah? You still sail dinghies?"

"No," I said. "Not anymore. We live in Manhattan."

"So? You could still get out on weekends."

"I guess."

"You guess? Come *on*, man, *frostbite* or something. At least keep
your hand in."

I shrugged.

"I mean, don't take this the wrong way," the kid told me, "but that's pretty lame of you."

He had opened a hatch to lay the line inside and when he came up he seemed to really notice Kate, finally, and she smiled at him across the cockpit in an anguished sort of way. "Hey, you!" the kid said. He went and sat down beside her and put his arm around her and squeezed her tight. "Hey, you!" he said again.

Harry came trundling up the companionway and announced: "I'd like to get a boat like this. How much did you say it would cost?"

No one said anything.

"Well, whatever it costs, if my company makes it, and it will, I'll buy a boat like this," declared Harry. "You guys should see it down there! It's got real bedrooms! And a fucking art collection! On a boat! The bathroom's made of marble! What do you say to that, Kate? Would you want me to buy a boat like this?"

Kate stared at him as if he were the most extraordinary person on earth.

"What kind of a company are you starting?" asked the kid, jumping up again. He remained in constant, deliberate motion. He didn't stand, he balanced; he didn't sit, he perched. They were all light on their feet, boys like Nick, from hopping around the bow in thirty knots of breeze.

"It's a software company. Has to do with navigation, actually."

"What do you mean?" said the kid. "Satellite navigation?"

"Naw, I'm talking about navigating computer networks."

"That's okay."

"Yeah?"

"It could still be cool," the kid assured him. "You looking for investors?"

"Oh, yeah. Say, maybe this dentist of yours . . ." Harry began speculatively.

"I can do better than that!" asserted the kid. He reached around into his back pocket and drew out a hundred-dollar bill and handed it to Harry. "Just got paid. Here—take it." The boy glanced at Kate; her big spender, and she hadn't even noticed.

Harry studied the bill for a moment. "Oh, no, you see . . ." he started to say. But then an embarrassed look crossed his face and he stopped himself. "Thanks," he said gruffly. "Thanks a lot. I appreciate it."

"You gotta get in touch with me if we make it big, okay?"

"Sure thing," said Harry. He tucked the bill carefully into his wallet. "Sure thing . . . care of *Oral Fixation*, right? Or maybe I oughta get your parents' address, case you—move on."

The kid wrote it out for him. "Now don't lose that, okay? And if you do buy a boat, and you, like, need someone to sail it for you—"

"I'll remember," said Harry, and, with a glance at the slip of paper, he added, "Jason."

"Jason?" Kate repeated, a puzzled expression on her face.

" 'At's right!" the kid said. "That's my name! So, who wants breakfast? How about you?" He addressed Kate. "You look like you could use something to eat."

"Oh, no," Kate said faintly. "I don't think I could eat breakfast right now."

"We've had breakfast," I said.

"Yeah? What about lunch? What time is it? I'm all messed up, 'cause of this delivery."

"We'd better get going," I said.

"Really?" said Harry. "But we were just—"

"It's time to leave," I interrupted.

The kid followed us back to town. I remember he took another hundred-dollar bill out of his pocket and held it in his hand and carried it that way, as if he were about to lay it down on odds or evens.

"Summer to summer, huh?" said Harry, revving up the car, his eyes following the lank silhouette up the road. "Must be a nice life."

"Yeah."

"Screwing around on boats. Probably dropped out of school. Those guys have it made."

"Excuse me," said Kate. "But you're not allowed to talk."

"What the hell?"

"No, please," Kate said mildly. "I mean it. Please don't talk. Only George is allowed to talk."

"What in goddamn hell do you mean?" Harry threw the car into a violent reverse. He stared at her, waiting for an answer, his hand on the gear shift.

Kate flipped her sunglasses down and stared ahead, motionless.

"Why am I not allowed to talk?"

"Because you don't know what you're talking *about*. Now, please don't say anything else."

"Are you all right, Kate."

"All right?" Harry bellowed. "Why wouldn't she be all right? What the hell's going on?"

"Shh . . . don't bother me. I'm sleeping." And she curled her slender arms around my neck and pretended to go to sleep.

Somewhere along the way Harry had lost his sunglasses. Eyes naked, he drove into the sun.

His mind must have been working, beating out a connection: he had never seen her this way. He didn't know enough to take that alone as some small measure of reassurance and leave it be.

"What about this Nick?" he asked. Groping, blind, he had hit on it. "This Nick that always gets mentioned. Did you know him, George?"

I nodded, acutely aware of Kate, pretend-asleep in my arms. I could feel her breath, the impression of her nose and mouth, at the base of my neck—could feel, with every minute shift I made, a corresponding shift down her body.

"So what's the big deal?"

"Well, they grew up together," I said slowly. It seemed to me I was speaking to her as much as to him. "Kate's grandmother has a house in Maine. In Cold Harbor."

"Where Chat goes—I know," Harry said impatiently.

"Right. And Nicko lived across the bay—the town's called Wamatuck."

Harry frowned, trying to understand how this fit in. I ought to have told him the endeavor was impossible. Or I ought to have told him a story—the same story Chat had told me to pass the time on a road trip to the city three years before. If the circumstances had been different, perhaps I would have—perhaps I would have given him the whole thing, all the information he could have possibly wanted, and then some. I might have added anecdotes here and there, that would have come to mean something to him. There was the time Nick taught me how to use a sextant, for instance, one dark winter afternoon when we were fooling around out at the Chatham boathouse. It's a simple thing, really. If it's night you get a moon sight or a couple of star sights and with those and the horizon you can pinpoint your boat on earth. Of course, you have to know what hemisphere you're in. What hemisphere, he said—as an afterthought, something that he might have left out, or that I might have failed to hear. I might never have had to learn that coming to the end of one half of the world in a boat, for him, simply meant crossing over to the other. The finite urgency of school, of youth, that I counted on didn't exist for him.

But Kate was wonderfully fair on my lap—

"And?" Harry demanded.

"That's just it," I said. "They grew up together." And I let the rest of it go.

There were two stories, actually—two stories Harry never heard. One of them was a story Chat told me on our drive down to New York, the summer after sophomore year. But the first was the story of the drive itself; we didn't go directly but stopped for a visit near New Haven. It wasn't till months later that the possibility occurred to me that Chat had undertaken the visit not by chance, as it seemed that day, but for the express purpose of making his subsequent narrative resonate. It's not something I have asked him about, however. It wouldn't have done any good then, nor would it now. I can't unlearn what I learned that day. Part of me thinks it's better, anyway, for a person like me to have his eyes opened periodically.

Dead August.

Chat and I had been at school all summer under the Dartmouth Plan, and would spend what would have been the fall of our junior year away. Chat was going to Mexico to try and pass the language requirement. I was going to New York to work at a bank, Fordyce, Farley, for the experience—or rather the money. But before Chat left, the two of us were going down to the city to set up camp at his parents'— they were still up in Maine—and hell around for a couple of weeks. We were going to see Kate there. She had graduated from Yale in June and was herself coming home from Cold Harbor just this week to pack before leaving for Europe. It was four years since I'd seen her. All the talk of a weekend road trip to New Haven had never amounted to anything. We couldn't seem to overcome inertia, Chat and I; each of us wanted the other to put his foot down and say, Let's go this weekend. "Anytime you want, Lenhart—just say the word." But I wasn't going to be the one to say it really mattered, and Chat would finally dismiss the idea: "Well, I'll see her in Maine." We talked of her less and less and eventually the subject died, like a crush that dithers too long. I had no claim on her attention, and I disliked the idea of a pilgrimage.

We got the Diesel packed the night before we left and went out till the wee hours with some Holyoke girls who were up in Hanover for the summer. Chat was so hungover in the morning I had to drive. He coughed awake in Hartford; croaked, "This New Haven?"

"Not yet."

"Get off in New Haven. I gotta get something for Kate. Take it down to New York for her."

And so I got to see how she'd been living the past couple of years.

She had an apartment off campus, in the old Taft Hotel—had it still, though she'd been gone three months: she hadn't had time to come back and move out yet.

After some discussion we got the key from the doorman and took the elevator up to her studio. Chat got the door to the apartment open with shaking hands. It was dark inside, with the shades pulled, and freezing cold. "What an idiot!" Chat stepped inside, indignant, and felt for a light switch. "She left the goddamn air-conditioning on all summer!"

The living room was straight out of a catalog. A white couch faced a bureau of laminated white wood. The carpeting was beige, the prints unobtrusive. In the far corner of the room a built-in closet stood in a state of explosion. It looked as if, rather than simply buying things to wear, Kate was collecting clothes for an exhibition. Fifty pairs of shoes jockeyed for position on the floor, a hundred sweaters bulged from the shelf, and in between an infinitude of sleeves begged to be called upon.

"Goddammit!" Chat began to hunt through the dresses for the one Kate had asked him for, and I wandered over to browse her bookshelves. There was nothing too highbrow, nothing too low—Cold War spy novels, bestseller-list nonfiction. She read the way a boy reads. I sat down on the love seat to wait. The white looked immaculate until you were sitting on it, and then you saw the cigarette burns and the liquor stains of a hundred parties. I thought with some envy of all the fun I must have missed in this apartment. Beside me was a little end table cluttered with photographs. She had all of the obligatory shots: the extended family ski trip on whatever mountain was "in" that year; the three brown-eyed little girls in smocking, Kate the eldest, sticking her chin out; the girl chums in bikinis by the pool, mouths open, chests flat. There was a great one of Nick and her sailing their 420 in a wild expanse of open water. Nick was gazing into the middle distance with his customary look, as if he were going to eat up the sea; Kate was all the way out on the trapeze, looking like she was having the ride of her life. She loved a howling, heavy-air day; she loved to go out and battle the elements and tell war stories afterward. Nick was different. He just sailed, and dealt with the weather as it came up. Even at Chatham he'd been like that: professional. I'd crewed for him once or twice myself, and he never said a thing beyond "Trim jib" and "Ready to tack?" whereas when I steered I would chat my head off to my crew, out of nerves and excitement.

Finally there was the picture I picked up off the table after a happy moment of recognition—I knew it well. It was of a large group of all ages in evening dress, the men in white tie, the women in gowns; they were imitating a chorus line, leaning forward on their right front feet, back feet in the air behind them, hands out with palms up—"Tah-dah!"—and in the middle of the chorus line (between ruddy Dad and stoically enduring Mother) a girl in a long white dress who had raised both of her hands in a kooky shrug as if to say, "Who, me?"

She had scabs all over her face. "Chicken pox," Chat had informed me. And with typical magnanimity: "She was the ugliest deb in New York."

Chat (second from left) had a copy of the picture on his bureau at school. Or had had it there till Harry stole it. We knew it was Harry because he was obsessed with it. There was no other way of putting it. I would drop by unannounced and find him studying the thing with an expression not of rapture but of fantastically intrigued puzzlement. Once I'd caught him trying it out for size on his own desk.

"I just don't get it!" Chat kept saying after it disappeared. "There are plenty of other pictures of Kate—way better pictures. Why in hell would he steal that one?"

The temper tantrums, the warnings not to scratch, the bedside battery of calamine lotion, vinegar, soap; the desperately whispered consultations between mother and aunt; Daddy's pep talk. . . . I set the picture down. Of course that was the picture he took. It is the oddest, the most melancholy form of envy I know: the desire to have had not another family's joys but its problems.

He got to keep the picture. The incident was too embarrassing to mention, even for Chat.

It happened around Christmas, and in January our Henry came back and announced that he wanted us to call him Harry. All his friends at home did, you see, and his father, and everyone, and the more he thought about it, the more he had realized, Hey, if you're stuck with a nickname, you're stuck with a nickname. I was almost impressed by it, in spite of myself—by the blatancy of the lie, of the admission that he was after something Henry couldn't get him. But he was adamant about it, and corrected us every time we said

"Henry," and despite Chat's initial ridicule, it worked so well that I see I have called him Harry the whole time here.

Chat whittled the dress competition down to three finalists, all of them blue, all of them short; the other adjective we didn't know, so we killed the A.C. and took the lot. Walking to the car, I wished I had not gone inside; it was foolish of me, I suppose, but I had expected antiques.

Back in June an arm of Chat's glasses had broken off—the other arm was bent nearly vertical—and he'd been wearing them like a two-paned monocle all summer long. "Now watch this bit of inspired engineering, Lenhart." Having reclaimed the driver's seat, he dug a pair of shitty sunglasses out of the glove compartment, put them on over the eyeglasses, and jury-rigged everything into place with a piece of duct tape. "I'm going to drive like hell," he announced, revving up the old car. "Unless . . ." He gave me a speculative look down his nose as far as he could, which wasn't far, lest the rig fall apart.

"Unless what? Let's get out of here," I said. It gave me the creeps to be in that deserted college town.

"Well, I just thought you might want to pay a visit to someone."

"Who someone?"

"An old friend someone."

I felt a wave of nausea, sitting there in the heat, last night's drinking hitting me at last.

"I thought we could go stop by, say hi to Nicko."

"Nick's around? You mean he's still here?"

" 'Course he's around."

"By himself? But Kate—"

Chat waited for me to finish.

"I don't know," I said, annoyed at being caught off guard. "I thought he'd be with Kate in Maine."

"I don't think so. I think I would have seen him or heard if he'd been up in Maine."

"But why wouldn't he be in Maine?"

"Search me."

I really hadn't thought about Nick's whereabouts at all. By that point, Nick was the kind of person who wasn't anywhere you could say, or from anywhere. He got jobs on boats and would be spotted in Montauk the same weekend somebody swore they saw him in Miami. Nick's mother lived in Maine, in Wamatuck, year-round, near Cold Harbor—that much I knew. But the fact had never had much resonance for me. He was like one of the big boats you saw in ports close to home, Westport or Rye; *Weatherly*, their sterns would say, *Nantucket, Massachusetts,* and in the next slip over you would see *Jamais, St. Barthélemy, FWI.* The ports of call were touchstones, that was all.

"So, what are you saying—he's not with Kate?" I said finally. Even considering the way he left Chatham—kicked out a year before graduation—I had never doubted they would be together as soon as they could. Chat was—well, I suppose the nice way of putting it would be to say that Chat was more practical-minded.

"Heading to Europe with Granny, you mean?" he said.

"No, of course not. But after—"

"In Manhattan, George?" Chat interrupted. "Kate's going to stay in the city, you know. Can you really picture Nicko with a New York desk job?"

I shrugged, more annoyed.

"So do you want to say hi or not?"

"Yes," I said. "I want to see Nick."

With a great roar Chat got the car in gear and pulled it out into traffic. "Sister lives in East Haven."

"His sister?" It struck me as preposterous that Nick had a sibling, had relations. To me he existed as a solitary player: have foul-weather gear, will travel. If anything, in my naïveté, I thought of him as part of Kate's extended family.

"Oh, yes," said Chat, and it was then that I discerned the merry hint of malice in his voice. "Don't you know Deb?"

Knowledge of the woman's existence, so strange to me initially, was to prove the mildest disturbance of the day.

It was a tiny brown house, one floor—the kind of place that hardly merits its freestanding existence. We parked next to a Plymouth Duster abandoned at the edge of the driveway. The hood of the car was propped open, exposing rusted guts. For a moment we didn't move, just sat with the windows open, looking at the water, twenty yards away. Then Chat got out and slammed his door and I followed him. There wasn't a breath of air, or a cloud, or the tap of a halyard or the cry of a gull, just the sun beating on the tar. Beside the house a little dinghy resting on a dolly had been stripped of its mast and left, bow to the ground. I walked over to it and propped up the bow on a pair of cinder blocks. A line of scum had formed around the tanks.

Chat peered through the sliding glass doors to see if anyone was home. He gave them a rattle, a couple of bangs. "Nicko, guy! Nicko! Open up! It's Chat!"

No one answered, so we went down to look at the water.

It is always that way with water. If you come anywhere near it, you will eventually walk closer and closer to it, to touch it, if you can. Even the driveway tar spilled over toward the little strip of beach, in a futile Tantalus grasp to quench its thirst.

From the right side of the cove, where the tar extended, a ramp led down to a long dock; I figured Nick would have set it all up. The tide was all the way out, remarkably far, and the ramp hung like a broken limb, snapped and dangling at an angle unknown to nature. It smelled like low tide, too—pungent, briny—the unmistakable scent of insidious things at growth. Where the water had receded, a layer of algae had settled on the tar, and a candy-bar wrapper had stuck there. Chat and I clattered down the ramp to get a better look out the cove.

The Sound had turned to a bowl of reheated soup, as it does in summer. The surface was flat and rippleless as far as you could see, except for the spot, about fifty feet off the dock, where a massive rock broke cruelly through the water. Someone had stuck a stake in the middle of it with a long fluorescent tape hanging from the end to mark the obstruction when the tide filled.

Chat slipped a foot out of his loafer and tested the water. "Oh, God," he said. "It's warm."

"I guess nobody's around," I said.

We were turning to go when I saw the Boston Whaler. The boat was tied to a cleat at the end of the dock. I wouldn't have noticed it, except that when a tiny swell rolled beneath us, she listed back to the end of her tether and the bow was exposed. The entire fore half was completely smashed, both lights blown, the nose crumpled flat: a head-on collision.

"Total no-air day," intoned a voice above us, and I jumped.

Nick was perched like a gargoyle on the top of the ramp. He seemed to have materialized out of one of the streaks of humidity in the air.

We shielded our eyes from the sun.

"Hey, guys," he said, barely audible, "whadda you know?"

"Jesus Christ!" said Chat, jovially.

From the dock Nick looked to be holding his side, like a runner with a cramp, and it wasn't until we were beside him that I made sense of the posture. His left arm was in a sling, and the sling was blue, the same color as his T-shirt, so that from a distance the two materials blended together.

"Nick," I said. I was awfully glad to see him.

"Georgie Len . . . Georgie P. Lennie P.—" He broke off into paroxysms of giggles. If possible, he was even thinner than before, thinner and browner, except for the top of his head, which was making a tentative gesture toward blond. His feet were bare, and he stood balancing on the outside of his soles, trading one foot for the other. "Tar's ouchy," he let on.

"Nick, Christ, let me tell you how George and I spent last night. So these three Holyoke girls were up all summer—Mount Holyoke, you know, girls' school—they come up to Hanover begging for action, right? And George has his eye on one, and I've got my eye on another, but first we've got to take care of Number Three." Chat launched into an account of our last-ditch attempts with the girls, only to come to a premature close, enervated, stopped dead by the heat.

"How very nice," said Nick, after a pause that lasted just long enough for me to realize he was stoned out of his mind.

"So you're still living here, Nicko?" Chat said.

Nick shrugged with his good shoulder. "Till Deb kicks me out."

"It's not too bad," Chat asserted, as if he were correcting Nick.

"Yeah . . ."

"No, Nick, it's really not. Hell, George and I would be thrilled with this. *Waterfront view*, eh, Nicko?"

Nick gave the giggle again as the three of us contemplated the water. Four or five pastel houses were crowded above the far side of the cove. In the distance, somebody with a hell of a lot of ambition was paddling a kayak toward Long Island.

"There's not—there's actually not tons of stuff going on here," Nick said. He tested the sling arm, extending it ever so slightly until he grimaced.

I felt spooked all over again, and I glanced back over my shoulder at the Whaler. "You guessed it," Nick corroborated. "I just got my cast off yesterday."

"God, that's awful."

"Ran right into Halftide Rock."

"Does it still hurt?"

"Not much."

"God," I said again. "When did it happen?"

He concentrated. "Must have been . . . oh yeah, it was Fourth of July." With an effort he focused bloodshot eyes on me. A thought seemed to have occurred to him from far away, something profound or original, and I had, for a moment, a pleasant sense of expectation. Then Nick said, with the most enthusiasm he had yet displayed, "Hey. Do you guys want to go inside and smoke a little?"

It was a mess inside of beer cans and dirty dishes, clean clothes piled in heaps metastasizing into dirty clothes piled in heaps; plastic cups and playing cards. It was just like any fraternity house, except that on top of the familiar reek of vomit and beer and cigarettes, there was a sickly sweetness that didn't belong, as if a commercial air freshener had recently been sprayed through the room, stronger even than the salty sea scent that followed Nick around. A particularly rank odor emanated from one of the couches, and I saw Chat hesitate before settling Indian-style on the floor.

"So you like my digs?"

"Oh, yeah, Nick," Chat affirmed. "You've got a great place here."

At that Nick looked up from lighting his bong and gave me one of his priceless grins, a grin that comprehended all the fantastic ironies of this hemisphere and the next. "Whadda you say, Georgie Len?"

We had each taken a couple of hits when from down the hall there came the incongruous sound of a child crying. Presently the door to the room swung open and a little girl in a diaper toddled in. She had brown curls with bows clipped to them. Babbling, she toddled to the end of the room and began to bang on the glass doors in a monotonous rhythm. Before I could begin to make sense of this apparition, it was succeeded by another: an obese woman in gym shorts and a bikini top who appeared on the other side of the glass. In one hand she held a bag of groceries, while with the other she banged savagely on the doors. The whole house seemed to shake.

"Lemme in, Nicko, goddammit!"

Nick got up in slow motion to open the door. I thought half-stonedly, *And now we have come to the entertainment part of the afternoon.*

"Nice fuckin' baby-sitter you ah! Yasit here gettin' stoned with yafriends, do fuckall for Katie-Lynn!" She heaved the groceries off onto Nick and with a display of exertion caught the child up from the floor. Nick paused barely a moment before letting the bag slide out of his hands and onto a broken desk.

"Day's a baby! Day's a baby! *Fuckin' ice cream'll melt!*"

The woman's body was blanketed in one of the cruellest sunburns

I had ever seen. Livid red flesh seemed to burst from her entire being. She was an oldish young woman of about thirty, with a massive head of blond hair springing defiantly from black roots.

"Fuckin' move yerass!"

Nick seemed not to have heard, his lips atwitch, amused by something only he could see.

"Deborah Beale?" inquired Chat, rising from the floor. "Are those your dulcet tones I hear?"

An expression of fear or delight seemed to freeze the woman into place. She hid her red face behind the baby, then came out for a peek. "Oh, my gawd! Chattie Wethers!" She looked as if she were going to cry. "Chattie Wethers! Chattie fuckin' Wethers!"

"Hello, darling," said Chat. He kissed her forehead. The little girl started to cry. *"Fine, then, yagoin down, yagonna learn a lesson!"* The toddler was viciously deposited on the floor, and Deb stood staring, overcome, at Chat, a hand to her mouth, her legs crossed as if she had to go to the bathroom.

"Lemme lookitya! Lemme lookitya!"

"Look all you please. Go on—get your fill."

I must have moved or done something to draw attention to myself, for all at once the woman seemed to become aware of my presence. She looked away shyly toward Nick. "Havin' a party without me, eh? Shoulda known, shoulda known! After all I done for you, right?" Deb held up a fist in mock threat. I stared at it blankly before remembering myself and struggling belatedly to my feet. Like many obese women, she had perfectly manicured nails.

Chat introduced us, but she was too shy to shake hands. Instead she leaned over and took the baby's hand and waved it at me. "Say hi, Katie-Lynn. Say hi to the nice boy. *Nicko, the goddamn groceries, I tellya!"* But now she was yelling uselessly, from habit or shyness; Nick had vanished into the back.

She and Chat settled companionably on one couch. "You boys up to no good, eh, Chattie?" I took a tentative seat opposite; the idea of the ice cream melting was driving me insane.

"Why, *Deb*—"

She cackled loudly. "Nicko's the same way. You know what I say, 'While the cat's away. . . .' While the *Kate's* away, ha-ha! While Kate's away—whoopsee!" She indicated me with a toss of her head. "He a friend-a Katie's?"

"I'm afraid he is, Deb," said Chat judiciously. "A very old friend."

"Yeah?" She looked directly at me. "You know Katie Goodenow?"

I nodded. "I do."

She seemed to weigh the evidence. "What's ya name again?"

"George," I said, clearing my throat. "George Lenhart."

Deb looked from me to Chat, suspicious, as if a joke were being played on her. "Yeah? Mine's Deb." As she spoke she redid the child's bows, taking them out one by one and smoothing the little pieces of hair over her fingers. "Deborah Moore. Used to be Beale. *Still oughta be, the fuckin' a-hole!*" She looked reproachfully toward the hall when she said this, and for one sickening moment I forgot where I was and thought the woman was Nick's former wife.

"Language, Deb!" Chat said reprovingly.

Deb made a face at him, sticking out her tongue, and cracked herself up. I laughed, too, to be polite. "Yanice kid," she told me. "Excuse my French, but I'm talking about this one's father."

"Her father?"

"Yeah. Split. Bastard lives over here in Pawanis. You know Pawanis?"

I shook my head.

"No? You sure? You ever go to the mall?"

"Yes, George, don't you ever go to the mall?" said Chat.

I felt myself turning red. "Sometimes I find it can be useful," I stammered.

Deb shrugged. "It's not that great," she said. "Only reason I go is it's close. And they got Kid 'n' Caboose now, and Katie-Lynn *loves* Kid 'n' Caboose. Don't you, Katie? Don't you, Katie-Lynn? There! You got all your bows, girl! And now you'll be a little heartbreaker!"

She held the child out proudly. Against my better judgment I glanced at it, and I happened to meet its eyes. I couldn't look away fast enough. Their expression was intensely bright, almost feral; she had pierced ears and looked the "little lady."

"Ya wanna hold her?"

"Oh, that's all right," I said.

"It's okay—g'head. She won't bite."

Blanching, I opened my arms and drew the child into my lap. "Hello."

Chat was trying to suppress his mirth. He sat himself down in front of Nick's paraphernalia to pack another bowl.

"She's a—cute little girl. You said her name is . . ."

"Katie-Lynn."

"Hi, Katie-Lynn."

"It's like Katie plus Lynn. You like it? It's a combination of my two favorite names."

"Very pretty."

Katie-Lynn's mother smacked her hands down on her thighs. "Fuckin' A!" she yelled. "I fagotaget cigarettes!"

"You shouldn't smoke, Deb," said Chat, languidly inhaling. "Not with the baby."

"Fuck you!" Deb leaned over and punched him in the chest. Chat coughed, laughed, then gave himself up to a full-on coughing fit. "You always did fuckin' cough," said Deb.

"George," gasped Chat, "help me!"

"Shut the fuck up!" Deb said good-naturedly. She groped around in her bursting handbag and a fist came up, clenched around a handful of bills. "Dannit! Will you lookit this? I'm poor already!"

"You've got to budget, dear—"

"Stick it up your ass! Three, four . . . Wait a minute: secret stash! I always have my secret stash." Her other hand felt inside the bikini top and removed a twenty, which Deb held up triumphantly. "They nevalet me down!" she cried, cupping her enormous breasts. "Neva-yet!" I felt a small cold hand finger my watch. "Ha-ha! You wanna go on a beer run wit me up the deli and get cigarettes while we're at it, Chattie?"

"In a sec," said Chat. He took another hit and laughed. "Where's Nicko? Contemplating the universe?"

"Conaplating his ass!"

"Kate come around much?"

"Every time she does she trashes shit!"

"How often would you say she came?"

"Who gives a shit?"

"Well, George and I—"

"Come *awun*, I wanna go up the deli and get a carton of cigarettes. I wanna get cigarettes! Now, Chattie, goddammit!"

"All right, all right, give a man a chance to recover."

"Pansy-ass!" shouted Deb. She dragged him to his feet.

"Excuse me, but . . . ?"

Deb laughed down at me, the angry sunburn undulating across her massive chest. "Yasicka Katie-Lynn? Yasicka Katie already?" Deb plucked her kid from my lap. "Yajust like her fatha!"

The moment they were gone, I stood up and dug out the ice cream from the bag of groceries and took it into the back. The tub was sweating and sagging from the heat. I put it into the freezer.

Nick was standing at the kitchen table fiddling with a piece of line. The table was covered in nautical hardware, pulleys and shackles and the long elegant rudder of an Olympic-class dinghy.

"Georgie Len," he said, taking in my presence anew. He had always been a little like this, like a kid you played peekaboo with. Every time you showed up, Nick would look glad to see you, whether he had seen you ten minutes or ten months earlier. He had his own inner timetable, and he functioned according to it alone.

"So Kate graduated," I said.

"Yeah." He stared at the array of hardware. "Pass me that shackle, will you?"

I passed him the fitting, and he spun it several times in his hands to see where it stuck.

"She's moving to New York, so we'll probably just see each other on weekends. Maybe . . . every third weekend." He sounded as if he were quoting someone.

"What are you going to do?"

"Me? I'm going to do an Olympic campaign, Georgie Len. Soon as I get the funding."

He was distracted for a moment, thinking, perhaps, about the force of a thirty-knot puff on a two-foot spar. There was the same entrancing economy to his movements that I remembered, and it struck me, as it often had before, that a hundred years ago he would have been a soldier or a sailor—a sailor, same as he was now, except doing two years before the mast; that he might have ended up a hero out of the sheer dexterity of his limbs. Except that he had been born into a generation that required of its youth no service. There was no place on earth, really, for people like Nick. And I thought with a sinking feeling of the office job that awaited me in the fall, and then again for good in a couple of years, and of all the years it would take to find out if the possibility of middle-aged comfort was worth it. Then Nick looked up and giggled, that little inward giggle. He kept chuckling to himself until finally I said, *"What?"*

I thought he was going to poke fun at me. But what he said was: "Utor, fruor, fungor, potior, and vescor take the ablative."

Startled out of my daze, I laughed out my breath. "You're right," I said, "they do." After a moment I said, "Goddamn slides of Pompeii!"

Nick tilted his chair back and balanced there on the back legs, his fingertips splayed on the table. "How many times did she make him show them."

"Must have been eight, ten . . ."

"So was Mr. Davis senile?" Nick said seriously. "Was that the problem?"

"I think he was, Nick," I said. "I think he was."

"Georgie Len, Kate and I still owe you, you know. We haven't forgotten."

That was for standing—or rather sitting—guard, with my pupil desk in front of the closet the slide projector came out of, to give them a knock when Vesuvius erupted. "Pater! Pater! Vesuvius fumat!" Kate would crawl out of the closet giggling, her hair in place, loving the game of it; Nick would appear a moment later, his eyelids at half-mast, and slink to his seat, as if in a dream. "Thanks, man," he used to whisper. "We owe you."

We talked boats for a while. Nick reheated some coffee, and we sat at the kitchen table and drank it black, because Deb had forgotten to buy milk. Nick kept remembering bits and pieces of school, and every few minutes would say something like, "*Muckrakers,* George—*The Jungle!*" in a tone of delighted disbelief. "Paris is well worth a mass!" or "*N'avez-vous pas vos vélos? Non, nous sommes à pied.*" I guess I reminded him of his education.

Chat and Deb were gone a long time. When we finally heard the Diesel sputtering in the driveway, Nick stood up and stuck his neck out the kitchen window, craning it toward the water. "You wanna go waterskiing," he asked. "It's a perfect day—no air, flat water."

"But the boat's wrecked, isn't it?" I said.

"Nah, it still works. You can still drive it."

"Oh, yeah?"

"It's not like she crashed into Halftide and blew up the motor, too."

At the word "she," I felt a coolness start at the base of my spine and creep up my neck. "How'd it happen?" I said dryly.

"Usual."

"Yeah?"

"Yeah, you know—night before Fourth of July. We were drunk. Forgot about Halftide."

"You and Deb."

"Deb?" said Nick. "No, sad part was, Deb was stone-cold sober, and was she ever ripped at me. It's her boat, see. She got it off Katie-Lynn's father when they split."

"Oh, really."

"See, I shouldn't have been standing up. That's why I flipped over the bow."

"And Kate?" I said, because that's the way you talked with Nick: you didn't have to contextualize anything, because he never did; you just tried to keep up.

"Kate was okay. She got a little whiplash. That was a good thing, see, 'cause she had to drive up to Maine the next day, and you know, that would not have been a fun drive with a broken arm."

"No, it wouldn't," I agreed. "No, it wouldn't."

"So, whadda you say, man?"

It wasn't the fact that Kate was responsible for breaking his arm that decided me, but the uninflected serenity with which he defended her. I still remember the false composure with which I stood up and said we had to be going. "Maybe another time, Nicko."

"Really?" I felt him looking at me. He hadn't expected me to be a phony like the others; to go with him only so far.

"Yeah, I've actually got to get Chat and we've got to get on the road."

Chat and Deb were having a companionable cigarette by the car when I came out. The baby on Deb's hip was looking around with that strangely independent look babies can have when they're being held—as if they're only using their mother for the lift. But the look on Chat's face, when I "reminded" him that we had to go, was equally strange, before he arranged his features into an expression of reluctant remembrance—it was very much like triumph. "You're right, George. We'd better get on the road." He dashed his cigarette to the tar. "So sorry, darling."

"You really have to go? Shit, guys," Deb lamented. "We were just stattin' to have fun."

Nick came out in cutoffs, carrying a homemade ski. "You're really going?"

"Yeah, sorry about that, Nick," said Chat.

"Sorry nothing. Deb'll take me, won't you, sis?"

"Yeah, I'll drive forya, Nicko." She threw her cigarette to the ground and shifted Katie-Lynn to the opposite hip. "You wanna take a beer for the road."

"Oh, that's all right—"

"You're damn right I do!" Chat said. "I paid for it, madam, in case you've forgotten."

Deb giggled. "Here's a six—it's cold."

Chat tucked the beer into the backseat. I could feel the baby watching me as I walked around to the passenger-side door.

"Nice meeting you," said Deb as I opened it to get in.

"Oh, you too. You too," I said. It made me ashamed that she had to say it first.

"I miss you, Chattie!" Deb started to weep. She leaned her heavy chest into the window. Chat patted her fried peroxide hair. The baby began to cry. Chat revved the engine with a glint in his eye, Deb stood back reluctantly, and we drove away.

We made it to Manhattan by dusk. I took a long shower in the Wetherses' creaky Upper East Side bathroom and stretched out on the divan and wished our plans for the evening would evaporate. Already I had my New York feeling on, of exhaustion and poverty, of not being up for the fight. I couldn't think of a thing that would cheer me up, least of all going out drinking with Chat's grade school buddies on my fake I.D. I wanted to go off alone somewhere and hoard the story Chat had told me to pass the time between New Haven and the Triboro Bridge, about when he and Kate and Nick were little. I had ruined Deb's day by insisting we leave. "We were just stattin' to have fun!" And when I closed my eyes to go over Chat's story and get it all straight, I would picture Katie-Lynn's mother instead, standing heavy and sad in the driveway, the color of the crayon nobody wanted—brick red—and, as Chat drove us away from their cottage by the sea, waving her daughter's hand like a doll's.

Then we went out and met Kate and her friends in a restaurant across town.

Just the sight of her made me instantly, profoundly optimistic. She was remarkably fresh, at any hour of the day. She was wearing her hair pulled back in a ponytail, and I remember it seemed to me as jaunty, as promising, as an ensign flying off the stern of a sloop, reaching through a fair day. Her eyes lit up when Chat presented me. "George! How *fun!*"

She was all collarbone and straight lines. I took her in my arms for as long as I dared.

We got an outside table, and Kate sat beside me and told everyone in the group—her and Chat's New York friends—how far we went back, she and I, six years, six formative years ago we had met, why we had practically grown up together (except that we hadn't)—and all I could think to say when it was my turn to speak was, "Did you hear we saw Nick today, too?"

I remember that she didn't answer me right away. It gave me time to search wildly for a change of subject—and to come up empty-minded. She took a long, unhurried sip of her white wine. It was a summer evening, the summer she turned twenty-two, and she was off on the grand tour with Granny come Labor Day. I'm sure she didn't need reminders like that, but then, they weren't going to throw her, either: she was out to have fun. "How nice for him," she said eventually. "How nice of you to stop by, George. I'm sure Nick appreciated that."

Her accent hadn't quite decided where to go. It was a good measure St. Chattlesex, which at that time derived from California surfer (the hurried, telltale "No, totally, totally"), but there had been other influences as well. Now it was hovering a few shades shy of the World War II–vintage dahling-dahling her parents no doubt spoke. I could have listened to it all night, and every time she said my name it sounded like a compliment.

At some point I made another brilliant contribution to the conversation by asking her what she had majored in. Still, I was curious to know.

"American studies."

"How'd you pick that?" I said.

"Same as anyone." But of the other couple hundred students who had graduated with that degree, I doubt a single one would have given the same reason Kate did. "I love this country," she said. I thought at first she was being disingenuous, but she got a look in her eye then which I have never forgotten. It was a look of highly intensified complacency—if that's possible—which I was certain no feast or threat of famine would ever shake.

We ended up at Chat's playing I Never, playing Thumper, playing Galley Slave—the version of Asshole that came out of Cold Harbor—and finally we ended up sitting around talking to one another in Nicko-speak, making decontextualized comments because we were too drunk to compose the lead-ins. Chat was trying to get some friend of Kate's into bed, and I found myself cornering a little sofa with her at the other end.

"You must miss those summers," I said. "You and Nick."

"Miss them? Oh, we still go there," Kate corrected me.

I struggled to explain. "No, but I mean—the high school summers, and before. They must have been—great." I was going to say "carefree," or something that I hoped would prompt Kate into giving her childhood a name, but somebody switched a light on behind us and at the illumination it gave to her clean, practical profile, I shied from the word.

"Yes, they were great," Kate concurred. She let herself have a smile over the memories—I think it was the closest I'd ever seen her come to nostalgia—and there wasn't anything more than contentment on her face when she added, "But now is so much fun, too. You know?"

"Oh, yes," I said.

The past was fun; now was fun. We cracked open some more beers from the case at our feet.

The thing was, I'm sure Nicko would have agreed.

CHAPTER 13

"Nick Beale was a very good-looking kid," Chat had said, turning to me at the first red light between Nick's sister's and the highway. "He never went through the awkward stage. It was very unfair."

That was the premise. The story followed. Chat must have told it over and over, polishing and embellishing, making it more his own. Each of the Cold Harbor kids must have had his own version; each of the parents as well. It was too good a story not to repeat.

"All the moms were in love with him when he was like eight or nine. They used to go down to the wharf and have him fish their lobsters out, and if he wasn't there they'd ask Ma Beale, 'Isn't Nicko working today?' 'Playin' hooky,' she'd say. 'Kid's just like his father.' Ma worked behind the short-order counter. She smoked when all our moms quit, and the ash always needed ashing and looked like it was about to fall on us or the food—the lobster rolls, you know, or the hot dogs. Pa Beale was a lobsterman. Oldest kid Timmy took after him.

Deb got pregnant, had an abortion, dropped out. Donny got away, went halfway through Maine on a hockey scholarship. Now he delivers boats for people, works some charter line down in the Caribbean. Nick was a mistake. Ma had him when she was forty-something and Pa was in his fifties, looked about a hundred. Fat. Could barely get in and out of the boat. Needed Nick to help him.

"It just happened there were a bunch of us Nick's age. Cold Harbor baby boom, I guess. There was me, Katie and Vivi, the Palls, Jess Brindle and the step-Brindles, Jay Cushing—he only came up every other summer—Tim Hertzlich (guy had a cute sister). And Nicko used to hang out with us. We'd play roofball down the wharf with him. Our moms would be like, Go and play with Nicko while I talk to Ma. He used to ride his bike over to Chillyick and rig a boat and take it out and sail in the fleet with us. Nobody said anything. One time this instructor tried to pull rank, and she got laughed off the water. We used to have races at the end of the lessons. Nick won more than anyone else, and at first I thought it was talent, but then I realized it was because he cared. It was kind of sad how much he cared. He wouldn't just win the races; he'd win, like, the cone drill and the tacking duels. He'd win the capsize drill, for God's sake. And he always got to the dock first and got his boat unrigged first. It was annoying as hell.

"The moms used to watch out for him, make sure he got invited to stuff. I remember one time my mom screamed my head off because I invited a bunch of kids to go sailing on my dad's boat for my birthday and there's Nick Beale standing on the shore watching us go off. Mom took him home and fed him my fucking birthday cake. He ate the whole goddamn thing. She said she felt so bad for him, he was so thin. The thing that pissed me off is he just was thin. It wasn't like he was starving. He wasn't some Victorian fucking pauper. Ma Beale fried him up a huge fried dinner every night, for fuck's sake. But you couldn't go telling that to my mom or Mrs. Brindle—they'd go ballistic. We all knew it was something about trying to make up for his having to stay there when we went away, but beyond that we didn't get it. Christ, what does a kid know. I hated going home in the fall. I used to cry in the car the whole way back to the city.

"We started partying when we were around twelve or thirteen. Nick knew about that, too. He was always one up on us. He could get Timmy to buy for us, and he could get pot off his sister. And he knew how to smoke it. Ha! Then he got to go on my dad's boat all the time. We'd have the launch drop us off at *Rum Punch* and row the dinghy back. We used to get baked off our asses and look at the stars and think up funny boat names. Charles Pall wanted to name his *Morning Wood*. Isn't that good? 'Morning Wood.'

"This was just the boys. The girls didn't party, really, not that young. They, you know, hung out at home more. They had slumber parties. Once in a while, one of the older girls would come out with us. One of the sixteen-, seventeen-year-olds. Marnie Pall—God, she was gorgeous. If anyone was getting any play, though, it was with the au pairs. There was this Swedish girl one summer. 'Please to help me with my rucksack.' Jesus. But mostly we'd see 'em—I mean the real girls—at square dancing Wednesday nights.

"Pa Beale was Caller. Every Wednesday at the yacht club, right-hand star, allemande left, allemande right, swing your corner, do-si-do your own. Warm up with Alley Cat. Close down with the Virginia reel. Dads and daughters. Old slacker kids with old slacker kids. Mr. Cushing with Mrs. Pall, *quel scandale, quel scandale.* So anyway, one night Pa doesn't show up. Guy's never missed a Wednesday in like forty years. They find him down the wharf, dead on the floor by a barrel of chum. Heart attack. It must have been his third or fourth. Big surprise, the guy ate lard for breakfast and smoked about a carton a day.

"Nick disappears. Steals a whaler and takes off for three days. Nobody knew where he went, and he never told. The girls wrote him these stupid little notes with flowers in them and like, haikus. They rode their bikes over to the Beales' and shoved them in the mailbox because they were too scared to knock on Ma's door. That's the first time I heard about him and Kate. Some stupid girl told me how sorry she felt for Kate Goodenow. I said, 'Why Kate?' And she was like, 'Well, obviously.' I bet she just liked him. I don't think Nick could have even said who she was. I don't think Nick could have told her from Jess Brindle or Heidi or any of them.

"Next Wednesday there's a big meeting, the dads go to the club to decide what they're going to do for Pa. I went with my dad because Mom was away. I was the only kid there. They planned a whole big memorial service, but I don't remember if they ever had it. Maybe they had it and the kids didn't go. That was it, we went up to the Hertzlichs' and partied—that was it. Played quarters on the kitchen floor, went up to Top of the World and got fucked up, probably, I don't know . . .

"At the meeting Artie Goodenow, Mr. Goodenow stands up and says what about taking up a collection to help out Ma—pay off the mortgage, put Nick through school, something like that. It's totally fucking crazy. Everybody jumps on the bandwagon. Everybody's forking over a couple thousand. My mom gave her own donation besides my dad's, and she wasn't the only mom who did. In less than twenty-four hours they've got fifty thousand dollars. Mr. Goodenow's the ringleader and he's taking suggestions, and next week when they meet again—still no square dancing—he stands up and says, 'Why don't we send Nick Beale to boarding school?'

"And that's what they did. St. Paul's? Exeter? No, that would have been pushing it a little. Katie and one of her friends from home were going to Chatham, and I'll bet you anything she begged her dad to send Nick there, too. Daddy Goodenow is loving it. Overnight the guy's a fucking Pygmalion. Calls up admissions, pulls the requisite strings, does the give-a-kid-a-chance routine, poor-family routine, says 'potential' a lot, Nick's in like Flynn."

Closing my eyes against the oncoming traffic, I knew the answer before the question, that one could never say was his going for the better or the worse.

"Now you know as well as I do, George," Chat went on, with the arrogant air of one who knows, "that a lot of people reinvent themselves in boarding school. The whole school knows you when you go in and the whole school knows you when you leave. Maybe you won't touch a drop when you go in and you leave filching the chapel wine. And maybe you spend four years as an Exeter loser and the next four years at Harvard name-dropping Exeter for prep-tool credibility. And maybe you go in wearing flammable slacks and leave wearing Nantucket reds. I knew a guy at Hotchkiss who got ragged on for wearing sixty/forty shirts. Guy's mom had bought them for him because she thought they'd be more 'practical' than hundred-percent cotton. Kid took those twenty practical shirts out behind the dorm one day and set them on fire. The disciplinary committee was like: 'Why didn't you at least give them to charity?'

"Nicko goes in, he's got dork-out L.L. Bean outlet-wear and this green blazer. It wasn't hunter green, either. It wasn't the green of the *forests*. I guess Goodenow was a little sketchy on the details of shipping the kid off. They made a big deal of presenting Nicko with a patch from the yacht club to wear on his jacket pocket. Never did inquire if he had a jacket. He was supposed to write letters to Mr. Goodenow, and Goodenow was going to forward them to the others—the Association, or whatever the fuck it was they called it.

"The unbelievable thing was, he pulls it off. He's just one of those kids who . . . pull it off."

For a moment the obvious pleasure Chat took in the narrative seemed to desert him. In the fading daylight his long white face registered the utter inequity of adolescence: that after five years, nothing intervening—not even the visit we had just paid Deb—had changed the fact that Nick Beale had been born cool, while Chat and the rest of us could only hope to achieve it.

"In about three weeks Nick's the big hero. By Christmas it's *the* thing to wear the green blazer. Guys fight over it. Everybody walks around barefoot the way Nick does until it gets too cold and they wimp out. In the spring Nick's the hot little skipper on the sailing team. They went undefeated and beat us in team racing for the high school championship. And of course it doesn't hurt that he and Kate are friends from Maine.

"She was the perfect little girl first year away. Sailed J.V.; reme-

dial math; French Three; string bracelet; Jerry-bears on her notebooks drawn by Charlie Pall . . . *headbands*. They started going out
around March break. Holding hands, smooching after the dance. No
one can decide who's luckier, him or her, her or him. He makes her
a tape, and every single girl who's even halfway friends with Kate
gets a copy made, and most of those girls still have that tape today,
'Groovy Toons for Kate from Nick.' Later there was a 'More Groovy
Toons.' 'Magic Carpet Ride,' 'Cowgirl in the Sand' . . . saw her at a
lacrosse game in the spring.

"They were king and queen all summer, too; the rest of us were
going to tennis camp, summer school—I guess we made some effort
at being productive. Kate and Nick were sailing instructors. They
just sailed their 420 and hung out on the porch of the yacht club.
Kate was such a baby. She still couldn't party with us. She and Vivi
had to be home at eight. Artie Goodenow didn't even know they were
going out, she and Nick. They used to sneak out to the big boat and
fool around. A couple times in the summer Goodenow had a talk
with Nick about getting his grades up, but everybody'd figured it
would take him a while to get up to speed, and they all commented
on his appearance—'vastly improved.'

"I only went up a few times that summer. I asked Nick how he
liked Chatham, and he said, 'It's all right. The sailing's decent and
Kate's there.' He didn't know he was supposed to have"—Chat
smirked—"great expectations.

"And now Sex—heh, heh—rears its ugly head." Chat cracked
open a can of beer from Deb's six-pack and took a long, thirsty swal-
low. "Nick was 'experienced.' The rumor was that he had lost it when
he was twelve with one of Deb's friends—as a joke at some party.
There was a girl in Wamatuck he was supposed to sleep with on va-
cations, and I guess at some point Kate figured it out. Nick said he
didn't understand what it had to do with her, he said it was two separate things—he told everyone who would listen, and I honestly believe he meant it, but that only made it worse, and anyway Kate had
convinced herself that she was going to have to sleep with him to stay

going out with him. And by now she wanted to keep him more than ever. Nick was—crazy. I heard he used to whip up frozen drinks in the kitchenette blender, and if a teacher came by, he'd offer them a glass.

"So she had it all planned out in her girly way. She wanted them to go down to New York some weekend her parents were away and sleep in her bedroom at home. But Nick didn't know that part of the plan. So one Saturday night he took her out behind the science building and had sex with her."

There was a long pause. I thought of a girl called Hallie Dryer.

"Kate was very . . . thin," Chat said finally. "Very thin. And she got thinner." With his free hand he picked absently at a blemish on his chin.

For the wrap-up Chat had adopted a soothingly businesslike tone, like the one Mr. Goodenow must have used to explain to his constituents that the experiment had failed.

"What can I say—you know the rest. Nick didn't get asked back after their junior year. The rest of us were gunning for the Ivies; Nick didn't care. Nobody had told him what came next. The money was mostly gone, and with Nick slacking his way through Chatham, nobody felt like putting up more. Mr. Goodenow told my dad he'd figured the kid would work hard, maybe get a scholarship somewhere decent. Nobody counted on his not caring at all, or his not ever caring."

After a moment, I said: "They let him finish out the year."

My interruption seemed to annoy Chat. He sped up, then cursed the car in front of him. It must have disconcerted him to be reminded that I had been there for this part of the story, that I could bear witness. He seemed to take no notice of the fact: somehow if I had been there, his story couldn't have been true. And yet it was. I knew, because I *had* been there.

"Memorial Day weekend they had the team-racing championships in Newport, and on Saturday night Nicko went down to Ida

Lewis and stole a boat. He stole a boat right off the pier. He tried to get Kate to come along. He was going to take her down to the Caribbean. Can you imagine? The kid had a vision!"

"But she said no."

"She said no, so he sailed *home.*"

"He had nowhere else to go."

"He came honking into Cold Harbor, 'chute up, soloing, ragging the main, cutting Little Otter closer than anyone ever cut it. And *nobody* has ever understood how he got through the Narrows at low tide."

"It was a Bermuda Forty," I remembered. I had memorized that. It had seemed important to me at the time.

"He had good taste in boats."

"He just had good taste."

"Wouldn't you know it turned out the boat he stole belonged to Kate's uncle. Goodenow patched it up with him, washed his hands of Nick. I think by then he'd finally figured out about Kate and Nick, and he didn't like it one bit. Goodenow's always been . . . *different* about Kate—he's more protective of her than he is of Vivi or CeeCee. Doesn't really make sense since she's the oldest, but everyone sees it and everyone agrees. Now this is funny: Nick made friends with Uncle Goodie, and he used to work for him, taking that boat from the warm places to the cold and back. The guy's pretty funny, actually. He said if Nicko could bring her home single-handed all that way and keep her out of trouble, then he sure as hell could do it again with crew."

"We lost the regatta," I said, "and drove back to Chatham without him." The whole school had gone into mourning over Nick. There was a strike to get him asked back; nobody went to class for a week—well, that part was fitting. In the fall it was the same thing. Everybody wanted to tell Nick stories. Kate had to hear them until she was ready to scream. They expected her to be the authority on the Nick Beale apocrypha when all she was trying to do was get her mind off him and get through. She applied early to college and she got in.

"Kate and I talked over Christmas break," Chat went on. "I called her up to congratulate her when I heard about Yale. She said Nick was talking about coming down to New Haven to be near her. Maybe at school in the dead of winter with him sneaking back on campus to take her out drinking, it seemed like a good enough plan. And when it clicked, in spring, that maybe the idea wasn't so hot, what was she supposed to say? I think at that point she still thought she owed him something.

"Kate didn't come up at all the summer before college. She got a job in New York—internship at a chick magazine, lived out in Greenwich at Uncle Goodie's. Maybe she made it up one weekend— I guess I did see her over the Fourth. She told me Nick was going to come hang out in New Haven for a while, maybe get a job working on boats. I asked her if she thought that would be a drag, since he wouldn't be going to school. She said she didn't know—she thought he would be fun to have around."

No doubt in the first year or two, he had been the ace up her sleeve. She wouldn't have had to bother with the orientations, the friendly overtures to her roommates—and Kate liked very much not having to bother. She would have had her own insulation in Nick. For him, nothing had changed. He had Kate, and New Haven was on the water. But in spite of the face she put on things, it must have been harder and harder to believe they would be together someday. Perhaps he had embarrassed her at a party, or perhaps it was simply the inconvenience, after a while, of having him show up in her real life at all. So she had gone on with her life—college, and college boyfriends—but she had created a space for him in which she believed she could always find him. She would see him from time to time in that space, which had nothing to do with her real life, and it would always be the way it had been when they were fifteen. Nothing would have to change.

CHAPTER 14

When Kate and Harry and I got back to the city, it was late afternoon and people were coming back from their weekends and running out again as fast as they could to fill up the cafés and murder the day and make it to Monday.

Through no effort of my own, I had made it back in time for my date with Delia Ferrier. I was glad to have somewhere to go, but I couldn't psych up for it, for the whole interesting, positive interaction between Mature Persons Numbers One and Two. I felt more like watching static on TV or going home and not talking to Toff. Everyone must feel like that once in a while, it's like getting take-out for dinner or putting a song on repeat—it's self-indulgent in exactly the same way. You just want to hoard your past in the luxury of your own room, to replay the stories over and over in darkness and not be bothered.

"Just leave me on the corner," I said.

"No, no, we'll drop you off. No trouble, George."

At my building Kate gave a good imitation of someone rousing herself sleepily. I deposited her on the seat and got out. "Oh, George. You're going, then. It was so good you could come along." Her smile seemed to come from far away, the way one smiles over a memory that is pleasant and will always be pleasant but is no longer compelling.

I took a dollar out of my pocket and gave it to her. "You won," I said.

"That's right," she said in a sleepy, vague, but happy voice. "That kid . . . was just a kid with a great job, wasn't he?"

"That's right."

"Well, I'll get myself something with this," she said, straightening up in her seat. "I'll get myself—well, what can somebody buy for a dollar?"

"Plenty of things!" Harry asserted, warming to the challenge. "A Coke or a candy bar—"

"He thinks of food," Kate remarked.

"But it's been hours since breakfast!" Harry said indignantly. "And we didn't even *eat* lunch!"

"You could buy a newspaper with a dollar," I suggested, leaning on the side of the convertible.

"Not today," Kate reminded me. "It's Sunday. And anyway, I hate that big, dirty thing."

"I hate it, too," I admitted. "I just about dread it."

"Oh, George!" she said helplessly, and the two of us started to laugh. Somehow Harry thought he was being made fun of, but there was nothing to be done about that.

I kissed her good-bye, then went around behind the car to shake hands. But I wasn't quick enough. Harry gunned the car into first and flashed his palm at me as he pulled away. I watched the car speed to the stoplight at the end of the block. I felt as if we had been going to run a race, a dumb little race between two boys in their own backyard, and that Harry had cheated in the stupidest way, by making a false start. I had suffered this very injustice from a fellow fac-brat at the Rectory, a neighbor of mine, when I was seven or eight, and even then I had been embarrassed for the kid, for thinking it meant anything if he won by cheating, and more than that, for being so stupid and obvious about it. Then as now, the lack of originality was depressing.

I was to meet Delia in a little French place downtown that Robbins had recommended. "I'm three for three with first dates there, Lenhart. You can't miss." I guess it was an oversight on my part that I didn't ask him why he was always going on first dates. There was a moment on the subway when I fantasized about telling her the whole story about Kate and Nick, just to have someone to tell—just for the satisfaction of telling it in its entirety. I managed to curb myself, but I am practically incapable of snapping out of a mood, and I'm afraid my preoccupation showed.

She was on time, which I appreciated but wasn't quite prepared for, and when we had squeezed ourselves into a corner table, the wine couldn't come fast enough. When it did, I ordered a gin and tonic as well. "You have to, you know, give it time to breathe," I said.

"Right."

"Would you like something?"

"I'll have the same."

We gulped them down and I remember I started off a bit wildly, by trying to convince her of my theory of Summer Displacement.

"Really," Delia said, when I had finished. "My friends and I never go anywhere. We stay in the city on weekends."

"Oh, right. Well, that's—different."

Then I rather rudely inquired, "So, does Harry take you out a lot?" For some reason I had the idea that Delia might have been his confidante.

But she said succinctly, "Not anymore."

The atmosphere was hopeless—hopelessly untenable. I could see the evening degenerating into one of Robbins's dates, during which he liked to "tell 'em the difference between a stock and a bond."

Then Delia said quietly, with the slightest jesting expression in her eyes: "He always used to say, 'Get whatever you want.' "

"Excuse me?"

"Harry—he used to tell me, 'Get whatever you want.' "

I gestured to the menu. "Get whatever you want," I said. "Anything. The steak—the surf and turf—"

"You shouldn't imitate him."

"I know."

"You're too good at it."

"Have you been out to his place in Southampton?"

"No."

And then all at once it was a relief, rather, to sit across the table from her after the long overnight of chaperoning. It was like moving to a new period in the Met. The palate was different, as Delia didn't tan. Her long brown hair hung heavily down around her pale, expressive face. And the tortoiseshell glasses were fascinating; I had an itch to reach out and remove them.

"I suppose you're opposed to the Hamptons in principle," I guessed, when our salads arrived.

"Oh no, not in principle," she replied. "You won't get me there. But I don't have any friends who go except Harry. And he's not likely to invite me."

"I would think he'd be begging you to come," I said.

"But he knows I won't sleep with him," Delia explained, "and he knows I would very much like to be invited."

We had finished our cocktails and started on the wine. I was glad to see she was drinking as fast as I was, so I wouldn't have to worry and pace myself.

"And because he knows I won't sleep with him but would very much like to be invited, he won't invite me. You see, he feels he'd be jeopardizing his position if he were to extend that kind of an invitation: he wouldn't *get* anything out of it."

"He'd be making a bad trade," I said.

"Precisely."

"It's funny, that's not the Harry I know," I said.

"Well, have you ever wanted anything from him?" she asked.

"No," I admitted.

"You see, if he did have me out, he'd have to assume I was only using him for his waterfront property."

"Well, would you be?" I inquired.

"No," she replied after a moment. "I like Harry. I mean, he's horrible, of course—in that way—"

"What way do you mean?" I said happily. "His manners?"

"Oh, no," Delia replied. "I don't mind if people are rude, really."

"You don't?"

"No, I'll trade manners for interesting. And I've dealt with much, much worse. No . . ." She looked up. "It's his new thing—he's become socially 'aware,' I guess you would say."

"You mean he's a social climber?" I said, because I thought she was being arch.

But Delia shook her head thoughtfully. "I don't mean that. Not exactly. Because that makes it sound as if it's calculated, and with Harry, I don't think it is. I think it's instinctive with him—he's always sniffing out the scent. But it's still embarrassing to be around. Like your Kate Goodenow," she said in a carefully neutral voice. "He's told me half a dozen times that she's got a house in Maine and a house in Newport and an uncle with a boat. Well, you know what I mean."

"Ye-es," I said slowly, "but I really don't believe it's the Maine ticket he's after." And I found I had spoken truthfully, whether or not Harry had realized it yet himself.

"I *think* I know what you mean," Delia said, but I could see she doubted me, or rather my motivation for making the statement.

I was hardly going to get into another discussion about Kate with her; anyway, I'm not sure I could have articulated it then. But that evening a theory began to form in my head about Harry's ambitions. It *wasn't* the obvious thing: it wasn't Maine or social access he was after, but something else about her, something utterly personal, that at the time I believed had nothing to do with money—it was Kate's complacency Harry coveted. And maybe he knew about the house in Newport and the house in Maine and Uncle Goodie's boat, but the need for information would not stop there—not if he had tried to look into Kate's eyes, as I had, and had instead confronted their opacity.

"But he is interesting," Delia was saying. "He's the most interesting person I know. And nobody's interesting anymore."

"Should we order another bottle?" I said hurriedly.

"Why not?"

It was one of those strangely agreeable dates. The whole evening I kept expecting Delia to say no. I figured she would decline a cocktail and say, "No, I'll just have the wine." I thought she would refuse dessert and drink an espresso with me. I even expected her to argue about the check, in a perfunctory way, after which I would insist. But I didn't have to insist. When the check came, she was good and drunk and hardly seemed to notice it. Nor did I have to insist on walking her home. She seemed grateful to take my arm and leaned on it comfortably as we walked the five blocks to her studio.

"Eh, *voilà*—the piano nobile," she announced, ushering me up a short flight of stairs.

She unlocked the door and I followed her into a rectangular room with a Murphy kitchen on one end. It was not a large room; a brown velvet couch and a pine-frame futon, facing off from opposite sides, occupied most of it, with a low table in between. The table was littered with magazines and coffee cups, and the rest of the room was crammed with a hodgepodge of collectibles: a shelf of cocktail shakers, a shelf of blue glass, a set of Dickens, a child's globe that glowed in the dark. There was a poster of Edith Piaf curling from the wall opposite the kitchen. It struck me as a friendly room, with character, but something about it alarmed me. It wasn't like my room, set up with no commitment at all, and it wasn't like Kate's apartment, which could have endured forever. There was some kind of truth in Delia Ferrier's apartment, some kind of reality I wasn't ready to reckon with. Delia herself was rummaging through the fridge. "I think I have some wine somewhere."

I opened my mouth to tell her not to bother—I had to go. "Oh, good," I said. "Do you mind if I stay for a minute?"

"I invited you in, didn't I?"

And when she joined me with two glasses, she had a look of wry expectancy as to how the evening was to continue. I hadn't expected that, either. Somehow I'd thought this young woman would be difficult—that she would put me in my place—and I had rather looked forward to being summarily turned down.

"Should I put some music on?"

"That would be nice."

And while there was a part of me that met each assent with a marveling at my luck, there was another part of me that dreaded the answer to why it didn't feel the same. The whole evening I'd had the idea that I would get through the date, push through it, the best I could, but then the strategy had proven unnecessary: she was good company, not taxing; she was better-looking than I remembered, not worse; she was happy to get drunk, not disapproving. And yet I couldn't seem to relinquish the mindset.

She had a giving body, Delia, when we embraced—it seemed almost thankful.

"Curves have gone out of fashion, I'm afraid," she said.

"My God—they shouldn't have," I said. I meant it, too. A whole world of possibilities presented itself to me when she took her shirt off. And once my hands found her breasts, I knew I was going to make it happen if I could.

"Really?" I inquired, sometime later. In the studio there had not, of course, been the sobering move from the living room to the bedroom.

"Well, we're not going to have ersatz sex all night, are we? I'm not fond of that."

"It does seem sort of pointless," I agreed.

Unfortunately, I'm sure the real thing proved just as irrelevant for Delia. Her face had been so animated all evening, but at the moment when I would have most liked specific reassurance, it went as neutral and pleasant as a mannequin's. I seemed to be alone in my sweaty, fleshy urgency, doing something I thought I'd forsworn once in adolescence, and once more since I came to New York—trying too hard: I couldn't seem to stop trying too hard.

Afterward, when I was lying on my back staring up at the ceiling, she said, "Don't stand on ceremony!" overly brightly, and added, "Don't you have to work tomorrow?"

"Yes. But—I'd like to stay," I got out miserably.

"Oh, no, please. Don't be silly. I really think it's time you got home."

She sounded like Mary Poppins, sending me briskly to bed, as she sat up and groped for her underwear. It was dusty in the room, and on top of the dust I could smell the kitchen spice rack a few feet away.

"Is my bra under there?"

I felt around for it. My father, I remembered, bizarrely, had always said "brassiere" on the rare occasions the word had come up, so now when people said "bra," to me it sounded like kids who called their mother "Ma."

"What is it with people?" I said weakly, as one is too apt to say, handing over the garment.

"People?" she repeated.

"Everyone's gotten so goddamn professional all of a sudden."

"Mmm . . . much easier that way."

We laughed a little, a little desperately. I hated to go, because then no matter what I did or said, that time with her would be over, and

I would have to start a new time, and all I could hear in my head was doubt, at the highest decibel.

"Look, I hate to say this—"

"Why? What do you hate to say?"

"No, it's not bad, it's just, it sounds wrong."

"Just say it."

"Well, exactly." I tried to think of a way out of the cliché, but there was no other way to leave. "I'll call you," I said finally.

She watched me get dressed by the light the street cast into the room. It was so bright it was almost like daylight. I pointed this out to Delia.

"Yes," she said. "It makes less of a difference when you sleep all day."

When I was ready to go, I thought I saw her expression change and admit some doubt, as well, but only for a moment.

"Listen, is it—?"

"No," said Delia, shaking her head as if dismissing a weakness of her own. "Nothing at all. I was just thinking—well, when I moved here."

"Uh-huh?"

She smiled wanly up at me. "It's just I had this idea that New York was going to be mostly cocktail parties where you would, you know, have the opportunity to recite 'Whan that Aprille.' "

I walked up the street toward the subway trying to do it so as not to think about anything else, but I got hung up where I always did—between "corages" and "Pilgrimages."

In our apartment I ran into Cara coming out of the bathroom, wearing one of Toff's T-shirts. "You're home late," she murmured sleepily, squinting without her contacts in.

"Yeah, you know."

"Get a little action, Georgie?"

"Cara, you've really got to stop—" But I couldn't hide the grin that crept, completely unexpectedly, across my face.

"Oh, my God!" Cara's hand went to her mouth. "Georgie got laid."

"Cara!"

"It's true, isn't it? Georgie—Georgie—Georgie got la-aid," she chanted.

I goosed her under the arms.

"Georgie! Owwwww!"

I wanted to thank her, really, or give her a kiss, for pointing out the possibility that it was that simple.

CHAPTER 15

Summer itself wore on like a doomed affair. One got through the days and emerged in darkness with the notion of doing something reckless, but it was hard to think of just what. It is hard to be reckless and still have one's shirts starched. That was how people our age wanted to play it: "wild" but safe. It seemed to me that Kate, at least, was giving it a good stab—I mean when she took up with Harry—until I realized that she was incapable of reckless behavior. It is next to impossible to be reckless with that kind of money as a buffer. Or perhaps it came down not to money but to one's personality. On the other side of recklessness lies remorse and after that regret, and regret wouldn't have occurred to her, really.

In the first week of the August heat wave, Robbins started sleeping with the only single woman in our Fordyce class because he said it was too hot to leave the office for courtship—well, he didn't say "courtship." Chat's air-conditioning broke—or rather Pam Allen's did, he was still camping out on her couch—so he checked himself into a midtown hotel, and when he called me he had been living there for two weeks. "It's great, George. You ought to check in yourself. I mean, I can get my *pants pressed* every night!" There was something about talking to him and knowing he would organize a crowd and we would go out soon that made me impervious to the oppression of work and of the heat. I found myself playing mind games with Daniels, being weirdly cheerful at home—complimenting Cara just for the hell of it—and eventually I asked myself why.

Of the fifteen or so young men and women Chat and Kate called their friends in New York, more than a few knew either Kate from Chatham or Chat from college (among other connections, and of course there was a great deal of overlap); in other words, I had gone to school with them, too—Billy P., Dick Scarum, Gretchen Willie— but I wouldn't have sought them out in New York. And had I known the others—the Cold Harbor kids, the Manhattan grade school friends—I think the same would have held true. In fact I had a hard time justifying to myself, though not admitting, their appeal. They were all attractive, certainly, and they all had good manners. And perhaps I am confessing my fatal flaw when I say that for long, long stretches of my life, this has often been answer enough. They weren't scintillating conversationalists; they weren't particularly talented. They certainly weren't hip. They did not have glamorous jobs. They weren't even rich-rich—not as rich goes in New York. What affecta-tions they did assume were so obvious as to be canceled out. But there was something about them. One night Harry told me what.

It was the night before the heat broke; I had met Chat after work in his room at the Drake. We played several hands of gin and ordered up room service and drank several glasses of gin, and from there we went to the Town Club. Chat had invented a new drink, which made its public debut that evening. The invention of the new drink called for us to make several phone calls and to rally Kate and Dick Scarum and his wife, Loribelle, and her sister, Amanda. Meanwhile Chat had made some friends: a man named Vincent, whose frequent, fervid appearances at the far right end of the bar belied the assumption that a certain type of character had died off long ago—the "Club man"; a thirty-five-year-old divorcée with a Palm Beach tan whose name I am sorry to say I have forgotten; and the divorcée's date for the evening, who turned out to be an undergraduate at Columbia. Just about the usual Town Club crowd on an off Wednesday.

Kate showed up with Harry in tow. Evidently she was taking him around with her now. His presence didn't seem to make any difference to anyone—perhaps we were all simply too hot. Even in Chat I could discern no real reaction; it was as if nothing had changed. Kate's friend Annie Roth (with whom, after the crank-calling prank, I had developed a phone camaraderie) had explained her theory to me: "He's like a coffee table that's a bit of a mistake, George, but once you get it home, you hardly notice because it holds your magazines so well."

"Lombardi, you want a Gin Wethers?" demanded Chat.

"No, I'm fine."

"Didn't ask how you were, Lombardi; I asked if you wanted a drink."

"Oh—yeah, heh, heh—make mine a Gin Wethers," Harry said.

"What's in these, Chattie?" the divorcée wanted to know. "They're *lethal*!"

"Get you another," giggled the undergraduate, who for reasons of his own was wearing black-tie.

After we had our drinks, Harry drew me to the side of the bar for the dreaded confidence. "Jeez, George, I been running around too much."

"Really."

"Yeah—boy, does Kate keep a busy social schedule!" He took a sip of his cocktail through the plastic stirrer.

It sounded like a line out of a mob movie: "a busy social schedule." I refused to take my cue.

Harry went on anyway: "Let's see, the other Wednesday, I guess it was, we hadda go to Annie's twenty-fifth uptown at—"

"La Boîte—I know. I was there after you left."

He nevertheless proceeded to account for the evening and for the last fortnight. When he told about a restaurant, he told what he ordered and what Kate had ordered, and whether the meal had been successful, culinarily speaking.

"So you and Kate are serious, then?" I broke in finally.

To my surprise he took the question, which I had posed intentionally to rattle him, with equanimity.

"Serious? Nah. She doesn't have a serious bone in her body. Or else she's all serious. I haven't figured out which. Oh, no. I don't pretend. . . . But listen here." He leaned in tight, as if offering me a tip on a horse: "Maybe if someone sprang it on her while she's young. She might go for it. Nobody else of her girlfriends has taken the plunge, right? I been noticing, and they're all on the brink, see . . ."

This time around I knew what "it" was. He thought that way; he would have had no interest in simply having an affair with her. He was the most goal-oriented person I had ever known. The present existed solely as a means for the achievement of his later goals. It was why people like Chat didn't get to him—not really. Strictly speaking, Chat had no effect at all on Harry.

"A lotta these kids weren't cool in high school," he went on, confidentially. "See, I was cool in high school. I had a car, I had a girlfriend—always had a girlfriend. I went to the junior prom when I was a sophomore and I went to the senior prom when I was a junior and when I was a senior, heh, heh, I had my own prom! You know, I lived with my dad after Mom split . . . this sicko batch pad. You'd wake up, nuke a hot dog, drink a Coke, tee off into Long Island Sound . . ."

He ambled back around to the point,—this idea he had—which struck me as strangely accurate: "It would mean something to her to be first," he said simply. "Uncharted territory. Pioneer spirit. And," he added obliquely, "we'd have a lot of money."

Before long the evening went the way of all Town Club evenings: desultory conversations in which points were too earnestly made; club soda'd attempts to make it all right. At some point Chat and I had adjourned to the library to have a serious talk.

"How serious are they?" I asked him.

"How serious do you think?" he spat out.

"Not marriage, then?"

"Are you on *drugs*, Lenhart?" He looked appalled.

"It's just—I heard a rumor."

"Oh, that's just Katie having fun." But a moment later Chat took a book from a shelf and hurled it violently across the room. It sat there where it landed, spine up, pages splayed, like a woman dropped on the dance floor, obscenely exposing flesh. "Beale, and now this!" Chat cried. "God, will she grow up."

"Why would she want to do that?" I said.

To his credit he saw the humor.

We went back downstairs to the bar. "Come on, we're going," announced Kate. "We're bored. Mr. Vincent is going to take us to the Racquet Club now. Two cabs—"

"I don't like that club," interrupted Chat.

"Oh, don't you?"

"No."

"And?"

"I'll think of something better to do."

"What are you? A dark cloud raining on all the fun?"

"Speaking of the fun, who's picking this up?" Chat looked imperiously from one to another of us. The undergraduate slurped his Gin Wethers in a hurry. I myself had a sudden, fervent wish to say coolly, "Would ten thousand cover it?" and write out a check. Chat had never made me feel uncomfortable about drinking on his tab, but I wondered uneasily if the two kinds of debt weren't associated now, in his mind.

Chat's eyes rested, presently, on Harry. "Lombardi. Are you a member yet?"

"No."

"For Chrissake! What's taking you so long?"

There was an excruciating pause. "I can give you the cash—" Harry began.

"For*get* it, man. Your money's no good here." Chat took a final survey and found us wanting. "Sammy! The check, sir!"

"Thank you, Chat," Kate said sweetly.

"Dammit, Katie! You run up my tab!"

"Well, what does a Gin Wethers cost, Chattie?"

"Ask your big brainiac here, why don't you? He's probably got 'em calculated in his head." He turned to Harry. "Do you? Could you tell me what a Gin Wethers costs? Fair market value, of course."

"I'd have to know what was in it," Harry said steadily. "How many kinds of alcohol."

"Ha, ha, ha, ha, ha!" Chat spouted his affected laugh. "I knew you'd try to get it out of me, and you never will! Nice try, buddy!" With a brutal pen swipe he signed the check.

"All right, two cabs to the Racquet Club," said Mr. Vincent, with a diffident air.

"We could walk," someone suggested.

"It's too hot to walk," Chat said.

On Park Avenue between Fifty-second and Fifty-third streets, on the block directly across from the Racquet Club, there are two long wading pools of about twenty feet by forty feet with fountains at the ends. They are not more than two and a half feet deep. A shallow breaststroke hits the bottom; I would recommend a modest dead man's float instead.

Chat was the first to take off his clothes. "I said I'd think of something better, and I did!" He stripped down to his boxers and pussy-footed around, testing the waters. When Kate joined him, the drivers got out of their limos to watch and leer, a joyful noise going up at the good story there would be to tell that night. Then the rest of us stripped down to our underwear and went in, all except for Mr. Vincent and Harry. Mr. Vincent stood watching from the corner of the block with a furtive, prurient interest.

Dick Scarum's wife had an elaborate hairdo and didn't want to get her hair wet, so Kate sneaked up behind her and pushed her under. "Oh, God *damn* you, Kate!" Loribelle came up, sputtering. "Would you look at this, Dick? Dick, *look at my hair!* I just had it *done!*"

"Aw, Lori, now, don't get mad at Kate."

"Don't get mad? Don't get mad?"

Kate had stood up dripping, exulting, in the middle of the pool. She looked around for her next victim and shouted at Harry to come in.

But he wouldn't be budged. "I got a cold, Kate! Summer cold! You don't wanna mess with temperatures when you got a cold!" And a little later, as I worked myself back into my clothes, he confided, "In the past I would have gone in. But now I don't have to." And then he continued in what I thought was a curious vein. "She doesn't know it, but Kate doesn't really want me to go in. See those guys out there?" We looked to where Dick and Chat and the undergraduate were continuing to romp semi-naked. "She doesn't want to marry a guy like that." He offered no apology for the comment. After a moment I found I agreed.

We watched the group of them leap out of the pool and seize their clothing. Chat picked Kate up, piggyback. She put her hands over his eyes and screamed when he tried to buck her off. "This is great, guys—this'll go down in history!" Dick Scarum yelled, standing up mid-pool in his boxer shorts. "This is like the time at Chatham my brother brought the cow into the chapel! That was before your time, guys, but you remember it, don't you?"

Dick was the last one out. He didn't want to get out. Loribelle had to plead with him to get dressed. Then she wanted to take him home, immediately, and give him hell. Before he left Kate's cousin put up a hand all around. As he waved good-bye, he seemed to me like a man defeated, vanquished by nostalgia.

"It's funny," I confessed to Harry. "I ought to get going, too. I don't know why I stay. I don't know what it is that keeps me—"

"They're that word you can't use anymore," Harry interrupted.

It took me a moment but I got it. They weren't exactly happy—that was too profound. "You're right," I said. "They're gay."

They were gay. If you went out with the crowd two or three times, you might notice a brittleness to the gaiety. You would not notice it the first time or the tenth time, but you would see it in new people who came out, the second or third time they came out, and you could see it in newcomers like Dick Scarum's wife. You would notice the brittleness hitting them and weighing them down in moments of repose, when they thought no one was looking at them.

The brittleness arose because theirs—ours—was a quoted gaiety. We were the last generation of the century to come of age, and the first one that wanted to be as much like our parents' as possible. We ought to have started a revolution; instead we bought cocktail shakers. Chat wanted to start a revolution: to bring back the old telephone nomenclature, PLaza 5 and MUrray Hill 4.

The fashions the girls wore, too, were in a fervent cycle of regeneration. Take Dick's wife, Loribelle, for instance. One night she was dressed in a forties-style outfit, and the next night the seventies, and then one disconcerting night the eighties. She wasn't the brightest girl, and Chat used to tease her, asking her once, "What if there was an early nineties revival?" Without missing a beat, she said, "You mean like mini-backpacks? That kind of thing?"

But somehow we must have sensed our failing, that we weren't making it new. None of us was. And that was where the brittleness came from. There was only one new thing and it didn't have a name yet. Harry Lombardi knew what it was. The way he was planning on making his money: that was new.

Bits of the idea had trickled down to me, until I had a vague grasp that the company was to help Luddites like me—"Just like you, George, I'm not kidding. People with no skills at all, even!"—access the coming network of information. One word that always came up when Harry discussed the infrastructure that would facilitate his plan was "protocol," and I found its recurrence somewhat comical. I remember a conversation we had that same night, when the group had adjourned, clammy and obnoxiously dripping, to the bar at the Racquet Club. Harry had a go at speaking what he assumed was my language. "Let's say you belonged to a country club when you were little, George."

"Sorry, I didn't."

"You didn't?"

"No."

"Really? Gosh." Harry frowned; banished the frown. "Well, let's just *say* you did."

"Okay."

"And maybe there was a certain way to act or dress at your country club that wouldn't have been the way to act or dress at the country club in the next town over. But let's say the two country clubs wanted to have a party together—you know, for, uh, the Fourth of July, with maybe, say, swimming and tennis. Well, then they'd have to get together and decide what the *protocol* would be."

"What if there was a dance afterward?" I said.

"Yeah, exactly!" Harry exclaimed. "That's what I mean—that's even better, George! You're really getting this. Well, the individual computer networks are like country clubs, and they've all figured out how to throw their big party. That's all been done! But not everyone knows how to find it, or how to get in. Let's say that *you* want to join. You want to go to this big party—*you*, George."

"I'm not sure I'd get in."

"Oh; you'll get in—with my help."

"It does sound fun," I agreed.

"I'm tellin' you, you're not gonna *believe* how fun it'll be."

At that point Kate had come tripping over to see what we were up to. "So serious over here in the corner. That can't be good!"

"Harry's going to show me how to get me into a country club," I couldn't resist saying.

"George!"

When Kate had taken him away to talk to Mr. Vincent about investing, I sipped another Gin Wethers and thought about the theory I had begun to form on my date with Delia—one that Delia herself would have taken issue with. Perhaps she was right; perhaps I was missing something insidious because through association I happened to be on the receiving end of Harry's aspirations. But it didn't make sense to me—his personality simply didn't add up. By all rights he should have been worried about protecting the ground he had gained with Kate, in Kate's world; instead he had invited Chat out for dinner to discuss investing. And even the company he was starting was too ironic: it was catholic in nature. It was all about letting people in.

CHAPTER 16

I later heard that a friend of the Wetherses had been passing by in a cab and had recognized Chat and Kate bathing in their underwear on Park Avenue. Eventually my name was also connected with the incident and Daniels looked at me with a new kind of respect. But that consolation, and laughable legitimization, came several weeks afterward; it always did.

For waking up after a night like that, one would feel like a banished soul. It was no use calling anyone. There were dictates on how much fun one was allowed to have, and one of them said that after having a great deal of it—like that, all at once—there would be no more fun for some time. One simply had to wait, alone and sweating, for the whirl to come around again. It was taking your medicine and everyone understood this and no one was so foolish as to call.

Labor Day rolled around and I skipped a train to Southampton, then two more trains, and finally went home and turned down a perfectly good offer to go out drinking with Toff and some friends of his.

The friends came over, they went out, and I was left alone. I knew I ought to have rallied and gone downtown with them, but I just couldn't face the idea of trying to make something of the night.

When it got dark, I skulked out to the deli to get a Coke. There was some initial comfort in the horror of it—alone in the city on the last Friday night of the summer—and I was beginning to feel rather defiant about it when, in the deli line, I recognized a girl from college. She was two ahead of me. Her hair was pulled back in a ponytail and the ponytail was stuck through the back of her Dartmouth baseball cap. She was wearing big Dartmouth sweatpants and buying a two-liter bottle of Diet Coke and a quart of ice cream and a bag of potato chips. "I don't need a bag," she mumbled, and looking guilty, she stuffed everything into the plastic bag she was already carrying, which bore the logo of a national video store chain. After she left I noticed that the guy behind her was wearing a cap as well, from his university, and had a bag from the same video store and was buying ice cream and beer. I was behind him wearing a Dartmouth T-shirt and buying Cokes. It struck me that all over the city the useless college graduates of American universities were skulking out of their apartments in sweatpants and falsely jaunty caps and returning with unsavory little plastic bags of junk food to stuff into their mouths while they watched their rented movies. And somehow I did not think that the same thing was happening all over Paris, but perhaps I was wrong. I had never spent a night there hoarding a little plastic bag of food watching a rented movie, but perhaps I had only been trying to live up to the context, while the native Parisian twenty-to-thirty-year-olds spent their evenings in just this way. Then I decided I would rent a movie, too.

There was nothing I wanted to see, however. Mostly I just rent the same two movies—one is about a hockey team and one is about a rock band—and both were gone. After sitting at the kitchen table and staring blankly at the salt and pepper for half an hour I came to the conclusion that something had to happen. It was a miserable thought, for whenever one thinks it, nothing ever does, and one spends an evening staring one's appalling obscurity in the face, and answers the telephone too brightly. Except for that evening, when the buzzer rang. "They've gone," I said into the intercom, but the ringing persisted. "Yes?"

"Gentleman here would like to come up."

"Who is it, please?"

After a moment the doorman gave the name, and I went to unlock the bolt. It was the second time that summer Harry had provided me with some distraction, and as always I knew I would disapprove of most of what he had to say and of whatever premise had brought him here. But I understood, too, how easily held my position was, and how false. I had always understood this, but it did not stop me from disapproving of him.

He was as haggard as I had ever seen him. The circles under his eyes were so dark they looked etched onto his face. He was wearing one of his custom suits, and it looked as if it had been slept in not just last night, as they often did, but all the past week.

He stood there poker-faced when I opened the door, the blue eyes the only living things in his face. "Is anyone else here?" he whispered, leaning forward a notch to peer into the apartment.

I assured him that I was alone.

Even in his strung out condition the fact made Harry wince. "Well, that's okay," he said after a moment. "It's actually you I came to see." He entered the apartment cautiously, as one enters the room of a patient when one is not quite sure how sick the patient is. I could see he was drunk, but not sloppily.

I showed him in and fixed him what we had—cheap vodka on freezer-burned ice; even the tonic was flat. To my surprise this produced no comment. He took the glass without a word, drained it, and walked unseeingly to the living room window. For several minutes he stood there motionless, as if trying to stare down the lights on Roosevelt Island. "George: sit down," he said, when he finally turned into the room.

I did so, on an arm of the couch, feeling that the order was given for effect, and more than a little repulsed by the theatricality of it. With difficulty I met his eyes.

"George, if I were to tell you something—I mean, not one particular thing . . .

"George, what I came here to say . . ."

After another false start or two, he found a way in. "George, do you know what my father does for a living?"

I didn't know the word for Mr. Lombardi's profession. "He's . . . an architect, isn't he?" I said.

"No," Harry said. "He's not an architect. He's a builder."

"Oh."

"He builds six-, seven-, eight-bedroom houses in Glen Cove, Locust Valley. . . . If one doesn't sell, we sell our house and move into it."

I nodded, uncertain as to the correct response.

"He started out working construction, and he moved up. Hit the market dead-on. It's all in the timing; you have that, you have it all. Timing's off, you got nothing. Now I'm going to tell you something, George, and I don't want you to take it the wrong way."

"All right."

Harry's eye contact was relentless, searching my eyes for a latent bias. "My father never went to college," he said. "I'm one of those kids who got into Dartmouth based on intelligence alone."

It was highly comic, the way he phrased it, and pathetic, too—not the information but his conviction that it was news.

"Didn't want Harvard. Didn't want Yale. I wanted the Big Green all the way."

"So you got what you wanted," I suggested, but he had warmed to his confessional. I could feel a headache starting behind my eyes, and I had to force myself not to look at my watch.

"You know, I used to tell people I was from Glen Cove. But I never lived there more than six months. We never lived in any of those houses long enough to set them up. And two guys—you don't really need much furniture, you know what I mean?"

"Sure," I said. "I know what you mean."

Evidently my empathy was not convincing, however, for Harry added hurriedly, "It's not that we didn't have a good time, don't get me wrong. Hell, we had a *great* time on our own. We threw some sick parties, let me tell you. My dad used to party right along with us. You know, it was a rite of passage at the high school to shotgun a beer with Daddy-o. I kid you not, George, I kid you not."

He paused as if to consider the implications of the fact, and there he was: trapped like everyone between self-pity and the brag. His mom had split for Florida when he was twelve, with the two younger brothers, but he had stayed on Long Island with Daddy-o. "I couldn't just *leave* the guy!"

Most people wouldn't have been able to pull it off, a monologue like the one Harry gave me that night; most people would have started apologizing for talking too much. But perhaps when confession is a part of your religion, it is only natural to want to run through the whole guilty spiel in front of an audience. And at the end, perhaps I would absolve him of being guilty of that happy American sin, of making a hell of a lot more money than he had grown up with—not that his dad had done badly!

"Not at all, don't get me wrong, occasionally there was a cash flow problem—"

And then of the sin that the first sin begot so naturally, of casting a belatedly covetous eye toward a new milieu—of upgrading from a Cara to a Kate. I suspect it says more about me than Harry that this was the absolution I thought he was after.

He touched in a desultory fashion on the salient points—his belated conversion, for instance, from heavy metal to classic rock—and as he talked I could see the shrunken concert T-shirt, feel the heat rising from the tar of the beach parking lots where he had hung out, trying to get girls like Cara McLean to give him a chance.

"I got that over with early, George, as it turned out"—the circumlocution was marvelous—"and all through high school I had a pretty good run. Now, I'm not a good-looking guy, I'm not saying that. But I was persistent, George. Persistent as hell. I learned that lesson very, very early."

That night I understood more fully the kind of man Harry was. He was the kind of guy whom girls would lie to one another about sleeping with, not simply because they had—anyone could get drunk and have a bad night, after all—but because they had enjoyed it.

It was a dark, trashed house, the house they went back to, the only one they managed to keep—tiny, with three or four cars in the driveway which together were worth twice the house. "My dad was really into cars, see."

Sometimes a girl would take a fancy to Mr. Lombardi. "Oh, no, nothing like that. But you know how sometimes one of these kinda lost girls will have a thing for an older man? The most he ever did was hug 'em a little, and if they really had no place to go, Dad'd let them sleep on the couch." In the morning the girl might do a little housekeeping to ingratiate herself with the Lombardi men, "or one time a girl made pancakes." But there were long stretches where it was just beer and microwaved hot dogs, and the families at St. Catherine's turning around in their pews to stare when the two skulked in ungroomed for a Saturday night Mass.

The computers he taught himself. It was the only thing he really liked to do, play video games and mess around with programs in the basement. It kept him busy when his dad was out and kept him out of the way when Mr. Lombardi was home with a lady friend. It wasn't even that he was good at it; he was, but that never occurred to him; it was just something he did.

"I guess that was lucky," I offered.

"Lucky?" Harry said quickly. He scrutinized me from his stance in front of the window. "In what way was it lucky?"

"Broder," I said, "of course, and now the company, and you're only twenty-four." But reassurance about specific accomplishments wasn't what he was after; it never had been. He wanted a grand pronouncement. He wanted to know how it would all add up. But only the green screen of his monitor could help him there, and I very much regretted introducing the topic.

"George," Harry demanded, "would you say that overall, I mean speaking in a very overall sense, I'm a lucky person?"

I don't remember how I got out of that one, but shortly thereafter Harry seemed to be seized by an internal claustrophobia. He loosened his tie in jerks and stuck his neck out through the shirt collar like a swimmer gasping for air. "Jeez, it's hot! What do you have the A.C. set on?"

"I don't know. It's in Toff's room."

"You mean you only got one? Jeez, George! What are you, some kind of twentieth-century martyr?"

"Do you want some water?"

This was dismissed with a shake of his head. He took a deep, shuddering breath, as if to calm himself, and when he did speak again, he clasped his hands pompously behind his back. With the interruption, the story of his childhood had been forgotten, tucked away and written off. Evidently it could hold his attention for only so long before his mind latched onto some new topic and he abandoned the previous one, as he had abandoned Cara McLean on the couch at our party.

"George—" There was an irritating note of condescension in his voice. He pronounced my name gently, gravely, as if he were afraid of spoiling some notion of mine with the hard facts he was about to present: that he had slept with my girlfriend, perhaps.

"George."

"Yes, Harry?"

He had the air of a child who has received an embarrassingly good Christmas gift. "Kate has accepted me."

It was gorgeous, the pomposity of the statement. I had a great urge to laugh. He sounded as though he had been practicing it for years—"Kate and I are getting married," "Kate said yes"—before settling on something he read in a book somewhere.

"That's wonderful!" I heard myself saying, and adding, irrelevantly, for we had none, "We—we ought to break open champagne!" I managed to stutter out a handful of inadequate congratulations and then asked, "When did all of this happen? I haven't spoken—"

"Last night," he interrupted, searching my eyes again, looking from one pupil to the other, yet oddly silent for a man who appeared to have the world to say.

"Last night? And where is Kate now? I want to call her."

"Oh, no," he said reprovingly. "Kate's gone up to Maine. She'll be asleep by now. Oh, yes"—he glanced at his watch—"definitely by now."

"Gone up to Maine? This weekend?"

"Of course. I wouldn't ask her to miss it."

"I know. I just meant—"

"She had it all planned, George."

"I see."

"I coulda gone!" Harry insisted. "It's not like I couldna gone!"

"Well, yes, of course, you could have gone. Next week, then. We'll have to have dinner together . . ." I groped on in a surreal fashion. "I had a feeling this might—"

Harry gripped my arm. "You did? This had occurred to you before, then?"

"You told me the other night."

"No, but before that," he pressed me. "Before I said anything?"

"When you started dating, of course I wondered, or expected—"

"Are you telling the truth?" he demanded.

I was spared from telling the whole truth when Harry's face cracked and every pretense of taking the fact in stride fell away. With a convulsive sob he sank down into Toff's reclining chair. I wished very much he had sat on the couch. It was hard to watch a man bawling on a La-Z-Boy.

"Look," I began, with no idea of how to continue. I myself hardly felt the effect of the news at all. It was like watching a play so thinly plotted that when the dramatic twist arrives, one only wishes it to pass as quickly as possible, to save the audience the embarrassment. But the actors go on saying their lines, because they have to. "What's wrong, Harry?" I asked. "You should be happy."

Harry raised his face. "It's not true, is it George?" he murmured. "I knew it was half a joke—I asked her on a lark! I got my stake out of China, spent fifty on the ring. One, two, three, sapphire, diamond, sapphire, little blue Tiffany box. I asked her on a lark, she must have said yes on a lark. She'll wake up tomorrow and it'll be off, won't it?"

He called seven years' labor a lark. And yet that was precisely it: she had said yes on a lark. And yet again, that did not mean it would be called off, that did not mean that the lark could not continue indefinitely. With Kate, that did not really mean anything. I think that was the first moment the news took on an element of reality for me.

"It's just new, that's all. And it's what you said: you're the first."

Harry's hands curled into fists and drummed the arms of the recliner. "We are the first. We are the first, dammit! There's that. She's beating all her friends." He began to tick off the names of Kate's girlfriends—Annie Roth, Jess Brindle, Vanessa Prince. It was curious to hear him recite the names of those girls, whom, except for Annie, I knew only enough to say hello to. It made him seem more entrenched.

I seemed to have hit the right note, however. He stood up abruptly and marched off to the bathroom. The tap ran for several minutes and then he returned, snorting loudly and swallowing. But when he spoke, his voice was hollow in his throat. "George, she doesn't want me."

"Stop it right now," I ordered, with, I thought, foresight of what was to come: a tiresome, sleepless night of consolation in which I would fail to convince Harry that he was good enough for Kate. "Don't go undermining yourself. It's boring."

"No," Harry said. I felt his eyes on me then, assessing me. His voice had turned cold, clinical almost. "I don't mean like that. I mean she doesn't . . . desire me."

I drew back, surprised into asking, "Don't you sleep together?" as Kate's rose and white bedroom floated up in my mind.

"Oh, yeah-yeah-yeah-yeah-yeah," he said, in the manner that he had said, "Don't get me wrong, we had a *great* time," and began to talk very quickly, pacing about the small room. I noticed how difficult it was for a short man to pace convincingly; there was something emasculating about it. He was better standing still. "I'm over there all the time. I practically *live* over there, George. You ever been there? Yeah, well, you know. You should see us in the mornings. It's so goddammed civilized! I read the *Journal* and the *Post* and she orders in coffee and—and it's like we're already married, you know? Like you know how when you're married, you read the paper together? We read the paper together. I read the sports pages and the financial section." He paused expectantly.

"And what—what section does Kate read?" I said inanely.

"Well, she doesn't really read the paper," he said, sounding annoyed.

"Oh," I said.

"We're going to work it all out when she comes back from Maine. We're going to go up to Maine together at the end of the month and see where we want to have the tent. We're going to have a long engagement—Kate likes that. She likes the fuss, you know?" The entire speech sounded like "gunna, gunna, gunna, gunna, gunna." "Kate could get married in New York if she wanted to, but we're going to get married in Maine. We both like it better in Maine. We're going to spend every summer up there. And our kids—our kids"—it took him three tries to get his head around the idea—"our kids are going to spend every summer there. They're going to grow up there."

He went on for another moment or two, building summer cottages in the sky, until he stopped quite dead. "And we're gunna—" But he couldn't think of another thing they were going to do. He looked across at me with the mute expectancy I'd been dreading. It was very awkward. He had chosen a confessor and evidently wanted this sin of omission coaxed from him.

"We have everything, George," he murmured. "Everything."

"But you don't . . ." I started reluctantly. There was only one way to put it: "have sex?"

For a moment Harry looked through me to a point on the wall, seeming to see the series of scenes that had led to this moment. He said hoarsely: "I *try* to . . . I don't know. Sometimes we . . ."

"Harry, don't tell me anything you—"

"It's so strange," he went on in an eerily calm tone, as if talking to himself. "We'll be out somewhere, and I can tell, you know, that she—I mean, if it were any other girl, I'd *know* that the minute we got home—!" He looked wistful as he said this, as if in memory of simpler times, with simpler girls. The look faded; he seemed to take himself in hand mentally. "But then once we're home . . ."

"You have trouble going—?"

"George," Harry broke in abruptly, "is there such a thing as a girl being . . ." He ran a hand through his thick, receding hair several times. "As a girl being frigid?"

I laughed, an unconvincing, foolish laugh. "It's such a fifties word," I said. "I don't know what it means, really."

"I mean a girl who doesn't like sex," Harry said clearly. "Who gets no enjoyment out of the act. The actual act."

"With the wrong person . . ."

"No, I don't mean that. I don't mean degrees. I mean is there a scientific diagnosis for—oh, *God*!"

He buried his face in his hands, I got up to make us another round, and that was how Cara found him when she let herself in with Toff's key.

CHAPTER 17

The door closed too loudly, as if she'd been going to slam it and had then thought better of it. Coming out of the bathroom once, I had caught her and asked her not to slam it again; our relations had been rather cooler since.

Cara's high heels clicked on the parquet floor and then she made her entrance: the righteously offended woman. It was lovely to see her modify this in a flash of opportunism when she spotted Harry weeping.

"Hello, Cara," I said.

"George, *hi*"—cozy, the good sport, finding nothing curious in the situation—"how's it going?"

Harry gave another great snuffle and arranged his features into a dull placidity. "Cara." He cleared his throat with determination. "Cara, how are you?"

"Fine, fine—just fine—great. Didn't expect to find *you* here."

"Yeah." Harry gave a forced laugh. "Keeping George out of trouble."

"We all do that! Georgie keeps us busy with that, don't ya, George!" Her lips turned up to indicate gaiety, but her eyes were working a million miles an hour, drawing conclusions—leveraging, as they said in the office, her assets. She pranced farther into the room. "Hope I'm not interrupting!"

From the couch Harry made a slow, indifferent assessment. "You look good," he offered.

"Aw, Henry—"

But he was right. The summer was the right time for a body like hers, and she was tanned to within an inch of her life. Everything else was frosted, her hair, her nails—I thought suddenly of the big boat in Sag Harbor: it wasn't my kind of thing, her look, but you had to give it credit.

"No, I mean it. How you been?"

"Good! I been good! Real good."

I was all set to ask her to leave, to save Harry more embarrassment. But as I got up to fix the drinks, it dawned on me that Cara was just the thing you needed at a time like this; she was just what the doctor ordered. I looked over at Harry, and he was kind of grunting and laughing at the things she said.

I found a stray beer for Cara and made two more feeble vodka tonics for Harry and me.

"That all you got, huh?" she said. "Too bad we weren't at my place. I've got my collection. I collect all kinds of alcohol, so no matter what somebody wants, they can always have it."

"That's a good idea," said Harry.

He dragged the recliner over and we all sat down and smoked a cigarette. It was static in the room, and yet comfortable somehow. "Hey," said Harry, "why don't blondes like vibrators?" He paused a beat. "Too hard on the teeth."

"My virgin ears!" Cara objected. "Please!"

"Ha, ha, ha," said Harry. "You used to tell—"

"Shut up!" she cut him off. Then she snickered and said, "All right, listen up. What do a tornado and a redneck divorce have in common?"

"You're bad, Cara, you know that."

"Somebody's gonna lose a trailer!"

"God, even George liked that one," remarked Harry.

They went on like that—blondes, feminists, rednecks. Then Harry wanted to do a card trick, so I found the cards. Then Cara tried to do one but it didn't come out right. "That's not your card?"

"It's not my card," I said.

"Are you sure it's not your card? It's gotta be your card!"

"It's not my card."

"Are you sure?"

"I think I know what card I picked."

"Don't laugh, it's not funny!"

"It is funny," said Harry. "It's fucking hysterical!"

"George, tell him not to laugh at me! I'm gonna kill you if you laugh one more time!" Cara stood up and play-punched him.

Her body had been stair-mastered and sculpted and treadmilled into its lean, taut, menacing form, and the very presence of it was like a compliment, and Harry was man enough to take the compliment. As for me, I liked her more that night than ever before. Cara could sense my indulgence and she began to tease me and tap my arm to emphasize a point, and then she and Harry put their heads together because they were going to set me up, they were going to find a girl for me, a really great girl.

"I got tons of friends for you, Georgie! If you'd only ever asked. If you woulda said something, I coulda had you introduced to all my girlfriends by now!"

"George wouldn't like your friends," Harry said.

"That's an obnoxious thing to say!"

"He wouldn't," Harry said, taking a last drag of his cigarette.

Some time later we had run out of card tricks and jokes and Harry had taken off his jacket and his tie and he was still hot.

"Whatta you have the A.C. on?" Cara asked me.

"I don't know—it's Toff's."

"And so you're not allowed to touch it? Please!" She rose and clicked into Toff's bedroom. "I cranked it way up," she said when she came back. "*Way* up."

"Thank God for that!" Harry said.

"C'mere." Cara scooted to the corner of the couch so she could lay a hand on his forehead. "Jeez, you're hot. You sure you're not sick or anything?"

"Naw. I'm not sick. I'm just hot."

There was a silence then, of a kind that I hadn't heard since college but that anyone who has ever had a roommate could not fail to understand. And as always with this kind of silence, I wondered how I had failed to hear it earlier, and I had the same sensation I had always had, though it lasted only a second or two. It was like being slapped in the face. I mumbled something about having to be up early and stood up to excuse myself, taking my glass with me.

"Don't go to bed now, George!" cried Cara predictably.

"Yeah, George," Harry breathed, "you should stay up with us."

With my back to them I raised my glass to demur and to say good night. I didn't want to turn around and see the guilty gladness on their faces.

In the early hours of the morning I woke to hear them moving on the couch. They were talking still, murmuring to each other in low voices. I heard Harry say, "You are truly heaven-sent." It seemed to me the one compliment that could make Cara blush.

But the night was not quite over. Coming out of my bedroom at six or seven, I met Harry sneaking through the living room.

"Jesus! I thought you were the goddamn boyfriend!"

"Toff's *home*?" I said.

"He's in bed with her! I've been hiding in the fucking closet for an hour!"

"So get the hell out of here," I hissed.

"I can't—I can't find my shoes!"

"Borrow a pair of mine," I said grimly.

"I can't! I can't! No offense, George, but these are four-hundred-dollar loafers from Italy that you can only buy . . ."

At the door he stuffed his tie into his pocket, licked his hand, and plastered his hair down against his skull. "How do I look?"

"Frightening." I meant to be funny, but I was sorry the minute I said it. He was crestfallen. You couldn't talk that way with Harry.

Wearily, I made the gesture of following him out to the elevator. "Listen, George," he began nervously. I knew what was coming, and in order to prevent him from saying it, I fixed him with as black a look as I could muster. But the bastard couldn't help himself. "Listen, George," he said again, passing his tongue over his lips, "don't tell Kate, okay? I mean, I would appreciate it if you didn't tell Kate. Don't get me wrong, it's not that I don't trust you . . ."

I think it was their lack of a sense of humor that tried my patience, more than the general sordidness of the evening. I had the sneaking suspicion both Harry and Cara saw this, their second and (one presumed) final episode together as the third act in a little tragedy about star-crossed lovers. Each of them had a dangerously melodramatic narrative bent, which the other's presence must have reinforced.

In light of what happened later, however, I have had to revise my opinion slightly. Cara's performance that evening was much, much better than either Harry or I observed. Even her body had underlined it, as if, like a Method actor, she had gotten into the right shape for the part. We had presented her with so many opportunities to give herself away and yet she had the wit to wait. I wish I could say to her now, Well played, Cara, well played.

CHAPTER 18

After Kate and Harry got engaged, Kate's crowd splintered for a little while. I didn't hear much from either of them, nor from Chat, but I had not expected to. I knew Chat wouldn't like to call me out of the fear that I would try to sympathize with him, which would have been intolerable to him, and I didn't like to call him for the same reason, lest he think I was checking up on him, to make sure he was all right. As for Kate, I gathered she was going around with her girlfriends most of the time; Annie Roth used to call me and keep me informed.

She was much too polite to say a word about Harry. "We're thrilled for Kate, we all are. It's just what she wanted. We couldn't be happier." And yet there was the slightest note of jealousy in her voice, which indicated Harry had been right: it did mean something to them that Kate was going to be first.

"And who are you saving yourself for, George?" she wanted to know. "We ought to get you out with us one night."

"Nothing would make *me* happier." She was great fun, Annie was.

She was one of those chubby, tartan-wearing lacrosse girls—the daughter, perhaps, of a man who had wanted sons. She was good-natured to the core, and could hold her liquor, too.

When I got off the phone I sat at my desk brooding. *Kate was engaged.* It was time I dated someone—Annie or the elusive Jess Brindle, if she would have me, or even one of Robbins's devotees. I guess it was just bad timing that that was the week Delia Ferrier got around to returning my call.

I had left the message weeks before, in an amnesiac moment, when the tone of our date escaped me. The words never matter, in books or on dates; it is the tone I've learned that survives. On the night we went out again, it came back to me with chilling clarity: ambivalence had been my attitude, covered up in desperation.

This time it was one of those dates on which you play out the entire relationship between seven and midnight. At seven, in a bar near her apartment, we were laughing about our first date, chalking it up to a ridiculous past.

"We shouldn't have—"

"But we did. It was stupid. My fault."

"But it doesn't matter. I mean ultimately—"

"No, but I have to apologize."

"No, but I don't want you to apologize."

At eight, we were having a burger across town.

"It's crazy about Harry and your friend Kate, isn't it?" she said.

"Don't you love just having a simple burger and a Coke? I think I could eat here every night."

"When are they going to get married?"

"Waiter! Next summer, I think. Kate wants a long engagement."

"That's not that long—it's already November."

At nine or ten we tried to go to the movies, but everything was sold out.

"Let's go to a bar," I said.

"Or we could just go somewhere and talk."

"We could do that," I agreed. We found a coffee shop. But I

couldn't think of what I wanted to order, and I had already slept with her. Dating was a farce, an utter farce. The only people worth dating were the people you already knew.

"Next week a friend of mine is performing a show she wrote—"

"Oh, yes?"

"I don't know if it's your kind of thing, but—"

"No, no," I insisted, "it sounds interesting." I gave up trying to decide what I wanted and smiled vaguely across the table at her intelligent face. I worried about that face. I had started something. I had put something in motion when I shouldn't have, and soon it would be too late to stop it. I remember a bunch of girls walked by outside then, laughing. One of them looked like Annie, but I couldn't be sure. I had a great longing to be out with them, making frivolous remarks. Then the waiter came to take our order. "The problem is," I told him, "I don't really want anything."

At eleven, we stood on the stoop of Delia's apartment building and broke up.

She invited me in again, and this time I hedged vocally. I hated what my pathetic hemming and hawing did to her expression, and determined to tell the truth. "It's just, I guess you should know," I explained. "I—I really just want to have fun right now."

"Fun," Delia repeated.

"It's just that I don't have much time. I work all the time, and when I go out . . ."

"I see." She frowned thoughtfully, looking down at her hands. "Is it still Kate Goodenow?"

It wasn't, actually, that simple, but how could I have explained it? What could I have said to Delia Ferrier, of the tortoiseshell glasses? Could I have explained that the only true gaiety in life was played out against a static background and that girls like Annie and Jess Brindle—and Kate—provided the background? I stammered on about work till Delia put me out of my misery. The last thing she said to me was, "I suppose you'll make vice president someday."

A week later I got the invitation to Kate and Harry's engagement party; the New York Yacht Club, *nos agimur tumidis velis*, cocktails, six to eight.

I went alone after a long dawdle at work but was early, or rather not late enough, and so I walked over half a block to the Algonquin to have a drink. It was the first time in my life that I had consciously fortified myself with alcohol for a social occasion. I sat at the bar fingering the invitation, a heavy card, bordered in blue, with blue sloops reaching into the lower corners. I kept thinking that they were the first, they were to be the first to take the ride and see what excitement could be summoned from its motion and turns. They were playacting, I thought, and yet long afterward, when Kate finally was married, the engagement party came to seem the only real moment in years of nuptial fuss. When I got other girls' invitations I would think, "Now why should Annie be making a big deal over her engagement? Kate is already married."

At seven I strolled over. It was late November, and what passed for foliage in New York was nearly gone. But as I started east on that treeless block I got a whiff of the true autumn that had gone on elsewhere. And as I walked, I no longer walked on the sidewalk but on a stone path between two dormitories, with a chapel bell tolling in the near distance. The school season came up and overwhelmed me, the streaming sinuses and the wool clothes and the notebooks. And in that meager half-block stretch, I remembered the day I met Kate.

I had passed a horrible first week away from home. All I wanted was to get my work done and get along with everyone. Instead I kept getting into trouble out of an eagerness to obey. One morning I had missed chapel because I had gone too early; another time I had helped a boy with his work program job and forgotten about required breakfast. I had consequently been warned by the dorm master about getting off to a bad start. As this was so far from my intentions, the week had left me profoundly shaken and a bit paranoid. At Chatham I lived, from the very first moment, in a morbid fear of being kicked out. For instance, I was certain that my much rowdier roommate's contraband would somehow be mistaken for mine, if and when one of the administration's notorious raids transpired. At the end of the week when I found myself alone in the chapel for the second time, I was very close to tears. I couldn't understand it; I had made a note of the time, I had come right over after English. It simply wasn't fair that I had somehow missed it again. Two absences from chapel meant a black mark and three black marks meant something very bad, though I could not remember what. We were reading *L'étranger* in French class, and, unlike most of my classmates, I identified wholeheartedly with the alienated, wrongly accused narrator. I heard someone walking in the sacristy— a teacher, I assumed—and without a second thought I jumped up, hurried out of the chapel, and ran across the campus to my dorm. That I might have pleaded my innocence and been excused never occurred to me. I went first to my room, but then I remembered the dormitory sweeps the teachers supposedly made. So I stole out to the common room and found a janitor's supply closet and opened the door to hide.

An electric bulb lit up the space. There was, to my horror, a girl inside, sitting on an overturned bucket; worse yet, I knew who she was: she was one of the five or six upperclassmen who had already been pointed out to me in dining hall and whose name I had heard repeated a sufficient number of times to have learned.

"You can't skip chapel here!" the girl said disdainfully. "I skip chapel here."

But I was desperate, and desperation gives courage. "Look, can you just let me in," I said wearily. "I can't get caught again. I've skipped already."

Kate Goodenow surveyed me coldly as I pushed my way in beside her. "You have to be quiet, *George*, so I can finish this." She had taken my name from my name tag; we were all required to wear them the first week. Embarrassed, I unpinned mine and stuffed it into my blazer pocket. She didn't have hers on, which confirmed my fear that nobody worth anything was wearing one.

The girl bent her head and proceeded to scribble answers on a Latin work sheet. The closet was narrow and extremely cramped with the mops and brooms, and it was all I could do not to touch or jostle her. I stood very still, pressed up against the door, and peered down at her paper. Presently she got a noun ending wrong and I told her.

I had spoken without thinking, and in the intervening silence I saw whatever hopes I still had of a future at Chatham ruined by the contempt of one pretty girl. But she said calmly, "All right, I've erased it. Tell it to me right." When I had finished she asked, "What Latin are you in."

"Latin Three," I said uncomfortably.

"Oh, really. So am I."

This surprised me; I was certain I would have noticed her.

"You're new?"

I nodded.

"Third form?"

"Yes."

"Pretty early to be skipping chapel, isn't it?"

"I tried to go! But no one was there."

The girl looked up from her paper with scorn. "It's Founder's Day. They have it out in the woods. Didn't you see everyone hiking out there after Father Grossman? Holding up the sacrament?"

"No."

"Time for a stronger prescription," she said rudely.

She opened up her notebook and began to doodle sailboats on a fresh page.

"Do you sail?" I said, eager to make a connection that might last beyond the next half hour.

"Do *you*?" she said.

"I do at home."

"I'll bet you do."

"I *do*—"

"So prove it," she said unexpectedly, after a minute. She glanced up at me with a menacing look. "Let's see you tie a bowline."

I watched in horror and fascination as she untied the knot in the line of rope she was wearing as a belt, and pulled it from the loops. "Come on, let's see."

It was green-and-white flecked quarter inch. I stared at the bitter end for a moment with the blind panic that comes of forgetting something so automatic that one could never hope to remember it consciously—one's telephone number, say.

"Rabbit runs around the tree—" the girl began patronizingly.

"I don't do it that way," I said, and remembered. Despite Pop's efforts, I learned the knot backward and have tied it that way ever since.

The girl examined it. "Bizarre method you've got there." She untied the knot and threaded the line back through her belt loops. As she was retying it she looked up and caught me staring, and she laughed wickedly.

I cursed her, Kate Goodenow, and her pathetic pop quizzes. Then she said indifferently, "Ever raced dinghies before?"

"Some."

"Where'd you learn to sail?"

"Knox Pond," I said.

"Knox Pond? I've heard of Knox Pond. Oh, you mean behind the Rectory School?"

"That's right," I said, surprised she had heard of it.

"What are you, a fac-brat?" she guessed, but the mockery in her voice was all but gone.

"My father's the headmaster."

"Really. Well, the men in my family, they all went right through the Rectory. They've all put their masts in the mud of Knox Pond, every one of them."

I laughed, not really at the substance of the remark, but at the girl's sudden generosity.

"It's different here," she said after a moment. "Open water."

"That's all right."

"Yes," the girl admitted, "you'll get used to it. Listen," she went on in a professional manner, "do me a favor: run down the hall to Nicko's room and give him this." She pressed the Latin homework into my hand.

"All right," I said.

"Then come back and get me if the coast is clear and I'll get you excused from chapel."

Even I knew where Nick Beale's room was. Everyone did. I can still remember the empty, echoing sound of the corridor as I walked down it to his room, clutching the paper. I have had ample time to wonder since then how different the texture of my life would have been if I had never taken that walk. I was a retiring fourteen-year-old, I was not athletic, I did not have brothers and sisters at Chatham to pave the way for me. It's true I was reasonably smart, but Chatham was no Exeter, and intelligence alone was not particularly respected there. I suppose I would have ended up like the kid who lived across the hall from me, David Henwood, the only other third-former in geometry. David played thirds soccer and acted in plays and founded the Latin club and went to Harvard. I have run into him in the city from time to time; first year out he was already editing a conservative political journal. And that he should somehow still defer to me when we meet has to do with nothing but my having been friends with Kate and Nick our third-form year while he was not. A lot of the older girls made pets of the freshmen, and I became Kate's; before I left Nicko's room that morning I had a sport and a nickname and more marijuana than I had ever seen or knew what to do with. It wasn't that I ever reached Nick's level—I wouldn't have even tried—but I had the credentials a little bit earlier than my class-mates. I was datable, somehow, when so many boys like me were not. I never partied much at school, but I didn't suffer from abstaining the way some people did; my teachers liked me too, and my final year the combined faculty and student body elected me Head of School. My whole career at Chatham was wildly beyond expectation.

And yet perhaps I sacrificed something doing things the way I did.

I remember an awkward exchange with Henwood in our senior year. It was just after the early acceptances came out. David came into the dorm looking as if he'd been knighted. It was clear he was too modest to say anything, so I said, "You got in, right?"

"That's right!" he exulted and brandished the letter. "The work paid off—it all paid off!"

When I congratulated him he began to look ill at ease. "Don't worry—I got in, too," I said, to reassure him.

"Jesus, I knew it!" He whacked me on the back. "I knew if anybody was going to get Harvard it was going to be you and me, Lenhart. We deserve it! We worked so goddamn hard! Hey, do you know what house you're in yet? Maybe we'll be together again."

"Oh, no," I explained. "I didn't apply to Harvard. I got into Dartmouth early. My dad went there and—"

"Dartmouth?" Henwood repeated, his face falling. "Oh, jeez, Lenhart, I'm such an idiot. I thought you meant Harvard."

"That's okay—you didn't know." I was as eager as he was to discuss college and what it would all be like, but David began to edge away down the hall. It irritated me when I realized afterward that he pitied me and that his pity made him think he had made a faux pas. In my yearbook, David Henwood wrote: "Sorry you won't be joining me in the fall—you were smarter than I was third-form year."

There was low, thumping music coming from Nick's room. I knocked several times but no one answered, so finally I pushed the door open and went in. Tapestries covered the walls. I nearly tripped over the guitar on the floor, and through a haze of smoke Nick Beale looked up from his book and nodded at me.

"I've brought your Latin homework," I announced.

He waited for me to continue. When I remained silent, he replied, "That's really, really nice of you." He set his book down and took the work sheet. I glanced at the cover; he was reading *Moby-Dick*.

"Oh, do you like it?" I said, to make conversation, for I felt that a great deal depended on the next few minutes.

Nick looked surprised, as if my question were beside the point. "I always like sailing stories," he said.

"Are you reading it for English?"

"No. I'm reading it for my own . . . personal edification. Are you reading it for English?" he asked politely.

"No," I said.

"Why not? You should always do your homework," Nick advised.

"No, I mean it hasn't been assigned. We're reading something else."

This didn't seem to make much of an impression on him. That was when I noticed that he was wearing two name tags. One said "Kate Goodenow" and the other said "Nicholas S. Beale." It was the first sign I got that he was not only cool; he had co-opted cool.

I explained that I had promised to go back for Kate.

"You do what you need to do."

I was now in the awkward position of feeling rude if I left to get the guy's girlfriend for him. "I could come back here, too," I said.

"Come back whenever you like," said Nick Beale. "You're always welcome."

When Kate and I returned, she began to tidy up the small room, folding sweaters and arranging pillows, as if it were the most natural thing in the world that she should be tidying up in a boy's dorm in a boy's room during morning chapel. Nick fiddled with a pipe and watched her with a bemused, far-off expression. "Nick, you should at least open a window. I mean, really." To get to the window she had to pass Nick. He reached out his long thin arms and slipped them around her and pulled her onto his lap. I felt myself blush. Our host seemed to have been asleep and in one gesture to have come alive.

"Nick!"

"Shut up—you love it."

"Right, I really like—"

Looking at her on his lap, I saw how small she was. Nick was so thin, but Kate, I saw, was one of those hipless girls whose figures were so in vogue. She was tan, too, like Nick, but in the freckly way blondes get tan. Her face looked like it had been sunburned over and over, until the burn had mellowed and sunk into her skin. It was nearly October, and they both looked like summer.

"Who's afraid of Kathykins?" said Nick hoarsely, his cheek against her back.

"I'm *serious!*" Kate protested when she had struggled to her feet. She yanked the window open. When she turned, she put her hands to her ponytail, adjusting it a notch. "Now are we going to play some cards before Latin? Nick? George? What should we play?"

We had crossed some bridge, on the far side of which all of the questions would be benign.

"How about hearts?"

"I don't know how to play," I admitted reluctantly.

"You don't know how to play hearts?" Kate sat down on the floor by Nick's feet and gave the deck an expert shuffle. "Did you hear that, Nick?"

Nick shook his head, grinning. I had pinned my name tag back on. "Georgie Len," he said. "Very bad, Georgie Len. I would call this a very bad omission in your edification thus far."

In the afternoon I went out sailing with them. While the returning students rigged boats, the coach gave us a pep talk about the long, proud history of yachtsmanship at Chatham School, thanking Art Goodenow for this season's new sails. Then he put all the new people into a Whaler and drove us out to where they ran the practice races.

It had been windy on campus and it was still blowing hard now, even in the harbor of the Bay; it seemed to me that Kate and Nick were the only ones who were doing much of anything, tactically—everyone else was just trying not to flip. When the breeze picked up another notch or two and two boats turtled, the coach—Tompkins—decided to call off practice. He cruised around in the Whaler, blowing his whistle to summon people to the docks. But Kate and Nick seemed not to have heard. Instead of following the others in, they headed up closer to the wind to make the point that marked the harbor entrance. Frustrated, Mr. Tompkins decided to drop us off and go after them himself. I turned around on the seat to watch them as we drove in. You couldn't see much of Kate. She was tucked in on the rail in front of Nick, hidden. Her ponytail would bob out on one side like a brush dipping paint, then bob out on the other as she flattened the boat for Nick. So I focused on Nick instead. He slouched his way through the tacks, but his was the finessed slouch of perfection. I imagined him learning to sail when he was very, very young and then, almost as quickly, learning the slouch. It was the combination of the two—the juxtaposition of skill and indifference—that I vowed I would appropriate.

At the far end of the inlet, the white triangle dipped once more and bobbed around the corner out of sight. Behind me I heard Mr. Tompkins curse Nick for his talent and his disrespect, and I thought: I will always watch till I can't see them anymore.

Just over nine years had passed since that day. I wasn't ready to draw conclusions, however. I had come to the address on Forty-fourth Street, and I went inside.

CHAPTER 19

Fifty or sixty of the Goodenows' family and friends, as well as Mr. Franklin Lombardi, Jr., and his live-in girlfriend, Rhonda, had assembled in the biggest toy room in Manhattan—the Model Room of the New York Yacht Club, with the half-hulls in all colors crowding the walls.

I had been nervous; at the threshold I wondered, about what? The crowd gave off the feeling of having just enjoyed a mildly funny joke. Nothing was going to happen, it seemed clear. In the middle of the room, Kate, in a square-cut black dress, was laughing up at a florid, gray-haired man whom I took to be her uncle. I felt a sense of relief that the party was in her hands; I have since reflected that she was the only hostess of whom I thoroughly approved.

I spied Harry at the bar and was making my way over when a stout woman in a pink suit stood herself before me. "Have you seen the article?" she demanded. A section of yesterday's *Times* was thrust into my hands. Under the caption NEW GENERATION SEES NO POINT IN WAITING, there was a picture of a young bride being fitted for a gown.

"Not the picture—read it: look."

I scanned down the column. It was, according to the piece, an emerging trend of my generation to be married earlier, defying the precedent set by feminists of the sixties and seventies to delay settling down until thirty or after. Katharine Goodenow, of the American paintings department at Sotheby's, was quoted. "It's silly to sit around saying 'Why?' for years and years, when you can just as easily say 'Why not?' My parents were married when my mother was twenty-three. I'm twenty-five now—I feel like a late bloomer!" Harry was not mentioned.

"Oh, Goodie! There you are!" panted the pink woman. "I've got to show Goodie, but make sure you finish reading it later. Don't forget," she ordered. "Come find me and read the rest."

Harry had vanished into the crowd, and after a couple of half-hearted steps in either direction, I spotted, across the room, the only person in the place I actually wanted to talk to. He saw me, too, and gave a bemused nod when I joined him.

"Where's your date, buddy?"

"She ran away," I said. "Yours?"

"She heard you were coming."

"But you've got two drinks," I pointed out.

Chat held up his two fists to examine them. " 'Deed I do, 'deed I do. You've got to protect yourself at these kinds of things. All the same," he added suspiciously, "I guess you'd better take one." I hesitated. To everyone else, perhaps, his courtship of Kate had seemed offhand at best. But I knew better, and if there was any night when a man was entitled to be double-fisting . . .

"Go on! They're brand new! Mixed 'em myself when the bartender wasn't looking."

We stood in our corner and drank. I tried to detect a brittleness in Chat's bemusement; he caught on immediately and ridiculed me for it. "You're the melodramatic freak—maybe *you're* bitter. That's it, isn't it? You're bitter. If you were in my position you'd be very glad to see Lombardi so high on life, Lenhart. So ambitious. He's a very ambitious guy, you know."

"Your position?" I inquired.

"I'm invested up to here." Chat held a hand to his jugular. "You ought to be, too, you know. He's moving into office space—he's got seed money for eighteen months. This thing gets big, baby—"

Everyone was getting in. Only I stood by, conservative; with my Christmas bonus I could pay Chat back. "Chat, I want to give you your money," I declared, without preface. "I'll have it next month."

Chat's answer sounded careless enough, and yet there was something surprising about it—its alacrity, I suppose. What I mean is that the reply was clearly something he had thought about: he knew what he would say if I mentioned it. He wasn't *surprised* to hear me mention it, as he might have been.

"Lenhart, p-p-*please*. This—this—this is an engagement party!"

"All right, but after," I insisted. "I want to make arrangements to pay you."

"Listen to me," Chat said. He was so rarely serious that I did his bidding. "If you're holding off on Lombardi's thing be—be—because of me . . ."

He let my silence serve as an answer.

"I thought so. I thought so. Well, forget about it. We're all going to cash in *big* on this thing."

"You really think so?"

"Hasn't poverty taught you anything, George?"

"All right," I said evenly.

"All right, then."

The woman in pink came by again holding out the newspaper. "Have you both—"

"We saw it," we said.

The crowd dithered, and shifted in a circular direction, like children playing musical chairs. "Oh, good," said Chat, refocusing. "We'll say hello."

I followed him to the side of an upright woman balanced on extraordinarily thin legs. The woman's hair was ash-blond, coiffed immaculately in a style quoting the 1960s. Her face was tan—the whole party was filled with parents who had better tans than their children—and she wore pink lipstick that sat on her lips and beamed when they beamed. Chat introduced Mrs. Goodenow.

"Isn't this a very nice occasion. My husband's brother's giving the party. Make sure you say hello, Goodie's right over there by Mrs. Pall. Lenhart, you said? There are Lenharts in Maine. Puce married a Lenhart. Chatland, have you managed to get yourself a drink? Oh, yes, I see that you have. You've probably had several."

"Oh, no, Mrs. Goodenow—"

"Now, Chattie, I want you to do me a favor, dear, and it's rather important." They didn't make voices like hers anymore, rich and clipped at the same time, drawling swallowed vowels to Boston and back, stowing R's away for safekeeping. "This young man can help you—Mr. Lenhart, you give Chattie a hand, will you. Mr. Lombardi is standing over there. Yes, go and talk to him, will you.

"Oh, *have* you met my other daughters. This is Vivi and Cecily."

I nodded at a Goodenow taller and more oblique than Kate, and then at a stocky brunette whom the milkman must have begotten. "Excuse me, darlings. I have *so* many people to see. Have a good time, won't you? Please enjoy yourselves. It's so *nice* to see you again. Vivi, have Chat remind you about Charles Pall, dear. He's a *very* good-looking boy. Chat, reintroduce her to Charles Pall."

"Hey, Vivi."

"Hey, Chattie."

"How's school?"

"Good."

"You transferred, huh?"

"Yeah."

"You like Denison better?"

"Yeah, way better."

"You playing tennis?"

"Number three."

"Good girl. That's what I like to hear." To me he added, "Kate could have played in college, but she didn't care enough."

The girl shrugged.

"Are you . . . in college?" I tried with the younger, stockier one, who looked older.

"Not yet."

"Are you at Chatham now, Celes?" Chat intervened.

Vivi spoke up. "No! She wouldn't go. She's such a baby. She stayed home."

"*No!*" Chat said.

The two girls nodded, showing teeth.

"Bad deal, Cees—you've *got* to go away."

"I don't want to."

"*Nobody* wants to at first—back me up here, George."

"It's true."

"*Sucks* at the beginning. But you gotta go. You don't want to be some homebody freak, do you, Cees? Huh? Huh?"

"I don't know."

"Those girls never turn out right. Coddled in day schools—"

"Neither do the girls who go away," I interrupted.

"You've got a point, Lenhart. For once in your life, you've got a point."

I left him grilling the Goodenow sisters and went to study the model ships in a case.

Kate came by and clutched my arm, laughing and grimacing by way of greeting, and left a girl in her wake: the willowy Jessica Brindle, delivered out of Kate's grossly untapped girlfriend world.

"I wasn't sure you'd be here," she said spacily, and rather disconcertingly.

"I wouldn't have missed it," I assured her. Presently the two of us drifted toward the bar, where a heavyset man was punching words into a crowd of boys. *"Henri père,"* whispered Miss Brindle in my ear.

"So I says, 'Kid knows which side his bread is buttered on!' Ha, ha, ha, ha, ha!"

"Remember," Jessica murmured, "we're not laughing at him, we're laughing with him."

I didn't laugh much at all.

All evening, people took their turns with Mr. Lombardi. A group would edge up, make his acquaintance, and go off pressing their lips together, their eyes large with seeking other eyes. Everybody wanted a story to take home—not the stories Mr. Lombardi told, but that didn't matter.

He was a short, shy man who drank to cover up his shyness. He eyed Jess Brindle sideways over the top of his drink. "Who's this you got, Chad?"

"Oh, I'm not Chat," I corrected him, and stuck out a hand. Mr. Lombardi pumped it with enthusiasm. "I'm George—George Lenhart."

"George is a good friend of your son's from college," said Jess Brindle, who seemed to be rather well informed.

"Yeah?"

"Oh, yes," said Jessica.

"Didn't know the guy had any friends! Except girlfriends, that is! Ha ha! Hey, Henry! Henry! Aw, he's busy talking—gotta get in good with the in-laws. I was gonna say, where's he been hiding you?"

"Why, thank you, Mr. Lombardi!"

Harry's father seemed to include me in a confidence. "You know, there's girls in Millport still call for him. Hell, there's girls in *Norwalk* still call! 'I hate to dis-o-point you,' I say, 'but my son is engaged to be married.' Disappoint them—what about disappoint me, ha ha? Kid had some pretty cute girlfriends. You two boyfriend and girlfriend? You make a cute couple. Speaking of girlfriends, where's Rhonda? Ha, ha, ha, ha, ha!"

By eight the waiters had stopped coming round with canapés, and Dick Scarum was saying wistfully that he wished he could come out late-night but ever since the splash on Park Avenue, Lori had been cracking down. Chat was suggesting venues, which the eligible Charlie Pall was dismissing, when an altercation at the room's entrance arrested the discussion. A young man was attempting to join the

party but had been stopped at the threshold by the bell captain because he was not wearing a coat. As we turned to look, a uniformed
employee hurried up the stairs with one of the blazers the club kept
on hand. But the boy protested. His face was so dark it looked black,
and I cringed, thinking it was some kind of racial incident, when
Chat's voice rang out into the hush: "*He* doesn't need a jacket, for
Chrissake!" He strode forth under every eye. "Nicko, good buddy!
It's Chat!"

Somewhere behind me a woman dropped a drink, dropped it flat
on the floor, as if she'd let go of it for fun.

Hush, murmur, hush, we went, like a roaring tide. Nick Beale had
returned from the tropics.

He stood as if the floor were hot tar, balancing on the far outside
of his arches. The hoarse question, when it came, was natural
enough: "Is Kate around?"

Chat grinned lustily. "*Sure*, Nicko—she's around!"

Everyone turned to his left or right, fifty adults trying to pretend
that if they could not see anyone, no one could see them. At last it
emerged that Kate had gone down to the bathroom. Through the en-
suing silence, one voice went on imperviously. ". . . to come up and
see us. And don't be stingy, Pris. We never seem to see you for more
than a day or two and that's not *long* enough. You promise me right
now you'll tell Boos that you're expected at Hedgeway for the middle week, Sunday to Saturday . . ."

Inexorably Kate returned with a giggling entourage.

"Kate, look—"

"Kate—"

"Oh my God, Kate—"

She took it all in with her eyes. They opened wide, marveling. She
moved forward as if to embrace him but seemed to check herself, and
in her hesitation a tall, gray-haired man cut through the group. The
man walked as if he were trying to catch up with the pointed index
finger of his right hand.

"Look here, Beale, I don't know who told you to show up, but
you've no right—"

"Dad, *Dad*!"

"—to come crashing in here. That's what you're doing, I needn't tell you."

Edging back a step, Nick did not meet the eyes of his former benefactor.

Mr. Goodenow spewed on, eyes goggling. "This is a private party. If you're trying to prove something—"

The spectacle was ridiculous. It was like watching someone yell at a servant.

"Stop it, Dad!"

I don't think Harry came forward out of strength of character or a moral propriety. It was just that he had been trained, growing up, to do the right thing. His behavior was automatic, like one of his computer functions. From the chair that he had claimed, Mr. Lombardi watched his son with slightly menacing eyes, ready to chastise if the boy should fail to carry out the instilled approbations of the middle class: "Say thank you to the lady, Henry!" "Elbows off the table, Henry!" "Don't you be rude to a visitor!"

And as he joined them at the entrance to the room, Harry's face assumed an expression I had never seen on him before: a pure emotionless tranquillity. It was as if his religion, too, had prepared him for those moments when life flashes its awkward intensity before our eyes. He could, miraculously, handle this—it was the pretty palaver over cocktails that he couldn't master. He acknowledged Mr. Goodenow with a nod.

"Hello, Nick," Harry said, holding out his hand. "Come in and have a drink."

"Come have a Mount Gay and tonic," Chat supplied eagerly.

In our little group conversation began again in earnest, like a bandage over a sore.

The attendants closed ranks; Daddy tried to reason. "I'll ask him to go, Kate. Right now."

"No, no, would you just stop it! Leave him alone!" In the background Uncle Goodie could be heard, proposing garrulous toasts.

"Quiet, dear! Quiet, Kate, quiet down." Mrs. Goodenow emerged from the wings to manage the scene.

"I want to talk to Nick! Let me talk to Nick!"

"Kate, darling, remember your guests."

"If you don't let me talk to him, I'll—I'll break something! I swear I will!"

"Art, she's hysterical. I'll take her downstairs."

"No, Mother! Nick and I are friends! We're still friends!"

"Don't forget that you're engaged, young lady!" Mr. Goodenow warned, with a hand around Kate's upper arm.

"Art, I will deal with this."

"You don't understand! Nick's my best friend! He's my best friend!"

But eventually Kate allowed herself to be led away. She cast an eye back. At first I thought she was gauging our reaction, and I raised my glass in a salute meant to imply good show in the face of adversity. But then I saw that her eyes sought out Harry—Nick had been urged on toward the bar by Chat—and, averting my eyes, I realized that she had just come as close as she could to loving him, for what he had done. She wanted him to turn around and console her with a glance.

Walking heavily forward, Harry passed a hand over his skull.

Slowly, one by one, the Cold Harbor mothers left their husbands' sides and surrounded Nick at the bar.

"Were you in the Caribbean, Nick?"

"Did you go to the Bahamas, Nick?"

"Did you go to St. Barth's?"

"What kind of a boat is it?"

"Did you cross the Atlantic?"

"Are you going back, Nick?"

"How'd you get so tan, Nick?"

Having settled his new guest with a drink, Harry withdrew a few paces and stood rocking forward onto his toes, sipping his drink through the plastic stirrer. No one noticed him, and he hardly seemed to notice himself. He looked a million miles away, utterly distracted, but with the air of someone who rather likes his distractions. Perhaps he was contemplating the fluctuations of the market, or the rate at which sand falls off a sandpile. It was November, and the wedding was set for June. He had less than a year to go before she was his.

I had wondered, going into the party, at the Goodenows' placid acceptance of their daughter's choice, why nobody seemed to mind doing business with Lombardi and Son. But it seemed I had underestimated everyone, most particularly the Goodenows. Like all surviving clans, they had an instinct for self-preservation; it was often said of Kate that she was a "smart girl." Nobody had doubted that she would pick a winner.

It was the last weekend of May when Nicko found out he wasn't going to be asked back, the school's way of intimating that he had flunked out. They decided to let him sail that weekend anyway. It was the last regatta of the season—the high school team-racing championships—and he could go home afterward; it was the least they could do.

The championships were in Newport that year. I had not been there since I was little, and I have returned only when circumstances have made it unavoidable. Once, in college, my girlfriend Ann Callow wanted to see the Astor mansion for a paper she was writing on the architecture of the Gilded Age. I drove her there and I sat in the car. I have never hated a town in quite the same way I hate Newport. I hate the crowds and the cruising Camaros and the ice cream stands and the fudge and T-shirt "shoppes," and the cigarette butts that line the cliffs around the mansions; but I hate the mansions, too. I used to muse about the source of my intense dislike, until one day I overheard Robbins telling somebody that Newport was the best town in New England for summer nightlife, and I knew at once why I cannot stomach that town: Newport doesn't belong where it is. The town has nothing to do with New England; it is like a girl who affects artlessness. It ought to be called New York Port. I met Kate in Massachusetts, in corduroys and Bean boots, and I always associated her with the northern virtues of cold, because the first thing I knew about her was that she spent her summers in Maine. And I often tried to forget that I'd seen her once in Newport, Rhode Island, in gold lamé.

They put us up in the barracks at Fort Adams. We were winning after the first day, and Mr. Tompkins took everybody out to dinner after we put the boats away for the night. Tompkins felt so bad about Nick's getting kicked out, and so sorry for himself that the sailing team was going to go down the drain, that he bought Nick his own beer and gave Kate sips of his daiquiri when the waiter's back was turned. It was a given at school that she could get away with anything. So could Nick, in a different way—at least that's what we had thought. Boarding schools were different then; they were stricter on the surface, but nobody really cared when you broke the rules, and the last thing any self-respecting parent would have considered was a lawsuit. After dinner we were supposed to go back to Fort Adams and hang out with the other teams till lights out. But Nick slipped away while Mr. Tompkins was getting the van, and Kate slipped away with him. They went down to the piers and waited till dark, and that was the night he tried to persuade her to run away with him. They were going to go down to the Caribbean—it was just as Chat had said—and live on a boat, and get jobs down there. Flip-flops, endless summer: he had it all planned out.

When it was over and she'd told him no, Kate sneaked into the boys' barracks and woke me up. She told me Nick was gone. He had taken a boat and left. I remember being conscious of having to rise to an occasion, something larger than myself, and of failing miserably. I wanted to comfort her but I was so tired and so sad—and now we would lose to St. George's for sure—that I started crying myself.

"Shut up! Shut up, will you? Shut up!"

"But they always beat us!" I cried. "And now they always will!"

Kate seized me by the shoulders and shook me into a teary, frightened silence. "Who cares about a stupid sailing team!" She took a handkerchief from a little evening bag and wiped my face with two strokes. A bracelet set off the fine bone of her wrist, and I noticed she had changed her clothes since dinner. She was all dressed up in stiff, glittery garments. "Don't you want to have fun tonight?"

I got hold of myself and told her I did. But what if we got caught? The fear was always, always there for me. I was never not conscious of the money my parents were spending to send me to Chatham; I could not afford to get into real trouble.

"Don't be stupid," said Kate, derisively. "I've got a note from Granny."

We sneaked out of the barracks. Outside there was a taxi waiting. She already knew how to do things like that—how to run her life at the utmost convenience, make the taxi wait, have things delivered. We got into the backseat. Kate gave the address and, groping on the floor of the cab, produced a bottle of vodka. "Now you have to do shots till we get there," she ordered. "To catch up." I did a couple of shots and Kate was satisfied. She sat back against the seat. "Where are we going?" I said.

"Granny's," she said. "I've just come from there." She took my hand and held it.

It was thrilling and yet too abysmally torturing to hold her hand and think of Nick. "Is Nick—?"

"Oh, shut up about Nick! He's gone and he's not coming back. And it's his fault. It's all his fault, don't ever forget. You can't help people who don't help themselves." She snatched her hand back and tipped up the vodka bottle to drink a long shot. "You're not allowed to mention Nick," Kate said. "That's the rule tonight." As quickly as it had come, the scorn vanished from her face. She lay her head against my shoulder. She smelled lovely—expensive. "We're almost there."

It was a great white house on top of a crag that jutted out above a private beach. The house had its own little guard station at the foot of the driveway, like a toll booth, with a barrier. Kate had the taxi drop us at the gate because she wanted the fun of sneaking past the guard. We ducked under the arm of the booth, and got halfway up the lawn when the man came after us with a flashlight. "Who is it? Who's there?" "Kate!" I urged, but she wouldn't say a word. I would be caught, blamed, dismissed—kicked out like Nick. She played every game to the death. The guard ran up and shined a flashlight in our faces. "Oh, it's you, Katie! Why didn't you say something?"

"You should have recognized me, Roger," Kate informed him.

"Well, whyn't you stop and say hello?"

"I'm busy, if you must know. I've had a terribly busy night."

"You got a friend tonight, Katie?"

"Yes! It's my boyfriend!"

"Your boyfriend, huh?"

"That's right!" Kate said, jutting out her chin.

"Aw . . . well, you kids go on and have fun."

" 'You kids go on and have fun,' " mimicked Kate.

We confronted the house. The first-floor windows had all been thrown open, and the synesthesia of warm light and clinking glasses and the high-pitched punctuations of laughter and the smell of the sea and the salty sea grass made me think I would forever conjure up this house, this moment, when anyone said, as Kate did presently: "It's the first party of the summer." Almost imperceptibly, her voice trembled when she added, "It always is." I glanced at her curiously. Her face in the moonlight seemed to falter; she looked daunted for a moment, as if even she doubted it was hers, as if even she doubted her capacity to rise to the challenge of taking her place over the next decade.

As we hesitated, a man and a woman emerged from the shadows of the front porch. They were in evening dress. The man lit a cigarette and leaned over the railing of the porch as he inhaled. The woman patted her hair into place, curving her neck like a swan. He made a joke out of the corner of his mouth and the woman laughed. She was silvery blond with long, thin limbs. I remember she seemed very vain to me. They both did, because they were oblivious of the sea, and of Nicko's being out on it. When they spotted us, the woman's face soured slightly and the man looked bored and drunk and annoyed—stupefied, rather. I felt the sick shame of the party crasher wash over me. But surely they would recognize Kate!

But they didn't seem to know her. And their rudeness seemed to settle something in her. Her face hardened. She tossed her head back as if to reaffirm her entitlement and led me up the steps to the porch and into the house.

The foyer was crowded with men and women lingering or traipsing glitteringly from one room to another. I had not yet gotten my bearings when Kate whispered, "I'll be right back!," squeezed my hand, and was gone.

I must have stood just inside the door for nearly half an hour. I tried to affect an impatient air of annoyance. I glanced at my wrist several times (I wore no watch) and pretended that I was greatly put out by the behavior of my date—so put out, in fact, that I was not to be approached. My discomfort doubled when I surveyed the throng of people having cocktails and realized that they were far closer to my age than I'd first thought. Many of them looked to be in college or their early twenties—not the age when a fourteen-year-old is more to be indulged than ridiculed.

When people began to eye me and whisper comments to one another, I couldn't stand it anymore. I made blindly for a room at the end of the hallway. When I reached the threshold, however, I saw that it was a dining room and that a dinner party was going on inside it. The older crowd, it seemed: I had a flashing impression of gray hair and a silver service. I backed away and turned the corner as fast as I could. I found myself in a little alcove underneath a massive stairway, and there I resolved to hide.

I had stood there no more than a minute or two when I heard a woman's shoes clicking up behind me. It was too late to move, and anyway, she giggled and said, "What are you doing under there?"

"I'm hiding," I said.

"I know you are." She chuckled. "I'm going to hide with you." And she ducked into the alcove with me.

She was a sweet, drunk woman—a lovely woman, I saw, when I stole a glance at her face, perhaps thirty-five or forty. She had a large cocktail in one hand, which she shot out for balance as, scrunching herself under the stairs with me, she tottered and nearly fell. I put out a hand to steady her. "My husband," the woman went on, having regained her balance, and taking a sip from the glass, "is out on the porch with Corny Murphy."

I considered this for a respectful moment. Then I said, "I'm George Lenhart."

"I know who you are." My companion giggled. "You're Jack's child."

"Jack?" I said reluctantly. "No—I'm sorry, but I'm not."

The woman smiled pleasantly at me.

"I'm a friend of Kate Goodenow's."

"Goodenow! Ah-hah! One of the cousins." She finished her drink and reached around and set the glass down on one of the steps above us. Then she ducked back in. "This is fun, isn't it?"

"Very," I said.

"Goodenow," she said again. "Are you with Vivi? You can't be with Cee Cee!"

"No, you're right," I admitted. "I came with Kate."

"Kate?" the woman said blankly. "Oh, *Kate*! It's funny," she observed. "One never thinks of Kate."

This was so far from the case at school, where everyone constantly thought, talked, and wildly conjectured about Kate, that I didn't know what to say.

"Kate hardly ever comes down to Newport," the woman volunteered. "And I have a pretty good idea as to why."

A waiter passed with a tray of cocktails. "One for me and one for you," said my new friend. We toasted. My drink was very sweet after the straight vodka in the taxi.

"She's a lucky one, Kate." That sounded more like her.

"Yes, she is," I agreed.

"*All* the money's Artie's. I mean, literally every dime."

"Is it," I said absently, flustered anew, because I had finished the drink in two sips and didn't know what to do with my glass— whether to hold it and pretend to sip out of it or carelessly demand another.

"Oh, God, yes. Viv didn't have a cent when they got married. Not a red cent. They've got that house up in Maine and that's divided three ways, and from what I heard it was practically falling into the sea when she and Artie got married."

"Gosh," I said.

"You know, people say Wills married *me* for my money, and I say I'd rather be married for my money and have money than marry someone with no money who—who doesn't have any." She paused, as if trying to understand the logic of that.

"Of course," I said, peering into her cleavage, which was eye level. "I mean, I can see why." She was an awfully sweet woman.

"But what happened to Viv would never have happened to me."

"Really. Why not?"

The woman drained her glass and smiled. "Because I don't go around screwing the townies, honey, that's why!"

At this point the meal in the dining room must have broken up, for there was a sound of chairs being pushed back, and people began to trickle into the hallway. A tall man with gray hair walked by us. Mortified, I shrank back as my partner-in-waiting called out to him. "Artie! Artie, come here! Look at us, we're hiding!"

The man stopped and looked around impatiently.

"In here!"

When the man saw who had called him, and whom she was with and where, the look on his face was both so contemptuous and so bored that I surprised myself by straightening up from the alcove and returning his glance with a sudden insolence of my own.

"This is a friend of Kate's, Artie!"

"Are you," said the man, turning indifferent eyes on me. "Linda, come out from there."

"I won't! We like it under here, don't we? We're playing Sardines! You"—she tugged at my sleeve—"you come back here."

I hesitated a moment, but the dinner-party group had come and surrounded Mr. Goodenow. His expression changed instantly to a host's condescension. He laughed deprecatingly at something one of the women said. He had taken less notice of me than if I *had* crashed his party—a real crasher, presumably, Mr. Goodenow would have taken the time to throw out.

Watching him go, perceiving the insult through her drunkenness, my friend remarked suddenly, "You know, Viv was a goddamn little bitch to me in school!"

"Maybe she didn't mean to be," I suggested, without much confidence.

"Oh, yes, she did! She did! She *hated* me. Because I had *sex* before she did. But I don't care. Why should I care when she got pregnant? To see her that way! To see her the way she was! Ha, ha, ha, ha, ha!"

"Is Mrs. Goodenow here tonight?" I inquired.

"Granny's here—it's her birthday. If you see her, you give her a big kiss for me! Granny and I have always gotten along."

"I'm sorry, I meant—Kate's mother," I said.

"Oh, Viv? Oh, no! Viv's not here! Viv *hates* Newport. *Nothing's* good enough for her but Maine. Well, you know what *I* say? I say Maine's a fucking cold bore!"

I noticed that it was quieter then. The grown-ups' party had passed through the hallway into another room, tucked away in the bowels of the huge house. Every few minutes you would a hear a car being started and the slurred comment of revelers as it drove away.

"That's them going down to town," remarked my companion, who had stopped to listen as well. "Are you going to go down?"

"I don't really know," I said.

"How old are you?" she asked suddenly. It was the first moment in our conversation that she had taken on anything remotely like a motherly air.

"Fourteen," I said.

The woman nodded, looking dimly into her empty glass. "I would have liked to have children," she whispered.

"Maybe you still can," I said.

"You think so?" said my friend. "I'd give anything—anything." We stepped from beneath the alcove into the deserted hall. "God-damn it, Wills is still out there on the porch with Corny Murphy!"

After Wills's wife went off to retrieve him, I wandered through the huge house listening for Kate's laugh. There were pockets of laughter here and there, but I had a dread of breaking in where I was not wanted, and eventually I found a small, dark library off the entrance hall. It seemed a safe enough place to wait without being noticed. I sat down on a ladylike sofa and switched on a lamp. When no one emerged from the shadows to accuse me of trespassing, I picked up the book on the coffee table and read it with all my heart. It was a history of the America's Cup. It was actually an absorbing read, and I was well into the first chapter when I became aware that I was not alone in the room. I heard a shifting in one of the corners, then perceived human breathing. I looked up from the book nearer to shrieking than I like to remember. The corner was dark, and so it took me a moment to make out the source of the noise. When I did, I felt foolish indeed. My companion was an old woman in a wheelchair. She had evidently slumped down—her head was bent halfway to her waist—and this had made her breath come stertorously. It was a pitiful position, not to mention untenable, and I was steeling myself to go to the woman's aid when the door to the library opened and a nurse or a maid in a gray uniform came in. "Hello," I said nervously.

"Yes, hello," she said, switching on an overhead light. "And what are you doing hiding away in here?"

Before I could explain, the old woman started awake. Her hand gripped the side of the wheelchair. "Bea!" she murmured. "Bea!"

"Yes, yes, I'm here," said the maid. "I come to take you to bed."

"Bea!" the old woman repeated.

"I'm here, crazy! I'm here, right in front of your face. Now, quiet down. I take you upstairs." She moved behind the wheelchair and released the stop.

"Where's Arthur gone?"

"Arthur, he go out." The maid shared an amused look with me. "Arthur, he have fun."

"Where? Where did he go?"

"Town. Everybody's gone to town. Now you go up to bed. It's past your bedtime."

The old woman frowned angrily, as if she had been duped. "Who is this boy? Who is this, Bea?"

"Why don't you ask him yourself?"

I stood up and said, "I'm George Lenhart, ma'am."

"Who invited you? Are you a friend of Arthur's?"

"Arthur? He don't know Arthur! He one quarter Arthur's age!"

"I came with Kate," I said.

"Kate! Where is Kate? Why didn't Kate come and say hello to me?"

I explained that I had lost track of her myself, a little while ago.

"He wait here all by hisself."

"You go and find Kate. She'll be upstairs."

"That's where the cousins hang out," the maid corroborated. "You go upstairs. You don't want to be hanging around down here with the old folks, do you?"

"Oh, no she won't, Bea," said the old woman. "Kate won't be with the cousins. She doesn't like her cousins. You know the only one she likes, Bea."

"Oh, yes, I do, crazy. She like Froggy."

"That's right, Bea," acknowledged Kate's grandmother. "She likes Froggy the best. And so do I."

"You go on up there," the maid said pleasantly. "You find Kate upstairs with her cousin Froggy."

Reluctantly I said I would go and look for them.

"Froggy's a little off," the maid warned me. "You know what I mean, right? You know Froggy?"

"Froggy's a good boy," countered her charge. "You be nice to Froggy, Bea!"

"I? I? I'm the nicest in the whole place. Froggy and I, we friends." To me she repeated gently, "Froggy not quite right, you get it, though."

"Oh, yes," I said. "That's all right."

"Then you go on and have fun! Don't sit here by yourself. You miss the party."

"Oh, I will. I'll go right up. Thank you."

"What's your name, boy?" demanded the grandmother.

"He already tell you, crazy! You forget already?"

"It's George," I said. "George Lenhart."

"Are you a friend of my son's?"

The maid smiled, rolling her eyes. "Come on. Let's go. Bedtime, Granny."

I held the door as she wheeled the chair through it.

"It's my birthday," the old woman said.

"Yes, I heard," I said. "Thank you for having me."

"Did you have a good time?" she asked eagerly.

"Oh, yes, Mrs. Goodenow," I said. "The best."

She nodded into herself, reassured. "Lenhart?"

"Yes, ma'am."

She nodded again. "Yes, I know," she said. "I know your name. There are Lenharts in Maine."

By that point instincts of self-preservation had overcome propriety; before I went upstairs, I ducked back into the library and took the America's Cup book and brought it with me for protection. Then I climbed the large curving stairs to the second floor. In a bedroom there, six or eight girls my age and some boys a few years older were lounging on a made bed and hardback chairs. They had evidently gone up there to drink; an arcane drinking game was in full swing, which seemed to involve elements of each of the ones I knew: telling the truth, kissing members of the opposite sex, laying cards down, recitation. I got an odd sensation watching them play. Then I realized that they all looked something alike, but in an odd way. Sitting on one of the beds were two girls who looked up at me when I came in. It wasn't just that they looked blank, their faces, for I was used to that. It was something stranger, and it wasn't till I compared them with Kate's that I formulated the thought, an ugly, inappropriate thought. They looked . . . inbred. Their eyes were a little bit too close together. I spoke up finally: "Has anyone seen Kate?"

"Upstairs," said the two girls, registering me and looking away.

I closed the door and went up another flight, and there on the third floor I finally heard Kate's voice.

"Kate!" I called. "Kate!"

They were playing inside a little bedroom, the kind every big old house has one of: the neglected bedroom, to which the lumpy twin beds are banished and the stuffed animals and the grammar school primers and the old athletic prizes. They were three: a grown man, a little girl of about five or six, and Kate. The man and the little girl were lying on their backs on one bed, giggling, and Kate was on the floor on her hands and knees.

"George!" she cried. "I'm a horsey! Come ride me!"

"No!" shouted the little girl. "I wanna ride!" She jumped down from the bed and climbed onto Kate's back and began to whip it with an imaginary whip. Kate reared and tried to toss her off, but the little girl screamed and clung to Kate's hair.

"Ow, you brat! You spoiled brat!" Kate's dress was bunched up above her knees and one of the gold straps was hanging off her shoulder. It was as if she had put it on just to ruin it.

In no hurry, the man on the bed rose and came over to shake my hand. He had a wonderfully warm face with a winning smile. And his handshake was firm. "I'm Fred," he said. "People call me Frog."

"Froggy!" the little girl screamed. *"Froggy!"*

The man removed a pack of cigarettes from a breast pocket and lit one while the two girls rolled around on the floor shrieking. There was a curious air of the invalid about Kate's older cousin. He was wearing slippers and an old cardigan. At the same time he reminded me of an old movie star; he moved through a succession of languid, rather debonair postures.

"You shouldn't smoke!" instructed the little girl.

"Say: 'You shouldn't smoke, Fred Goodenow Brown!' " Kate ordered.

"You shouldn't smoke Fred Goodenow Brown!"

Mr. Brown bent over with the cigarette between his lips and exhaled pointedly into their faces, whereupon the little girl plucked the butt from his mouth and threw it on the ground.

"Hey—*crazy*," Mr. Brown rebuked her, picking it from the rug. "That's a lit cigarette! You want to start a fire and burn down Granny's house?"

"I *hate* Granny!" said the little girl, and stamped her foot.

With a lazy, disapproving shake of his head, the man picked the child up and thrust her bodily from the room, shutting the door and locking it behind him. "That little bitch," he said.

I must have looked alarmed, for the man smiled suddenly and said, in a low, rather seductive voice, "Do you live here? I mean, would you like to live here? We have plenty of room, now that *she's* gone." He indicated the door with a nod.

"Frogs," Kate said warningly. "Don't start. You don't know George. George isn't family."

"Family, shmamily."

"Kate, we should probably get back," I suggested.

"Aren't you having fun?" snapped Mr. Brown. The change in tone was so fast, it was almost as if a different tenant had taken up residence in the man's body.

"It's not that," I began, when Kate's eyes flew strangely up to mine. "Kate." Her face was miserable. She looked inconsolable, and more: as if she had just realized she was inconsolable. "I miss Nick," she said. Outside the door the little girl had begun to cry.

Fred knelt down beside Kate, momentarily his former self again. "Katie, Katie, Katie, what's the matter? I'm sorry. I'm sorry, darling. Did I do something to upset you? I'm sorry—"

In the midst of the confusion, there was a knock at the door. "There's a child out here wants to play," said a woman's voice.

I instinctively took a step back as Mr. Brown sprang up and wrenched the door open. It banged terribly. "Whadaya want?" he demanded.

"This little girl wants to play horse and rider," said the woman.

"All right," sighed Fred. "Come on, you little bitch," he added, in a gentle, resigned tone that didn't match the words, and laughed at what he evidently considered to be a joke.

When the woman stepped into the room, I recognized my companion of the alcove. "Oh—*hello,*" she said. Then she noticed Kate. "I see you found Katie!" she added brightly, retreating from the room.

"Don't call me, Katie, Linda," Kate said. "And you're interrupting."

"All right, Kate. I'm sorry, I'm very sorry—I was just trying to sleep next door and I heard the little girl crying—"

Now Kate rose from the floor, her dress hanging in distorted folds. Before I could even guess what her expression meant, she had gone to the door and, astonishingly, slammed it in the woman's face. "How do you know her?"

"We met downstairs," I answered.

"Linda Van Wijck is a slut," Kate said.

"A big slut," Mr. Brown said gaily.

"A bigger slut!" the little girl cried, clapping her hands.

"But you're a slut, too, Katie." Mr. Brown gave a wink in my direction.

"Ha ha, that's very funny." Kate was sitting on the bed, picking carpet shards off of her gold top.

"She's not a virgin, is she?" taunted her cousin. "Is she? Is she, is she, is she?" By now he was pointing at Kate and dancing a little jig around the room. "You've had it in you! You've had it in you!"

The little girl was banging on the bedpost with one of Kate's shoes.

"Kate, please—let's leave," I urged. "They'll be wondering where we are—"

Mr. Brown walked toward Kate, his arms outstretched like a sleepwalker's, his hands fixed in a strangle grip. There was a horrifying moment when I went to pull Kate up from the bed and away from him at the same time that her cousin grabbed hold of the gold top. Kate shrieked as the material ripped away from her. Mr. Brown held up the top, brandishing it triumphantly. "I capture the castle!" he cried. "I capture the castle!"

For a second or two, like the stunned expression of a child that falls down, Kate's face could have gone either way. Then she went with laughter. Her arms folded defensively over her bare flat chest, Kate sat on the little twin bed and laughed. They all did, all three of them, and they had the same laugh—Mr. Brown, Kate, and the little girl. I don't mean the same timbre or that they laughed on the same vowel—I mean that the intensity was the same. I felt like a real spoilsport. I had to push and push myself to keep laughing while their laughter went on effortlessly into the night.

They played for hours. I sat on the floor outside the bedroom and read the history of the America's Cup. I learned all kinds of things, such as who the first skipper was, and what year they invented the Park Avenue boom. At two or three a maid came up and told them to quiet down. Mr. Brown picked a fight with the woman and was sent to his room, and the little girl's mother finally came back, drunk, from town and took her daughter away. I had a bad feeling, crashing in the room with Kate, that the adults in the house would think I'd try to take advantage of our solitude up there on the third floor, but in retrospect I'm sure no one gave it a thought.

I never mentioned my conversation under the alcove to Kate, or heard the rumor Linda Van Wijck told me confirmed or denied. I am sure I probably misheard the woman, or misunderstood her—or more likely, that she misspoke out of drunkenness, or some lingering envy from her school days with Kate's mother. For what I thought I heard her say was that Mr. Goodenow was not Kate's father. It is strange, perhaps, that I did not try harder to learn the truth. But the idea of doing so behind Kate's back was more inconceivable only than asking her to her face. I had trouble believing it was true, and yet there were times later on when I felt it would have explained a great deal. A third possibility occurred to me the next morning, when Granny's car drove us over to the regatta: maybe it was true, and they had never told Kate. Or perhaps—I stole a look at her, dozing lightly across the seat from me, at the jaunty chin, which no messy, irrelevant past had ever brought down—perhaps poor Linda Van Wijck knew more than she knew she knew: maybe it was true, and the women had never told Art Goodenow.

In any event, in the wake of Nick's dramatic departure, there were no repercussions about our overnight absence.

CHAPTER 21

After Kate's engagement party Nick found a job steering a boat from Rye, New York, down to the West Indies. At my urging, he'd waited around for a week while I did what I could to penetrate the Goodenow fortress that had sprung up to protect Kate. But it was no use. They wouldn't take my calls; they wouldn't let him see her. Kate didn't answer at home or at work, and it was only when an aunt mistook me for someone else on the phone that I learned she had taken a leave from Sotheby's.

Nick put off the job for a weekend, but then they had to go and one Monday in November we had our last breakfast. During his stay in my apartment I'd gotten back into the habit of a morning meal. Nick had learned to cook going down to Bermuda on one of the maxis and he said it was funny now, using a stove that didn't tilt. He made omelettes for Toff and me every morning but he tried to keep it healthy, leaving out a yolk every other white.

"I guess I'm not going to see Kate this visit." Nick had a habit of sopping up his eggs with toast, of combining several dishes into one and eating them as a kind of stew, of finishing his juice and using the empty glass for milk, but with him you attributed all this to the galley, and you admired the practicality.

"I'll tell her you were here, that you waited," I said.

"Sure. I'll be back."

We finished our coffee.

It was true that Nick had gotten married, just like the kid told it— on a boat off Anguilla one Race Week. At odd times his wife's name would come up. I would be on the brink of asking, "Now, who's Stacy again?" and then I would remember. "I'd like Kath to meet Stacy," Nick said, pushing his plate aside. "I think they'd get along."

"I'll tell her," I said. "I'll tell her you said that."

He nodded reflectively. "That guy she's marrying. Harry. He's a nice guy, isn't he?"

"Oh, sure," I said.

"Seemed it. Seemed like a really nice guy."

"I'll tell *him* you said that. I don't think anyone's told him that before."

"Yeah? Why not?"

"Oh, I don't know," I said. "He's very . . . ambitious."

"Ambitious?" Nick said, after a moment, as if he hadn't heard right. "But that's great, George. Ambition is great."

"Sure it is, Nick."

"Who doesn't know that? Don't people know that?"

"They know," I said. "But sometimes they see it in someone else and—I don't know—it bothers them."

"Why would it do that?"

"It's stupid, I guess."

"It is. Stupid." Nick tipped back from the table and used his fingertips to balance on the back legs of the chair. I picture him that way, suspended in an adolescent's posture that he had never outgrown.

"Maybe I should have had more ambition," he suggested finally, in the manner one might say, "Maybe I should have taken a cab," and let the front chair legs back down to the floor.

"Come on, Nick," I argued, "you're doing better than all of us. You've got it figured out. You do what the rest of us only—"

"But, George," Nick said, with a patient smile, "we don't know where I would have been if I had had ambition. Yes." He nodded solemnly. "Ambition is good and people shouldn't knock it. I'm going to write that guy a postcard and tell him so."

I was late by then so I took a cab down to work. On my way down, I thought about my second, abortive date with Delia Ferrier, and the excuse I had made of my job. It was a breezy day and the wind seemed to mock me and my ambition—the puffs rippling down the East River; the pointless, metropolitan gust. Since coming to the city, I had done my best to ignore the wind, but sometimes it found me anyway.

Harry was anxious on the phone: "I'm-unna—I'm-unna— I'm-unna see her soon. Soon as she's back. She can't be bothered, George, and I can't tell you any more. She's resting, all right? Leave it at that. I'm-unna see her soon, and soon as I do, I'll tell her you were asking for her. You and she are very good friends, I know. You and she go way back, and I know she'd want to see you if she was seeing anyone. But right now she's not seeing anyone. So leave it at that, okay. Leave it at this." I suspected Harry didn't know where they were keeping her any more than Nick or I did, but felt he had to keep up a semblance of being in the familial know. I didn't blame him, nor did I press him. I left it at that. For I felt rather lucky to have gotten rid of Harry for the time being; I always did.

It was nice, chatty Annie Roth who finally filled me in. Kate was indeed gone from work, and the rumor was that she and her mother had gone away somewhere warm. "We tried to visit her in the hospital," Annie volunteered, "but they wouldn't let us in." I very nearly asked her what had happened—I was picturing Kate with a broken leg or arm—before I grasped the truth. "But Mr. Goodenow took Jess and me out to lunch at the yacht club. Wasn't that sweet of him? Poor guy, they're *really worried.* I mean, this is the second time, you know. You see, Kate never had any of the adolescent rebellion problems the rest of us did. Well, okay, there was the eating thing, but hell, who wasn't starving themselves in high school? I just wasn't very good at it! That's sad, isn't it, George? A would-be anorexic!"

Cara, whose presence of late had been refreshingly muted, resurfaced after Nick left. She seemed to be possessed of a great, secret energy, and this energy prompted her to bring over her vacuum to clean the living room, and to mop the kitchen floor and go around spraying spots on the wall. The apartment had never looked so good. She found a torn flannel shirt of Nick's in the couch he'd been sleeping on and used it as a dust rag and then threw it out. "Good riddance!"

"He is coming back, you know," I told her. "He's coming back tomorrow, so you'd better get used to sharing your space, dear." I loved to needle her.

"What?" Cara cried, pausing with spray bottle in hand. "How long's he gonna stay?"

"Two, three months. Probably for good."

"What? How can you say this? Don't you know you're being taken advantage of?"

"Um . . ."

"But he was here on the couch every night!"

"Ye-es. Well, so have, ahem—"

Cara was the kind of girl who looks surreptitiously into every reflective surface she passes, and she had been fixing her hair in the window. But now her hands flew to her hips as she spun around. "That's different! I'm Geoff's girlfriend!" Till the very end, she was always Geoff's girlfriend. "I have a right to be here! He's not . . . anyone!"

"He's a friend of mine."

"Well, you should tell your friend to clean up his act. You know he *smokes* all day! That's very bad for me. For . . . someone like me," she finished rather meekly, momentarily deserting her indignant stand.

"Come on, you smoke yourself."

"Cigarettes!" shrieked Cara. "And not any*more*."

When I didn't reply she positioned herself between me and the television. "Yes?"

"I quit."

"Congratulations."

"Well, it wasn't hard," she conceded. "Considering."

Three years afterward, and I can still remember the exchange. She kept dangling pointed remarks in front of me which I kept batting away. It was fun not letting her get a rise out of me. And she— she must have been dithering between fear and triumph, dithering at such a fever pitch that she held back and held back and held back, almost in spite of herself. I remember telling her she ought to go take an aerobics class, to get rid of some of that excess energy, and she mentioned her "condition." She must have been out of her mind not telling me, and yet for the first time in her life she must have sensed the security that a great secret affords: time. You can wait and wait and wait; for once, you have enough time. You can detonate the bomb any time you wish, and it still explodes and ruins things.

Of course I deserved to miss every clue. I paid her no heed, I never did; because she was Cara.

I consider myself a fairly perceptive person, I mean when it comes to dime-store psychologizing. I'll admit I take a certain pride in understanding the desires and fears that drive the behavior of my friends and acquaintances, in understanding where these feelings come from and how they are manifested. All too often I am aware of the ulterior motives beneath the thin veil of convention or cant that people use to explain their behavior. But as an analyst of human nature I have one critical failing. And despite my awareness of it, I cannot seem to correct it. I cannot seem to teach myself otherwise. Year after year I go on assuming the wrong thing: I never expect people's lives to fall into cliché. I never expect a man to cheat on his wife, I never expect a woman to run off with a lover, and if someone were to tell me that a beautiful girl was marrying a rich old man for his money, I would dismiss the idea as too Hollywood. When time and again I witness just such trite scenarios played out around me, I am amazed. Amazed and a bit abashed, too, that whoever it is could get it into their heads not only to act at all in such standard situations, but to act in so hackneyed a fashion. The predictible is the thing I am incapable of predicting. I don't know where my own predilection for originality—my expectations—comes from, but I am betrayed by it, nearly always.

I worked Christmas Eve and spent a freezing, endless New Year's Eve with Chat. The actual hour of midnight we spent in the all-night post office on Thirty-fourth Street, express mailing Chat's business school applications, which he'd been too drunk all Christmas to finish.

"Bastard. It's A.A. for you."

"I don't need to drink to have fun."

Afterward we went outside and did shots of vodka with the homeless, on the steps of that massive gray building.

"Good," I said. "Because we're too late for Annie's and too early for Twelfth Street." Not that I minded, really. New Year's, like all evils, was made worse by New York. We ought to have skipped the rest; we ought to have called it a night then and there.

"Have you met Roth's new boyfriend?" asked Chat. He took a final drink. "Now, that man is a serious alcoholic."

We capped the bottle and started down the steps, coats and scarves flapping. Then we were running for the warmth of the subway stairs—there wasn't a cab to be had anywhere.

"You know what Kate told me about her father? 'Dad says Alcoholics Anonymous is ruining this country, and Mom and I just say . . .' " I quoted drunkenly.

Chat's teeth showed in the night. "Goodenow?" he cried. "Now, that bastard is an *old-school* alcoholic. You should see him when he can't get a drink. He punched a neighbor once! Mr. Godfrey! In Maine!"

"Something to work toward!" I cried. In the meantime, I suspected, the general rule of thumb would continue to prevail: anyone who drank more than you was an alcoholic; anyone who drank less was a crusader, a cramper of styles, or simply odd.

All night we were too early for the party or too late. The people we wanted to see had not arrived. The people we wanted to see had just left in the only available cab in the five boroughs. "This is no good, George," Chat complained as we stood in a fluorescent hallway watching another apartment empty out. "Find us a party."

We picked up Pam Allen and a friend of hers in the vicinity of Murray Hill, and the four of us went, around three in the morning, to a Fordyce party in a rented bar. The line to get in was so long it had turned into a party itself. A nervous, one-night-stand camaraderie pervaded, of the sort that is particular to the largest cities during holidays and disasters.

"I'll be damned if I'm going to stand in line to get into a bar," Chat said disgustedly. "Let's go back to my place. There's plenty to drink."

"You mean my place," Pam corrected him.

"Oh now, Pammie, don't be *stingy*! It's New Year's Eve!"

"You guys! You guys!" A voice, dogged and eager, broke out of the line and then the man claimed it, trundling forward, gesticulating with a bottle of booze.

Chat's eyebrows rose in merriment. "I do believe we have found our ticket to ride."

"Who are you?" said Pam, listing a little to one side.

"May I present Henry Lombardi, Junior," Chat announced with aplomb. "This, Pamela, is Kate Goodenow's fiancé."

"Oh, *you're* the one?" said Pam. Her friend could barely rouse herself to nod hello.

"Where is the little woman this evening?"

"Kate's in Saint Kitts," Harry said dully.

"Oh, is that where they took her." Chat nodded. "I *see.*"

"She's coming home tomorrow."

"Ahh, start the new year right? Clean slate? Fresh plate? Ring out the *old*—and yet one might think that down in the Caribbean, certain, pernicious *influences* of old—"

"Where are you headed, Harry?" I broke in.

"Oh, I don't know. How 'bout you guys?"

I gestured to the stalled line. "Are you going in here?"

"I don't know. I was, but . . . but now I don't know."

"D'ya know of any other parties?" Chat demanded.

"No. No, I don't know of anything."

"The hell with it. Let's go to Pam's," Chat decided. "We can drink there."

"How are we even going to get up there?" Pam's friend wailed, seeming to lose patience with our scene all at once.

"She's right. There aren't any cabs."

"God*dammit*, New Year's *sucks!*"

"I hate it too," I said.

"I'll take you guys," offered Harry.

"Take us?" Chat said. "The hell you mean?"

Harry shrugged and stuffed his hands into his pockets. He wasn't wearing gloves or a scarf; I guessed it was an old habit from high school—that back then, keeping warm hadn't been cool. "I have my car."

"Your *car*? Well, that's . . . crazy!" slurred Chat.

"Heh, heh, heh."

"Where is said car, er, situated?"

Harry gestured up the block. "Garage."

"Garage? Jesus! That is fucking incredible, Henry. You guys—Lombardi has his car. Did you hear that, George? Lombardi has his car." Chat looked balefully at the rest of us. "Well, come *on*, everyone; we'll take the car."

"Oh, say," I said quietly, walking up the block with Harry while

Chat played sweep with an arm around each girl, "I have something for you."

Harry gave me a look like the one I imagine a father would give a son who has finally taken his advice after all these years. He knew exactly what I was referring to. "George—you're a good man, George. And a smart man. Send it to me at the office."

"Office?"

"Yeah. I'm finally outta the apartment. Got office space now." He pressed a business card into my hand.

"It's not much," I warned.

"It'll do," he said. "It'll do."

Halfway to the garage the girls cut their losses and decided to go back and join the line. Deserted, we waited unhappily for the car. "This is—this is *tragic*!" Chat wailed. "I mean, there's got to be a party somewhere! It's New Year's Fucking Eve!"

"I know of a party," said Harry after a moment.

"You do?"

"Yeah."

"Thought you said you didn't. *I* thought that *you* said that *you* didn't know of anything."

"I just remembered."

"So what is it? What's the party?"

"It's a Millport party," Harry said. "I was going to go there later."

"It *is* later!" Chat complained. "It's four—five—four in the morning!"

"If you want to go, hell—let's go."

I asked him where it was.

"Jersey City."

Chat's face lit up, his eyes reflecting the infinite possibilities indicated by this location. "Jersey party?"

Harry nodded.

"Woo-hoo! Woo-hoo!" exulted Chat. "New Year's Eve! Jersey road trip! New Year's Eve! Jersey road trip!" He did a little drunk, anticipatory dance in the parking lot. I had forgotten that about

Chat: how sour he was, how put out and difficult, and yet how frequently affable underneath.

There was some dispute over who would ride where.

"Look, I'll go home and you two go."

"Oh, no," said Chat. "Oh, no, Lenhart. I saw that coming two hours ago and I'm not letting you off the hook. It's New Year's *Eve.*"

Harry wouldn't hear of it, either. "No, listen. You two take my car and I'll take a car service. It'll be better that way. No, really—really. I'll give you directions and when you get there, just tell 'em you know me. Just tell 'em you know me, they'll let you in."

"We'll be sure to tell 'em!" Chat promised. "We'll tell 'em Harry Lombardi sent us. Good ole Lombardi!"

Had I been sober, I hope I would have had the grace to beg off. But as it was, it seemed reasonable enough that Chat and I should take the convertible and that Harry should follow in a car service, despite it being his car, his friends, his party, his everything. I insisted on driving, as the lesser of the two evils, and as we left Harry pressed a twenty into my hand. "For gas and tolls, George. She might need a top-off."

It took an hour to get through the tunnel, and Chat, after turning on the radio and changing the station twenty times, fell fast asleep. Seeing the two of us in that cream puff of a car, the beefed-up drivers of more than one lane-changing vehicle called us some very uninspired names. When we got past the tolls it was nearly five. I was so relieved that it was still dark out I didn't care. I drove about ten miles an hour and stopped at every stoplight for years; I made a few circles, puzzling out Harry's directions, but it's funny how one's sense of direction kicks in when the other senses are dulled. I felt my way there, down real little streets of real little houses to a yellow one with a mesh fence around it. Cars were parked at rakish angles up the street and on into the yard. The party was on the second rickety story. Chat stumbled up the stairs, chanting, "Lombardi sent us. We friends of Lombardi." As we went in, I had a flashback to college fraternity parties: the familiar smell of beer and bad carpet; the familiar shock at the spectacle of a house, not just a dormitory room, getting trashed.

It was a good, friendly crowd inside—Harry's friends from home, not the Catholic WASPs of Manhattan and Westchester but the lower-rent partiers who made Thanksgiving and Fourth of July such crazy *"You kids!"* bashes every year. I fought my way through the pink, sweaty faces to a keg in the bathroom. Automatically I had picked up an empty pitcher to fill—get the most beer possible—and when the guy who was manning the tap apologized for the head on it, it seemed like the kindest thing anyone had said in a year. Chat had made a noisy entrance and then headed for a bedroom, presumably to pass out. I just wanted to be allowed to stand in a corner and drink my pitcher of beer.

A girl was putting on a show in the middle of the room, demonstrating a new dance that people did together in a line, not touching one another. A few rhythmically minded young men had stood up behind her and were echoing her movements. It seemed like a sweet, safe party, where the worst thing anyone did was get trashed, smoke a lot of cigarettes, maybe have sex. I went to refill my pitcher.

The dancing girl joined me presently. "Aren't you going to say hi?" she said, giving me a genial elbow.

I stopped pumping the tap. Of course she was there. "Cara," I said, giving her a kiss. "Happy New Year."

"That's right, Georgie, Happy New Year. It's gonna be a *big* happy new year for me. Lemme see that; it's all foam." She took the pitcher and poured it off into the grimy bathtub, then refilled it with an expert tilt. Perhaps it was the hour, or the idea of the new year, but I seemed to be falling into a soppy frame of mind. I found myself thinking Toff ought to stop screwing around—she would make some man a good wife.

"Thanks."

"No problem." Her face was red from exertion, and she looked uncharacteristically bloated.

"So, Geoff is here, too?"

"No! The asshole wouldn't leave Manhattan."

"Oh, no?"

"He doesn't love me," Cara added.

In view of the rest of the evening—day, rather; dawn was threatening even as we spoke—I remember our brief discourse about my roommate as a blessed moment of convention; it seems polite in retrospect, how we discussed whether Toff loved Cara or had ever loved her, as if we were discussing the weather at a funeral. "It's a nice day, isn't it?"

"Yes, it is: perfect. I know Toff just used me for sex."

"Oh, dear, are you hot? But there's such a nice breeze. Come toward the window."

"Why did he do that, George?"

"Toff would have enjoyed this party," I said. "Beer?"

Cara held up a cup. "All right, now, where's Henry hiding?"

"He's not here yet."

"No, I saw the car. *She's* with him, right? I knew that the minute he didn't come right up."

"Who—you mean?" I said, purposefully omitting Kate's name. "Well, they are . . . *engaged.*"

"I'm right, aren't I? Where is she?" pressed Cara.

"No, she's not here. God—she wouldn't come out here."

"No? No sense of adventure, huh? Just like Toff. Maybe she doesn't love him, either," Cara speculated.

"I drove the car," I explained. "With a friend of mine. Harry's coming in a car service."

She was highly doubtful of this explanation, as well might she have been. "Oh, yeah? Well, soon as he gets here, tell me, okay? I got a surprise for him."

"What do you mean you've got a surprise for him?" I said coldly. I envisioned Harry, come out to Jersey for a final, *final* nostalgic tumble. It was getting a bit ridiculous, even for them.

"You'll find out soon enough."

"Lenhart!" Chat had rallied from the dead. "Man-man-man here says he knows you. Name of Lombardi. Should we let him in?"

The telltale giggle was like the bass line to Chat's chorus: "Heh, heh, heh. Heh, heh, heh."

Cara flinched at the noise. She stepped tentatively into the middle of the room. Her heels were so high I didn't know how she could balance on them. "I have an announcement to make!" she said in a strained voice. "I have an announcement to make!"

"Heh, heh, heh. Cara: heh, heh, heh."

"Henry, this concerns you." With the room's attention, Cara looked around rather wildly, like a child at an audition, who suddenly finds herself alone on the stage. "I hope everyone's listening—"

"Who're you?" Chat asked rudely.

Cara focused on him as if she couldn't quite believe what he'd said. She stared, astonished, digesting the question. It seemed oddly to inspire her. She threw her shoulders back. "I," she declaimed, patting her abdomen instead of her heart, "am the future mother of the son of Henry Lombardi."

"What does that make you, his aunt?" cracked a guy in the background.

At the door where he had come in, Harry's face was motionless. Only his eyes were alive, moving, in intense perception.

Noting the rather blank reaction that her revelation had prompted in the rest of the crowd, Cara relinquished her front-and-center stand. She put her hot face close to mine and said, menacingly—and somewhat bizarrely—"He made his bed, he can lie in it!"

After a moment, Harry turned to a group of people by the door and wished them a Happy New Year.

CHAPTER 22

It is a source of perpetual vexation to New Yorkers who live and work in Manhattan that the best views of the city are had by the outer boroughs and New Jersey. But this geographical injustice can be turned on its ear: "We *create* the view," I have heard a man rationalize, "and they all look at us." And yet one remains suspicious, heading back in, that they do nothing of the kind; that one is a rat on a wheel whose observing scientist has gone home for the night. We spin and we spin and we spin, and no one notices.

It was dawn when I drove Harry back above Chat's protests; it was, finally, dawn. It was a lead gray, ashen dawn, more a diminishing of darkness than an infusion of light; an anticlimactic dawn. I kept the car lights on, for safety's sake, as if there were anything left to protect. Harry had asked me to drive, he said so he could think. But I recognized the gesture for what it was—a concession to my agitated state, which he knew the driving would help assuage. And Harry did not think. He sat quietly with his hands folded in his lap, taking steady, modulated breaths. It was the first time I had sat beside him and not watched him bite his nails or touch the back of his head or drum his fingers on the nearest surface. I gunned the car down the back streets. When we got to the highway Harry cracked his window. "Is this too cold for you?"

"No," I said. "So, let me see now. You're entirely decided, aren't you?" At the party, he and Cara had disappeared for half an hour. When they returned, she was leaning on him tearfully. He wanted to drive her back, but she wouldn't hear of it. "Beer and bagels," she had sniffed. "I can't miss the beer and bagels. I promised."

"You're going to be quite the martyr, aren't you?" I said.

"It's funny, we throw that word around—"

"Don't, Harry! Don't subject me to it!"

He was silent several minutes, contrite.

"Do you ever go to church?" he asked.

"Twice a year," I told him.

"Of course." He beamed. "The Christmas and Easter Episcopalian."

"Yes," I said. "I believe in a God who looks like a cross between my father and my high school headmaster. I believe in the Nicene Creed with a couple of hymns on either side. Why can't you leave your theology at that?"

"Oh, George . . ."

"But she planned it! She plotted the whole thing!"

"The only thing she 'plotted,' " Harry objected quietly, "was keeping it. I would have asked her to do that."

I ranted on: "Are you going to let yourself be sucked in? Are you going to be stupid enough—"

"See, that's where we differ, George," Harry interrupted. "I don't think of it as a question of my intelligence."

"Kate needs you, you know," I said a little later, but I could feel my belligerence ebbing from me. "She had some kind of—breakdown when Nick showed up. You ought to remember that. You ought to remember the raw deal you would be giving Kate."

"Yes," he said seriously. "I know she needs me. I'll have to be a very good friend to Kate in the next few months."

"God," I said. "I hate religious people."

He smiled faintly, in an infuriating way. "But we *love* you," he said. I think it was the first joke I ever heard him make.

It felt like a funeral—the way one ends up telling jokes on the drive there, understanding precisely how long the reprieve will last, the length of the drive, and exactly why one tells them: it makes life easier to bear.

In Manhattan we drove up Eighth Avenue past Penn Station, where in high school Harry must have waited, carded at every bar, for the last train out. On the East Side the sidewalks were crowded with the old frat boys stumbling home, straggling out of bars like it was any town in America, and the lone girls doing the walk of shame in prom dresses and tennis shoes, carrying their pumps and awake to see the dawn.

I stayed the morning with him. He didn't want to go home, so we went to a diner. It was packed with the morning-after, demanding Bloody Marys. Harry ordered one. "Come on, George! Hair of the dog!"

"No," I said, "I'm never drinking again."

He looked at me curiously. "*You* didn't cause this."

"It was a joke."

"Oh."

We hadn't slept, of course. Harry wouldn't touch his food, and after three or four cups of coffee he had worked himself into an ecstatic state.

"I can learn to love her, George. I do love her in a way."

I stared stonily at my cup.

"She was the first person who ever gave me a chance." This last remark he made completely without irony, as if he'd forgotten the nature of the chance.

I was furious by now, and I couldn't do a goddamn thing. Harry made me feel as if I were going to throw a temper tantrum in front of a psychiatrist, or a priest. Even the way he had taken the news had been alarmingly calm. He had not lost control for a moment. If one had had a tape of Cara's announcement, of her immediate and appalling marshaling of the evidence to prove it was his, one would have had to zoom in on Harry's face and replay his reaction half a dozen times in slow motion even to see that there had been one at all.

I sat at breakfast with him that morning, and it occurred to me that in the days to come I would mourn the passing of the old Harry. It was too early for him to go! But they had gotten him so young. That sinner had been looking all his life for the sin to fit him.

I had found a Bible in the end table of my room out in Southampton. I recalled it suddenly, my amusement at finding it there, as if Harry had taken his cue from the Holiday Inns and wished to have a summer house as nice as . . . any cheap motel! It was what I generally think of as a Roman Catholic Bible, covered in white with color plates of Moses at the sea and Lazarus getting a second go-round with a funny expression on his face. Harry had marked certain passages for further study. One of the bookmarks had a Technicolor sunset with a psalm embossed on it, and on the back Harry had written:

> BAD: *Doing* _____.
> WORSE: *Thinking about* _____.
> WORST: *Lying about* _____.

It was all there in the omissions and the ordering, the relationship to the sin a greater offense than the sin itself. Kate would have absolved him of it, of all of it, and he couldn't bear it. He had to go back and root around with Cara in the trashed house in Millport, with his dad upstairs getting some, too, praying he wouldn't get caught— doing—thinking about—. It was a congenital curse: for some people getting off scot-free was unbearable.

"God damn you!" I said presently, not quite knowing whom I was talking about. At that point it could even have been Kate.

"Heh, heh, now, George—"

Harry excused himself then; his cellular phone was ringing and he had to take the call.

CHAPTER 23

I'm still not sure how he persuaded me to go over and wait with her, except that it was Harry, and at my first show of reluctance, I swallowed the feeling and stammered out guilty apologies. The breakfast over, Cara had gone home and changed her tune. She had called sounding "hysterical." She didn't want to be alone; she was worried she might "do something."

"Like what?" I said, highly skeptical.

"I shouldna let her ride back alone. She's worried and upset, George. She needs somebody with her."

"I'll bet she does."

"Now, George . . ."

"What?"

"I want you to— I'm *asking* you to go and see her."

"All right, all right!" I conceded. "Just don't look at me like that."

"Good." He was satisfied. "You just go over there and make sure she's all right, and I'll be there as soon as I can."

"You want me to *stay* with her?"

"Yes, George. Try to be charitable, George. You have the day off, don't you? Take the car."

"But where are you going?"

"Coupla things I've got to do. I've got to go talk to a priest."

"Oh."

"And then I've got to talk to Kate."

I was settling the check when Harry came panting back to the table. "Oh, say, George, don't forget," he reminded me. "I mean about the money."

"The money?" I said suspiciously. "It's only twenty bucks."

"No, you know, the, uh, investment. You didn't lose my card, did you?" He put up a hand to stop my protests. "Good, good—just checking. Send it to me at the office this week, soon as you can."

She lived four flights up, on First Avenue in the Seventies. It was one of those staircases that seem to have been built especially to insult one's pretense of physical fitness. The landings didn't come fast enough. On each of them, unsavory plastic bags of garbage had been set out, and a smell like rotting Chinese food grew stronger and stronger as I climbed, until I was holding my jacket over my nose and breathing into that. But soon, I guessed, Cara's walk-up days would be over. She'd move into Harry's high-rise, start ordering the doorman around. . . . On Cara's floor, an old woman opened a dilapidated door. She peered out at me for an instant, disapproving, then retreated into the darkness of her apartment.

I suppose Harry had told her to expect me, but the alacrity with which the buzzer had sounded outside, cutting me off before I could say my name, gave me the impression that they were in the habit of buzzing, oh, just about everyone up. The door was open, propped on its dead bolt, and I pushed my way in, wondering what pose she would have struck. Her apartment was a two-bedroom serving as three; one person—Cara—had the living room for a bedroom. There was something indecent about it, about stepping into someone's boudoir without a hiatus of even six feet of hall.

She was sitting up in bed, spooning frozen yogurt out of a Styrofoam cup. She was wearing a tunic over the black leggings, and except for the position she was in, I wouldn't have guessed her condition. Cara was one of those pregnant women who only get the stomach, while the rest of them stays thin.

Beside the bed, on top of a stack of milk cartons, was a large framed photograph of Geoff Toff. "Hello, George," Cara said weakly, affecting a deference to me, as she used to do when she greeted me in my own apartment.

"The two of you survived the festivities, I see." But I had promised to be charitable.

The room itself was rather pitifully neat. The main piece of furniture besides the bed was one of those pine stands that ought to be used as bookshelves but more often hold, as the one in Cara's apartment did, a glass bowl, a teddy bear, a picture of a bunch of girls, and a row of yearbooks and photo albums plus five books of popular fiction.

"Do you want something to drink?"

"God, no." I looked around. Above her bed were two collages made of photographs and magazine headlines, the kind girls make for one another for high school graduation.

"Not thirsty?"

"No." I was disappointing her, I knew, by not getting more into the spirit of things. *Her* work was done: this was supposed to be the fun part. Probably I should have volunteered to run out for ice cream and pickles.

"Well, I'm gonna have something." She slid off the bed and went into the kitchen. She was still wearing her party shoes, balancing precariously on the tiny heels. She poked her head out and beckoned to me. "Come see my collection."

A little card table had been wedged in between the stove and window, with a lace doily on it, and two folding chairs pushed underneath, as if to prove that the advertisement had not lied—that one could, indeed, "eat in." Cara opened the cupboard above the sink. It

was filled with miniature shot bottles of alcohol, forty or fifty of
them. "I collect them," Cara said proudly. "I bring them back from
all my trips. See? I've got Tia Maria, I've got Frangelico—I could
probably make you any drink there is. I could make you a White
Russian, or a Long Island Iced Tea—anything. Anything you want."

"Wow."

"So you don't want something?"

"Not today, Cara."

"*Boring*. Boring, boring, boring." After some deliberation she
mixed herself a Kahlúa and milk and got back into bed.

I followed her back into the room, and that was when I noticed
another picture, hanging on the wall opposite the bed. It was a drawing of a pair of rampant lions on either side of a cross. In cursive
script below the drawing (which appeared to be a page torn out of a
guidebook) the caption said: THE MCLEAN FAMILY CREST. The absurdity of that endless day was now complete—or so I thought.

"Whatever you think about this, George, you're wrong," Cara
said petulantly. She was now sitting Indian-style on the bed with her
back up against the wall. "I didn't plan anything. Not a thing! When
we hooked up the night of your party, I had no idea—"

"You know, you shouldn't drink when you're pregnant," I interrupted.

"Big deal! It's New Year's Eve."

"It's not, actually."

"New Year's Day, then!" she snapped. "Don't be so pedantic!
Anyway, one day isn't gonna kill her."

"Her?" I said curiously.

"It's a girl. I was kind of hoping for a boy so we could name it
Henry, but now I know it's a girl we can name it—"

"Cara?"

"*No*. Priscilla."

"Priscilla?"

"Yes. Priscilla."

"Er, why—?"

" 'Cause I *like* it! That's why!"

Somehow we got through the day. Cara turned the football on and we argued stats and rooted against each other. I tried Harry a couple of times, but his phone was turned off. Still, it gave me a funny picture: "Father, I have sinned. I—oh, could you excuse me a moment? I've gotta take this call."

Eventually I did run out to the deli for snacks, a long list of them, from barbecued potato chips to a chocolate bar I brought the wrong version of. "You got nuts and raisins!" wailed Cara. "I hate nuts and raisins! I wanted plain!"

"I'll eat it."

"Good! You take it. Good riddance! Hey! What are you smiling about?"

"Never mind." I'd been thinking that it was all working out rather well, that Harry would be working off the errors of his ways for a lifetime, pushing a stone up the hill of nuts and raisins and barbecued *rippled* and the *good* kind. . . .

"Well, I do mind!" She sucked on the straw like a pacifier, her eyes moving back and forth with untold wounds. Every so often a hand would move to the little bottle of Kahlúa on her bedside table. It would dash a few more drops into her drink and return to rest, complacent, on the inflated abdomen. It terrified me, the idea that she had been able to go out and get herself pregnant, seemingly by herself—Harry's involvement almost seemed superfluous.

But the heat was cranked up and the television was large. And by late afternoon I was sufficiently settled in to resent the harsh ring of the buzzer. I remember thinking that at least I would get Harry to give me a ride home before he did anything else. He owed me that.

Cara labored out of bed and made for the door as if I were going to race her for it.

"Hello? Hello?" she said breathlessly.

"Maybe it's Toff," I suggested.

"Ha, ha."

"This is Arthur Goodenow," said a grim voice. "Let me in."

If Cara had recognized the name, perhaps she would have had the sense not to let him in at all. But her finger was poised over the buzzer, and in the instant before she pressed it, she appeared to feel only a deepening of the excitement that she alone had caused. Instinctively she turned to me, a question on her face.

"It's her father," I said as she let the man in.

"Kate's father?" She looked around wildly, and straightened a perfect pile of magazines before retreating to the bed. Cara was a demon tidier, a fact that gave a curious pathos to the caught-in-bed artlessness she affected.

"George, he can't do anything to me, can he?"

"What could he do?" I said. But I myself relinquished the sagging armchair and stood up. I didn't want to be caught sitting down by Kate's father; I knew that.

"I don't know," she said nervously. "I just mean—he can't do anything to me, can he?"

He had Kate with him.

The sight of her tan, erect figure in the doorway made me think that everything was going to be all right, in the end—that the situation could be resolved in a professional manner, and then we could all go out and have a drink together—call Harry from the bar to come and join us. I went to Kate and kissed her. But from the query in her voice I understood that I had been caught off-sides. "Why, George," she said, drawing back and making a quick, critical survey of the room. "How funny to find you here."

Unlike his daughter, Mr. Goodenow showed all the signs of being painfully, angrily hungover. He had slicked his gray hair down and was immaculately shaven—all the exterior efforts undertaken to put things in place. But his hand, as he raised it to point at Cara, shook wildly. "I'd like you to tell us, Miss McLean: just what in hell do you think you're going to accomplish with all of this?" Without taking her eyes off him, Cara's hand closed around the shot bottle, and she shook alcohol into her glass.

"Dad—"

"Let me go on, Kate!" He moved farther into the room. The poor furnishings seemed to cower in the presence of an older man in a very fine dark suit. "If you think for one minute that this contemptible little ploy of yours is going to see one *dime's* net gain when I'm through here—"

"Dad, *Daddy*—"

"Kate, let me talk to her. I know how to handle the situation. Now listen here—"

"It's all right, Cara," interrupted Kate. "We're not mad at you. We—"

"*I* damn well am!" shouted Mr. Goodenow. "You must think you're pretty clever, pulling this stunt! I don't think you're clever at all. I think you're a goddamn little conniving—"

"Dad!" cried Kate, her two hands on his arm. "Don't talk to her like that! You're not going to get anywhere!"

"I'll damn well talk any way I please!"

"Dad! *Dad!*" Kate forced him to look at her. "Dad, please—will you wait outside?"

Mr. Goodenow frowned. The man had a look of stupid anger, as if he'd forgotten the cause and remembered only the emotion itself.

"Yes, you go and wait outside. Here, I'll go with you, all right?"

"If that's what you want—if that's what you want, K. . . ."

Kate turned momentarily to Cara. It occurred to me that she must have come straight from the plane. It was January first and she was wearing a sundress and sandals. "I'm so sorry. I'm terribly sorry. Please excuse us. I'll be right—right back. I'm so sorry to trouble you like this."

Cara stared at Kate's retreating back with a look of increasing marvel. One thing she had not expected that afternoon was Kate's apologizing to her. We could hear Kate muttering angrily to her father on the landing outside, and then she returned, smiling slightly and shaking her head a little.

"First of all, I just want to repeat that I'm not mad at you—Cara.

I know what happened—Harry has told me what happened, and I want to say that I'm not going to blame you and I'm not going to blame Harry. That would be silly. It's not . . . important." She paused, concernedly. Cara, sipping softly, was spellbound. "What is important is that Harry and I are going to be married next summer." Kate paused again, letting the fantasy establish itself; the striped tent; the striped ties. I remember wondering, in that illogical way that one considers the future as if it were tomorrow, whom I would be seated next to at the reception. Jess Brindle, I hoped.

"Cara, I'm not mad. I'm not mad"—she tilted her chin up—"but I do think that what you did was low." Kate looked the older girl in the eyes quite calmly. "I know that we aren't good friends, but I would never, ever have done the same thing to you—or to any woman. I believe that there are standards, you see, moral standards . . ." But the patrician mask fell away for an instant as she snapped, "Frankly, Cara, I would have gotten an abortion!"

For all my mainstream notions, the word was uglier on her lips than I ever could have imagined.

"You can forget about that," Cara retorted, but Kate was hurrying on.

"What I'm about to say may sound incredibly tacky to you at first. But I've talked it over with both my mother and my father and we feel it's the right thing.

"I know you're—" Kate started and then paused, with distaste. "I know you don't have—" It was fascinating to watch her struggle to bring up the subject. She shot a peremptory glance at Cara, as if she expected Cara to have the good manners to finish the thought and save her having to wallow. Cara, however, didn't know the code. There was the pathetic sound of her slurping up the end of her drink, after which Kate laughed and said, quite directly, "The point is, we want to give you some money."

A curious look crossed Cara's face then, which she quelled as fast as she could. But in the moment that she seemed to prick up her ears, I realized that the idea of a bribe had never occurred to her. Once the opportunity came, she had plotted a scheme around it but never once had money entered into it—at least not that kind of money. She had contrived and connived, with the oldest trick in the book, and yet I stood there, ashamed, in the face of her relative innocence.

Once it was out, Kate seemed to enjoy the idea. She stood very naturally, as if they were haggling over Broadway and Park Place. "I was thinking . . . a hundred thousand," she offered.

It was just as ridiculous as one would expect, hearing someone put a price on a life, as dismal and funny at the same time; and coarse, ultimately—that, too. But an even coarser thought immediately occurred to me: that a million would have been more like it. A connection established itself in my mind, but I managed to refrain from asking if Nick Beale had gotten severance when they cut him loose.

"Forget it. He's marrying me."

"Yes, Harry has—has spoken to me of his honorable intentions," Kate said, "but you see I'm appealing to your sense of what's fair, Cara. You know that we have been engaged for some time and that Harry wishes to marry me."

"I don't know that. I certainly do not know that. What I know is he wants to marry me."

Kate pressed her lips together patiently. "He would say that, you see, because he knows he has to—"

"No!" Cara said. "He *wants* to!"

"You're wrong, you see," Kate said. Her voice was growing quieter and quieter, milder and milder. "He's wanted to marry me for years and years. And he'll be miserable—"

"Says who? You don't know the first thing about us! Henry doesn't want a prissy girl like you. I bet you're no good in bed! Otherwise why would he come to me? Answer that! Answer me that!"

For a moment no one said anything.

Then Kate said, "George," appealing to me, as one adult to another, to reason with a stubborn child.

"Kate," I said gently, "why don't we get your father to take you home now."

Kate argued a little while longer; she was a good competitor, after all, and hated to lose an argument. Then, when it dawned on her that her case was hopeless, she clutched at the wall. "Daddy!" she sobbed. "Oh, Daddy! Daddy!" She began to shudder, as if the sudden return to the winter weather was too much for her.

"Kate!" I said.

"My God," cried Cara, pushing herself to the edge of the bed. "Are you all right?" I think she was genuinely worried. She hurried unsteadily to the alcohol cupboard as I made for the door to get Mr. Goodenow. "I'm gonna find you some whiskey. You're overwhelmed, I know, at losing Henry. I was, too." Cara went on, chattily, rummaging through her collection, oblivious to the tone in the room. "Girls understand these things! Kate," she said, bringing the little bottle. "You and I have a lot in common."

The repugnance on Kate's face when she raised it was so bald that Cara took a step back. But even after Mr. Goodenow had cursed her name and taken his daughter into his arms, Cara wasn't quite ready to relinquish the fight. She had discovered the winner's graciousness; she had taken that from Kate, and she was determined to act graciously toward the Goodenows.

"Leave it alone, Cara," I said.

But she tottered after them out to the landing. "Can't we talk this over? Don't you wanna have a drink or something?"

In response, Mr. Goodenow turned from the top stair and viciously batted the shot bottle of whiskey from her hand.

"Hey!" said Cara, relinquishing her politesse at last. "I collect those!"

"Do you. Well, I'll be damned if I'm going to drink dime-store hooch with a two-bit whore!"

"Watch what you say, you hear me?" Lunging for him, Cara tottered on her high heels.

"George!"

Mr. Goodenow was not too hungover to recoil from contact with the flailing figure. Shielding Kate, he pressed himself to the railing. I caught a glimpse of Cara's stomach-flesh as she tripped off the top step and the tunic billowed out like a sail. "Fucking Christ!" With the added weight, the fall made a loudish noise, part whack and part thud.

"Cara?"

The landing now seemed quite far down indeed. Cara's neck was skewed at a ridiculous angle—a wildly obtuse angle that a geometry teacher would make up for the test, an obnoxious angle that you would never see in real life. And there wasn't one of us looking down at her who didn't think the silence that followed her scream might have been for effect.

CHAPTER 24

So few days into the new year, and yet when I got home I had no idea what day it was. Only by counting intermissions of darkness and light could I figure that I had been at the hospital one full night, at the precinct house one full day, back at Lenox Hill another full night, and that it had been three nights and three days since I'd left for New Year's Eve with Chat.

Chat Wethers. The very name seemed part of a social experiment, a comic utopia in which I had dwelled a very long time ago. I could not remember, or had never known, what had become of him. Perhaps he was stranded still in Jersey City, hunting around the party for cigarettes, trying to beg a ride back to the city with a couple of girls.

I sat in Toff's armchair in the weak winter light and wondered idly if I had, at last, been fired. My excuse wasn't so great after all: "My roommate's girlfriend—" "The one-night stand of a guy I know—" The answering machine was blinking like mad, and that would have Toff worried. It made him nervous when I didn't play the messages and write them down in a timely fashion, the way he did. Then I remembered that Toff would not be worried about the answering machine at all. It was difficult; there had been two camps at the hospital—the extended McLean family, who referred to Toff as their daughter's fiancé, and Harry and Mr. Lombardi and Rhonda and I. So I hadn't had much opportunity to talk to Geoff.

I was stumped. I couldn't see myself going in to work, but there was no real reason to stay home, either. I went to lie down on my bed. Then I thought of what to do. It was all I could do to force myself into the shower, make myself shave, find a pair of pants and a clean shirt, lace up my shoes. I had to see Kate. There was something I had to tell her before it was too late. The conviction came to me that she was waiting for me, at that very moment, that she had been waiting for me all along. It was so simple, so obvious, that we hadn't seen it. But wasn't that the way it was supposed to be? You never saw what mattered until something happened that was bigger than yourself—like a death, a tragedy—and then you saw it clearly. What was always left for Kate and me was the way we had been before. If she didn't see this now, she would never see it. I had to make her understand. I prayed—to my Episcopalian Christmas-and-Easter God, I prayed it wasn't too late.

The funny thing, if there was anything funny about the eradication of Cara McLean from the universe, was that I still had Harry's car. I had been using it to chauffeur Harry back and forth to the hospital, to take Rhonda to the grocery store and so forth, and so that morning I had simply driven home. It was parked outside, illegally, but like any good chauffeur I had gotten brazen about that.

So I drove over to Kate's. I had the idea that I would get her to come out riding in it, and then afterward I would tell her what I had to tell her.

The same roadblock of an aunt was standing guard and I had to plead with her, via a very suspicious doorman, to let me up. She showed me into Kate's white living room.

"You know Kate has not been very . . . *well*."

I explained that I was an old friend and asked to be allowed to see her.

"Yale friend?" the aunt inquired coldly.

"No. We went to boarding school together."

"Oh, *Chatham*?" the woman panted, with a sudden fond interest. "Are you a Chattie as well, then? What year did you graduate, dear?"

The apartment wore signs of being overloaded by visitors, just the way Harry's did. There were suitcases half open in the foyer, and a cosmetic case resting incongruously on top of a bookshelf. Catching my glance, Kate's aunt confessed, "I've been sleeping on the couch," and I felt a sudden well of sympathy for the Goodenows, that they should have to camp out for a child in need, like everybody else.

Eventually Kate was produced, and Aunt Kate—Kate was her namesake—removed herself to run errands.

"George," said Kate faintly. "You came." It took me a moment to recover from the shock of seeing her. She was wearing a nightgown and slippers, and behind her head a mat of hair stuck out. But I only felt more tender toward her, and more sure of my conviction. "Won't you sit down? I've been hoping you'd come. You know, I haven't been particularly well."

I watched, incredulously, as Kate took a feeble seat on the couch and drew her knees up to her chest. "I know I'm not much to look at right now—"

"Kate! Kate!" I cried. I crossed the room and took her in my arms. She let herself be hugged, limply, with a wan smile on her lips. I released her but held her icy hands still. She had begun to weep.

"George—"

"Oh, Kate, it's been a mess, it's been a mess!"

"It's been horrible!"

"I know, Kate! I'm so—I'm just so sorry!"

"But it's all right now. You came."

"Come take a ride with me," I urged. "I've got Harry's car outside. It would do you good to get out."

"Do you think?"

"I'm sure of it. You've been cooped up in here with Aunt Kate . . ."

She laughed a little. "Should I get dressed?"

"Only if you want to," I said, stroking the smooth part of her hair. "Park Avenue has seen you nekkid before, remember."

"Why didn't you come sooner?" she asked, looking up at me as if she wanted to be kissed.

"I was at the hospital," I murmured, "with Harry—"

"All this time?" she broke in. "There wasn't very much to be done, was there?"

"Not to be done, but—" I stopped and looked at her. "You know they saved the baby."

Kate drew away slightly. "I'm sorry?"

"The baby," I said gently. "They think it's going to live."

"But how could that be?"

It was curious, her tone. It was very much like annoyance.

"After a certain point, the—the fetus has developed enough—"

"I didn't mean literally!"

"It will be a miracle if it lives," I said after a moment, though I didn't believe in them. I just wanted to say something to close the subject.

Kate seemed to be thinking of something very far off. "A miracle," she repeated thoughtfully. "Do you think so?"

"For Harry's sake," I said.

"Hmm. I suppose."

A black, sobering thought occurred to me. "Were you thinking of going back to him, Kate?"

"Why wouldn't I have?" She frowned. "We were *engaged* before all this started, as you may remember. None of this business is *my* fault."

There was a long silence. "If you'd rather not go out today," I began finally.

"It's just that—" Kate cleared her throat, rather affectedly, and smoothed the old white nightgown over her knees. "Well, I think it's a bit of a shame, really." She spoke reflectively, musing aloud: "A child like that . . . not much of a start in life, really. Do you know keeping children like that alive costs some unbelievable amount of our taxpayer dollars? And is it really worth it?" Her face, clearing, dismissed the unattractive subject. "But shall we? Shall we take that ride?"

It had been so long since I'd had a good night's sleep. Now it was my hands that grew limp. Kate tightened hers around them, as if to press them into reassurance. "I knew you'd come, George," she said softly. It was just as I had hoped. She began to say all of the things I thought she would never say. "You and I, we've always been the most alike. We think the same. We're the only ones who realize that what they taught us at school—that's what matters. *Esse quam videri*, isn't that right?" As she spoke she grew more animated. She rose and walked to the bathroom, still chatting as she ran the tap and splashed water on her face. When she returned she had a white robe on over her nightgown. "Look! It's from the Ritz! Dad got it for me for Christmas. Mom didn't want me to have it, but I kept begging . . . George?" She swooped in front of me and struck a pose. "Should I go like this?"

At Chatham they said Kate Goodenow could get away with anything. She could get caught with a bottle in her room, drink blatantly in her room on a Saturday night, and the teacher on duty would say, "When I come back you'll be at the dance where you ought to be, won't you?" The more cynical among the students attributed her seemingly unpuncturable state of grace to the fat checks Artie Goodenow anted up each semester, but Kate's friends never paid attention to the naysayers. We knew it was just Kate. Money had nothing to do with it. She was like that—that was all. It had not occurred to me that without money there would have been no Kate Goodenow. That Kate Goodenow without money would, in fact, have been a different person. And until that moment I think I had always believed that my own upbringing had been just like theirs, like Chat's or Kate's, that *except for the money* we had been raised in just the same way. Anyway, I had tried to believe it. But it was like Nicko had asked me, trying to get a couple of facts straight for his history class in what was to be his last term of school: "So, except for the sun being in the center of the universe, his plan was pretty much the same?" And I wondered, sitting on that white sofa in that white room, if Cara's parents, when they came to pack up her things and take them away, had enjoyed a moment of comfort when they took the McLean family crest down from the wall, and if her mother had perhaps intimated to Mr. McLean that, unlike other people, they at least had that.

I realized that I was not going to drive Kate anywhere and that, in any case, to do so in Harry's car was a low notion, badly thought out.

"Well, should I, George?"

She had asked one question, but I answered a hundred. "No, Kate," I said, my mouth dry. "I don't think so."

"All right," she said indifferently, "then I'll change." Her face registered my response, and then she looked a second time: registering my response.

She had been well taught, Kate had, to look beyond the rudeness, the slight, instead of trying to answer it directly. "All right," she said again. She was trembling slightly, and to steady herself she sat down and laid her hands on a book. It was the catalog from Sotheby's sale of Americana. "It was a good idea, but I don't much care what I do. I never do. I'll go for a run or I'll—I'll read a book."

Certain things one did not forget, and they were more real than any religion. At Chatham, it was assumed, fresh air and honest prose could cure the most malcontent of souls.

"They can't take that away, can they George?" cried Kate, rising again. "We were *there*. I was there, and you were there. We put our boats away side by side."

"We did," I said.

"That's the truth, isn't it? And you know, I'm right about you. You'll see it more, as you get older. You're just the same as I am—you are! You really and truly are!"

I had been in such a hurry to see her; now I wanted to leave while there was still time, while I could still remember what had brought me there in the first place. When she was sixteen and I was fourteen—

"You'll know what I mean about what matters!"

As I rose and walked to the door, I could sense her flitting about the apartment, looking into her closet, throwing open a window. I stopped and went back into the room. She had taken out a comb and was working vigorously on the snarls in her hair. I took both of her wrists and stilled her hands.

"Yes, George? Yes, what do you want?"

"Kate, I'll always—" I started to say.

But her eyes laughed that off. She was better than that and we both knew it. Kate played to win; the other girls could keep the consolation prizes. I dropped her wrists. I would always—nothing.

The elevator took so long I nearly gave up and went down the stairs, but it finally stopped on Kate's floor.

The doors opened and Chat Wethers got out with a bouquet of flowers.

"Chat." I was glad to see he had brought something for her. Kate appreciated those concrete displays of affection more than any girl I knew. She loved gifts, even Hallmark gifts like boxes of chocolate and lingerie; she was like Cara that way.

I assumed the two of us would linger a moment, and remained standing in the hall, but Chat held the elevator door for me. "Why, let it go!" I said.

He did so, with a disgusted shrug. "You," he said. *"You."*

"You're lucky you got here now," I said. "There's a terrifying aunt who keeps everyone at bay—"

"Excuse me."

"Chat?"

He looked bored. "Kate is expecting me."

"Expecting you?" I said, failing to understand. "But I was going to take her for a ride," I considered aloud. "If you had come any later—"

"What are you talking about, Lenhart?" he said dismissively. "No one's going anywhere. We're all staying right here."

"We are?"

"Not you. We. Right here, where we've been."

"You've been visiting?" I said.

"No, I haven't been visiting. I've just *been* here. Taking care of Kate."

Kate had come to the door. She stood watching us from the threshold. "Excuse me." Chat went to her, presented her with the flowers, and kissed her affectionately on the cheek.

"Oh, Chattie, these are sweet of you."

"I'll be just a moment, dearheart."

I waited until Kate had retreated into the apartment. Then guessing, finally, at the nature of my offense, I explained, "I wanted to come sooner, but I've been at the hospital with Harry."

"Yes," Chat said coldly, "you've been with Harry."

"Christ, Chat, you know I would have been here—" But even to me the words sounded hollow. I stopped abruptly, for suddenly there was nothing further to say. He had every right to be offended. He had stuck by her. "I'm sorry," I said.

"Sorry's not quite good enough," Chat said evenly.

"All right. If that's the way you feel."

That he would not deign to accept my apology did not really surprise me. In fact, I rather respected him for it. As he disowned me as a friend, I wished to salute him: *Esse quam videri.* Instead I pushed the down button.

It was understandably awkward as we waited. I wished Chat would simply go, if he had made his point. But he shifted his weight uneasily from one foot to the other, the kind of physical tic he was always mocking in the Lombardis of the world. "I believe you owe me some money," he said.

CHAPTER 25

For eight or nine generations my father's family lived on the island they had settled and got their living from the sea. They were fishermen and whale fishers. They sailed their whaling ships as far north as Greenland and as far south as the coast of Brazil. In the winter, when the ships were laid up, the men took up a trade. One was a blacksmith, one a cooper, a block and pump maker, a painter, a house carpenter. Boys were taught a trade, as they were taught to read and write, and while they grew they practiced tying a wondrous array of knots: the clove hitch, the sheepshank, the double-sheeted carrick bend. In spiritual things their creed was the opposite of intricacy: they belonged to the Society of Friends and worshiped God on plain wooden pews.

When whaling declined in the middle part of the last century, my ancestors emigrated off-island. They bought property on the closest cape and in Boston; they turned-coat Episcopalian and crept down the coast to New York. There they applied themselves to getting and spending with the customary zeal of converts. Of these latter, my father's father was one, an importer, who made and lost more money in the tea trade than any of us could reckon. When I was old enough to realize that my father had been rich as a child and that I might have been too, I felt I had been done a great disservice, and said so to him. It was the only time I spoke to him of money. He set me straight right away. At the time what he said was little comfort to me, and there were many years afterward when I dismissed the advice as something only someone from the Ice Box Age would come up with. My father had told me that I would always have my good name.

And I suppose when I missed Kate and Chat, I missed the gaiety and the shared history of a hundred touchstones. But mostly I missed the silent tribute they had paid me all these years—of recognizing my name.

Lacking other ideas, I went back to work. Toff must have done the same, for I never saw him now. One night I came home and there was a note on the refrigerator. It was our preferred means of communication: the cable bill taped up at the end of the month, *Yr. share: $15.07.* Toff was scrupulous about the odd penny, and alternated who paid $.07 and who $.06. But from now on I would be paying it myself. *I am sorry about the lack of notice,* he wrote, *but in view of the present situation, I will be moving out.—Geoff*

The future progressive was pure Toff; in fact, he was already gone. He had taken the couch and the television, packed them off in the middle of the day, as the most agreeable way to go. The recliner was gone, too. There was only the coffee table atop the blue carpet, stained now, and stretching dully into a deserted bedroom. I took to sitting on the floor with my back up against the wall, looking at the place where the television used to be. Toff had forgotten one important thing, and I suppose had been too shy to return for it: sometimes I would pretend to switch channels with the Cara McLean Memorial Remote. And occasionally I would turn the pretend television off and just sit there, and at those times it would occur to me that I would probably make vice president some day.

I lived out the lease. In March I found a studio closer to midtown, in a no-man's-neighborhood advertised as "Walk to Work!" It took me one cab ride to move. There was the problem of furniture, but that, too, was presently solved. The answer came in the form of a letter from my father, the envelope addressed in his curious World War II, typewriter-like script. It was the first letter I'd had from him since I went away to Chatham a decade before. I didn't open it for nearly a week, the way one puts off a bill in the hopes that it will go away. When I did, I saw that it was a joint letter to my sister and me. We were advised to come home before a certain date to claim what of the remaining furniture, dishes, clothes, books, and boxes of school papers we wished to keep. Pop was retiring from the Rectory, the letter said, and they would have to give up the headmaster's house come summer.

So that I wouldn't worry what was to become of them, I'm sure, my mother had added an encouraging postscript: "Your dad and I have found a lovely place in the condominium complex on the edge of town!"

I got some good stuff. I got the armchair I wanted and its ottoman, the painted bureau, the partners' desk, and a vast mahogany sideboard. But when I took it all back to the city, I felt as if I'd broken into one of the decorative arts salons at the Met and was living there on the lam. Robbins said there was a simple answer to my problem: "Storage." So I joined the ranks of the dispossessed owners that people New York.

The books I kept. Among them were a number of children's picture books that I didn't need—*Babar*s and *Madeline*s; the entire *Frog and Toad* oeuvre. I made up a separate box for them, and on the first nice Sunday I brought them over to Harry.

He had kept the same apartment, an unapologetic bachelor pad on the West Side below the park. Things hadn't worked out with Rhonda, and so his father had moved in temporarily. Mr. Lombardi acted as a kind of personal assistant to his son, referring business calls to the office, dropping off and picking up the dry cleaning, keeping the refrigerator stocked. They had a woman for the baby, but Harry liked to come home at lunchtime and see how she was doing. It was part of the whole new kinder, gentler entrepreneurial approach: family time was just as important as grind time. Supposedly the new breed of entrepreneurs wore turtlenecks to work, as well. But not Harry. "Oh, no, George. I'm in a suit every day. You gotta be—it's professional, right?" He had learned all the rules only to find that they no longer applied.

We sat in the kitchen and played with the baby, and Harry showed off her pictures. "The way she's looking up like that? You oughta be in pictures, baby!" He swung her up in her white nightie and bounced her and clapped her hands together. Self-promotion, so lacking in the man, was happily justified in the father. The baby was called Marie, after his mother and an old Dartmouth girlfriend; as far as I knew, I was the only one who knew that Cara had decided on Priscilla.

She was more like Harry every day, and yet his looks translated remarkably well into a girl's face: the big eyes, for instance.

Eventually the nanny took the baby away, and Harry and I sat and drank a beer at the kitchen table.

What an odd life he was going to have! I suddenly thought. He of all people had veered wildly, inconceivably off track. What on earth were they saying at his old firm?

"You wanna come in, Dad?"

"Naw," called Mr. Lombardi over the television. "I'm watchin' the game."

"How about that, George, huh?" Harry said.

"Yeah," I said noncommittally, as I hadn't a clue what he was referring to.

"Never thought I'd have a kid with a trust."

"Aw, come on," I said. "Sure you did."

"Shoulda gone in with the ten, George," he said later, shaking his head. "We're going to make a lotta people rich."

"Maybe next year," I said, but I knew I would never invest now. I had missed my opportunity by settling an old debt, and I had never learned to put much faith in second chances.

"Next year? *Next* year?"

I took the ribbing, and then I said: "You know me, Harry. I'm just too conservative."

"You gotta get over that, George," he said, "if it's the last thing you do."

We went in to watch the baseball with Mr. Lombardi. Harry dragged the box of books in and squatted down to examine them. He took them carefully out of the box, one by one, occasionally stopping to flip through one. He wasn't much of a reader himself. A certain book piqued his interest, though, and he sat down heavily in a leather armchair to read it, turning the pages without a word. When he got to the end he asked, "Do you know this one."

I glanced at the cover. "Let's see . . . the girl loses a tooth . . . and then what?" I tried to recall. "Oh, I know, her father takes her to town in the motorboat and they get ice cream cones."

I looked at Harry for corroboration, but he was lost in the black-and-white world of a Robert McCloskey picture book where traffic "cops" make way for ducklings and "Sal" picks blueberries and a couple of kids spend one morning in Maine. He finished and set the book down on the coffee table. He said, without emotion, "Their childhood was *One Morning in Maine.*"

When I left he came down in the elevator with me and we lingered outside the building, looking across the street at an empty play-ground. I didn't feel like going back to my starter studio. I didn't feel like making another start.

"School's out, I guess," Harry observed. "About time. They keep them forever. That's public school for you. I 'member one year on Long Island we had like twelve snow days and went till the Fourth of July. . . . My dad was like, 'Fuckin' bureaucrats!' "

But he couldn't hold the expression. His mouth dropped and then his eyes. "Did you know she kept the same date?"

"I saw the paper," I admitted.

Then both of us spoke at the same time, pronouncing the name we had never said aloud, had never heard till we read it that morning.

"Strange, isn't it?" He turned to me with a kindly, searching expression. "It's funny, you and she were always so close. I'd've thought she would've—I mean, afterward, George, when—"

"You know what Chat would say," I broke in. "Bit of a random choice, eh?"

"Chat Wethers," Harry said. He shook his head and laughed, as if the name were the punch line to a grand joke.

"Chat, indeed."

"Supposedly the new guy has a lot of money," Harry added, his voice speculative. For a moment he seemed to be on the verge of making a connection. He raised a thumb to his mouth and worried a hangnail. But with an emphatic sigh he gave up the effort. "Anyway, you can't blame her."

"No."

"There'd be no point." I braced myself for the platitude that was sure to come. "All you've got is your youth and your hobby, right, George?"

But I wasn't going to let him get away so easily. "Isn't that all anyone has?" I said.

"No." Harry frowned in surprise. "Oh, no. I never had a childhood."

I had a sailboat when I was little, bought for my tenth birthday, though we couldn't afford it. She was a wooden catboat, gaff-rigged, twelve feet from bow to stern. She was called *The Bluebird* for the usual reason, that she had a navy hull. On summer weekends I used to sail her in the races the faculty got up on Knox Pond, and one year we decided to campaign her a little, so I went around to all the local regattas. I was never very good, and I was terrified of anything over ten knots, but I went anyway and Pop would drive me there to watch. He loved going to the regattas. He loved the color and the motion and the fresh air.

The summer before I left for Chatham I tried to tidy up the life I was leaving behind. I thought that if I could get my papers into folders and my pictures into albums I could finish with the years they represented as well. In the end the mess got the best of me and all I managed to do was clean out a few shelves of my bedroom closet. Buried there I found a box stuffed with the sailing trophies. A second place from the Sunrise Pond Annual Summer Regatta. A First in Fleet from the Junior Division at the Lake Ponkapog June Series. And so on, until I had counted five or six of them. So I had done all right, I thought. But all I could remember, sitting on the floor and holding the cheap metal in my hands, was the white dread of the drives to the regattas in the mornings and the gorgeous satisfaction of the rides home afterward—taking off my hat and laughing at my plastered hair, eating the soggy lunches out of the cooler, Pop and me stopping for ice cream. . . .

Habits creep up on you in childhood. I got so used to packing up my gear and going—going, going, going every weekend—that when the regattas ended for the fall and later, when *The Bluebird* was sold and they ended for good, staying at home seemed strange, wrong, like going to the movies on a nice day. I missed the going, with the indulgence of "after."

With Kate you always felt like you were going.

I walked across the park and I thought about what Harry said. If he was right about youth and hobby, then weren't the Goodenows to be commended, and shouldn't we all do as they did, practice one and preserve the other, like so many Fairisles in camphor?

The announcement had been a rather long one, as the editors had to spend a good three paragraphs summarizing the Goodenows' history of achievement and benefaction in this country before going on with all the irrelevant details about Kate herself—how she'd graduated with honors, and worked at Sotheby's. Somehow they'd managed to leave room at the end for a couple of lines about the groom, I suppose to explain why he had felt himself at all justified in staking his claim.

The picture showed Kate alone, of course. It became a habit of mine to take it out and to study her face for the clue that the text omitted. But it revealed nothing. It was just Kate—Kate in the costume of a bride. She didn't look noble or exalted, the way some brides do, transformed for a moment by a consciousness of their role in the human drama. No: Kate would have called that nonsense, and she was too well bred to be beautiful. But the square, correct Goodenow chin was thrust forward, and her eyes were full of mirth.

Mother New York went on spinning us to the
far ends of her web. Occasionally you
crossed through the center again, and when that happened you ran
into Kate. Coming home from a weekend last year, I happened to
meet Mrs. Carter Smith.

In New Haven the train from Boston stops for ten minutes to allow
the switch in power from diesel to electric. The lights go out; somewhere a baby always cries, and frequently a passenger is left pro-
claiming fatuities that ought to have been drowned out, such as: "I
don't care how it looks! We're moving!"

There was the sound of a couple taking a mass of luggage down,
then walking it up the aisle. I had one of the double facing seats at
the middle of the car, now to myself, as a pair of Yale sweatshirts had
just departed.

"George?" cried the man's wife. It was as if she were calling me to
service, the way she said my name, for some yet to be defined purpose of her own. A passing trainman caught her imperative wave,

and as the bags were hoisted up over our heads, Kate and I sat down like old friends.

"What a miracle that we found you! Carter had us sitting in front of an awful woman with two horrible, screeching children." The man himself joined us, his oblong face set in dull disapproval.

"Yale friend?" he inquired.

"I'm afraid not."

"Carter thinks all Yale people are communist liberals," Kate explained.

"That's not true," interjected her husband. "I think you're all fags!"

The Smiths chuckled. Kate wanted to be caught up on all the news and all the gossip. I told her I had left Fordyce for Fayerweather, Dean, and she congratulated me on the implied promotion. We went through the list of mutual acquaintances, a larger number than I remembered.

"Oh, here's something, George. Listen to my brilliant idea. Carter and I were thinking of chartering a boat in the Caribbean this winter, and I was thinking, wouldn't it be fun if we chartered the one Nick works on?"

I seemed to have turned into a spoilsport these intervening years. I simply couldn't make the effort to nod and agree.

Kate began to hedge. "I mean, not that we'd make him do anything—"

"We sure as hell would! *I* sure as hell would! Those boats go out for fifteen, sixteen thousand a week! You think at that price we're going to watch the crew sit on their asses while we grind winches?"

An irrelevant thought came to mind: that if Cara had taken Kate's money she could have rented a luxury yacht in the Caribbean—for about two months.

"Carter, where are the cards?" Kate was asking.

"I don't know—left them in Maine."

"Can you go and buy some? Do they still sell cards on trains? Will you go check?"

When he returned with a new pack, Kate started to deal three precarious hands on the empty seat. "So, George, tell us," she said coyly, "where on earth are you coming from? You seem . . . lost in thought."

"I'm sorry." I laughed. "A wedding in Boston."

"Oh, yes? Anyone we know?"

"Friends of the family."

"Well," Kate said generously, "they're the best kind."

"Depends on what family," Carter Smith asserted.

"How's your family, Kate?" I asked.

Kate grimaced, neatening the piles of cards. "I guess you could say—not terrific. Cees is having a little trouble . . ."

"A little trouble! She ought to be committed!"

Kate giggled. "She just got kicked out of Miss Porter's."

"Oh—sorry."

"That's all right." She raised her face to me, disarmingly, and the two of us laughed, the way we used to, at a thing that no one else would find amusing.

"The money your dad has spent trying to get that girl a goddamn high school diploma—"

"Oh listen," Kate went on contentedly, ignoring him, "have you heard about Chat's latest scandal at the Town Club? George, *you* will appreciate this . . ."

We picked up our hands and began to play.